ORGONE GIZMO

Orgone Gizmo

A Novel

Richard Gartee

Lake and Emerald Publications

Books by Richard Gartee
—Fiction—
Orgone Gizmo
Atlantis Dying
Atlantis Obsession
Lancelot's Grail
Lancelot's Disciple
Ragtime Dudes at the World's Fair
Ragtime Dudes in a Thin Place
Ragtime Dudes Meet a Paris Flapper
—Poetry—
Mountain Breathing
Watching Waves
Canyon Falls
Arbor Encore
—Non-Fiction—
Skating on Skim Ice
The Hippodrome Theatre First Fifty Years

A complete list of currently available titles by the author can be found at www.gartee.com

Published by Lake and Emerald Publications, LLC
Gainesville, FL

ISBN 978-1-7363957-7-6

Library of Congress Control Number: 2024909537

"Time Koan" was previously published in *Arbor Encore*.

To Anthony Capitano
who first turned me on to the work of Wilhelm Reich

CHAPTER 1

"Where's Gizmo?"

"Over here!" I looked up from my drafting table. I was working on schematics for a line of radar installations along the DMZ, the no-man's-land that served as a buffer between the North and South Korean armies.

"Gizmo," my staff sergeant said, "I don't know what the hell you did, but they want your ass at headquarters, pronto."

I made a quick stop at the barracks, where I kept a fresh-pressed uniform and spit-shined shoes ready in case of an inspection. Whatever HQ wanted, I'd be better off showing up with sharp creases and polished brass rather than ink stains on my cuffs.

When I arrived, I was put in a small room that held only an empty desk and two chairs. By this point, I'd been stationed in Korea almost two years. I got along well with my fellow airmen and noncom superiors and made friends with my tinkering.

The war ended before I even got there. An armistice was signed and the US began shipping GIs home. But not me. The Air Force had invested in my engineering training and intended to use it. They flew me to Seoul and assigned me to a group building airfields, flight control towers, and radar installations. My God! I had been only eighteen years old when they started me drawing electrical schematics for South Korea's defense.

I waited in that empty room for an hour, watching dust motes drift through the sunlight streaming in the window. Why had I been told to get here "pronto?" Waiting heightened my anxiety. I tried to remember anything I'd done wrong—at least, anything the Air Force might know about. I drew a blank.

Finally, the door opened. A naval commander entered, carrying a blue folder tucked under his elbow. He closed the door and locked it.

What a Navy man was doing on an Air Force base, I couldn't imagine. But I breathed a sigh of relief. I wasn't here for a reprimand. I stood and saluted.

He sat down at the desk and pointed to the other chair. "Take a seat, Carson."

He laid the blue folder on the desk and opened it. "I am Commander . . . Smith."

I noticed the standard military name tag which should have been on the right breast of his uniform was absent. Between that and the hesitation, I smelled "Military Intelligence," an oxymoron in any GI's mind.

He took a retractable pen from his inside jacket pocket and clicked it. "I have a few questions."

I leaned forward to glimpse what was in that folder, but my chair was too far away for me to see.

He then asked me a lot of nonsense questions: Which factory had my father worked at during World War II? When had my mother's parents emigrated from Sweden? Had either of my parents attended a communist party meeting?

"I don't think they would do that." But how the hell did he expect me to know if they did? I was just a kid back then.

Strangely enough, he didn't write any of this down. He just made check marks on the sheets inside his folder, as if my answers were already there.

"According to your record, your first name is Sven. Is that Swedish?"

I nodded. I'd always despised my first name. When I was in school, I tried to get kids to call me Kit, like Kit Carson. They didn't. Instead, they called me "Sven the hen" or equally stupid names. It wasn't until I was stationed in Korea that my fellow airmen gave me a nickname I could love.

"Why are you using the alias Gizmo?" he said.

"It's just a nickname. The guys call me that because I have a knack for getting things running, or jury-rigging a quick fix."

"For example?"

"I can revive a dead radio. Once, I made a toaster oven out of an empty ammo box and a heat coil."

My most popular invention was a cocktail mixer I made by drilling a hole in a jar lid and attaching strips of tin flashing to a shaft connected to an electric motor. But telling him that would be an admission that we drank in the barracks.

After another ten minutes of inane questions, he unlocked the door and told me to return to my duty station. I went back to work and gave no more thought to the matter.

Then, a few weeks later, I was working on wiring schematics for a new hangar when an airman entered my office and handed me orders from the captain to report to transport at sixteen-hundred hours.

"Lucky bastard," he said. "You're being sent stateside."

Yeah, with two hours' notice. The papers didn't say why. Just that I was being flown to Edwards Air Force Base in California and would be reassigned from there. "Any hint as to what this is about?"

He scratched his head. "Nope. Kind of mysterious."

But the one desire of every GI in Korea was to get the hell out of Korea, so best not to question the wisdom of the upper echelons. I left to pack my duffel.

Going home made me think of my sister Nora's husband, Tom. Drafted, yes, but he'd served his two years and was now out. I'd enlisted, so I still had twenty-three months left.

I have two older sisters, Nora and Sophie, who took care of me during World War II while our parents worked in defense plants. I'd just started first grade when Pearl Harbor got hit. Sophie was in fourth. She'd pack my lunch and walk to school with me. Nora turned fourteen in the spring of '42. She was learning to cook—using me and Sophie for guinea pigs. That continued until the August before I was to start fifth grade, when, to everyone's relief, the war ended and Mom took over the kitchen again.

Nora graduated from high school the following spring and got a job cooking at a diner. I guess all those years practicing on me and Sophie paid off. She went through a number of "beaus," as she called them, until 1950, when she married Tom. By then, the Korean War had started, and men were once again being drafted. She and Tom thought he'd get a deferment if they were married. In '52, he got drafted, anyway.

In 1953, I turned eighteen and had to register with the Selective Service. That caused me to look at Tom's situation. I didn't much want to get drafted into the Army and wind up sitting in a foxhole. I had good grades in science and math and really wanted to study engineering in college, but our family didn't have the money for that. Dad had been working for five years at a local company that made wheels and brake drums for Ford. We weren't poor, but we weren't rich, either.

An Air Force recruiter promised if I enlisted, they'd train me in electrical engineering—I could start as soon as I graduated high school that spring. They kept their part of the bargain, but when my training finished, they shipped me straight to Korea. Now I was on my way back, hoping I'd get to serve my remaining time stateside.

The flight lasted sixteen hours, counting a refueling layover at a base in the Aleutian Islands, where we weren't even allowed to leave the plane. Tired as hell, I reported to the Officer of the Day at Edwards, who shook his head when I asked him what I was doing there.

"Carson, I don't know any more than you do," he said. "I've had guys like you arriving all day. Find a bed in the west barracks and get some shuteye. Report back day after tomorrow. By then, I'll know what the brass wants to do with you."

This wasn't my first time in California. I had basic training at Parks Air Force Base up near Oakland, and in Korea I took a lot of guff from my fellow airmen over it. Nearly everyone else had trained at Lackland in Texas, and they were quick to remind me Parks didn't even have a functional runway. But California was a big place and Edwards, being in the Mojave Desert, wasn't anything like Parks. Not that it mattered. Three days after I arrived, I and two dozen others were told to report with our gear to an empty building. There we were harangued for half an hour by a naval officer, who, like "Smith," bore no name tag.

"Men, you have been thoroughly vetted, and are being entrusted with the highest level of security clearance assigned to any military man," he said. "Where we are about to go and what you are about to undertake is top secret. From this day forward, you are operating under the Defense Secrets Act. Conveying any information with the intent to interfere with the success of the armed forces or naval operations of the United States is punishable by death or imprisonment."

Jeez, thanks for nothing. After his stirring speech, they issued us photo ID tags that denoted our top secret clearance. From there, we boarded a C-47 and were flown to an undisclosed location in Nevada, which I later found out was Indian Springs Air Force Auxiliary Field at Groom Lake.

The C-47 landed on one of two unpaved 5000-foot runways. Scenery at the base was much the same as at Edwards—a salt flat surrounded by desert. The biggest difference was that it sat on the southwestern edge of America's primary test site for the nuclear bombs our government had been exploding with regularity since World War II.

Our job there was to build a base some desk jockey with a warped sense of humor had named Paradise Ranch. Maybe he thought it would fool men into wanting to be stationed there, but just a glance out the window and any nitwit could see it wasn't paradise.

While we were getting our physicals, the ground shook, and the sky thundered. And I knew that, somewhere nearby, a mushroom cloud was rising.

"I'd say the name refers to the certainty that the nearby nukes are going to send us into the afterlife," cracked a wiseacre in front of me.

The corpsman giving us physicals said, "Don't worry. These days, nuclear tests are mostly underground and hundreds of miles from us."

"Mostly?" I said.

"On the plus side," the corpsman said, "after a man's been here awhile, we can measure the size of his balls with a Geiger counter."

Great.

If there is a more isolated, desolate place than Groom Lake, I haven't seen one in all my years. When we arrived, the base had only a few huts for dorms and workshops for our small team and a couple of house trailers where the brass lived. For the next three months, we worked day and night. By the time we finished the base, it had a paved runway, three hangars, a control tower, and fuel storage tanks. For the personnel, there was a mess hall, better accommodations, plus a movie theater and volleyball court for recreation. But it'd take more than that to make the place hospitable.

Suddenly, one day in July, we were all furloughed. Everyone who'd come from Edwards was told to pack our duffels, get off base, and never come back. No explanation. But then, when did the higher-ups ever give a GI a reason for anything? And we had no desire to question it. A month's leave was all that mattered.

The nearest city where you could catch a bus or train home was Las Vegas. The Air Force loaded the lot of us on a creaky olive green bus, obviously left over from the days when the Air Corps had been a branch of the Army. Three hours in blistering midday heat in that rattletrap got us to "sin city," from where they expected us to dutifully go straight home. This was the 1950s, remember.

Look, I was twenty-years-old and inexperienced as hell. Vegas seemed like the place to remedy that. A bunch of the guys were laying over there, so we pitched-in and rented a couple rooms in the cheapest dump we could find. It was crowded, but we'd spent three months jammed together at Groom Lake, so this was no different. Besides, we didn't intend to spend much time in our rooms.

CHAPTER 2

Las Vegas wasn't the strip of luxury high-rise resort hotels you see today. It was basically just Fremont Street and Las Vegas Boulevard. Still, it was like no place else in America.

In 1955, the large cities were New York, Chicago, Philadelphia, Los Angeles, Detroit—none of which I'd ever visited. Pretty much everywhere else were rural villages or towns centered on small manufacturers. Everybody's mom dressed like Barbara Billingsley on *Leave it to Beaver*. Dads were farmers, factory workers, salesmen, or white-shirted businessmen. People attended church on Sunday, and nobody but the town lush went to bars except on Friday or Saturday night. Gambling was illegal everywhere outside of Nevada, so the only way to indulge was in some shady backroom or a private lodge where you had to be a member to get in.

Certainly not on a street glaring with bright lights and neon signs, where every other doorway offered entrance to a room full of gaming tables and slot machines. I had not only never seen anything like this, I'd never imagined it.

The guys I came with decided to get right into the action on Fremont Street. On one end was the Golden Nugget, and on the other end the Pioneer Club, which had a distinctive sign—a cowboy, forty feet tall, outlined in neon lights. You had to be twenty-one to drink or gamble, but we were in uniform and no one asked soldiers for their ID. In fact, they usually bought you a drink. And the first place we entered offered drinks for free.

We thought either we were really special, or they were really patriotic. But back in those days, the casinos gave gamblers free booze. It took us a while to figure that out, and by then we had a good buzz on. Two of the guys teamed up at the craps table. One would bet Pass and the other No Pass. Usually that meant when one guy lost the other would win, so between the two of them they could stand there all night drinking for free and barely lose anything.

Not me. The dice game completely confused me and I lost every time. I moved over to blackjack, which seemed simpler. I was good at math and all you had to do was not let the value of your cards exceed twenty-one. Still, you could lose money at the turn of a card. I thought about all the free booze and glittering lights and realized they weren't paying the bills by letting rubes like us win.

Someone suggested we should go to the Silver Slipper, where they featured exotic dancers, as they were called then. The drinks weren't free, but they had musical numbers with showgirls dancing around in what amounted to their bra and panties. For a small-town boy, that was pretty damn exotic. Again, this was about five years before the bikini, so even at the beach women wore one piece bathing suits which had little skirts for additional modesty.

The final number in the show was a lone woman who came out wearing a floor-length dress and long white gloves, like a girl would wear to senior prom. She swayed her hips and shimmied around the stage, slowly removing her gloves, then her dress. When she undid and dropped her bra, they stunned me. I mean, we kind of knew what was coming, were hoping for it. But there they were in all their glory.

So, yes, I'd never seen bare breasts before—in real life. Barely even in a photo. When I was in Korea, the first issue of Playboy Magazine came out featuring Marilyn Monroe in the centerfold. We thought that was just breathtaking. This sexy screen goddess, whose movies always left you imagining what she must look like undressed, lay across a three page spread with a staple in her middle. But this was visceral. This was live. A mere eight feet away, and with every step she took, they quivered like Jell-O. It drove me out of my mind.

I returned the next night, and the next.

After three days of partying, I realized if I stayed much longer, I'd piss away my pay before my leave was up. Besides, I needed to see my folks. I came back to my room to pack and saw a guy with a bunch of stuff he'd bought in Korea spread across the bed.

"What ya got there, Smitty?"

"Silk scarfs, fans, jewelry boxes . . . your basic Korean trinkets."

"So many."

"Gifts for the ladies. Women love this stuff. I'm picking out something for a cocktail waitress I've got a date with tonight."

Suddenly, I realized I'd spent all that time overseas and was going home empty-handed. "It looks like you've got quite a stash. Would you sell me a few? See, I've got my mom and two sisters. It never dawned on me to do any shopping over there."

"Sure, Gizmo, pick out anything you want."

I chose an ornate black lacquered box and two silks scarfs printed with large flowers. "How much for these?" I pulled out my wallet.

"Aw, put your money away. They cost me practically nothing over there."

"No. That wouldn't be right." I handed him two dollars.

"Shit, Gizmo, you could buy ten scarves for that."

"Yeah, but I didn't. And I can't buy them at that price here."

"Okay." He accepted the bills. "But let's go have a steak—my treat."

After we ate, I went to the train station and bought my ticket. I had a lit-tle time to kill and needed something for dad. It didn't have to be from Korea. There were all kinds of shops between the casinos. You see, if you did manage to win, they wanted you to spend it in Las Vegas while you were still feeling flush. I entered one place that sold cowboy stuff—hats, boots, big silver buckles. My dad worked in a wheel factory. I couldn't imagine him showing up at the plant in a cowboy hat. I walked out.

A little further on, a store had a display of turquoise jewelry and hunting knives in the window. Dad didn't hunt and I couldn't feature him wearing a bolo tie with a big turquoise stone to church, but I wandered in. A Zippo lighter with a Marine Corps emblem on it caught my eye. Dad smoked. Well, everyone did, then.

"Have you got those for other branches of service?"

The salesman looked at my uniform. "Air Force?"

I nodded.

He fished around in a cabinet, brought out a white cardboard box, and opened it on the counter.

Nice. Enameled on the case was the roundel we put on our planes, a white star in a blue circle flanked by red and blue stripes on either side. He wanted twice what it would have cost at the Px. But I wasn't at a Px. I coughed up his price and returned to the motel for my gear. I said farewell to the few fellows who weren't out on the town and told them to say goodbye to the others for me.

CHAPTER 3

After two days on the train, I reached home. I caught a lift to our house from a fellow passenger. I opened the front door, dropped my duffle on the floor, and yelled, "What's for supper?"

Mom, wearing an apron, dashed from the kitchen. I hugged her, lifting her feet off the ground.

She kissed my cheek. "Put me down and let me look at you. I can't believe you're here. Why didn't you write that you were coming home?"

Actually, I had been writing, but wasn't allowed to mention being in Nevada, and the military somehow snuck our letters into the postal system without a postmark.

She laid her hand on my face and smiled. A single tear leaked from her eye. "So handsome in your uniform—" She wiped her cheek. "Are you hungry?"

"I can wait for supper. What time does dad get home?"

She always wore a small watch with a thin gold band on her left wrist. She glanced at it. "In about an hour. Put your bag in your room while I call your sisters. Won't they be surprised?"

I grabbed my duffle and climbed the stairs two steps at a time. Ours was a modest two-story middle-class house identical to its neighbors except for the color of the shingles and whether the yard was landscaped with flowerbeds or hedges. The subdivision was one of thousands thrown up at the start of the baby boom. We had three bedrooms. Mine was at the far end, with a window that looked out on a detached garage in the backyard.

I leaned my bag on the wall next to the closet door. The room smacked of a seventeen-year-old kid who now seemed like a stranger. Baseball cards, comic books, the full set of Tom Swift books—a time capsule my mother had carefully preserved. I opened the closet and studied my choices. Home on leave, I was allowed to put on civvies. I tried on several old favorites, but nothing fit. Some were too small. Most were just too young.

"Sven," Mother called up the stairs, "I just spoke with your sisters. They're coming over for dinner."

I put my uniform back on. I'd go clothes shopping tomorrow. Meanwhile, Mom would like it if I came to dinner in uniform.

Sophie arrived first, and was as big as a barn. I knew she'd married while I was in Korea and that she was expecting. But her stomach bulged out so far I thought it might burst. Just trying to hug her was a challenge.

She grinned. "Hi, little brother."

I glanced down at her belly. "Hello, huge sister."

Mom pulled her into the living room. "Sophie, come, sit down."

As soon as she settled, Mom lifted Sophie's legs and pushed the ottoman under her feet. "Your ankles, dear."

I looked at Sophie's legs. Her ankles were nearly the same size as her calves. The skin was white and puffy as a marshmallow. Wow. I wasn't the only one undergoing changes.

Mom headed for the kitchen, fretting over whether she'd prepared enough food.

Sophie called after her, "Mom, I doubt Nora's left home yet. Why don't you ask her to bring a dish?"

"No, no, she's got enough on her plate with Tommy Jr. I'll peel more potatoes and open a couple jars of the peaches we put up last year."

I grinned at my sister. "Jeez, Sophie, did you swallow a pumpkin?"

She grimaced. "Well, it feels more like lugging a bowling ball that won't stop rolling around. And I'm not due for another month, if you can believe that. I never knew a person's skin could stretch this much." She laid her hand on her stomach. "He's moving right now. You want to feel?"

"Naw."

I was already uncomfortable enough. Back then, men and women rarely discussed pregnancy with the opposite sex, except when a girl told her boyfriend he'd knocked her up. I felt like I was being thrown in to the middle of the mysterious world of women.

"Will your husband be joining us for dinner?" I hoped so. They hadn't started dating until after I enlisted. He grew up in the next town over, and I'd only ever seen him in the wedding picture she'd sent me. In the photo, he kind of looked like the younger brother of the Everly Family. I bet he'd made Sophie swoon.

"No. Eddie's working the swing shift. He won't get off until eleven." Prairie View, Iowa, was a company town on the Wisconsin border. It had one large factory that employed pretty much everyone.

Sophie glanced at the kitchen where Mom was busy cooking. She lowered her voice. "Sven, are you in trouble?"

That hit me completely out of left field. "No. Why?"

"A while back, some government men came around asking questions."

"Oh. That was for my security clearance."

She leaned toward me conspiratorially. "Is there something top secret going on in Korea?"

I was glad she'd ask it that way. We had orders never to mention our job in Nevada, and I'd never been able to outright lie to her.

"Not that I know of, I wired a line of radar stations facing the DMZ, but that's not a secret. It's probably that ever since the McCarthy hearings, they have to make sure guys working on military technology aren't communist sympathizers."

Mom appeared in the doorway. "Sven?"

That name jolted me back to unpleasant memories of my childhood. "I go by Gizmo, now."

Sophie laughed.

"I will not call my son Gizmo. Please go to the garden and pick any ripe tomatoes. There's a basket by the backdoor."

I jumped to my feet. "Love to." Oh, man, I hadn't had fresh sliced tomatoes since I joined the Air Force. In my opinion, there's nothing better.

The vines were loaded. I filled a peck basket with the reddest ones, my mouth watering the whole time. When I brought them into the kitchen, Nora was there, holding a tiny person on her hip. She grabbed me in a hug, squishing Tommy Jr. between us. He looked at me with eyes the size of cantaloupes.

I took him from her and ruffled his hair. "Hi, Tommy. I'm your Uncle Gizmo."

"Gizmo?" Nora said.

Tommy cocked his head and pawed the silver stripes on my shoulder patch. Nora pulled his chubby fingers away and took him back. "I brought a cake. It's still in the car. Would you bring it in?"

"You didn't have to," Mom said.

"I'd already made it for Tom. But when you invited us to supper, I thought I may as well bring dessert."

"I'm glad you did," Mom said. "I had no chance to bake. Sven caught me completely unprepared."

"Where is Tom?" I said.

"He's setting up the playpen in the living room."

I gave Nora an affectionate squeeze and left to find Tom, who was snapping together the corners of a small wooden prison. Two Masonite panels fell into place, forming the floor. He stopped to shake my hand and then laid a quilt in the bottom of the playpen.

"Wait until you have kids," Tom said. "You have to haul a carload of crap to go anywhere."

I laughed. I didn't figure on having children anytime soon.

"You're on leave," he said. "Why aren't you in civvies?"

"I tried. All my clothes are too high school. I'm going to have to go shopping."

"Don't waste your money. Come by the house tomorrow and Nora will loan you some of my pants and shirts."

The door opened and Dad came in. "What's all the hoopla? The driveway looks like a used car lot. I can't even get to the garage." He leaned over and kissed my sister on the forehead. "Hi, sweetie, how you feeling?"

And then he saw me. His mouth dropped open. "Well, aren't you a sight for sore eyes?" He rushed over and pumped my hand. "How long are you home for?"

"A few weeks," I said. "How have you been, Dad?"

"Staying vertical."

"Beats the alternative." An old joke between us.

"You want a beer?"

This was the first time he ever offered me a drink. It marked a milestone in our relationship, his way of acknowledging I'd become a man. "Sure. Thanks, Dad."

Sophie smirked. "Tell Dad your new name."

He looked at me and raised his eyebrows.

"Gizmo. Guys in service call me Gizmo."

His face cracked into a broad smile. "I like it. Good handle for an electrician."

"Actually, I'm an electrical engineering technician."

He slapped my back. "Is that a fact? Well, we're all damn proud of you. Aren't we, Tom?"

Tom nodded and looked away.

I was torn. Thrilled to receive Dad's praise. On the other hand, he seemed to ignore that Tom had actually been shot at and all I'd done was push a pencil.

"I'll be right back," Tom said. "I left Nora's cake in the car."

"Oh. She asked me to get that. I'm sorry."

"Forget it. Stay and talk to your dad." And Tom streaked out the door like an F-86.

But Dad had already gone to the kitchen, leaving only Sophie and me.

"Eddie will be off Saturday. You can meet him then."

"I'd like that."

"If the weather's nice, we'll have a cookout."

Dad returned carrying three beers. I was glad to see he brought one for Tom. He handed me a bottle and clinked his against mine in a wordless toast. Tom carried a chocolate frosted cake past us and returned carrying Tommy Jr. Dad handed Tom his beer and did the same clink of bottles. Tom responded in kind and then turned to me and did the same. So apparently my pencil-pushing status wasn't an issue for him.

He bent over to set the baby in the playpen, but Sophie said, "No. Give him to me."

"Are you sure?" Tom said. "He's heavy."

"It'll be good practice," Sophie said.

Before he could make the handoff, Mom called us to dinner. So he left the baby in the playpen and pulled a blanket over him.

Sophie held out her hand. "Gizzard, help me up."

"That's Gizmo, madam colossus."

"Don't be mean," she said.

After dinner, while we were having cake and coffee, I slipped up to my room and got their presents. The scarves delighted my sisters, and I think Mom liked the jewelry box, though she wouldn't have said so if she hadn't. Dad seemed really pleased with the lighter. He flipped the top open and spun the little wheel. Sparks flew and . . . nothing. He tried again. Same result.

My face grew hot. "Sorry. I forgot to fill it."

"That's okay. There's lighter fluid in that cabinet right behind you."

I leaned my chair back on two legs, opened the door, retrieved the can, and handed it to him. While he filled his lighter, I said to Nora, "I'm sorry I didn't bring my nephew a gift, but while I'm home, you can help me find something appropriate."

Sophie patted her stomach. "Don't forget this one, too."

"I won't." But I had. Tom and Eddie, too. I didn't know the rules about brothers-in-law. I probably should have consulted Emily Post.

My face must have shown what I was thinking, because Tom said, "Don't worry about it. What you brought was just right."

Dad nodded and passed his lighter around the table so everyone could see the enamel Air Force emblem. I imagine that in the following weeks he offered to light everyone's cigarette at work, providing an excuse to talk up his son in the Air Force.

CHAPTER 4

Rain Saturday forced Sophie to cancel the cookout. Her and Eddie's apartment was too tiny to fit all of us, so everyone met at Mom and Dad's again. While I was overseas, they'd bought a television, and the baseball game was supposed to be televised. So the women stayed in the kitchen talking and cooking while the men gathered in the living room. Such an arrangement might not fly in today's world, but back then everyone thought it was normal.

Their TV was in a cabinet of fine wood with a pair of doors that hid the knobs and screen when it wasn't in use. That's the reason I hadn't noticed it the night I arrived—it just looked like a credenza. The fancy cabinet cost extra, but Dad said Mom didn't want to look at a glaring eye all day. They received all three channels where they lived. Two came in all right, but the third had a lot of static.

When the game was called on account of rain, we turned off the TV and ate early. Afterward, it was still raining. Eddie suggested we go to a bar. The women passed, so Dad and Tom and I piled in Eddie's car—a shiny, new blue and white '55 Ford Fairlane. It was gorgeous, low and sleek with V-shaped chrome trim that ran the length of the body, and divided the two-tone paint job. The front fenders raked forward, making the car look fast as hell, even standing still, and that's the way Eddie drove it. Tom predicted a baby would bring an end to that.

Our small town had only two drinking establishments, and truth be told, they were both pretty much the same: linoleum floor, long wooden bar lined with stools, booths along one wall, and a handful of Formica-topped tables with chrome-legged chairs in the center of the room. At the far end was a pool table, and near the entrance were a cigarette machine and a jukebox. We sat in one of the booths while Eddie went to the bar. He returned with a pitcher and four glasses. Once again, no one asked to see my ID.

Our first pitcher was all small talk—cars, baseball, the plant. The pool table freed up, so we shot a couple of games. Dad and I weren't bad, but Tom and Eddie licked us handily, twice. After turning down a third try, we returned to our booth. A waitress brought us a new pitcher. "On the house," she said. "Eddie says you just came home from Korea."

"Th-thanks," I said. People in the 1950s treated GIs like that a lot. If I had to hitchhike somewhere and I had my uniform on, there wouldn't be two cars passing me before someone gave me a lift. Of course, I wasn't in uniform that night. I was dressed like everyone who worked at the wheel and brake factory. Just like Tom, in fact, because I was wearing his clothes.

The waitress refilled our glasses, set the rest of the pitcher on the table, and left.

"Have you thought about what you'll do when you get out?" Dad said.

Actually, I had, but I wasn't sure quite how to tell him my plan. "I've still got nineteen months to go."

Condensation from his beer had created a wet ring on the table. He slid his glass in a circular motion, expanding the watery circle. "I'm just saying, son, with your electrical training, you could get a good position at the plant. Something higher up than us."

I bit my lip, then took a sip of beer. "Er . . . I might go to college."

He glanced into my eyes for a half second, then blinked and stared into his beer. "I'm sorry I couldn't do better by you . . ."

In an unusually familiar gesture, I reached over and touched his hand. "You did fine. I'll have the GI bill. It'll cover tuition, books, even my dorm."

Eddie, oblivious to Dad's distress, said, "But, Gizmo, you'll be four years older than everybody—eight years older by the time you graduate and begin work. Forget college. Buy a nice car, find a wife, and start living while you're young."

Sophie had really picked a winner. I turned to Tom. "What about you? You have GI benefits, too. Did you ever consider going to school when you got out?"

He shrugged. "Did you forget I'd already married Nora before I got drafted? So when I got out, college wasn't an option. Besides, you were always the smart one in the family."

"That's true," Dad said. "He could count to ten before he was two."

* * *

The following week, with the men back at work, I tried to keep myself busy. Raised by Nora and Sophie while our parents worked, I'd never developed a habit of chit-chatting with Mom. Sure, I admired and loved her, but we didn't have that kind of relationship. So, most mornings, I'd sit with her for an extra cup of coffee, and then go find something that needed doing. The first day I weeded the garden. When I finished that, I climbed up on the roof and adjusted and reground their antenna to improve their TV picture. Now it got all three stations with hardly any snow. The next day, I mowed the lawn and cleaned the garage.

When Dad saw what I'd done, he said, "You shouldn't be working. You're on leave. Have some fun. Drive me to work tomorrow and you can have the car to go visit some of your high school buddies."

In the morning, I dropped him at the plant, and tried to reconnect with old friends. But they were all either married and working at the plant, or away at college. Those who'd enlisted in the military when I did were still in. So I ended up at Sophie's. We talked for a while, but she said she was really tired and needed to take a nap. I visited Nora, but her attention was divided between housework, tending Tommy Jr., and preparing dinner for Tom. Somehow, she'd turned into Mom. Or maybe she always had been.

She invited me to stay for supper, but I said, "No, I have Dad's car and have to pick him up from work."

That was true, but I had hours to kill. I took the car home, changed the oil, cleaned the spark plugs, filed and set the points, and tightened every belt on the engine. I picked up Dad, and after dinner, the three of us watched TV. This was apparently their weekday routine.

I'd not grown up with a TV, so at first it was kind of charming to see many of the stars I recognized from radio and movies horsing around on a little black-and-white screen. Eventually, it bored me. I liked the movies because the theater was dark, the picture was larger than life, and there was camaraderie in a room full of strangers all laughing with you at the same joke. TV felt isolating.

So I did what I often did when I was bored. I started taking the TV apart in my mind. I realized the picture tube worked on the same principle as our radar screens and tried to explain the concept during a commercial for Lucky Strike. They indulged me until the commercial ended, when Dad said, "Let's see if Marshal Dillon figures this out."

Of course he did. Just like he had every week I'd been there. Don't get me wrong. I loved my family, and it was great having a break from military life, but I was getting restless. It was hard to admit, but I'd outgrown the little town I came from, and my family's routines were not mine.

After I'd fixed everything there was to fix at home, I began helping my sisters. Sophie and Eddie didn't have a record player, and she relied on a little AM radio for music. It sounded terrible. I took it apart and found the speaker had a tear in it that rattled with every note. I spread a thin layer of Elmer's glue over the cone and applied a sheet of tissue wrapping paper, smoothing away any wrinkles. After it dried, I put the radio back together. Sophie couldn't believe the perfect sound. You'd have thought I'd invented Rock 'n Roll.

I was ready to be somewhere else. But I couldn't report to my next post early, and I sure couldn't afford to go back to Las Vegas. So I stuck it out, making what fun I could. One day, Nora and I took Tommy Jr. to the lake.

He was too young to swim, so one of us sat on the blanket watching the baby, while the other swam. Other than that, I went for long walks or read in the town's small library.

By the time my train pulled out after a final weekend of drinking beer and shooting pool with my brothers-in-law, I vowed my future visits home would forever be much shorter.

CHAPTER 5

My new posting was Holloman Air Force Base, about six miles southwest of Alamogordo, New Mexico—they'd stuck me out in the desert again. I soon learned our base was the cornerstone of White Sands Proving Ground, where they'd set off the first atomic bomb. Was the Air Force that determined to irradiate me?

Even though the Trinity Site was up near the northern border of the proving grounds, and mostly we tested missiles and rockets, I still got very familiar with Geiger counters.

Alamogordo was a military town whose economy thrived on its proximity to Holloman and White Sands. When we had liberty or a weekend pass, it was the nearest place to go. Some officers lived there with their families.

I arrived during the monsoon season, which lasted from July to September, and supposedly the regular rains cooled the temperatures below a hundred degrees. Outside of those months, it rained little, but in the wintertime it got as cold as home. No snow, though.

Much of what we did there seemed ordinary, but they ordered us to keep our lips zipped when we were off base—that every bit of it came under the Defense Secrets Act and the McCarran Internal Security Act. Although most of it has been declassified by now, I'm not going to discuss my work there. I will say that being stationed there was the best thing that had happened to me up to that point in life. But I'm getting ahead of myself.

The officer in charge of electrical engineering was a WWII vet, coming up on his twenty-year retirement. One August afternoon, he met with a half-dozen of us and told us that if we wanted to get anywhere in this field, we should take evening classes at the college in Las Cruces, which was about ninety minutes away. He offered to write passes for anyone who wanted to attend. Every man did.

"How will we get there?" I said.

One of the guys, Evans, had a '38 Plymouth. He said he'd drive if we'd pitch in for gas. So six of us crammed into his car three nights a week. His car was nearing twenty years old, and I became the de facto go-to guy to make sure we made it there and back. Fortunately, its L-head-six engine left a lot of elbow room to work under the hood.

That worked fine for two semesters, but then Evans' enlistment was up. The rest of us didn't know what we'd do for the remaining semester. Yes, I've already said hitching was easy for a man in uniform in those days, but not five of us at once. Plus, the road through the Chihuahaun Desert didn't have much traffic.

We started missing classes.

The captain found out and gave us an ass-chewing. "I'm not writing you passes so you can cut class."

"Sir, we're not doing it on purpose," I said. "Ever since Evans left, we've had to hitchhike, and some nights we never catch a ride. With your permission, I'll go into Alamogordo and find a jalopy to fix up."

He wrote me a pass, and the next day I hitched into town. I thought I'd buy a newspaper and check the classifieds. Then I spotted a blue Volkswagen Microbus in someone's yard, with a sign: "For Sale $350." That seemed incredibly cheap for something that large.

I took a closer look. It was shaped like a motorized shoebox with a pair of doors on one side. Most importantly, it had three rows of seats. I'd heard Volkswagens were reliable, simple to work on, and the lowest priced cars on the market. Even so, $350 seemed like too little. There had to be something wrong with it. But what the hell, I could repair most things.

I knocked on the door. A middle-age lady answered.

"Excuse me, ma'am. Is your husband home?"

"He passed away."

"Oh. I'm so sorry. I wanted to ask about that VW in your yard."

"It was his."

"Does it run?"

"It did when he was alive. I don't know if it still does. I can't drive a stick-shift. That's why I'm selling it."

"Your asking price is far less than what it's worth, so . . . pardon me for wondering why."

"This town is full of retired vets who fought the Nazis. None of them is about to buy a German car. I kept lowering the price, but you're the first person to ring my bell."

"What model year is it?" I had to ask because Volkswagens looked the same from year to year.

"1956."

This was 1957. The van was almost new. How many miles could it have on it? I chewed my lip and gave it serious consideration. It'd use up all of my savings, but I wouldn't be buying an old clunker, which is about all you could get elsewhere for three-hundred-fifty bucks.

I'd heard enough about Volkswagen to know the engines were in the rear. I opened the back and looked. It was clean. Strange, but clean.

She brought me the key, let me start it, and take it for a test drive. It cranked a while until gas hit the carburetor, then it sputtered to life and purred along smoothly. I put it in gear and drove down the street. By the time I got back, I'd made up my mind. I asked her to hold it for me while I returned to the base to get my money.

"How are you going to get there?"

"Hitch."

"Take the car. It'll save us both time."

"Really?"

"Sure. If I can't trust the US Air Force, who can I trust?"

I kept that VW Microbus for many years, rebuilding its motor twice. I could remove eight bolts, a few screws, then drop the motor out of it and push the bus away from the motor. When I was done, I could remount the motor myself with nothing more than a jack. It wasn't going to win any races. It might reach seventy miles-per-hour on a flat road with a good tailwind. But it got 32 miles per gallon, when most cars those days barely got nine.

As my discharge date drew near, the Air Force pressured me to re-up for another term. But I had some college credits now and figured if I attended school full time, I might finish my degree by the time I was twenty-five. Besides, I'd joined up with the idea of getting an engineering education, and I intended to get one.

Then one day, an executive from a private firm who held military contracts at Holloman took me aside. "Gizmo, we've had our eye on you and think you'd do well at TWC."

"What's that?" I said.

He looked slightly offended. "Texas Western College—best engineering school in Texas."

"I'm already enrolled in college at Las Cruces."

"We know that. Your credits will transfer, and we can arrange for you to test out of any classes your Air Force technical training already covered." He pulled out a business card and handed it to me. "We need smart electrical engineers with top secret clearance. We're headquartered in El Paso where TWC is. If you go to school there, you can work for us part-time while you get your degree. When you graduate, you'll already have a job."

I glanced at his card and recognized his firm as one of our main subcontractors. This was just the opportunity I was looking for. I shook his hand and accepted on the spot.

Once I was discharged and enrolled at TWC, I went home again. Only for a week this time because I wanted to get back and situated before classes started.

Dad and Mom were so proud. I was the first person in our family to go to college. Sophie'd had her baby, and as she predicted, it was a boy. He was a year-and-a-half old now, and spent a lot of time with Nora's son. The two of them acted more like brothers than cousins.

Tom's prediction that having a family would change Eddie had been wrong, though. Eddie still had his Fairlane, and still drove fast, at least when we were with him. I told Eddie I'd bought a VW, and he made a farting sound with his lips.

Sophie insisted I come over for dinner before I left.

The prospect of another night of watching TV with my folks wasn't that appealing. I told her I would.

Sophie made pot roast, and after she got it in the oven, we listened to music and laughed like teenagers until Eddie walked in carrying a six pack of beer and a road atlas. Sophie pushed herself up from the couch and gave Eddie a kiss. "Sorry, honey. I lost track of the time. Let me go put supper on the table."

"That's all right, babe." He removed two bottles and handed her the carton. "Put these in the fridge, will you?" Eddie fished around in his pocket and came out with his key ring, which included a bottle opener. He popped off the caps, handed me a beer, and sunk into the couch with a sigh.

"Long day?" I asked.

"Same old, same old." He took a long pull, swallowed, and belched.

I pointed to the atlas. "Planning a trip?"

"I wish. No, I got to thinking about your stint in New Mexico, so I looked up Alamogordo on the map." He flipped it open to a page he had dog-eared and spread it out on the coffee table. He drew his finger eastward across White Sands and stopped on Roswell. "It's not that far, as the crow flies. My guess is, it'd take only minutes in one of those fast fighter jets."

I stared at the map. He'd lost me. "I suppose, but why would you want to? Holloman is a much bigger air base."

"Flying saucers, Gizmo, UFOs."

Oh. "I don't know anything about that."

Eddie raised one eyebrow. "Don't know, or are forbidden to say."

"I have no idea what you're talking about."

"They really keep it that hushed up after all these years? Gizmo, Roswell is where that UFO crashed in 1947."

"Hell, Eddie, in 1947 I was twelve years old. The only thing I knew about New Mexico was the state capital. We had to learn that in geography class. And I still can't fathom why they make kids memorize all the state capitals."

Sophie called us to supper.

We barely got our plates filled when Eddie started again. "You were stationed out there all this time and—"

"Honestly, Eddie, I'm sworn to keep secret the things I saw at White Sands. But I swear, flying saucers aren't one of them."

"So, no one ever said nothing?"

I shook my head. "That's Buck Rogers stuff. Nothing more. An airman starts believing in flying saucers, he'd be up for psych review and lose his security clearance real quick."

Eddie got us each another beer. I hadn't finished my first one.

He looked at Sophie. "What have I been telling you? When they cover it up, they hide it from everybody. Gizmo, we get done eating, I'm going to give you an education."

After dinner, Eddie brought a scrapbook from his bedroom that contained pages of clippings from supermarket tabloids, all pasted neatly in place. He rehashed each one while Sophie washed the dishes. I thought it was all bullshit, but I didn't say that to Eddie. Yet, if there was one thing I learned in four years of military service, if the brass said it was a balloon, you damn sure saluted the balloon.

My chair legs made a scraping noise as I stood up. "Sophie, can I dry those for you?"

"No. I just leave them to dry in the drainer. You boys go ahead and talk."

CHAPTER 6

My first foray onto the Texas Western campus came as a shock. For a minute, I thought I was back in Korea. In stark contrast to the adobe-colored, red-roofed buildings of the Las Cruces college, TWC's buildings weren't Korean, but oriental enough that it momentarily threw me for a loop. I soon learned the campus architecture was based on Bhutan and Tibet, though it overlooked the Rio Grande with Juárez, Mexico just across the river.

I had just started fall semester, when the Soviet Union launched Sputnik, the world's first satellite.

Perhaps they still teach about the Cold War in school, I don't know. But following the victory in World War II, countries that had been allies divided into opposing camps, with the USSR on one side and the Americans and British on the other. The two sides got into an arms race, and political tensions ran high. News that the Soviets had a piece of hardware circling the globe and passing over our country every ninety minutes was unbearable. It took the US four months before we got our first satellite, Explorer I, into orbit. Meanwhile, Sputnik continued to beep, beep, beep.

Texas Western had been coed for years, but men seriously outnumbered the women, and my chances of getting a date were slim. When I transferred in, I was years older than my classmates and in a hurry to graduate before I reached the ripe old age of twenty-five. So, I didn't date much in college. I kept my nose in my books. But I loved college. Even the required English Composition helped improve my writing skills. That class also had a higher percentage of female students than my chemistry or calculus classes. Although I might not have had time to date, I enjoyed a class with women.

I lived in the dormitory until graduation because my GI Bill covered it. When handed my diploma, I suddenly found myself homeless and ill prepared for bachelorhood. Up to this point, my parents, then the Air Force, and then the dorm, had provided my bed and meals. When I looked at an apartment with a two-burner stove, I realized I didn't know how to cook. Mom, Nora, and Sophie had always taken care of that. Most guys would think the solution would be to find a wife. But I was late starting on that, and it would require longer than I had at the moment. Instead, I found a landlady.

Senora Jimenez was a plump, cheerful woman about Mom's age and stood barely taller than her front gate. Her husband had died in combat during WWII. She supplemented her widow's pension by letting rooms in her home. The deal included breakfast and dinner—you were on your own for lunch. That suited me, as I was now working full time, and the company had a decent cafeteria.

Mom and Dad couldn't make it down for my graduation, and that wasn't a big deal anyway. I had my photo taken holding my diploma and sent it to them.

During my college years, I hadn't gotten back out to Hollman. Although our engineering firm had contracts with bases all over the southwest, my part-time work was limited to the El Paso office. But I heard things. White Sands Proving Ground had been testing rockets since WWII, when 100 captured German V2s were shipped there for study. It had since been renamed White Sands Missile Range and began testing the Redstone rocket, which would eventually carry America's first two astronauts, Alan Shepard and Gus Grissom, into suborbital space.

My department wasn't involved in rocket science, though every one of us wished we were. The firm's government contracts required Top Secret/Sensitive Compartmented Information protocol, which meant even those with top security clearance were limited to knowing just what they needed to work on their portion of a project.

I'd been full-time about five months when, one October afternoon, I was given a polygraph test.

"You passed," my boss said. "Pack your bags for an extended stay."

"Stay where?"

"That's above my pay grade."

The following morning, two carloads of us left El Paso. This was before they had finished the Interstate highway, and it took us two days to drive there, wherever there was. As we neared our destination, military police patrolling the area stopped us and checked our credentials. At a security checkpoint further on, another set of guards verified our papers and IDs again. As soon as we drove on base, I knew where we were. I was back at Groom Lake. But I didn't know whether I was allowed to talk about having been there before, so I decided to keep mum. If someone at the base recognized me from my Air Force days, I would own up to it. Otherwise, I would just keep my past to myself.

It was designated "Project 51," and I was more than surprised to find the Navy was now in charge. This was still an Air Force base, wasn't it? We were told we'd be working double-shifts for ten months. As soon as I realized how long we were going to be there, I sent Mrs. Jimenez a letter telling her she could rent my room to someone else and asked her to store my things until I returned.

The project was about half done in April, 1961, when we heard that Soviet Lieutenant Yuri Gagarin became the first human to orbit Earth. Shit, our guys hadn't even gotten off the ground. It was humiliating.

We continued working, finishing in August. A new hanger was constructed, then the hangers built when I was there in '55 were converted into maintenance and machine shops. We added administration and storage buildings, a control tower, fire station, and three surplus hangers for the Navy. A new 10,000 foot runway ran diagonally across the salt flat. Seven new jet fuel tanks held 1.3 million gallons.

The Navy also moved 130 duplex housing units from Babbitt, Nevada. During WWII, these had housed civilian workers at the naval ammunition depot. The duplexes were old, but ready-made and still sturdy. It looked like they planned for a large contingent of personnel.

Elsewhere on the grounds, they spruced the place up, planting trees around a reservoir pond to create a recreational area, adding a baseball diamond, gymnasium, and movie theater. Were they still hoping to convince people this was Paradise Ranch?

Security was enhanced, and for the second time in my experience with that place, I was told, "Thank you very much for your assistance, now please leave."

Fine with me.

When I got to El Paso, I went to pick up my stuff from Mrs. Jimenez and find myself another place to live.

"Come in. Your room is all clean and ready. Have you eaten supper?"

"Didn't you get my letter?"

"I did, but my sister came for a visit, and I let her use your room."

"Mighty long visit." I couldn't imagine staying at Nora's or Sophie's for ten months.

"Her husband . . ." She brushed her hands like she was dusting off flour.

Ah. "Where is she now?"

Mrs. Jimenez shrugged. "Reno."

"Oh." I didn't know anyone who'd gotten divorced. Movie stars, sure, but not ordinary people. Of course, I didn't know Mrs. Jimenez's sister, either.

"Put your bag in your room and wash up. I've made green corn tamales."

My favorite.

After we ate, I felt bad about not paying her rent. I knew she couldn't live on her pension alone. I was flush from a bonus I'd received for Project 51, so I laid ten months' back rent on the table.

"That's too much." She pushed it back.

"No. It's fair, and I can afford it."

"But you never slept or ate here."

"I got a place to come back to. That's worth something."

We haggled a bit longer and settled at half.

That night, the Soviets announced that they'd sent up another cosmonaut and kept him in orbit for twenty-five hours. Alan Shepard and Gus Grissom had made suborbital flights earlier that year. Suborbital wasn't the same thing, but we pretended it was. After Thanksgiving, the US managed to put a manned capsule in orbit, but its passenger was a chimp.

It wasn't until February 1962 that John Glenn succeeded in orbiting the Earth three times after his previous launch attempts had to be scrubbed because of a problem with the rocket fuel tanks, and again due to weather. I remember it was a Tuesday. I was out at Holloman Air Base—this time as a private contractor. Worked stopped, and we gathered around a TV someone had carried over from a barracks. About a quarter to nine, our time, his rocket took off without blowing up. There was a collective sigh of relief.

Finally, Glenn was away and riding high. His flight lasted almost five hours. None of us got any work done. We were all glued to the TV.

In those days, the launches were covered live and preempted regular TV programming. NASA also gave the networks unfettered access to the live audio transmission between the capsule and ground crews. This one caught everyone's attention:

> "This is Friendship Seven," Glenn said. "I'll try to describe what I'm in here. I am in a big mass of some very small particles that are brilliantly lit up like they're luminescent. I

never saw anything like it. They round a little; they're coming by the capsule, and they look like little stars. A whole shower of them coming by. They swirl around the capsule and go in front of the window, and they're all brilliantly lighted. They probably average maybe seven or eight feet apart, but I can see them all down below me, also."

I couldn't help but think of my brother-in-law's scrapbook about a UFO crash back in '47. It had set off a flying saucer craze that still lingered with people like Eddie fifteen years later. Now, here, our first man in space has spotted a spooky phenomenon.

"Roger, Friendship Seven," answered a cool customer at Cape Canaveral. "Can you hear any impact with the capsule? Over."

"Negative, negative. They're very slow; they're not going away from me more than maybe three or four miles per hour. They're going at the same speed I am, approximately. They're only very slightly under my speed. Over. They do, they do have a different motion, though, from me because they swirl around the capsule and then depart back the way I am looking."

That set the saucer believers' heads spinning and earned Glenn ribbing for years afterwards.

Then, near the end of Glenn's mission, ever-dependable Walter Cronkite, with carefully chosen words, told us that a loose heat shield could potentially cause Glenn's spacecraft to incinerate as it reentered the atmosphere. "Capcom at Cape Canaveral has advised Glenn not to jettison the retro-rockets after they fire, in hopes that the straps holding the retro pack will keep the heat shield in place."

After Glenn fired the rockets to leave orbit, he plunged into radio silence, and I swear none of us watching breathed.

Capcom's words came out of the TV speaker, "Come in, Friendship Seven, come in."

Nothing.

On and on, Capcom called, with no response.

On TV, Walter Cronkite, the coolest head in America, looked worried. Guys around me who set off rockets and H-bombs for a living started to panic.

Finally, seven grueling minutes later, "Friendship Seven, do you read me?"

"Loud and clear, Capcom."

"Roger that."

The room collectively resumed breathing. Splashdown was a little off target, but a nearby Navy destroyer had him aboard in minutes.

We Americans felt Glenn's accomplishment had put us on even footing with the Soviets. Then in September, President Kennedy threw down the gauntlet, giving his now famous speech committing us to putting a man on the moon by the end of the decade.

It was heady stuff, and I started wondering if I could get a job in the space business.

Chapter 7

President Kennedy's challenge to reach the moon changed the world conversation from an arms race to a space race. Although countries continued building bombs, the news shifted from reporting who tested the biggest hydrogen bomb to who had the latest space rocket. Briefly.

Our firm had engineering contracts at numerous military bases. Because of my previous posting at Holloman, they often assigned me projects there. It was about a two-hour drive, so if I got on the road by seven o'clock, I could be on base by nine. One such assignment came in October, when temperatures in El Paso typically dropped into the lower eighties or high seventies. Hemlines on coeds walking to early classes were above the knee and trending shorter. I didn't mind a bit. It gave me something to think about on my daily commute. I'd been dating, but trying not to get tied to just one girl.

My work week started off normal. We were connecting a new radar system in the control tower. Late in the day, while we were still testing, it started picking up increased blips. Either there was a sudden jump in air traffic or a glitch in the new system.

"Gizmo, you gotta get this fixed," the commander of the control tower said. "I can't tell if these are some of John Glenn's fireflies or the entire Strategic Air Command is in flight."

"I'll have our guys switch you back to the old system and we'll run some diagnostics on this one tomorrow."

Tuesday morning, I was delayed because cars backed up outside the gate while MPs checked everybody's credentials.

"What's going on?" I asked a young airman on guard duty.

"Just doing what I'm told."

"Is this going to be a regular thing?"

"No one tells me and I don't ask." He handed me back my ID and waved me through the gate.

A thin veneer of tension hovered over the base, like a high-pitched background noise you only notice when you concentrate, but never goes away. We could find absolutely nothing wrong with the new radar system. The increase in airborne traffic was real, and no one knew why.

"Probably some large-scale training exercise," the tower commander said. "I should have been informed. White Sands is a closed air space. One of our test missiles hits one of their planes, and I'll have the Pentagon up my ass."

"They're not passing through your air space, sir," I said. "This advanced radar just picks up objects further out."

Pressure did not ease up the rest of the week. They put the base on high alert, and the scuttlebutt was, it included all bases across the south. I had to leave for work a half hour earlier every morning just to clear security. Still, no one said what was up. I was glad when the weekend came. The following week, I was to work in the El Paso office instead of driving to Holloman.

Monday morning, Mrs. Jimenez's urgent rap on the bathroom door startled me while shaving, and I nicked my face.

"Gizmo!"

"Yes, ma'am?"

"Something's happened."

"What?" I wet the tip of a styptic pencil and staunched the bleeding.

"Come. I show you."

I'd have to finish later. I wiped the shaving cream from my face, put on my shirt, and opened the door. She handed me the morning newspaper. A bold typeface headline spanned the front page: "CRISIS President to Address the Nation." I skimmed the article, but it contained no information beyond that President Kennedy would speak at seven p.m. on a matter of the gravest importance. That'd be five o'clock our time.

She wrung her hands and looked at me. "I know your work is secret, but will you at least tell me if I should leave?"

I took her hands in mine. "I don't know anything. We'll have to wait and hear what the President says." To be honest, I did know the Air Force was on high alert, but that happened almost every time a Soviet general farted.

She slipped her hand from mine and rubbed her forehead. "Will you drive me to the market when you get home from work tonight?"

I nodded. "I'll take off early so we're back before the President's speech."

She made huevos rancheros for breakfast, but I felt too agitated to eat more than a forkful and left for the office early. Little got done that day, as all anyone wanted to do was speculate on what the crisis might be.

I left work at three and drove Mrs. Jimenez to the Piggly Wiggly. She gave me a shopping cart to push and took a second one for herself. I followed her through the store as she filled both of them to heaping. Like my parents, she'd lived through the Great Depression and World War II. Her instinct at the first hint of crisis was to stock up—flour, sugar, rice, beans, coffee, cornmeal, and canned meat. We might get nuked, but we wouldn't die hungry.

We'd just put the groceries away when the President came on TV. Normally, she and I sat at separate ends of the couch. That night she squished next to me.

Our handsome young President's voice was eerily calm, yet somehow direct and forceful as he informed us that the Soviets had placed rockets and missiles in Cuba capable of delivering a nuclear warhead to most major cities in the Western Hemisphere. Mrs. Jimenez trembled. I patted her shoulder and concentrated on Kennedy's words. He told the Soviets in no uncertain terms to get the missiles out. His speech ended with a threat. "It shall be the policy of this nation to regard any nuclear missile launched from Cuba against any nation in the Western Hemisphere as an attack by the Soviet Union on the United States, requiring a full retaliatory response upon the Soviet Union."

Ominous. Both of us had witnessed two wars. Nuclear bombs had only been used twice, back in '45. Still, everyone had seen pictures of what they could do. She was too shaken to sleep and stayed up late, talking nervously about anything and nothing.

Finally, I said, "I have to work tomorrow."

"Oh, of course you do." The way she said it implied that I might personally be called upon to stop a war.

She was mistaken. Our firm had nothing to do with the Cuban Missile Crisis, as it came to be known. We were spectators, like the rest of America. The way top secret information was compartmentalized, none of us knew any more than what Walter Cronkite reported, and if anyone did, they couldn't have said anything, anyway.

The next morning, the newspaper featured full page photos taken by our U2 planes of the Cuban missiles. Mrs. Jimenez spread them over the dining table and studied them.

At the office, projects lagged. Rumors circulated, some true, some not, no way to tell which was which. The first true thing we learned was that our military bases worldwide had been raised to DefCon 3, a state of increased force readiness that many assumed was a prelude to war. The next day, they raised the Strategic Air Command to DefCon 2. That might not mean much to someone outside the military, but to put it in perspective,

DefCon 1 means nuclear war is imminent or has already started. So, two was one step away from annihilation.

The ordinary citizen may not have known these codes for force readiness, or what they represented, but driving the streets of El Paso, I sensed palpable fear emanating from everyone.

One measure the President announced was a quarantine of Cuba by the US Navy. All ships bound for Cuba from any port would be stopped and searched for offensive weapons. The blockade was to start at ten o'clock in the morning. The television networks broadcast it live, as they would a space launch. One of my coworkers brought in his Sony portable TV—a new invention shaped like a miniature canister vacuum cleaner. Most of us had never seen one, but we huddled around and watched its eight-inch screen.

Cronkite gave a play-by-play report as ships approached the quarantine line and our destroyer moved to intercept.

I gripped the edge of the desk so hard my fingernails left marks in the polished wood. This was it. If the freighters didn't stop, our destroyer would fire on them. If that happened, a Soviet sub would sink our destroyer. Then we'd retaliate, and things would continue to escalate until one of us decided to use "the bomb."

The entire Cold War had rested uneasily on the threat of mutually assured destruction—the only probable outcome of thermonuclear war—so devastating for both sides that neither side would dare it. It was the reason the US kept setting off ever larger nuclear tests in Nevada. But "nuclear deterrent" was only a deterrent until someone pressed "the button."

After a tense half hour of drama on the high seas, Cronkite reported the Soviet ships had turned back. A cheer went up. But for the rest of the week, apprehension continued to afflict the world.

Finally, on Saturday morning, the news reported that Soviet Premier Khrushchev had broadcast a message on Moscow radio stating that work would cease on the Cuban missile sites, and the weapons would be returned to the Soviet Union. Mrs. Jimenez jumped up from breakfast, ran around the table, and kissed me on the cheek.

"I had nothing to do with it," I said, but I was grinning.

"I know. If Kennedy was here, I'd kiss him. But he isn't."

Khrushchev kept his word, and in early November President Kennedy gave a radio and TV address informing the nation that the missiles were gone from Cuba.

Things actually got a little better then. Stepping to the precipice of nuclear war impelled both sides to reduce the odds of planet-wide destruction. A "hotline" between Moscow and Washington was established to provide instantaneous, direct communications to avert future crises. Over the next nine months, a partial Nuclear Test Ban Treaty was negotiated that prohibited testing nuclear weapons in the atmosphere, under water, and in outer space. Underground tests were still permitted, so the guys north of Paradise Ranch would keep having their fun. On August 5, 1963, the US, USSR, and UK signed the treaty.

The next day was the anniversary of Hiroshima. I wondered if that was intentional.

CHAPTER 8

Throughout that fall, Mom and my sisters kept asking what I was doing for Thanksgiving. Nora and Sophie had new babies and wanted me to see my latest niece and nephew. They'd each had three by now, and I would have thought the novelty had worn off. I knew everyone expected me home for Christmas, and I wasn't sure I wanted to make two trips in a row.

A local El Paso woman I'd been dating sporadically was also pressuring me to spend Thanksgiving with her family in Dallas, so I could meet them. I didn't know if I was ready for that.

Don't get me wrong, I wasn't a virgin—I hadn't been totally tied up in work. But I hadn't dated as much as some of the guys. In college, between my job and trying to graduate early, I rarely had time for girls. After graduation, frequent extended out-of-town work assignments kept me from getting too serious with any one woman. Also, the girls back then all seemed in headlong pursuit of a husband. Maybe it was the constant threat of nuclear destruction hovering over us, maybe because they had few other choices, but they acted like marriage was the end-all be-all. They were sweet girls, but they made me feel like prey and I resisted.

All week, I'd been hemming and hawing, unable to decide about Thanksgiving. Mrs. Jimenez, overhearing my dilemma, said, "You don't have to go anywhere. I'm having my whole family over. You are most welcome to eat with us. Lucinda will be here."

That was a very kind offer, but not without strings of its own. She'd hinted more than once that her sister's daughter, Lucinda, would make a good wife.

I began to hope that the firm would assign me a job far enough away that I could truthfully say, "Sorry, I have to work." Unfortunately, no such assignment materialized. All of November, I worked in the El Paso office or out at Holloman, which was too close to serve as an excuse for anybody.

Friday came. Thanksgiving was the following week, and I still hadn't decided who to disappoint. I had to work at Holloman that day and spent the entire drive there considering alternatives. I got so lost in thought it surprised me when I pulled up to the gate.

I parked, went inside, and resumed the project I'd been working on. About an hour later, a sudden tension arose on the base, as if we were on high alert. There wasn't anything I could put my finger on. No klaxons going off. No fighter jets being scrambled.

Radar was showing increased air traffic, but no one at my level of clearance had an explanation. But something was up. That was for sure.

A memory of the heightened state of tension preceding the President's announcement of the Cuban missile crisis only a year before came unbidden. A sense of uneasiness became so strong in me that I did something I'd never done in the entire time I'd had Top Secret clearance. I called Mom.

"Hi Sven, this is a pleasant surprise. Are you calling to say you're coming for Thanksgiving?"

"Er . . . that's still up in the air."

"Oh."

"I'm not saying no. I just don't know yet. Besides, I'm coming for Christmas. That's not too far off."

She didn't sound panicked or even afraid.

"Is Dad home?"

"Of course not, he's at the plant."

"So . . . nothing's going on there?"

"Well, Nora's coming to take me shopping. It'd help me know how big a turkey to buy, if I knew your plans."

"Anything on the radio?" Mom always listened to the AM radio on her kitchen counter while she cooked or washed dishes. Her favorite station broadcast a couple of minutes of news on the half hour.

"Just the weather report." A tone of concern crept into her voice. "Are you all right?"

"Yeah, I'm fine. I just felt like calling." Perhaps my imagination had gone wild from a work life privy to too many secrets. "I've got to get back to work. I'll let you know about Thanksgiving real soon."

We said goodbye, and I hung up the phone feeling pretty foolish. I had another hour until lunch. I walked over to a coffee pot we kept on a table in the corner and poured myself a cup. Someone had brought donuts. I ate one and got powdered sugar on my tie.

At the exact second I was brushing off my tie, a red-faced airman rushed into the room, screaming, "The President's been shot! Someone's shot Kennedy!"

Those of us who could leave our desks rushed to the nearest barracks with a television. The set was already on when I came in. Walter Cronkite was sitting at a desk in a newsroom cluttered with typewriters and rotary telephones. He held up a photo that showed a motorcade with Jack and Jackie riding in the backseat of a convertible. "This is a picture that has been transmitted by wire. It was taken a few minutes before the incident."

"What incident?" I said.

For the next hour we stayed glued to the barracks TV while Cronkite peered at us through his black-rim glasses. His sonorous voice spoke measured phrases in a careful manner, repeating everything that was known at that time, which wasn't much. "In Dallas, Texas, three shots were fired at President Kennedy's motorcade. The President had been hit and was rushed to Parkland Memorial Hospital."

He continued to fill time, much as he had done during the Mercury space launch delays, while awaiting further news. He'd remove his glasses to talk to us, then put them back on when he needed to read something. Suddenly, someone off-camera slid a piece of paper in front of him. He put his glasses back on, but could barely look at us as he read it. "From Dallas, Texas, the flash, apparently official. President Kennedy died at 1:00 p.m., two o'clock, Eastern Time. . . ." He glanced up at a clock. "Some thirty-eight minutes ago." His voice cracked, and I thought he was about to cry. He put his glasses back on and looked away from the camera. I could see him visibly swallow his emotions. He wasn't alone. A wave of grief crashed over the barracks, and hardened military men around me openly wept.

A few minutes later, a lieutenant entered and told us the base was on lockdown and all civilian contractors were to leave. I nodded and walked to my VW. Men in the parking lot were speculating wildly. Some were certain Castro was behind it. Others claimed it was the Soviets. None of us knew anything but the pain of sudden loss, as if a brother or father had just died.

My microbus chased down the desert road to El Paso as fast as it would go, spawning little dirt devils in its wake. At home, Mrs. Jimenez was a tearful mess, fervently working her rosary beads as if she could personally lift Kennedy into heaven.

"Do you want me to drive you to church?" I said.

She sniffled, wiped her nose, and nodded. So I did. By the time we got back from church, the nightly news said they'd captured his assassin.

* * *

The next three days the nation mourned, and television let no one forget it. All day, every day, something was being said or shown about the man, his upcoming funeral, or the murder of his assassin by Jack Ruby.

Back then, TV stations went off the air every night. But NBC, with cameras inside the Capitol rotunda, decided to broadcast uninterrupted coverage all Sunday night of a quarter-million mourners passing on both sides of the coffin two and four abreast.

Monday, the day of the funeral, I woke up to find Mrs. Jimenez still watching. "Didn't you sleep?"

"How could I, Gizmo?"

"But it's just people, quietly walking past the casket. They've been doing it since yesterday."

"I know, but I was helpless before. This makes me feel like I am there, walking beside them. They have stood in line all night in freezing weather to carry my condolences with their own."

It was apparent she didn't intend to cook breakfast, and I still hadn't learned how. I made coffee and carried two bowls of corn flakes into the living room.

"Gracias," she said.

An announcer with a map showed the route the funeral procession would take from the Capitol to the White House, to St. Matthew's Cathedral, and then to Arlington National Cemetery. All three networks would carry the solemnities in their entirety.

I'd had enough grief and needed a break. I swallowed the last of my coffee and set my cup in the sink. "I'm going for a walk."

"Be back by ten-thirty," she said. "That's when it starts."

I shook my head. "That's eastern time. It'll be eight-thirty here." A short walk, then.

The streets of El Paso were eerily quiet for a Monday morning. Every business was closed. With school canceled, a few kids were riding bicycles, but other than that, I had the sidewalks to myself. Early morning air was cool. Walking felt so good, I momentarily forgot what lay ahead. It wasn't hard. I'd said losing Kennedy was like losing a brother. But I only had sisters. My grandparents had died before I was born. I had no idea what it was like to have someone you loved die.

When I got home, Mrs. Jimenez was wearing the black dress she wore to funerals and wanted me to put on a suit and tie.

Just to watch TV? That didn't make sense.

"You'd better hurry and change," she said. "It's nearly time."

I could see she was deeply upset, so I compromised and put on a dress shirt and tie. When I came out of my room, she'd set glasses of water and a second box of Kleenex on the coffee table. It turned out to be a good thing she had.

The procession, led by a riderless horse and accompanied by military bands, began a four-hour solemn and sorrowful ordeal that had us both weeping. It ended at Arlington with Jackie lighting a gas flame at his grave, which we were told would burn eternally. By that time, we'd used up every tissue in both boxes. Now, I was beginning to understand what it was like to have someone you love die.

She stood up. "I think I ought to change clothes and cook something for us to eat."

Truthfully, I was too upset to have any interest in food. Besides, I didn't think she'd slept since the night before last. I tried to protest, but quickly grasped that she needed some practical, nurturing task to overcome the heaviness hanging over our hearts.

I nodded. "Okay, but don't make too much. I'm not very hungry."

She left to change, and I picked up the wastebasket of used tissues and carried it out to the burn barrel in the backyard. I dumped in all but one, which I lit with my lighter and threw onto the pile. I made sure the rest caught and then walked back into the house.

I turned off the TV and relished the silence.

After twenty minutes, Mrs. Jimenez still hadn't come out of her room. I knocked lightly on her partially closed door, causing it to swing farther open. There she lay on her bed in her slip and stockings, softly snoring. I pulled her door shut and went to the telephone.

"Mom," I said. "I'm flying home for Thanksgiving. Ask Dad if he'll pick me up at the Madison airport Wednesday night."

I needed to see the people I loved.

CHAPTER 9

The year following Kennedy's death, a gray pall settled over our nation. The Kennedy family had brought a youthful glamor to the stodgy old White House. Eisenhower, however great a general he'd been, was the kindly old, bald grandfather you didn't know very well. He spoke softly, had a wan smile, and played golf.

Jack and Jackie had lit the country up like the opening night of a Broadway hit. Magazines called their reign Camelot. Jackie gave the nation a televised tour of the White House—the first glimpse the average citizen ever had inside that august residence. *Life* magazine ran photos of the Kennedy brothers playing touch football on the lawn. Those years felt enchanted, like we really were in Camelot.

Three shots in Dallas, and it was over. Lyndon B. Johnson, the loud, cantankerous, crude Texan, took over, and the country slipped into a funk. The only bright note that entire year was the arrival on the music scene of the Beatles. Leading the "British Invasion," they dominated the airwaves with hit after hit. Though a decade older than the average Beatle fan, I found I liked their music. I had come of age at the birth of Rock 'n Roll, when performers like Buddy Holly, Chuck Berry, Jerry Lee Lewis, and Elvis stole the music scene from the Dorseys and Crosbys. Twelve-bar, three-chord songs, infused with the rhythms of backwoods Mississippi boogie-woogie, won our nickels in the jukeboxes while earning our parents' disdain.

What the Beatles succeeded in doing was to find the heart of us first generation Rock 'n Rollers, then add musical sophistication without undermining the primitive appeal. They dragged us out of the bland pap that pop music had become.

For the next few years, there were always two or more Beatles' songs in the top ten charts. I'll admit lyrics to "I Want to Hold Your Hand" seemed lame to a grown man. Others, like "Please, Please Me," and "Love Me Do," carried a not too subtle sexual connotation, at least from the male perspective. The same hint at "original sin" had caused our parents to denounce Elvis's early music—too sensual, and certain to lead youth into moral decay.

Then, too, there was the Beatles' hair. Today, if you look at their early photos, you'd wonder what all the fuss was about. Boys in church choirs have hair that long nowadays. But aside from Albert Einstein, Americans hadn't liked a man with long hair since Custer. Newspapers and comedians poked fun, saying they looked like girls, but girls treated them like gods. And not just shrieking adolescents in the Ed Sullivan audience, either. Secretaries and young homemakers alike engaged in serious debates over which of the "Fab Four" was the cutest. That didn't go unnoticed by young men. Boys started dressing like Beatles and letting their hair grow.

I opened the *El Paso Times* one morning to learn that when school started in the fall, principals were going to suspend any boy whose hair extended over his collar. I thought that was absurd. My generation had James Dean. Bad boys we called greasers combed their hair into "duck tails." Elvis had long sideburns until he went in the army.

I, of course, couldn't let my hair grow. While I wasn't in the service anymore, I did work for a military contractor and had to keep it cut like Perry Como—or an insurance salesman. Same haircut, really.

Oh, and there was one more thing happening then. While newspapers squandered ink obsessing over Beatles' hair styles, President Johnson got the Gulf of Tonkin Resolution passed, and we were at war for the third time in my short life.

I felt like a hypocrite, working in the heart of what Eisenhower called the military-industrial complex, accepting their money hand over fist. I knew it was time for me to move on. And I knew just where. The first integrated circuit had been built in 1959, and they were now entering production. Computers seemed to be the wave of the future.

I found an opening at the company that had once built adding machines. Now it built computers. I put in my notice, said a tearful goodbye to Mrs. Jimenez, and drove my VW Microbus to Paoli, Pennsylvania, home of the company's Defense and Space Group Division. Space had a powerful draw for me. I'd tried to get hired at NASA, but learned you needed a PhD just to get in the door. I hoped this job would provide me a backdoor into the space program. Maybe develop a computer for them.

Instead, my new employer assigned me to design Defense Department circuit boards. And I was back in the military-industrial complex. My Top Secret clearance was my albatross.

Still, I was making good money and spent lots of it on records. These were 45s—mono recordings on seven-inch platters that had a large hole in the center. When the Beatles began to concentrate more on albums, I invested in a stereo. I hadn't bothered before, because until then, most singers with a hit song put out an album with that one hit and a bunch of fillers. If I already owned the 45, why buy the album? Right from the get-go, the Beatles were different. Nearly every track on their first five albums topped the charts.

I was living alone in an apartment without a TV, but I owned the best stereo system in town. Most nights, I'd invite a girl over to eat dinner, drink wine, and listen to records. I still couldn't cook much beyond toast, so I got to know the best takeout services in town.

Different women came on different nights. I wasn't a playboy or anything, only the beneficiary of a drastic social revolution. Women taking "the pill" could choose to have sexual relations without fear of pregnancy. This shift took me by surprise. When and where I grew up, men and women held adversarial positions—the man trying to get the woman to give in, and the woman trying to get the man to give her a ring. Suddenly, both sexes found themselves on the same side. Instead of saying, "No," women in my circle were saying, "Can I spend the night?"

One of them, Claudia, was a free spirit who called herself Sparrow. She thought the Beatles were all right, but she was into the folk music scene coming out of New York City. She had her own record collection and would bring over songs by Peter, Paul, and Mary, The Rooftop Singers, or Tom Paxton for me to hear.

As we dug ourselves deeper into the Vietnam War, folk songs became the medium of pacifists and antiwar protesters. Music split into two branches—mindless romantic tunes and erstwhile messages of import. At the forefront of the latter category was Sparrow's favorite, Bob Dylan. I didn't think the man sang well, but his lyrics were anything but pap. One night, she brought over *Freewheelin'* and played me "Masters of War." I listened to it and wondered again about my current work on a computer for the Defense Department. In fact, I was beginning to wonder about my entire life's work up to that point.

Labor Day neared, and Sparrow wanted us to take a three-day trip to Greenwich Village. New York City was only a couple hours north on the Interstate, so I said, "Yes."

"We'll bring sleeping bags," she said. "In case we need to sleep on someone's floor."

"I have money," I said. "We can afford a hotel."

"You never know. We might meet someone cool who invites us to stay with them."

The whole concept of sleeping on someone's floor by choice was so far outside the range of my experience that it never occurred to me. In that moment, I realized that except for three days in Las Vegas once upon a time, I'd gone only where sent, never stayed anyplace that hadn't been prearranged. Yet, here was this Sparrow ready to take wing on a whim, unconcerned about where she'd land.

"I'll bring snacks for the road and a thermos of coffee." She kissed me on the mouth and pulled me into the bedroom.

CHAPTER 10

Greenwich Village lay at the south end of Manhattan, far from the towering skyscrapers of midtown, or the glitzy lights of Broadway. It was a world unto itself, with architecture dating back to the nineteenth century. I drove through narrow side streets until I found a parking spot. We locked the van and mingled with the tourists and beatniks. The differences between the two were easy to spot. Beatnik men wore goatees, horn-rimmed glasses, and sandals. The women wore black leotards or capri pants and had long, straight hair. Both sexes wore berets. So did many tourists, bought from numerous shops selling beatnik accouterments.

A couple on a bench in front of St. Mark's played acoustic guitars and sang a cheerful duet. Several other beatniks sat at their feet on the pavement, playing bongos and tambourines. We stood for a while, listening. My plans for enjoying the Village didn't include sitting on a dirty sidewalk in my clean slacks. A stringy-haired girl wearing too much eye makeup handed us a mimeographed flyer promoting a poetry reading that night. Kerouac and Ginsburg were long gone. Columbia students, Columbia drop-outs, artists, folk musicians, and self-proclaimed poets had taken their place in the beat movement.

Sparrow, with her long straight hair, fit right in even though she was wearing a skirt instead of capris. I, on the other hand, worked at a white-color firm. Casual wear meant removing my tie and unbuttoning my shirt collar. Among the beatniks, I looked like a refugee from Madison Avenue or Wall Street.

Sparrow decided to remedy that. She led me into one of many apparel shops in the area and convinced me to buy a pair of brushed denim pants and a burgundy shirt. A lot further out than I was used to—in my world, a pale blue dress shirt was considered radical—but I went with it.

My Florsheim wingtips screamed, "square." Sparrow wanted me to get sandals, but there I drew the line. Eventually, we compromised on a pair of loafers, worn without socks. I changed into my new togs in the store dressing room and put my regular clothes in the van.

We ate lunch at a pizzeria that sold it by the slice on a paper plate. I learned how New Yorkers ate pizza—slice folded in half lengthwise.

That evening, Sparrow took us to "Café Wah?" where Bob Dylan had frequently introduced his new songs. Dylan was too famous for that place now, but newer folk singers played there. After every song, a basket was passed around the room. If you liked the performance, you put in a small contribution. It seemed very egalitarian—letting the audience decide the payment.

Each act had an acoustic guitar, and sometimes a banjo or flute. If there were several members, they sang harmony. Some songs were originals, others, covers of popular folk tunes. It seemed most sets included a rendition of "Blowin' in the Wind," and the exceptions sang Pete Seeger's "Where Have All the Flowers Gone?" Both songs I recognized from Sparrow's records. I had to admit there was real talent there.

Curiously, many of the "cool cats" wore sunglasses indoors, even though it was nighttime and the room dimly lit. Around us, several people rolled their own cigarettes. I'd only ever seen that done in cowboy movies and Bogart films.

A gregarious couple joined us, following the apparent custom of sitting at any table with empty chairs. We became instant friends. Lisa was an abstract painter and Geoff a writer working on his first novel. I didn't mention my defense work. Sparrow carried the conversation for both of us.

After a time, I guess Geoff figured out I wasn't a cop. He showed us a skinny, hand-rolled cigarette. "Do you partake?"

I cocked my head and looked befuddled. Why was he offering me a hand-made cigarette when there was a pack of Marlboros lying right there on the table?

"Is that . . ?" Sparrow said.

Lisa nodded. "Let's step out back."

Sparrow hooked my elbow. "Let's."

We walked into an alley. Geoff glanced both directions, lit up, took a long pull, and passed it to his girlfriend. She took a puff and handed it to Sparrow. The smoke had a strange, heavy, not unpleasant aroma.

I didn't just fall out of a truckload of soybeans. I put it together pretty quickly that they were smoking marijuana.

Sparrow handed it to me. I hesitated, but *what the hell*. I was here for new experiences, and this qualified. I put it to my lips, inhaled, and coughed. Definitely not tobacco.

"You have to hold it in," Sparrow said.

I took another drag and held my breath, choking and trying not to cough. Geoff reached over and took it from me.

We continued to pass it around until it was too tiny to hold. Then Lisa removed a hairpin from her hair and slid what remained between the prongs. We each got one more "toke," as Geoff called it. With only a small burning ember left, Geoff spit on it and then swallowed it.

I burst into laughter, unable to contain myself.

Sparrow looked at me, glassy-eyed. "What's funny?"

At first, I couldn't stop laughing long enough to form words. Finally, I managed to say, "Never seen anyone eat a cigarette butt."

Geoff laughed. Then Lisa and Sparrow joined us. Laughter became contagious and grew until we became hysterical. Fortunately, we had the alley to ourselves.

By the time we reentered the café, the place had filled up to see that night's featured performer, Phil Ochs. Although I'd never heard of him, he apparently had a lot of fans. Our table had been taken during our absence, but Geoff and Lisa found us seats with their friends.

Ochs came on stage and sang several songs, mostly lampooning society or the government. I found his lyrics hilarious, but that was probably the marijuana. Near the end of his set, he performed an anti-war song, "I'm Not Marching Anymore." It spanned the entire history of US wars from 1812 through the current war in Vietnam. The crowd cheered between each verse.

I realized then that I was in the midst of a room full of strangers vocally denouncing the Vietnam War. Because of my job, I was still very much marching *for* the war effort—a sobering thought. I wished I could be so brash as to say, *I'm not marching anymore.*

Those at our table seemed unaware of my consternation. After Mr. Ochs finished, Geoff and Lisa invited us to their apartment.

"We'd love to," Sparrow said, without consulting me.

But I didn't mind. I was still high. "Should I move my van?"

"It's up to you," Geoff said. "There might be a parking spot on our block. You never know."

At this point, I was too stoned to remember where we parked that afternoon and decided to leave it. "The city won't tow it or anything, will they?"

"Not unless you've parked somewhere illegal," Lisa said.

I took that as a "no," though again that might have been the marijuana.

We left the café and walked as a quartet a few blocks over to an old red-brick house subdivided into several apartments. Lisa asked us to take off our shoes as we entered.

It was a small place, a combined kitchen/living room, plus one bedroom with a bath. What surprised me was they had no furniture. A large Persian carpet covered the living room floor. Along the wall were cushions and pillows. The wallpaper exuded an almost subliminal scent of sandalwood incense. An orange crate standing on its end held records and books. Atop it, was an old style record player. Next to the crate stood a tarnished brass floor lamp with a cracked lampshade. The kitchen didn't have a table. A counter with stools served in its place.

"Sit anywhere," Lisa said.

I couldn't imagine my mother inviting guests to sit on the floor. I peeked through the open bedroom door and saw it was equally lacking furniture—just a mattress covered with blankets on a Persian rug.

Lisa opened the refrigerator and removed a gallon of what I assumed was cheap white wine. After all, good stuff wasn't sold in gallon jugs. She set a carafe on the counter next to the sink.

"Can I help?" Sparrow said.

"Sure," Lisa said. "Hold the carafe while I pour. Jugs are too unwieldy to fill glasses with, so I like to decant the wine into something smaller."

The word *decant* cracked me up. As if Gallo was vintage wine that had to breathe.

Geoff kissed the back of Lisa's head. "I'm going next door to get Hodae."

I didn't know what "hoe day" was but thought it might be another slang word for pot, like Mary Jane.

On his way out the door, he pointed to the record player. "Gizmo, why don't you put on some music?"

I nodded and got down on my knees in front of the orange crate. They had an eclectic mix of albums. Dylan, Joan Baez, and Peter, Paul, and Mary, I expected. Also were jazz and be-bop artists whose music I didn't know, even though their album blurbs called them jazz greats. Next to an album of Indian Ragas, I found the Beatles' *Rubber Soul*—a pleasant surprise. The album had come out the previous Christmas. Critics had hailed it as a synthesis of folk, rock, and soul. I owned a copy myself and thought listening to it on this strange night in this strange place would ground me.

I carefully slid the platter from the sleeve and set it on the turntable. I blew a piece of dust from the needle and gently set it on the outside rim. As it spun into the first track, the acoustic riff opening of "I've Just Seen a Face" burst from the speakers. The vocals kicked in and the tempo brought forth a flurry of words. My mind connected it with the folk sets in the café earlier.

I'd been listening to the album for months and recognized from the day I bought it that it was a major shift by the Beatles from the basic rock of their previous albums. As I waited for Geoff to return with more pot, the next track, "Norwegian Wood," with its droning sitar, played. I'd never heard a sitar before *Rubber Soul* came out. I had no idea what the instrument looked like, I only knew its name because it said so on the back cover.

A sudden pot-fueled realization dawned. The Beatles were not only reaching beyond the confines of pop music by introducing new instrumental sounds and rhythms, but were now leading music in a new direction.

Sparrow carried in two glasses of wine and handed me one.

Lisa turned on the floor lamp and draped a silk scarf over the shade. "I hope you don't mind white wine. We used to drink red, but every time we have a party someone spills wine on the carpet. Red is so hard to get out."

I took a sip—sweet, tart, sharp on the palate. Not as bad as I feared from the size of the jug. "Thanks."

Sparrow curled up on a cushion next to mine. Lisa kept moving around the room, lighting incense and a candle stuck in an old Chianti bottle, the kind sold in woven straw, its sides covered with hardened wax drippings. She turned off the overhead light, brought her wine and a plastic sandwich bag of dried leaves, and sat across from us. "Gizmo, pass me that album cover."

I scooched across the floor on my butt, handed it to her, and returned to Sparrow.

Lisa took a pinch of leaves from the bag and crumbled them over John and Ringo's face. She pulled a cigarette paper from a pack of Zig-Zag and used the package flap to scrape the crushed weed into a line, then scoop it into the fold of the paper. I wondered where the pot had come from since Geoff hadn't returned yet.

Quicker than any cowboy in a movie, Lisa licked the edge of the paper and held up a perfect joint. She scraped the loose remnants on the cover back into the bag, then leaned toward the candle flame and lit up. She took a long pull and handed it to me. I took a drag and passed it to Sparrow. The smell of the smoke commingled with the fragrant incense.

The door opened. Geoff and someone else entered. They kicked off their sandals and closed the door. Once I got a better look, I thought Geoff must have woken the poor man from his sleep, for he was wearing a long, white nightshirt, like people wore to bed in the 1800s.

Sparrow offered Geoff the joint, and he accepted it. "This is Hodae." He took a toke, then passed it to Hodae. Geoff exhaled and pointed to us. "That's Gizmo and Sparrow."

"Pleased to meet you," I said. So Hodae was a person.

"There's wine on the counter," Lisa said.

"Hodae has something better," Geoff said.

Hodae picked up the glass. "Wine is fine."

I laughed at his rhyme. The pot was kicking in.

Hodae had longish hair and a beard. He seemed completely at ease wearing a nightgown in front of strangers. He flipped off the kitchen switch, casting the apartment in pastel rays streaming through the colorful silk scarf covering the living room lamp. Flickers of yellow danced from the wavering candle flame.

Side one of the record ended. He smiled and nodded toward me.

A little too stoned, I struggled to my knees, turned it over and started side B.

"You like the Beatles," Hodae said. It sounded like a statement rather than a question.

I nodded, mouth too dry to speak. I sipped some wine. "Very much."

He walked over and stood in front of Sparrow.

She turned her face up to him.

He slipped small squares of paper from a pocket in the side seam of his garment. Okay, so not a nightshirt. Maybe some sort of robe or cassock, like monks or priests wore.

"Stick out your tongue," he said to Sparrow.

She did. He laid a postage stamp size paper on her tongue and tipped his glass to her lips. "Drink, ye child of the cosmos."

The Catholic echoes in the ritual weren't lost on me.

He turned to Lisa and did the same, then repeated it with Geoff. I had only an inkling of what might be going on, but by the time my turn came, I'd made up my mind to commit.

It wasn't bad. The paper melted in my mouth, and the wine washed it down.

Hodae sat on a cushion next to Lisa.

"Aren't you taking any?" I said.

He shook his head. "Can't tonight. My job is to guide everyone through. Don't worry. Leary says it is all about set and setting. Geoff's place is perfect—soft light, sweet smells, nice music."

Guide everyone through what? So far, nothing was happening—just the effects of the marijuana I'd been feeling all night.

The Beatles' record ended and Hodae put on the Indian raga album. At first, it reminded me of "Norwegian Wood." Later, it just became irritating. "Can we please put on something else?"

Hodae came over, lifted the needle off the record, and stroked my head like he was petting a dog. I shook his hand off. He put the record back into its sleeve and looked through the albums. "Everyone stay here. I'll be right back." He went out the door.

I noticed his sandals by the entrance amongst our pile of shoes, and I worried he hadn't worn them. The silence in the room was profound. I wondered if my companions shared my concern over Hodae's sandals. "After all," I said. "What good are shoes if you don't wear them?"

Lisa and Geoff just looked at me. I turned to Sparrow, who was tracing swirls in the carpet pattern with her finger. I watched her finger for a while. What wonderful colors some skilled Persian family has chosen. It felt connected—us on this flying carpet, and those in the Mideast whose art lay beneath our bare feet.

"Creativity spans all borders," I said.

Time had become unimportant, so I can't say if it was a long while or a mere moment before Hodae returned carrying albums. I only know I experienced a wave of despair when I saw him standing there. The quiet had been peaceful. The records under his arm meant it was over.

My fears were unfounded. He put on Beethoven's Sixth Symphony, the Pastoral. The flutes and strings of its opening bars lifted my mood, and judging by their smiles, also those around me. I don't mean to imply that I had any knowledge of classical music. I only learned what we were listening to because it was on the album jacket. When he laid it down, I picked it up and tried to read the liner notes. I stopped on my fourth pass through the first paragraph—I'd reach the last sentence, forget what the first was about, and have to start again.

I set the album down and stretched out on the floor, listening to the music. Its passages painted pleasant images in my mind. Hodae had made a wonderful choice, and because of that, I started to feel like I trusted him to guide our journey.

Hodae rinsed out the carafe and filled it with water. He poured some in each of our empty wine glasses. "Don't drink any more wine tonight—just water."

I raised up on one elbow and took a sip. It tasted sweet and cool, with a faint hint of the Chablis that had been in my glass earlier.

Sparrow, who was sitting cross-legged like an Indian, scooted toward me, lifted my head, and rested it in her lap. She leaned forward, her face filling my vision, breasts lightly pressed against my scalp. Her long, straight hair fell into a curtain around us. "Did he just turn water into wine?"

That was a heavy thought. Had he? I contemplated it for some time before answering. "No. I think he turned wine into water."

Sparrow's pupils, shiny like pools of liquid tar, studied my own. I felt part of my essence flow into her eyes and intermingle with hers.

And we became voyagers through the blackness of space.

CHAPTER 11

Dawn light slipped into the room around the edges of the window shades, bringing with it the sounds of early delivery trucks. The candle in the Chianti bottle had long ago sputtered its final flicker. I was still high, but starting to come down enough to realize we'd stayed up all night.

Sometime during the night, after the music ended, Hodae had read aloud from a book of poetry by Kahlil Gibran. Heavy stuff that set our minds spinning.

I wanted to sleep. The others were yawning, too.

"You'll be fine, now." Hodae opened the door and light spilled in over his bare feet. I had a vague memory of something to do with his sandals. "I'm going home. If you want to talk about your experiences after you wake up, my apartment is next door."

"Thank you, man," Geoff said. "You're one cool cat."

Hodae picked up his sandals and left.

Geoff turned to us. "Lisa and I are going to bed. You cats are welcome to crash here."

Lisa walked into the bedroom, returned with a quilt, and gave us both a hug.

Sparrow gathered all the cushions in the room and set about making a nest, then spread the quilt over it. Next, she pulled off her clothes and stood naked. The fantasy light from the floor lamp lent a pinkish glow to her white abdomen and breasts. I'd been naked in a barracks full of GIs, but I could never imagine baring my body in the middle of a stranger's living room. Until I did it.

I undid my belt, dropped my new brushed-denim jeans to my ankles, and stepped out of them. I unbuttoned my new burgundy shirt and tossed it aside. I hesitated at removing my skivvies, but I was still pretty high. When in Rome. . .

Sparrow lay down on the quilt. I turned off the lamp and joined her. She grabbed an edge of the quilt and pulled it over us.

* * *

A familiar domestic noise woke me. Lisa was in the kitchen making coffee, wearing nothing but a tee shirt. I glimpsed the round cheeks of her bare butt as she reached for a canister on the top shelf.

I sat up. "What time is?"

"Six-thirty."

"In the morning?"

"No."

"You mean we slept all day?"

"Geoff's still at it," she said. "You want coffee?"

"Love some." I needed to pee, but my pants were by the record player where I'd dropped them. "Er . . . would you mind turning around for a second?"

"Why?"

"I'm naked."

"I've seen a penis before."

"Not mine."

"Why, is it something special?"

My face grew hot. "No. It's just . . . I don't know, the way I was raised."

"Man, that's the Puritanical shit we're trying to overcome."

"Listen, I really need to use the bathroom. Humor me. Turn around for two seconds while I get my pants."

She turned toward the wall. "One-thousand-one, one-thousand-two."

I dashed over, snatched up my pants, and turned my back to her while I put them on. To reach the bathroom, I had to go through their bedroom. Geoff was snoring as I passed by.

After I relieved myself, I put down the seat and flushed. I washed my hands, splashed water on my face, and studied myself in the mirror. Same Gizmo. I'd read articles in *Time Magazine* about LSD. Yet here I was, neither enlightened nor schizophrenic.

The door opened. Sparrow came in, still naked—apparently a freer bird than me. Especially when she sat on the toilet and began to go. I cleared my throat and slipped out, closing the door behind me.

In the kitchen, Lisa pressed the plunger of the French Press and poured three cups of coffee. I lifted one to my nose and inhaled the fragrant aroma. Nothing better than the smell of coffee in the morning—even if it was evening.

"You take cream?"

"No, black." I blew on it to cool it and took a small sip. It was strong. I held out my cup. "Just this once."

She added cream to both our cups and handed me a teaspoon. "What about Sparrow?"

"She'll definitely want cream."

Sparrow came up behind me, pressing her bare breasts against my bare back and wrapping her arms around me. She planted a kiss behind my ear, let go of me, and took a sip from my cup.

"Do you want to borrow a tee shirt?" Lisa said.

Sparrow shook her head. "A towel. I'd like to take a shower, if you don't mind."

"Not at all. Towels are in the cabinet under the sink."

Sparrow gathered up her clothing and tugged on my elbow.

I shook my head.

"Come. We'll save hot water."

"You go ahead. I'll take mine later. I want to finish my coffee." Well, that was true enough. Besides, I wasn't high anymore and a little too uptight to shower with a woman who wasn't even my steady girlfriend, while a stranger snored in the next room.

Never one to be discouraged, Sparrow skipped off to the bathroom like a happy-go-lucky child.

The living room was quite a mess, which gave me something to do. I took apart Sparrow's nest and distributed the pillows and cushions around the room the way they'd been when we arrived. Lisa set her cup on the counter and helped me fold the quilt. Perhaps she wasn't aware that her pubic hair peeked out from below the hem of her shirt as she moved. Perhaps she didn't care. I kept my eyes on her face until we'd finished and she'd left to put the quilt away.

By the time Sparrow came out of the bathroom—dressed this time—I had the room shipshape, Lisa had the dishes from last night washed, and Geoff was awake, sitting on one of the counter stools drinking coffee. He opened a tin can labeled "English Breakfast Tea" and removed a bag of pot. Geoff rolled a joint and lit it. He offered it to me. I hesitated. Were we just going to repeat yesterday?

Sparrow reached for it, took a puff, and handed it to me. Okay, I guess that's what we were doing.

We passed it around until it was gone. This time Geoff didn't eat it. He put it out, dropped it into the bottom of the tin can, and put the lid on.

After I showered, I came into the kitchen and found Lisa bent over, staring into a nearly empty refrigerator, her bare ass showing again. Man, I wished that woman would put some pants on before I got an embarrassing erection.

"Is everybody as starved as I am?" I said.

She straightened up.

"Yes," Sparrow and Geoff echoed from the living room.

"Let's go out," I said. "My treat."

"You don't have to do that," Geoff said.

I caught Sparrow's eye. "No, you guys gave us a place to stay, and . . . well, everything else. It's only fair."

"Yes," Sparrow said. "Let us return the favor."

"Gizmo, you're a cool cat," Lisa said.

I smiled at her. "You'll have to put on pants, though."

She lifted her shirt tail a few inches. "Didn't you know? Pubes are in fashion this year." She laughed when my face turned bright red and then dashed into the bathroom.

Geoff paid neither of us any mind. Maybe she was that outrageous around everyone.

"We should invite Hodae to join us," I said.

"The more the merrier," Geoff said. "Give me fifteen minutes to wash up."

I put on my shoes and went to the apartment next door. I pressed the button for the buzzer, but couldn't hear anything. I knocked. No one answered the door. I knocked louder.

Sparrow came out. "Doesn't seem like he's home."

Lisa joined us. "Got everything? Geoff's waiting to lock the door."

I glanced at Sparrow, who nodded.

"Good to go," I said.

"Geoff, they're ready to split," Lisa said.

They led us to a neighborhood bistro that served clam chowder and Cuban sandwiches. Only, because of the whole missile business, they called them "hot pressed," instead of Cuban.

Marijuana makes people hungry. I already kind of knew that. But to be fair, we hadn't eaten in twenty-four hours. Everything on the menu looked so good, we ordered way more than necessary. After we'd eaten as much as we could, I took what we had left to the man at the counter and asked him to wrap it to go. Lisa, Geoff, and Sparrow waited outside on the sidewalk.

I came out carrying one of those large brown paper grocery bags. The others were trying to decide where to go next, but I really wanted to make sure my van was all right. So they walked us around the Village until I found where I'd parked it.

"I'm relieved they didn't tow it. And look, I didn't even get a ticket."

"It's Sunday," Lisa reminded me.

I unlocked it and opened the side doors.

Geoff leaned in. "Man, this is the coolest."

I handed him the grocery bag. "Hop in. I'll give you a ride."

We drove to their apartment, but all the parking spaces on their street were taken. I put the VW in neutral, set the brake, and left the engine idling. We got out and stood around in the street. I hugged Lisa, thanked her, and said goodbye.

She frowned. "You're leaving?"

I turned to Sparrow. "There won't be as much traffic tonight as there'll be tomorrow. If we get on the road now, we should be in Philly before midnight and have all of Monday to recoup."

Sparrow was okay with anything.

"Well, let me roll you guys a joint for the road," Lisa said.

I didn't need it, but Sparrow said, "That'd be cool." She took the grocery bag from Geoff and walked inside with Lisa. Geoff and I wandered behind the van, and I opened the engine compartment to show him. That's what guys did. I don't think he was particularly mechanically minded, but as I waxed on about how the Germans had so cleverly fit the whole motor in a small, self-contained space, he looked interested. Or maybe he was just stoned.

The women came back outside, and I closed the engine cover. We all hugged and promised we would write. Sparrow and I waved out our respective windows as we drove away.

CHAPTER 12

Okay, I'd tried LSD. It was still legal then. I won't say I wasn't affected, but I didn't become schizophrenic or check myself into a loony bin. Although I wasn't itching to try it again, "Turn on, tune in, and drop out," was a popular quote from Timothy Leary at the time. Quit my job? Not just yet.

But Sparrow did.

We saw each other sporadically after we returned to Pennsylvania, about as often as before. Then one night, she told me she was moving to Greenwich Village to be part of the "scene."

"When?"

"After I get paid on Friday."

"Why?"

"You're kidding! You saw. It's a happening place. Paoli is nowhere-ville. Come with me."

I shook my head.

"Suit yourself." She brightened. "You can visit. I'll send you my address as soon as I score my own pad."

I smiled. "That sounds nice." But I didn't really expect it would happen. And I was right. She disappeared into the Village, and I never knew where.

The memory of the folk singers protesting the war stuck with me. I did consider changing jobs. A company outside Boston was developing the first computer small and cheap enough for a mid-size business to use. I thought it'd be cool to be in on something that groundbreaking. Up to then, a computer filled an entire room. These minicomputers were no larger than a modern refrigerator. The electronics industry had changed from tangles of wires to the use of printed circuit boards. I had experience designing printed circuits like this company was using in their systems, so I put out some feelers.

Located where they were, the company had a ready supply of talent from MIT, so I really didn't think I had a chance. But what I had over recent graduates was nine years of experience. I'd cut my teeth on transistors as their use crept into modern electronics. The company saw my value and hired me.

I flew home for Christmas. We pretended things were normal, but they weren't—on many levels. Mom was not doing well. An unexpected heart problem had surfaced the previous week and laid her low. Nora and Sophie took over holiday preparations, which saddened Mom. Dad's gray hair had turned whiter and his eyes sagged. I suspected the doctors had told him more about Mom's condition than he'd shared with us.

Mom's grandchildren lifted her spirits. My sisters now had three apiece, and the kids' attempts to guess the contents of the wrapped packages beneath the Christmas tree made her smile. But she slept a lot, and when she was out of bed, she usually had to lie on the couch after being up only a few minutes.

While I was there, the doctor prescribed Mom a new medication. Nora asked me if I wanted to ride with her to the pharmacy.

"Sure." I was glad to get out of the house. Besides, I suspected she wanted to get me alone to talk about Mom's health.

Nora and Tom had prospered and now had two cars. Hers was the family station wagon, complete with fake wood panels along both sides. She braked at the stop sign, turned right on Main Street, and said casually as you please, "I've been seeing an analyst."

"You have?"

She nodded. "In Madison. I drive up there two mornings a week after the kids get on the school bus."

"Does Tom know?"

"Yes. He doesn't think it's helping. 'Waste of money,' he says. If he'd let me work, I could pay for it myself."

"Tom won't let you work?"

"He's afraid people will think he can't support his family."

"No one would think that."

"He would. Says a woman's place is at home with the children. The problem is, the children are busy with Scouts, and basketball, and hockey, and everything else. I'm stuck in the house, alone, and frankly, Gizmo, it's depressing."

"Well, sis, you started taking care of me while Mom and Dad worked during the war. That was twenty-five years ago. I expect you're good at it by now."

"That's the problem. I have the house cleaned and dinner planned by ten a.m., then nothing to do until school's out, when I become the chauffer. I know being a good homemaker is supposed to be the pinnacle of womanhood, but I don't believe it. So, I started psychoanalysis."

"Has it helped?"

"Not much, maybe not at all. I just lie on his couch and talk. It's better than sitting home talking to myself, but I don't feel we're even close to figuring anything out."

She pulled to the curb and parked in front of Rexall, the town's only pharmacy. We got out of the car, met by an icy wind that cut right through my coat. Snow flurries whipped past our faces.

"Maybe we'll have a white Christmas," I said.

"Not if this wind keeps up. None of it will stick to the ground."

I realized that she was seeing the negative in everything and wondered if her psychiatrist would consider giving his patients LSD. I didn't bring it up. He was her doctor, not me. Besides, I didn't plan to tell my family about my Labor Day adventure.

When we returned with the medicine, Mom was looking peaked. Nora gave her one of the new pills and went home to cook Tom's supper. I sat with Mom until Dad came home, but she mostly napped. Then I went to the kitchen, trying to puzzle out what to do about dinner, as she seemed too indisposed to cook. Prairie View was too small to have anything in the way of takeout, which is what I lived on. The only thing I made at home was cereal and toast, and that didn't seem like dinner. Then I found a package of chipped beef in the refrigerator and thought we could have chipped beef on toast. The package had directions for making a white sauce.

Before I started, Dad came into the kitchen carrying a casserole dish covered with foil. "Sophie sent this. She says all we have to do is heat it."

That, I could manage. I had plenty of experience reheating takeout and set the oven to 350 degrees. "How was your day, Dad?"

"Same as ever. How was your mother's?"

"She slept a lot. Nora picked up the new prescription and gave her a pill around four o'clock. She said to give her the next one at eight."

Dad slid the casserole into the oven. "Tom said he'll bring Nora and the kids over after supper."

"Good. Mom's happy with the grandkids around."

"Yep, kids are a blessing. You'll see. When are you going to give us a couple?"

"Well, I'd need to talk to my wife about that. And before that, I'd need a wife."

"Anyone in mind?"

"No one special."

"Don't wait too long, son. You'll be an old man before you know it. Then who will want you?"

I laughed that off and changed the subject. "How's your health, Dad? No offense, but you seemed to have aged since I saw you last."

"Have I? Don't look at myself in the mirror too often."

"Not even to shave?"

"I can do that blindfolded."

A clamor from the front room sounded like Sophie, Eddie, and their brood had arrived. She came into the kitchen, hugged Dad and then me. "Haven't you eaten yet?"

"Just got it in the oven," Dad said.

"Mom's up," she said. "Go be with her while I get dinner on." She began pulling lettuce and salad vegetables out of the refrigerator. Dad and I left her to it.

Mom was sitting up, looking much better, like the new pills were working. Sophie's kids nestled with her on the couch, showing her Christmas projects they'd made at school. Dad leaned over them, kissed Mom, and ruffled the hair on each grandkid's head.

Eddie shook my hand and offered Dad and me a beer from a six-pack of Schlitz he'd brought with him. We accepted, and he put the rest in the fridge. When he returned, he wanted me to go out to his car and see his new eight-track tape player. These had just come on the market. He started the engine and handed me a plastic case about the size of a paper-back novel. He pointed toward a rectangular slot in the dash. "Push it in."

I did, and wonderful sound filled the car—as good as my home stereo. At that time, cars radios were AM mono, which delivered tinny treble-y music. He pushed a button, and the music changed to a different song. He handed me one of the tapes to examine. It was sealed all the way around save for a one-inch hole in the bottom and a gap on the end where I could see an inch of brown magnetic tape.

"That thing holds an entire record album," Eddie said.

I read the list of songs on the front label. It was impressive. "I've got to get one of these." I imagined how the sound would fill my VW Microbus. It'd be like driving down the road inside a speaker cabinet. "Where'd you get it?"

"The auto parts store installs them."

"Oh." I didn't have my VW with me. I'd flown in.

"But you're an electrical wiz, Gizmo. You could install it yourself, I'm sure."

Dad came outside without a coat on and tapped on the window. Eddie rolled it down.

"Sophie's got dinner on the table. Says for you to come in." He shivered and hurried back to the house.

Eddie rolled the window up and turned off the engine.

"Thanks for showing me that, Eddie. I might buy one to take back with me."

"I'm sure they sell them in Philadelphia."

* * *

Christmas Eve, we all went to church, even Mom. Christmas morning, about five, I heard noises in the kitchen and came down to see if Mom was all right. It was Nora, come to put the turkey in the oven.

"Merry Christmas," I said.

"Merry Christmas." She slid the big blue-enamel roaster into the oven and closed the door. "Sorry, I'm in a rush. I've got to get home before the kids wake up. I'll be back at nine. Everybody's meeting here for breakfast."

Sophie and Eddie's family arrived just before nine. Nora and Tom returned with their kids. Sophie had baked two large cinnamon nut rolls, which she sliced and served for breakfast.

"This is delicious," I said. Sophie beamed.

My niece and nephews, eager to open more presents, begged the adults to eat quickly. We finished our rolls and carried our coffee into the living room. Fifteen minutes later the room was ankle deep in wrapping paper, and every kid was clamoring to show Uncle Gizmo what they'd gotten. Dad and Eddie gathered up the wrappings and took them out to burn while the women headed to the kitchen to start dinner preparations. Tom made the older boys clear the breakfast dishes from the dining table, and the younger ones set the table for dinner.

With everybody else gainfully occupied, I wandered into the kitchen. My sisters didn't want Mom to overdo it, so they had her sitting in a chair cutting vegetables for the relish tray. She finished and reached for a sack of potatoes.

"Mom, you ought to rest for a bit," Sophie said.

"I'll sleep when I'm dead. Peeling potatoes won't kill me."

"The doctor wants you to take it easy." Sophie took the paring knife from Mom and handed it to me. "Gizmo can peel the potatoes."

"Can I? I've never peeled a potato in my life."

Sophie raised her eyebrows. "Not even in service?"

I shook my head.

"Well, a brainiac like you shouldn't have any trouble figuring it out."

Nora, stirring a pot on the stove, turned toward me. "What do you cook at home?"

"I don't. I never learned."

Nora frowned. "That's my fault."

"No, it's not. I enlisted right out of high school."

Mom grabbed my arm. "Aren't you eating?"

"I eat plenty. Takeout most nights, restaurants sometimes. There's a cafeteria at work for lunch."

She picked up a potato and tried to take the knife back. Nora shook her head.

"Mom, I've got this," I said. "Cut off the brown part, keep the white part. Right?"

* * *

Christmas fell on a Sunday that year, so Dad's plant gave employees Monday off as well. Eddie suggested the guys should go out for beers Monday evening. I didn't want Mom to be alone, so I said, "Let's buy a couple of six-packs and play cards at Mom and Dad's."

Dad looked relieved. "Good idea. I'll make popcorn."

Tom and Eddie arrived just as Walter Cronkite did his typical sign off, "And that's the way it is, Monday, December twenty-sixth." Dad turned off the television. Mom was already in bed, though it was early. I set up the card table while Dad popped corn. We chose partners and started playing Euchre. An excellent game because the play is fast, yet it's not demanding enough that you can't talk at the same time. Dad was my partner, for which I was grateful because he was hard to beat. He'd played Euchre for over fifty years and knew every trick and strategy.

We won the first two games, but Tom and Eddie weren't about to give up. I had to fly home the next day and decided this was my last chance to tell Dad I was moving. It was Tom's deal. While he shuffled the cards, I said, "As soon as I get home, I'm moving to Massachusetts."

Dad set down his beer. "You're what?"

"I'm starting work at a computer company outside Boston right after New Year's."

He furrowed his brow. "Do you think that's wise? You've only been on your present job for a couple of years."

"It's a good opportunity. I'll be designing the newest type of circuits."

Dad shook his head. "I don't like this idea modern young people have of changing employers all the time. Sure, after the war I had a number of jobs, but that wasn't by choice. Companies kept laying people off. Things are stable now. You find a good place to work, stay there for thirty years, and they give you a pension when you retire. That's what I'm doing." He nodded to my brothers-in-law. "Tom and Eddie, too."

"It might be that way in factory work," I said. "But the fastest path upward in my field is to find companies developing the latest technology and get in early."

He tapped his temple with his forefinger. "Think, Gizmo. Keep switching jobs until you reach my age, and you won't have any pension."

"It's too late to change my mind," I said. "Anyway, a week from now, I'll have a new address. I'll send it as soon as I know."

"Well, don't tell your mother. Let me do it. We can't upset her."

I didn't see why my having a new job would upset her. He was the one getting bent out of shape.

"Are we playing cards here, or what?" Tom said.

I glanced at the card he'd turned up. "I pass."

Eddie passed.

Dad said, "Pick it up. Can't make points by passing."

Chapter 13

The following week, I loaded all my possessions in my van and moved to Massachusetts. One drawback of VWs, you had to drive a long while before the slightest amount of heat came out of the vents. That meant, if I wanted to keep warm, I couldn't stop often or for long.

I'd only been at my new job for a week when Sophie called me at work, in hysterics. "Mom died."

I took the receiver from my ear and stared at it. The tinny sounds of Sophie crying poured out of the earpiece. I put it back up to my ear. "When?"

"A few minutes ago, you're the first person I called." She let out a sob. "Gizmo, come home."

"I will."

I hung up and told my new boss what had happened. He was very understanding. Even though I'd only started there, he told me to take all the time I needed. I raced to my apartment, threw my suit and other clothes in a suitcase, and drove straight to Logan airport. I left my van in long-term parking and bought a ticket at the counter. While I waited to board, I got change for a buck at a newsstand and called Nora from a pay phone. We didn't talk long. She had a million things to do. I gave her my arrival time and flight number and asked her to have Tom or Eddie pick me up at the airport.

Mom's sudden death made me doubly glad I'd gone home for Christmas. I changed planes in Chicago and the layover gave me too much time to think. Was there some sign I'd missed? Could I have stayed with her longer instead of heading off to Massachusetts?

Dad was waiting for me when I got off the plane. I hugged him. He patted my back twice and pushed me away. This was before men started hugging.

"I told Nora to send one of the guys," I said. "You shouldn't have had to."

He pulled out a handkerchief and blew his nose. "It was my idea. I needed a long, quiet drive."

"What can I do?"

"Nothing. There are too many hands and too few things for them to do." He fished out his keys and handed them to me. "You can drive us home. I'm beat."

Conversation on the drive home was minimal. Just basic facts—she'd gone into the hospital last night and died this afternoon with him, and Nora, and Sophie around her. The funeral would be the day after tomorrow, with a viewing at the funeral home tomorrow night.

"I didn't know she was that bad," I said.

"None of us did. I thought the medicine would give us more time. I was wrong. It was only to help her chest pains." He blew his nose again and never spoke another word until I parked in his garage an hour later.

* * *

I woke the next morning with the strongest urge to see Mom, probably because I hadn't been with her when she died. It felt like I'd left something unfinished.

At the breakfast table, Dad and I sipped coffee. Neither of us felt much like eating. "Dad, is there anything you need for me to do for you?"

He looked up from staring into his cup. "No. It's all arranged. There's nothing for any of us to do but wait."

I couldn't do that. "I'd like to see Mom. Can I borrow your car?"

"Visitation doesn't start until six."

"I know, but I want a few minutes alone with her."

He stood up like an old horse on its last legs and leaned against the wall next to the kitchen telephone. "Let me call the funeral home and tell them you're coming." He removed a business card tucked behind the rotary dial, picked up the receiver, and dialed.

He was still on the phone when the doorbell rang.

"I'll get it."

It was Louise Brockport, a widow who lived two doors down. She handed me a casserole and a gush of sympathy. I thanked her and returned to the kitchen. I opened the refrigerator and found it crammed to the gills with covered dishes from apparently every neighbor and church lady Mom ever knew. I shuffled them around a bit, making a hole for Mrs. Brockport's.

"They don't have her ready yet," Dad said.

"Who?"

"Your mother. But the funeral director said you can come at one o'clock."

I made us toast and cereal for breakfast, mostly to fill the time. We drank coffee together and waited. Eventually, Dad dropped his spoon into his uneaten bowl of raisin bran and left to take a shower. I phoned Nora and Sophie, who both wept while we spoke. That got me started, too. Intermittently, the doorbell rang and more food arrived—cakes, pies, and Jell-O salads.

At noon, I made us sandwiches, but neither of us was hungry. I wrapped them in wax paper and set them in the refrigerator on top of a casserole. "Dad, you want to come?"

He shook his head. "No. This is your time."

I felt bad leaving him. He'd never seemed so alone. "Ride with me, then. I'll drop you at Nora's and pick you up afterwards."

He shrugged and patted his pants pockets. "Car keys must be upstairs on my dresser."

I glanced at the kitchen clock. It was a quarter to one. "Meet me at the car. I'll get them."

* * *

After the funeral, the house filled with relatives and neighbors. Nora, Sophie, and several ladies from the church kept replenishing food as guests consumed it. There were more tears until it seemed none of us could cry any more. Then some new arrival with the best of intentions would say something, and Sophie, or Nora, or Dad, or I would burst into tears. Then, the rest of us would get caught up in the emotion. By the time everyone left, we were wrung out.

The next day, Nora and I talked about who would take care of Dad.

"I suggested he move in with me or Sophie," Nora said. "He nixed that right off the bat, saying, 'I've lived in this house since before the War, and I see no reason to move.'"

"So what's the plan?"

"Sophie and I will take turns having him over for dinner. Other nights, we'll leave a casserole in his refrigerator. He'll have at least one decent meal a day."

"What about laundry and housekeeping and all the things Mom used to do?"

"I'll do it. My analyst thinks I have too much time on my hands, anyway."

"Well, I can help financially, at least. You said you wanted a job and Tom wouldn't let you work. Let me pay you."

"Gizmo! You really think I could accept money for taking care of my own father! Tom and I are doing quite well, thank you. I didn't need the income. I just needed a job to help me feel . . . you know, worthwhile."

"My mistake. Well, taking care of Dad will fill the bill."

"Taking care of people is all I do now."

I squeezed her arm. "I'm better at transistors and resistors than understanding what women are saying. Tell me in plain English what you want, and if I can do anything about it, I will."

She patted my hand. "If I knew that, I wouldn't need a psychiatrist, would I? Just go back to your computers and don't worry. We'll be fine here."

But I couldn't help worry. I'd left here two weeks ago thinking Mom was fine, and look how that turned out. Nora already seemed deeply unhappy. I could only imagine what Mom's death would do to her mental health.

* * *

At Easter, I flew home for the weekend. I hadn't been going home that often before, but I wanted to see how Dad was doing. "My job and the grandkids keep me hopping," he said cheerfully.

When I visited Nora, I asked her if he was putting on a false bravado for my benefit. We were standing next to her sink. She shook a yellow tablet from a prescription bottle, popped it in her mouth, and took a sip of water. "No. We're happy as clams."

Were clams happy?

I nodded toward the bottle. "Are you ill?" She'd been my second mother. I couldn't lose her, too.

She patted my cheek. "Don't worry. I'm fine. These are just something the doctor prescribed for my depression."

"Is it helping?"

She shrugged. "I call them 'happy pills,' and they take the edge off. But I don't think he understands what's really going on with me. I lie there twice a week and talk and talk. He takes notes, but he never gets it."

"What doesn't he get?"

"My profound emptiness." She absently gazed out the kitchen window. "Magazines tell you having a husband and children make women fulfilled. I suppose when the kids were small, and I was busy nursing and changing diapers, it did feel like I had a purpose. Now I'm almost forty. There'll be no more babies. So what am I to do for the next thirty years? Clean the same floors over and over again? Cook dinner by five? Take pills?"

I didn't have an answer for her.

Nora baked ham and scalloped potatoes for Easter dinner. Our holidays had always been at Mom and Dad's, but Nora said, "That will only bring up painful memories. From now on holiday dinners will be at my house."

No one disagreed.

CHAPTER 14

I returned to Massachusetts confident Dad was adjusting to being a widower. I put my head into my work, glad to be developing computers for civilian use for a change. The younger guys in my office, all MIT alumni, often took me to parties in Cambridge. The fact that I was a decade older didn't matter when we talked about magnetic core memory or 12-bit processors. But I quickly learned to keep my past to myself when the topic turned to the Vietnam war. And in those years, it always did.

Despite President Johnson's claim we were winning "the hearts and minds" of the Vietnamese people, an ever-growing number of Americans were sick of the war. It became increasingly uncomfortable to admit my prior association with the military, especially in left-leaning Cambridge.

The nation became polarized and the collective grief so intense that everyone needed a break. In May, the Beatles gave it to them with *Sergeant Pepper's Lonely Hearts Club Band.* It broke in at number one on the charts and remained there for fifteen weeks, leading us into, and all the way through, what came to be called the "Summer of Love."

I bought the album the day it came out and invited several guys and girls from work over that night for a listening party. The album cover depicted the Beatles wearing colorful Edwardian military band uniforms, standing in front of a collage of celebrities ranging from the Marx Brothers to Mae West. The picture made you smile and turned the prevailing gut reaction against men in uniform into a bit of a lark.

They had again turned pop music on its head. I won't say the songs were un-Beatle-like; they'd hinted of coming change with the odd sounding "Strawberry Fields Forever/Penny Lane" single released a few months prior. But the new tunes were a mix of vaudeville music hall, circus, and psychedelic. "Lucy in the Sky with Diamonds" openly told the world the four lads had taken LSD. Many nights I'd lie on my couch listening to it with my eyes closed, and re-experience that night in Geoff and Lisa's apartment.

Were any Beatniks left? Everywhere, the new hippie phenomena were cropping up. Men wore their hair much longer than when the Beatles first shocked the world. Women threw away their bras, and both sexes wore beads. They were much more happy-go-lucky than the earnest, black-clad beatniks and professed peace, happiness, and free love. It had started in San Francisco's Haight-Ashbury district, which soon became the mecca for thousands of young people with their thumbs out hitchhiking cross-country. *Time* and *Newsweek* featured hippies on their covers. A new generation trotted out Jack Kerouac's *On the Road*. I imagined Sparrow lived in San Francisco by now.

One didn't need to go to Haight-Ashbury, though. Hippies were a national phenomenon from Cambridge to Austin and every burg in between. No doubt some kid attending my old high school was smoking pot and going barefoot on the streets where I grew up. Dad and Eddie and Tom wouldn't like it, but I saw it as a good sign.

Although people still opposed the war, those same people approached passersby with a smile on their face, holding up two fingers, and saying, "Peace." Indeed, 1967 was a Summer of Love, and I sat at my drafting table, drawing circuits and humming "With a Little Help From My Friends."

At a party in Cambridge one Friday night, I saw a flyer advertising free mediation classes at the Unitarian Church. It promised to be a simple method to realization of the inherent worth of self. I thought of Nora and wondered if it might be a cure for her discontent. I knew she wouldn't find it at our small-town public library.

I showed the flyer to the woman giving the party and asked if she knew anything about it.

She glanced at the paper and shook her head. "I don't know who left that here."

According to the flyer, classes began the following day. I decided to check it out. If it worked, I'd share it with Nora when I went home for Christmas.

Saturday, I returned to Cambridge and located the Unitarian Church. A sign for the class directed people to the fellowship hall. I entered and found the typical collection of hippies—women in peasant blouses and long skirts, others wearing miniskirts and knotted blouses that bared their midriffs. A white guy in an African dashiki sported a huge afro. Another had shoulder length hair and a beard that nearly reached his belt. In fact, most of the men had facial hair—if not a beard, then at least mutton-chops or a mustache. I felt naked with my clean-shaven, Midwestern look.

A majority of the crowd were in their twenties, with one glaring exception, a man I judged to be my father's age. Although his look was as far away from Dad's as I could imagine. Long gray hair stuck out wildly, Einstein-like. A gray bottlebrush mustache cemented the image. He had on an India-print shirt and bell-bottom trousers.

Chairs had been pushed to the sides and back of the room. Most people sat on the floor. The man with the afro said if sitting on the floor bothered anyone, they were welcome to use a chair. It would not hinder the meditation practice he was going to teach us.

Okay, so now I knew who was giving the class.

The old man who resembled Einstein ignored the offer of a chair and sat on the floor with his legs folded like a pretzel. Someone turned off the overhead lights, and I sat down where I was, near the back of the crowd, on a chair.

"Everyone sit erect, spine straight," said the afro guy. "Inhale deeply, and let it out. Relax your muscles and let the tension flow out of you."

His instructions seemed contradictory. To stiffen one's spine naturally required tightening the back muscles. Was that part of the tension we were supposed to release?

"Close your eyes and concentrate on the movement of your breath. During inhalation, mentally think the word 'so.' As the breath flows out, think 'hahm.'"

I started thinking *sew . . . hem . . . sew . . . hem . . .*

"So . . . hahm . . . so . . . hahm—like calm with the 'el' silent," he intoned in a sonorous voice.

Oh. So and Hom like hominy. Now I got it.

"When the mind wanders, gently turn your attention back to the breath."

I did my best, but I admit my mind frequently roamed.

Eventually, I managed to stay focused on my breathing. And by the time the meditation ended, I was in a very peaceful state, so much so that I was not in the slightest hurry to leave. Around me, people stood and put on their jackets. From behind me, a pair of cool hands clamped my eyes shut. "Guess who."

"Sparrow!"

She took her hands from my eyes and came around to stand in front of me. "How did you know?"

How *did* I know? I'd had dozens of women friends in Cambridge, any of them more likely to be here than Sparrow.

I shook my head. "Your name just came to me."

She held out her hands, took mine, and pulled me up. We embraced. "I thought you'd be living in California," I said into her hair.

She held me at arm's length and looked into my face. "I was. I caught a ride with a group of folk singers from the Village who were to perform at the Monterey Pop Festival. That was a gas. You should've seen it. A real Be-in." She had picked up the lingo. "Afterwards, the band went back to New York, but I didn't want to miss San Francisco, so I caught a ride there and crashed with some hippies."

I smiled at her. "All summer, every time the radio played that song, 'San Francisco (Be Sure to Wear Flowers in Your Hair),' I pictured you doing just that."

She grinned. "And I was. Flower-power, baby."

"So, what are you doing in Cambridge?"

"Woody came here to invite some philosophers from the college to his place in Vermont. We saw a flyer for this class and decided to check it out. Wild coincidence, eh?"

"Woody?" Of course, Sparrow would be with someone after all this time. Undoubtedly, there had been many since I saw her last. We were in the middle of the sexual revolution, after all.

"Oh! You have to meet Woody!" She pulled me across the room, all the while talking a mile a minute. "Woody and I met at a poetry reading at City Lights Bookstore in San Francisco. He and his commune had temporary use of a place in Haight-Ashbury, and said I could crash there until they left."

I thought meditation calmed people down. Not Sparrow.

"When it was time for them to come home, I rode along, and I've been in Vermont ever since."

At that point, we'd reached a cluster of hippies surrounding the Einstein-looking old man. Sparrow wedged between them, dragging me with her. "Woody, this is an old friend of mine from Philadelphia, Gizmo."

He turned and looked at me. Wise eyes crinkled as he smiled. "Hello, Gizmo. Good name. Did you come up with that yourself?"

I sheepishly looked at my shoes. "No, the guys in the service started calling me that because I could fix things."

I'd said it without thinking. At the mention of being in the service, those nearest us stepped back as though I had cooties.

Yet Woody did not. He threw his arm over my shoulder and laughed. "Always good to be someone who fixes things." He turned to a hippie girl. "Sunshine, a map please."

A haversack sewn out of the kind of flowery upholstery material you'd find on some grandmother's couch hung from her shoulder. She glanced at me warily, then lifted the flap of her bag and pulled the top sheet off a sheaf of paper.

Woody took it from her and passed it to me.

"Free Vermont Vacation!" printed in large letters, reproduced in that purple ink of old-fashioned ditto machines. "Join us for a week or a weekend in a beautiful Green Mountain National Forest retreat." The rest of the page was a hand-drawn map of roads in the area.

"Why don't you come Thanksgiving weekend?" Woody said. "It's a time for the tribes to gather."

Tribes? I looked at him. He didn't look Native American. More like, he came from one of the ten lost tribes of Israel.

Sparrow grabbed my arm, enthused. "Yes, Thanksgiving, perfect."

Woody nodded. "Thanksgiving it is." As though I'd agreed.

"Away, friends, let us away," he said, and the cluster of hippies around him migrated toward the exit.

Sparrow held back. "You still drive that old VW van?"

I nodded.

"Good. There isn't a lot of room at Woody's. Bring a sleeping bag." She kissed me and promptly skipped away like a mouse following the piper.

Thanksgiving in Vermont? I thought they'd decided for me, but I realized my answer was "yes" before I even left the church. Woody intrigued me, and running into Sparrow seemed less like coincidence and more like destiny. I folded the map in half and tucked it above the van's sun visor.

* * *

During the weeks before Thanksgiving, I kept attending the meditation classes, partly because they did help me relax, but also in hopes of seeing Sparrow again. Sparrow and her commune never reappeared, but it got easier and easier to focus on my breathing.

The week before Thanksgiving, a surprise snow and ice storm paralyzed Boston right in the middle of the evening rush hour. If it was like that here, what would I find in Vermont? I didn't *have* to go. I could just stay in my apartment and eat a TV dinner.

By Monday, the snow had melted, and the weather report predicted mild temperatures for holiday travel. Wednesday morning, I packed up the VW so I could leave straight from work. I snuck out early, grabbed a sandwich and coffee to go, and ate while driving. The news came on the radio, and the announcer reminded listeners that on this day four years ago, President Kennedy had been murdered.

I didn't need that in my head. I was off to have a fine weekend with new friends and one old one, not a walk through gloomy memories. I changed the station, but that one was also in the middle of a memorial for JFK. Massachusetts wasn't letting anyone forget their favorite son. I turned the radio off, regretting I hadn't installed an 8-Track tape player like Eddie's.

Darkness fell early, and traffic was heavy on I-91 in northern Massachusetts. I unfolded the map Woody had given me and read the directions by flashlight. "After crossing the Vermont state line, exit the interstate at Brattleboro and drive west on Route 9 toward Bennington." I did.

I came to a sign for the National Forest just past Wilmington and entered a wilderness area a few miles farther. I passed a large reservoir, turned north on a forestry road, and then onto several ever smaller dirt roads. As I bounced in an out of ruts, I started thinking that it would have been wiser to have waited until Thanksgiving morning when I'd have daylight to find my way. Then, next to a dirt driveway, I spotted a mailbox with the name Woodbridge painted on it. Could that be his actual name? I turned and followed an even more rutted dirt lane until it ended in front of a small house. The siding was tongue and groove, painted a dark color—gray, I thought, but colors are deceptive in moonlight.

A warm, inviting orange glow emanated from the windows. I approached the door and knocked. Sunshine, the young woman I'd met at the meditation class, opened the door and invited me in. The house had a large main room with a kitchen sink, counter, refrigerator, and gas range along one wall. In the center was an old-fashion farm table that could easily seat twenty. At the far end of the room was an expansive open area containing two couches, numerous chairs, an upright piano, and fourteen or fifteen hippies.

I spotted Sparrow on the couch and waved. She jumped up and ran to hug me. We joined the group, and she made introductions. "Sugar Bear, Autumn, Misty, Leaf, Squirrel . . ." The list went on, sounding like characters in a kid's cartoon. Everyone had nicknames—not a single Sam or Sue.

"Where's Beaner?" Sparrow said.

"Bathroom," Leaf said.

In Texas, Beaner was a derogatory slur for a Mexican. Were these supposedly loving hippies racist? I decided to put the old man to the test. "Uh .. . where's Woody?"

"Meditating in his room," Sunshine said. "He'll join us when he's finished."

The bathroom door opened, and Beaner came out. He didn't look even vaguely Latin. I felt both relieved and confused. Sparrow introduced us, and he gave me a bear hug. "Gizmo—cool name. Wish I'd thought of it."

I pried loose from his hug. "It just kinda got laid on me." I thought not to mention the service.

"Gizmo fixes things," Sparrow said.

Beaner smiled at her. "Handy dude to know. Gizmo, give me a hand in the kitchen."

He removed the lid from a five-gallon plastic container and replaced it with a large sheet of cheesecloth. "I'm going to strain this over the sink. Your job is to keep the cloth in place."

Not as easy as it sounded. As he poured the water, something heavy inside the bucket pushed forward, trying to come with it. Once the water reduced to a trickle, he set the bucket in the sink, spread the cloth on the drain board, and began laying white, cheese-like blocks onto it.

It didn't have a smell. "What's that?" I said.

"Tomorrow's dinner."

"Huh?"

"Haven't you ever seen tofu?"

"In Chinese takeout, I guess. Cooked, not raw."

"Making soybean curd is how he contributes to the commune," Sparrow said.

"Oh. Now I get it."

"What?" she said.

"Why his name is Beaner."

Woody came out of his room and said hello, but was strangely reticent, as if he hadn't fully returned. I'd been meditating the last few weeks and understood how he might not want to leave a peaceful state.

Musical instruments appeared. Leaf played the piano, two guitars joined in, and everyone sang. The merriment continued until late. When the music ended, Sparrow said, "Did you bring a sleeping bag?"

I nodded.

"Good. Take the seats out of your van and I'll join you."

That surprised me. Not that we'd be sleeping together—I'd kind of hoped for that. But out in the VW? A temperature/clock on a bank I'd passed in Wilmington read forty degrees. The weather had surely cooled further in the hours since then.

She opened a double-door, revealing a storage area, pulled out a foam mattress, and handed it to me. She retrieved a stack of blankets and said, "Good night, everyone."

Volkswagen designed the bus seats to come out easily—a couple of clamps held in with thumbscrews. I set them outside and put the mattress on the floor. Once we got in and burrowed beneath her blankets and my sleeping bag, things warmed up quickly.

CHAPTER 15

Thanksgiving morning, the microbus windows were completely fogged. Sparrow and I dressed under the covers, waiting until the last second to leave that beautiful warmth our bodies had created. I opened the side door, stepped out, and immediately regretted it. The air was nippy enough to make it hard to breathe. Sparrow grabbed a Navajo blanket and wrapped it around us. I closed the door, and we ran to the house, swathed in the blanket, like two natives coming to dine with Pilgrims three hundred years ago.

A propane furnace had the house toasty. Everyone was up and moving around. I aimed straight for the bathroom, only to find a line of women waiting their turn.

"Pee outside," Squirrel said. "You've got an entire National Forest. Any tree will do."

Not something I was accustomed to, but I nodded and walked outside to find a secluded tree. Now that I was up and moving around, the cold wasn't so bad. The area behind the house looked like a used car lot. I was trying to pick my tree when the back doors of a panel van opened and two of the people I'd met the night before tumbled out. They flashed a peace sign and headed to the house. Parked next to them was an old delivery truck with the faded image of a loaf of Wonder Bread barely visible on its side. There were also several station wagons, an old hearse, and a school bus with tie-dyed window curtains.

I picked a birch tree and just started to release the flood when Woody came over and stood at the tree next to mine. "Sleep all right?" he said.

I nodded, finished quickly, and zipped up. Woody finished and walked to a spigot on the outside of the house and washed his hands. I shrugged and followed his lead.

Jesus! That water was cold enough to make my fingers hurt. I dried my hands on my pants and stuck them in my pockets to warm them. I nodded at the parked cars. "Are all these yours?"

"No, of course not, they belong to my friends. I'll explain inside where it's warmer."

Fine with me. We entered and sat on one of the couches. Springs poking into my back betrayed its age.

"My grandfather owned this place before the National Forest was here," Woody said. "When the Federal government nationalized the area in '32, existing homeowners who didn't want to sell could keep their property as a residence, and pass it on to their descendants. But it could be sold only to the Department of the Interior."

I looked around the room. "Your grandfather built this place? It doesn't seem that old."

"It's not." Woody stood up. "But that's a longer story. Let's see if there's any coffee."

Men and women crowded the kitchen, preparing various dishes for the feast.

"Don't get in the way, Woody," Sunshine said. "And we don't need advice."

He pinched her cheek. "And you won't get any. Just give Gizmo and me a cup of coffee, and we'll be out of your hair."

"Your arm broke?" She pointed to the coffeepot. "You know where the cups are. Get it and git."

He filled a cup, handed it to me, poured one for him, and then pointed toward the door. On his way past Sunshine, he patted her butt affectionately. She must have been a third his age.

Outside, he stepped off the porch. "Let me show you around. In a few hours, more friends will arrive. You'll want to park out back with the others."

"Oh, sure. You started to explain that earlier."

"Well, I told you the arrangement I inherited with the deed. Here's the rest of the story. The commune was growing, and I wanted to add onto the house. Give people rooms. The forestry service didn't relish having a bunch of hippies here and blocked the construction permits. I dressed like a lawyer, went to court, and presented my case—that we had every right to build on private property."

"What happened?"

"The judge is elected to office. Someone political put pressure on him, and he denied the permits." Woody smiled. "He was an old codger. I surmised he'd grown up in a time when outhouses were common. I pointed out that when people switched to indoor plumbing, the government raised no objection to my grandfather adding on a bathroom. Hadn't that set a precedent?"

We turned the corner of the house and two smaller buildings came into view. I hadn't noticed them because I'd arrived after dark. I zipped my jacket all the way up. The sun hadn't warmed the morning yet, and Woody's story seemed to be taking the long road.

"The judge mulled my argument over, then modified his ruling. He said we had the right to maintain, modernize or restore the existing structure, so long as such construction did not increase the building's square footage. So, we tore out several non-load-bearing interior walls. That gave us more floor space."

"Are you getting to why the backyard is a parking lot?"

Woody's eyes twinkled. "That, Gizmo, is the loophole. They can't stop my friends and visitors from sleeping in their vehicles. So we use the house as a communal kitchen and meeting area. At night, everyone gets out their bedrolls and sleeps on the living room floor or goes to someone's van if they want privacy."

He stopped, picked up a piece of limb fallen across the path, and chucked it into a gulley. "You don't have to sleep out in the cold again, by the way. You're welcome to find an empty place in the house tonight."

We came to a good-size outbuilding. He opened the door and gestured for me to enter. "This ought to interest someone who likes to fix things."

I looked around at a very complete woodworking shop. He had a table saw, band saw, radial arm saw, router, and lathe. There was an electric planer, three types of sanders, and a drill press. "What do you make with all this?"

"Furniture, custom cabinets, sometimes picture frames for artists in Bennington—brings in a little extra bread for the commune. Sparrow says you're good with tools. Is that right?"

I shrugged. "Actually, more in the mechanical and electrical realms."

"Good. Look at this lathe, will you? It keeps changing speed while it's running, and that's not good." He clamped in a length of wood, turned the power on, and guided a cutting tool against the rotating wood. Chips of wood shavings flew, some of them sticking to my trouser legs.

I could hear from the whine of the bushings that the speed was indeed slowing down whenever he put pressure on the cutting tool. "Have you checked that the belts are tight?" That was a frequent problem with car engines.

He shut it off and handed me a screwdriver. I kneeled in the sawdust and removed screws holding a cover plate over the drive belt. I pressed the belt, testing for slack. It seemed taut. I hooked a finger around it and pulled. No slack there. "Turn it on and let me see if anything is out of sorts down here."

Woody flipped the switch and this time wood shavings sprayed on my head, and intermittent sparks flew from the motor. That explained it. I stood up and shut it off. "One or both of the motor brushes are shot. I can rebuild it for you, but I'll have to take it apart."

He brushed woodchips from my hair. "Wait until tomorrow. Today's about camaraderie and good food."

We walked back outside. I dusted the sawdust off my clothes while he closed up the workshop. I pointed toward another smaller building. "What's that?"

"That's a whole different thing. It used to be a woodshed."

Sugar Bear came over. "Gizmo, can I have the keys to your van? People are trying to get in the driveway."

"Oh! Sorry. I'll move it right away."

"It looks like you and Woody are in the middle of something. I'll do it, so you can continue with whatever."

I shook my head. "Nothing important. Where do you want me to park?"

"You're staying the whole weekend?" Woody said.

"If that's all right."

"It is. Park next to Sugar Bear's school bus so the day trippers can have spots nearer the driveway."

I turned to Sugar Bear. "So, that's your bus?"

"She'd old, but she's homey. After you move your VW, come over and I'll you the five-cent tour."

Moving my VW involved putting the seats back in. I wasn't sure if I'd be sleeping on the floor in the house tonight or if Sparrow wanted to share the van again. She'd left the mattress, so maybe that was a sign. I stood it up against the side opposite the door and stacked the seats in haphazardly without fastening them in place. Driving a few hundred feet wouldn't hurt anything.

The inside of Sugar Bear's bus smelled like pot and patchouli. He'd stripped out all the seats, replaced them with a double bed across the back and a couch along one side that unfolded into a second bed. With a quick lift and shove, he converted it back into a couch. "Have a seat."

"Thanks. It's actually warm in here."

He pointed to a stove pipe rising from a ring of blue flame and exiting out the roof. "Propane heater. I've also got a small two-burner stove for cooking when I'm on the road."

"You don't live here?"

"Just summers. I don't care if people call me a snowbird, Vermont winters are too damn cold. We'll head to Florida right after Thanksgiving."

"We?"

"Me and a couple of lady-friends. As yet to be determined."

I hoped Sparrow wasn't one of them. Not that we had any special commitment, but running into her again had been a happy discovery, and Vermont was a hell of a lot closer to Boston than Florida.

Sugar Bear fished around in his shirt pocket and out came a joint.

Jesus, it was ten o'clock in the morning—at the latest. I looked around the bus for confirmation, but didn't see a clock. Sugar Bear didn't seem concerned. He struck a match and lit up.

What could I do but partake?

Bear's shit was very good and wrecked me with just two tokes. After staring for a while at the patterns in an India-print bedspread he had fastened to the ceiling, I decided to take a shower and put on clean clothes before Woody's other guests arrived. I thanked Bear, and retrieved my shaving kit and fresh clothes from the VW. Inside the house, aromas from dinner preparations filled my nose, and I was seized by serious munchies. I grabbed an apple from a bowl and ate it down to the core.

No one was in the bathroom, so I closed the door, stripped off yesterday's clothes, shaved, and stepped into the shower. Still stoned, I pictured myself standing in warm rain. I didn't find a washcloth, so I worked the bar soap into a lather and washed with my hands. The shower curtain moved and Sunshine joined me in all her naked glory. "You don't mind?"

I didn't. Maybe Sparrow and her friends were having a good influence. Or maybe it was the pot. I rinsed off my face and stepped aside to let her get wet. "Your house, your rules."

She handed me the soap, gathered her hair in both hands and held it atop her head. "Wash my back, please."

I soaped her back from top to bottom, hoping Sparrow wouldn't get jealous. When Sunshine turned around to rinse, her breasts rubbed against mine, giving me the start of an erection.

"Let's trade positions, so I can let go of my hair and not get it wet." She took the soap from my hand. "Now, I'll do your back."

The shower curtain parted behind her and Beaner stepped in. My budding erection wilted faster than Jell-O in hot water. "Uh . . . Thanks, but I was about done when you came." I jumped out, dried quickly, dressed, and left. Sure, in the service all the guys shared one big shower room, but this wasn't the Air Force. And Sunshine sure wasn't one of the guys.

Chapter 16

Thanksgiving dinner was vegetarian, but plentiful. Even sampling small portions of the many dishes made me stuffed. Beaner had baked slabs of his tofu on a layer of sliced onions, drenched with an umber color gravy he'd made from nutritional yeast. Different, but delicious. All the arriving guests brought casseroles or wine to share. I felt bad I'd brought nothing to contribute, but no one had told me.

So I offered to wash dishes. There were a lot of them, but others joined me and I had a merry time playing in the dishwater and laughing with new friends. Memories of doing dishes with Sophie when we were kids came to mind.

The afternoon continued with music, laughter, marijuana, and wine, until the curtain of night began to fall. After the day trippers, as Woody called them, departed, Sunshine called everyone into the living room. "Woody's going to tell some Zen stories."

I had no idea what that meant. But so far, I hadn't run into anything Woody offered that wasn't enjoyable, so I was in.

Sparrow, seated on the floor, handed me a cushion and pointed to a place next to her. Woody wasn't there yet. Probably in his room meditating, which I assumed was his evening routine. Then the outside door opened, and he came in, rubbing his hands. "Temperature's dropping." He removed his coat and hung it on a hook. "Gizmo, I apologize for keeping you waiting. One of our afternoon guests gifted us an ounce of weed. I needed to bury it in the woods."

I must have looked confused, for after he sat in the armchair in front of me, he explained. "The government would just love a reason to bust us. So whenever there is more than a joint or two, I hide it across the property line in the National Forest. That way, even if they raid us, it's on their land, not ours."

I wondered about Sugar Bear's school bus. I suspected there was more than a joint or two in there.

He grinned. "It's like Joseph Heller said, 'Just because you're paranoid doesn't mean they *aren't* out to get you.' Have you read *Catch-22*?"

I shook my head.

"You should. It's a satire on the Army Air Corps. You'll relate."

Okay, I'd never mentioned which military branch I'd served in. I glanced at Sparrow. Had she told him?

Again, he read my mind from my face. "I've always assumed the government sends undercover agents to infiltrate us." He laughed. "Some dress just like you. So I asked around about you."

Everyone turned and looked at me. My face grew hot, and I regretted wearing a button-down shirt. The burgundy one Sparrow had bought me in the Village got lost in the move to Boston.

"No, no, I don't mean Gizmo," Woody said. "He doesn't work for the government. I read his aura. He's a sincere person, definitely against the war."

Well, I was now. But you couldn't have said that if you'd met me a few years ago.

Woody smiled. "What's more, I think we converted more than a few of their spies. After their agents get to know us, they go back and quit. Eventually, they're gonna run out of people to send."

His audience laughed. I was glad to have their attention shifted elsewhere.

The reprieve didn't last. Woody picked me out of the crowd and shot me a Cheshire cat smile. "Gizmo's problem is that he can't get free of his mind. He's a good thinker—but there can be too much of a good thing."

Again, I found myself at the center of attention, and the temptation to escape to my VW was strong.

Sparrow took my hand in her lap. I stayed.

"Gizmo needs a trip to the woodshed," Squirrel said.

Woody gave him a sharp look, then settled on me. His eyes softened, reminding me of an old family dog. "Meditation will help you, but breaking the habit of thinking requires effortless effort."

What? What the hell did that mean?

"Zen involves continuous concentration on what you're doing at the moment, and meditation on a koan. Koans are stories or unsolvable riddles intended to free the disciple's mind by provoking it."

Disciples? The word sent up red flags. I looked at the hippies around me, all of them at least forty years younger than Woody. I squeezed Sparrow's hand. Had she joined a cult?

"Let me give you some examples." Woody started with a story of an important professor who visited a Zen master. Customary to such meetings, the master made tea. When he filled the professor's cup, he continued pouring until it overflowed.

"'Stop!' cried the professor. 'My cup is full.'"

"'Ah,' said the master. 'So it is with you. How will you receive my wisdom unless you first empty your cup?'"

In light of Woody's earlier comment about being caught in my mind, I supposed the story was aimed at me. I had to stop thinking so much to make room for . . . whatever Zen was offering.

Next, he gave me what I presumed to be a Zen koan. "Without the heavens, there are no stars. Without stars, without sun, without moon, what time is it?"

I scratched my head. What the hell did *that* mean? If this was Zen wisdom, I wasn't getting it.

Woody continued, telling stories that made no sense, yet sometimes brought on laughter. I admit he was a charming storyteller, and I thought he was making them up. Years later, when I came to know Zen, I realized he'd gotten them from a book.

"Now, a koan for Squirrel," he said. "To journey a thousand leagues, take the first step. To know the path to perfection, be the one neither leaving nor remaining."

I looked at Squirrel to see if this meant anything to him. His leg jittered like a man who'd drunk too much coffee. I returned my attention to Woody. He yawned. "I believe I'll retire, now."

Sparrow again elected to sleep with me in the van. I hadn't meditated that morning, and frankly, we didn't get to it that night. In meditation class, they'd said to practice twice daily, but a pretty woman in my bed sidelined my best intentions. Besides, wasn't it a holiday?

But I awoke in the morning, determined not to let skipping become a habit. "I'm going to meditate," I said. "You're welcome to join me, or I'll meet you in the house when I'm through."

"Okay. I've got to pee first." She opened the door, squatted in the frosted grass beside the van, and peed like a female dog. Living in nature had certainly changed her. I think it was starting to change me, since I wasn't as shocked as I once would have been. I could only imagine what my sisters would have thought.

She crawled back inside the van, closed the door, and began rubbing her bare feet. "It's cold out there."

"I'll bet."

We pulled the blankets from our bedding and wrapped one around each of us. The cold morning simplified meditation on breath—we could see it. For fifteen minutes, we sat doing "so" and "hom" like two steam kettles.

We went into the house for breakfast. After we ate and did dishes, the whole commune lazed about in the warm living room except Sugar Bear. "He's still crashed out in his bus," Squirrel said.

Throughout the day, people came in and out, ambling through the forest and returning when they chose, snacking if they were hungry. When it grew dark, leftovers from the previous day were reheated, and a second feast commenced. After the supper dishes were washed, everyone gathered for another of Woody's discourses.

Woody was well read and seemed to know something about everything. "Freud wasn't always right, but he was the first Western doctor to see our mental psyche as interaction between the conscious and the unconscious." He tapped his forefinger against his temple.

Okay, so no Zen today.

"Of course, the authors of the Upanishads understood consciousness three thousand years before Freud. But let's not get into that."

"Why not?" I said.

Woody ignored my question. "Although Freud identified a fundamental energy innate in all humans that he termed 'libido,' he thought it was limited to sexual desire. His ideas drew many doctors to his Vienna clinic, among them, Wilhelm Reich."

Woody smiled like a professor. "I'd give Freud a B minus because he failed to pursue his original notion that the cause of neuroses in the genital stage was incomplete sexual release. Reich understood this, specifying the orgasm as the criteria of healthy function."

"I'll buy that," Sunshine said.

Woody winked at her. "A medical doctor as well as a psychiatrist, Reich found his patient's problems weren't just psychological, but physical.

Suppressed, repressed energy bound the muscles, hardening the body like a suit of armor. Reich observed that if he loosened the muscles, the repressed emotions behind a neurosis surfaced. Release of tension not only brought hidden feelings to light, but patients experienced unexpected pleasurable streaming energy in their body."

I nodded. I'd taken psychology as an elective in college. Reich's *Character Analysis* was one of our texts, and I recognized a lot of what he was saying. I later came to see this conversation as typical Woody. His exposition on a wide range of subjects made him seem all-knowing, but I wondered if he just had a good memory for things he'd read.

"I actually met Reich," Woody said.

Okay, maybe not in this case.

"When the Nazis came to power in Austria and Germany, they tried to imprison Reich for his sexual theories. The fascists didn't care much for Freud's ideas, either, and ordered his books burned. Freud successfully escaped to Britain, and Reich to Denmark. From Denmark, Reich moved to Sweden, then Norway, and eventually to the Unites States. In Norway, he studied the orgasm and identified a bioenergy sequence: mechanical tension to bioelectric charge, then bioelectric discharge leading to relaxation."

"Not very romantic," Sunshine said.

"No, but important, for it dawned on him that this sequence of body movements—tension, charge, discharge, relaxation—was similar, or possibly identical, to those of microscopic protozoa. Was this rhythmical four-beat formula a common function of all living matter?"

"Was it?" I asked. "Is it?"

Woody nodded. "At first Reich thought bioenergy was a form of electricity. While studying microscopic bions, he observed that the energy emitted by some of them didn't seem to obey the known laws of energy. He found larger, more complex organisms, even humans, emitted the same energy. Reich believed it was a previously unrecognized physical phenomenon, a special energy common to all life. He stopped using Freud's term libido and named it *orgone*."

Woody smoothed his mustache. "In humans, Reich found that bioenergy varied by how much the patient was free from or bound by neurosis. The freer the person, the more they experienced the streamings and exhibited a natural liveliness."

Though he spoke to the room at large, it often seemed like Woody was speaking directly to me. Now, he made it clear he was. "Gizmo, have you ever felt energy streaming from your feet to your head?"

Suddenly, I felt all eyes upon me and knew I'd turned red as a sunburn. "If you mean the rush of an orgasm, yes, frequently." I nodded toward Sparrow. "Ask her."

"Not just that," Woody said. "There's life force energy flowing through everything. Some people can feel it when they're meditating. I just wondered if you ever had."

I stammered a bit before Woody let me off the hook. "Reich continued his study of orgone after he came to America. When I met him, he still thought orgone was limited to living organisms. Then he discovered its presence in our water and atmosphere and concluded it was ubiquitous. Just focused more in living organisms."

I wondered how much farther Woody was going with this story when he stood up. "That's enough for tonight. We'll take this up again tomorrow."

Everyone began to stir.

"Time for the woodshed?" Squirrel said.

Woody shrugged. "Can't rush these things."

It was the second time Squirrel brought that up. What was his obsession about an old woodshed? Or was it a euphemism for stern discipline?

Sparrow took my hand and pulled me toward the door. As we left, I noticed Sunshine draw Woody into his room and close the door.

Once Sparrow and I got the VW bed ready and snuggled under the covers, I propped myself up on one elbow. "Does Woody sleep with the people who live here?"

"Not the men."

This was long before gays were open about it, and if I'd ever met a homosexual, I wasn't aware of it at the time. So, her remark seemed like she was deflecting. "You know what I'm asking. What about the women? Does Woody—"

"Make us? No. It's a very open commune. Anyone can have sex with anyone else, so long as that's what they both want. If a woman wants to sleep in Woody's bed, he wouldn't object, but he would never be the first to suggest it."

I sat up. "But . . . God, he's old as my dad, at least twice the age of any woman here. It can't be any fun. At least for them."

"You'd be surprised. That orgone energy he was talking about tonight? He's loaded with it." She pulled me onto her. "Now, are you going to lie here worrying about Sunshine sleeping with Woody when you've got a horny, naked woman under you? Shut up and kiss me."

Chapter 17

The next afternoon, Woody and I walked around his property. The day was surprisingly warm for November. I suspected he saw I still had questions about the energy he was talking about last night.

At a certain point, I felt comfortable bring it up. "If this energy is out there, why haven't other scientists found it?"

"They're not looking," he said. "Nothing Reich discovered was ever disproved, only dismissed. Orgone may not move planets or make lightning or hold atoms together, but it is the fundamental creative life energy that charges and radiates from all living beings. It also streams freely through the atmosphere and outer space. Its effects make us us, but that's not the direction modern physics is taking. Although we're immersed in a sea of it, we may be like the fish who doesn't know that it swims in water."

We moseyed behind the house, toward the woodshed. "My grandfather used to store firewood in there. When we remodeled the house, I replaced the fireplace with a propane furnace. Now we've repurposed the shed."

Sided with rough slab wood, the infamous shed had a sloped roof and looked too short for a man to stand up in. It also wouldn't have held enough cords of wood for an entire New England winter. Maybe enough stove wood to keep the fires going for a week in case of a blizzard. An old-fashioned hook and eye latched its wooden door closed. The door failed to cover the doorframe, having a four-inch gap at the top and bottom, like a lavatory stall in a public restroom.

Woody unlatched the hook and swung the door open. Inside, it was even smaller, with dull, galvanized sheet metal walls crowding in on an old wooden chair with a cane seat.

"What is this place?"

"It's an orgone energy accumulator," Woody said. "Reich invented a special metal-lined cube for his bion experiments, but after he removed the bions, orgone continued to accumulate within it. His further research revealed that orgone is most strongly attracted to living things, to water, and to itself, and reflected away by ferrous metal. His hypothesis was that the orgone that built up within the accumulator would flow into living matter placed inside. Investigations progressed, and he eventually made a box large enough to hold a person."

"Like this?" If I sounded skeptical, it was because images from old prison movies jumped into my head of some convict in the electric chair.

"The device is purely passive, employing neither electrical, magnetic, nor radioactive energy," Woody said. "I thought you might like to try it."

I hesitated, shifting from one foot to the other.

"Another reason conventional science misses orgone? A theory is proven by experiment, and Reich's opponents refused to try his experiments. Of course, if you don't want to try, no one is going to make you." He turned and made as if to walk away.

What the hell. "No. I'll try it. What do I do?"

"Well, if it was summer, you'd take off your clothes, but it's too cold for that. Just have a seat in the chair, close the door, and relax."

The shed was too small to stand in or even to turn around, so I backed in and sat on the chair. Space was tight. The ceiling was only a few inches above my head and the walls mere inches from each shoulder. A larger man wouldn't have fit. "How long do I have to be in here?"

"Don't stay longer than thirty minutes. You might build up more energy than you can tolerate at first. Meditate or read, if you want to pass the time."

I didn't see any books in there. I guessed I'd meditate.

"I'm shutting the door now," Woody said. "There's a hook inside you can latch to hold it closed. Someone will come and knock in a half-hour in case you lose track of time."

He closed the door, and I latched myself in. The inner face of the door was also galvanized sheet metal. The dark claw of claustrophobia gripped me. I turned my eyes up toward the gap at the top of the door and saw clear blue sky.

I took a deep breath, closed my eyes and started doing the so-hom meditation. What else could I do?

After a time, I experienced a tingling all over. A mild sensation of energy streamed rhythmically from my scalp to the soles of my feet. Was this what Woody was describing the other night? Nothing like an orgasm, though. Could have been the power of suggestion. Whatever it was, I found it very pleasurable.

It didn't seem I'd been in there more than a few minutes when fingernails gently tapped on the door. "Gizmo?"

"Yes?"

"You can come out now."

I really didn't want to, but I undid the hook and the door swung open. The sky seemed a deeper blue, the leaves carpeting the forest a brighter orange.

Sparrow, more beautiful than ever, stood waiting. "What do you think?"

"I didn't think. I felt." I kissed her, letting it linger, experiencing a sense of well-being, fully alive. More so even than our trip in Greenwich Village.

When I let go of her, she latched the shed door closed and pointed to the cloudless sky. "What do you see?"

I looked up, expecting to just see sky. But there were tiny points of light which, if it had been nighttime, I might have taken for distant stars. Except that they moved in and around each other like a dance.

"Vesicles of orgone energy in the atmosphere," she said.

An inkling at the back of my mind told me I'd seen them in the past, long before I ever sat in an orgone accumulator.

Sunday morning, I helped Sparrow carry the foam mattress and blankets we'd slept on into the house and store them. I reinstalled the seats in the back of the VW, and we ate breakfast. Afterwards, Woody and Sparrow walked me to my van. Sugar Bear's snoring rumbled from his school bus. All three of us laughed.

I looked up and saw little pinpoints of orgone still dancing in the clear azure sky. It made me happy.

"Come back anytime," Woody said.

Sparrow wrapped me in her arms. "Yes. Do."

"Thank you. I will, and I'll bring the parts to fix that motor in your workshop. But it won't be until after the New Year. I have to go home for Christmas. My mother died earlier this year, and my dad's been living alone."

Woody patted my shoulder and Sparrow kissed me. I kissed her back, then got in my VW and left.

I'd crossed the Vermont state line into Massachusetts when I stopped at a Friendly's restaurant to use the restroom and buy a cup of coffee.

"Coffee to go," I told the waitress.

"Regular?" she said.

"No, black." First thing I learned after moving to New England, 'coffee regular' means with cream and sugar. If you want it without, you have to specify.

She filled a paper to-go cup, the kind with little flaps you could pry out to form handles. I paid her and walked outside. A newer VW Microbus had pulled in and parked next to mine. A square section of its roof was sticking up a couple of feet. I'd never seen one like it. I walked around to the side doors, where a woman inside stood at . . . a small sink?

"Can I help you?" said a male voice from behind me.

I whirled around. "Oh, hi. I was just admiring your VW. That's mine." I pointed to my aging vehicle. "I've never seen one like yours. Did you customize it yourself?"

He smiled like the father of a newborn. "No. It's a Westfalia camper. Would you like to see it?"

"I would."

The left outside door had built in storage shelves, and just inside it was a neat little wardrobe for hanging clothes. The right door had a shelf that folded flat when not in use. His wife came out, and he invited me to step inside. With the roof up, there was ample clearance for me to stand upright. Next to the sink, the dinette had a fold-down table that converted into a bed.

"This is really cool," I said.

"Let me show you how easy it is to set up and take down. Duck your head." He reached into the pop-up and pulled gently on two handles to lower it. Next, he fastened four elastic restraining straps. "There. We're ready to go."

"Does it have heat?"

"It does. Plus a three cubic foot icebox and six gallon water tank connected to the hand pump on the sink."

I thanked him, and we headed our separate ways. The rest of the way home, I contemplated how I could modify my microbus. I felt certain I could make a fold-out bed. Did I really need a sink? Probably not, but definitely a heater. I wondered if I could buy the pop-up unit and install it myself. I might have to hire a body shop to cut the hole in the roof.

By the time I got home, I'd made up my mind to see if the Boston VW dealer could order the pop-up parts and what they would cost. Then, I remembered the camper had jalousie windows with screens. I'd been concerned about a heater, but when the weather warmed, I'd need to open the windows, yet keep out mosquitos.

All this conceptualization meant one thing. My subconscious was definitely planning to revisit the commune.

CHAPTER 18

Christmas fell on a Monday that year. I flew home Saturday morning and Dad met me at the airport. I had five nephews and a niece now and needed to buy presents for them.

"Dad, I wonder if we might stop at Sears and Roebuck on the way home. I don't have gifts for Nora's and Sophie's kids and thought you might help me choose."

He shook his head. "I'm helpless." He pulled a large white handkerchief from his back pocket and blew his nose. "Your mother always did the Christmas shopping."

I grabbed my suitcase from the baggage carousel. "Surely you bought your grandkids Christmas presents."

"Nope. I gave Nora the money, and she bought and wrapped them." He pointed toward the pay phone. "Call her. Ask her if she has time to go shopping today. I'll drop you at her house."

Nora answered, sounding frazzled. I regretted calling and had about decided to just borrow Dad's car and muddle through on my own.

"Oh, Gizmo, of course I will. Tom's home. It won't kill him to watch the kids for a few hours. Have Dad let you off at the store and I'll meet you there."

The company had given me a raise and the largest year-end bonus I'd ever received. I felt inclined to be extravagant, but Nora damped the inclination down. "That's too expensive," she said when I started to buy Sophie's oldest a two hundred piece Lionel train set.

I shrugged. "I can afford it."

"Sophie and Eddie can't, and you don't want to make them feel poor. Here, buy this smaller set. He'll be just as delighted with it."

Later, a box with a pink ribbon caught my eye. I showed it to Nora. It wasn't expensive, but it contained a shiny, chrome-backed mirror, hairbrush, and comb. "Do you think Sophie's daughter would like this?"

"Are you kidding? She'll love it. Uncles' gifts don't have to be expensive to have a high squeal factor."

"A what?"

"When children open a present that delights them, they spontaneously go, 'Eeeeee!'"

Shoppers in adjacent aisles turned to stare at Nora.

She didn't seem to care. "I call that the squeal factor. And this gift is going to burst your eardrums. Wait 'til Christmas morning, you'll see."

Once she'd given me a measurable standard by which to gauge gifts, shopping got easier. I'd pick up a toy and imagine its squeal factor. Nora said I chose exceptionally well, which pleased me. She drove me back to Dad's, helped me wrap everything, and then went home to relieve Tom.

Nora hadn't been gone long when Eddie burst through the door. "Gizmo! I heard you were here. Get your coat. Come see my new car. You too, Dad."

In the driveway, a shiny red Mustang sat parked on the newly fallen snow, sticker still on the window.

I walked slowly around the two-door coupe. "Does Sophie know?"

"Not yet. I just picked it up from the dealer. It's a Christmas surprise. Come on, I'll give you guys a ride."

I tilted the passenger seat forward and climbed into the backseat so Dad could ride in front. I had to scrunch my legs up. Definitely not a practical choice for a family of five. But when it came to cars, Eddie wasn't realistic, and in terms of squeal factor, Mustangs topped the rest.

Snow hadn't been cleared from the side streets, but that didn't slow Eddie down. Once we turned onto Main Street, which had been plowed, he shifted into fourth gear, going fifty miles-per-hour through downtown. Dad braced himself on the dashboard as Eddie wheeled into a church parking lot scraped clean for Christmas Eve services. Eddie spun a half-dozen donut circles and then took us back home.

He left the engine running and popped the hood. All three of us got out and stood in front of the car, studying the throbbing big-block V-8 engine. Dad walked around to the sticker to read the specs. When he saw the price, he whistled.

"Oh. I didn't pay that," Eddie said. "The '68s are out, and the dealer needed to unload his '67s."

That wasn't my understanding. The way I heard it, dealers couldn't get Mustangs fast enough to keep up with demand. But that was Sophie and Eddie's business. He left to show Sophie and the kids their surprise while it was still daylight.

I followed Dad into the kitchen.

"How about grilled cheese and tomato soup?" he said.

"You cook?"

"Have to, don't I? Time you learned. Nothing to it." He set a saucepan and a frying pan on the stove and turned on both burners. He opened a can of Campbell's soup and shook a red lump into the pan. From the refrigerator, he took a quart of milk and a package of American cheese. He pointed to the bread. "Butter four slices." While I did that, he filled the soup can with milk, poured it into the saucepan, and stirred. "Just lay two slices of bread in the pan, butter side down, then put a couple slices of cheese on each."

The butter sizzled when I dropped the bread in the skillet. I didn't need further instruction. Obviously, the other two slices of bread went on top. I wasn't an engineer for nothing.

"Take the spatula and lift one corner high enough to see the color underneath. When it's golden, flip the whole sandwich over." Dad continued to stir his pan. "Trick is, don't let the soup boil. When it's well mixed and steaming hot, take it off the burner."

One side of my sandwiches got darker than it should have. "Aw, that don't hurt nothing." Dad held the sandwich over the kitchen sink and scraped the black off with a dull knife. "See? Perfectly edible."

Over soup and grilled cheese, he said, "Don't be like I was, son. Learn to cook for yourself. After your mom got sick, I depended on your sisters. But opening a can of soup or boiling a hot dog is something any man can do. If you want a better meal, buy a cookbook and follow the directions. I told myself that a man who can assemble his grandkids' swing set ought to be able to put together a pot roast. They write cookbooks simple enough for women, you know."

I hoped he never said that to my sisters. They'd throw the book at his head.

He gathered our dishes, washed them, and set them in the drainer. "Gizmo, unless you've got a wife on the horizon you haven't mentioned, it's high time you stopped living out of restaurants."

"You're right, Dad." I picked up a dishtowel and reached for a plate.

"Don't bother drying those. I don't know why your mother insisted on that. Air dries them perfectly well."

Christmas morning, everyone gathered at Nora's. Squeals of delight filled the room. Not just over my gifts, but from everyone else's, too. Except for the underwear—the boys weren't too happy to get those. But my niece, Patty, loved opening a box and finding seven pairs of panties, each embroidered with a day of the week.

Nora prepared as good a feast as Mom ever made. Afterwards, Tom, Eddie, and Dad retired to the living room for after-dinner drinks. I went into the kitchen to help clean up. Nora shooed me out. "The kids are old enough to do dishes, just like we did." She got the youngsters organized, and we joined the other adults. Dad and Sophie were playing Euchre against Tom and Eddie.

I picked up my gift from dad—*Culinary Arts Institute Encyclopedic Cookbook*—over a thousand pages thick and heavier than a brick. "Night before last, I hinted at what you were getting," he'd said when I unwrapped it. It wasn't a manly gift. All the photos featured smiling housewives showing how to roll out dough or whisk meringue. Interspersed were sections on how to select meat, tell which vegetables and fruits were ripe, and plan a meal "your family will love."

Nora pointed at the cookbook in my lap. "I have the same one. Come over one day this week and I'll teach you."

Eddie slipped out to his car and returned with a Wolverine Work Boots shoebox tied with a ribbon. He handed it to me.

"What's this?"

"A bonus present for you. Open it and see."

I untied the ribbon and removed the lid. Inside was Eddie's 8-track tape player.

"It's used, but I didn't think you'd bought one yet."

"No, I haven't."

"I knew the Mustang had a factory-installed tape deck. So I took mine out before I traded in my car. You'll have to buy a pair of speakers. I had to leave mine in the Fairlane."

"Wow, Eddie, thanks."

"From your sister, too. She said it couldn't be your Christmas present because it wasn't new."

"Thanks, Sophie, this is great." I fingered the harness of wires coming from it and studied the connectors. It looked pretty straightforward—black and white for power, pairs of red and black wires for the speakers.

Eddie fished a sheet of paper out of the box. "I saved the original instructions that came with it. You won't have any trouble installing it."

Dad smiled at me across the card table. "Easy as cooking."

Tuesday, the menfolk returned to work. Dad dropped me off at Nora's for my cooking lesson while Sophie took all six kids ice skating.

Nora opened the kitchen cabinet, got a prescription bottle from the top shelf, and tipped out a yellow tablet into her palm.

"You still take those?" I said.

She popped it in her mouth and sipped some water.

"You know there's an alternative," I said. "It's a new thing called meditation breathing. I learned it this fall in Cambridge. Let me show you."

We sat for a short meditation, me telling her what little I knew. When we finished, she said she felt good about it. But maybe the "happy pill" she'd just taken had kicked in.

"It's subtle," I said, "but I found it helped me. Practice it every day and you may not need those pills, or psychoanalysis, for that matter."

"Tom would like that, but I don't see how I'll do it with three kids around."

"Well, this week you'll have to wait until they're in bed, but next week you can meditate in the mornings after they leave for school."

"I'll try. Now, let's get cooking."

We worked all day. Nora taught me how to make an entire basic meal from scratch—meatloaf, mashed potatoes, braised carrots, and brownies for dessert. She marked pages in my new cookbook where it showed how to measure things like shortening and brown sugar. She said I could buy frozen vegetables, parboiled rice, and cake mixes to save time.

Dinner was pretty good, even if saying so is patting my own back. But, Lord, it'd taken the whole day. I'd never be able to work all day and then come home and do this. So much easier to stop by a restaurant after work and order tempura to go. Then I remembered Nora telling me how boring her days were, that she had the house cleaned and dinner made by ten in the morning. If I was going to cook for myself, our next lesson would have to be how to do it all in an hour.

I stayed through New Year's eve, but I had to fly back on New Year's Day. Nora drove me to the airport while the men watched football.

I half-turned in my seat and watched her drive. "You never said if the meditation helped you."

She glanced away from the road in my direction. "Tom won't let me. He thinks it's unchristian."

"Tell him I learned it at the Unitarian Church in Cambridge."

"Unitarian's not going to change his mind."

"If you meditate in the morning after everyone's left, how would he ever know?"

"A good marriage doesn't work like that, Gizmo. I couldn't do something that he opposed behind his back."

"So he'd rather you quell your unhappiness with pills?"

"They're prescribed by a doctor."

"That doesn't make them good for you." I was tempted to tell her about how orgone streams from our feet to our head, but we didn't have enough time to explain it adequately, and it would sound like something even weirder.

She focused on the road ahead. "Let's not quibble. We're almost at the airport."

CHAPTER 19

After I returned from Christmas vacation, a new project at work kept me busy, so I didn't get back to Vermont as soon as I'd intended. Anyhow, January was too cold to sleep in my van, and I wasn't ready to spend the night on the commune's living room floor in a tangle of bodies. I'm not saying they had orgies, but my puritanical Midwest mind couldn't be sure they didn't.

In February, newspapers and magazines reported the Beatles had gone to India to study meditation. Like every trend the Beatles had started in the past four years, meditation and yoga instantly went mainstream. Attendance at the Unitarian mediation classes swelled. I needed to arrive there early to even get a seat on the floor. I wondered if the fact the Beatles were meditating would change Tom's mind.

One Saturday, I came across the 8-track tape player Eddie had given me for Christmas. The weather had been too cold for me to work outside installing it. Besides, I still needed speakers. That'd make a good Saturday errand. I drove into Boston looking for an automotive electronics place. Up ahead, I saw the VW dealer. What the hell, I'd stop in and see what their parts department wanted for a pop-up roof.

The parts man said, "We don't stock them. Let me make some calls and see where I can order it."

While I waited, a salesman came into the service department, introduced himself, and shook my hand. "I heard you're looking for a camper."

"I'm thinking about converting my microbus."

He made a low whistle. "That's a lot of work. What year is yours, '56?"

"Good guess."

"Man, that's twelve years old."

"True, but I keep it in perfect running order, and VWs last forever. Just rebuild the motor when it needs it."

"I can't argue with that. It's one of my chief selling points. Tell you what, why don't we take a walk out to my back lot? I've something that'll interest you."

The parking lot had been scraped, but there were snowdrifts between the vehicles where it was too narrow to plow. In front of the dealership, someone had shoveled paths around the cars so potential buyers could inspect them. No one had bothered with those parked in back. It made them look a little forlorn and abandoned.

The salesman led me to a red Westfalia camper. "Wait here. I'll pull it forward so you can open the doors."

He waded through calf-deep snow to the driver's side door and climbed in. The starter turned the engine over several times, but it didn't want to catch.

"It'll be fine," he said. "It's just been sitting all winter."

He cranked it again, and the engine coughed. Third time was the charm. He put it in first gear and it putt-putted onto the plowed portion of the parking lot. He cut the engine, jumped out, ran to the passenger side, and threw open the side doors. Inside, he undid latches and raised the roof. Unlike the camper I'd seen at the restaurant, this one's roof was hinged at the back and the entire thing rose at an angle, like a drawbridge. Snow that had accumulated on the roof slid off the back of the van.

He invited me in, and spent considerable time opening all the storage compartments to show how cleverly they'd utilized every bit of space, including the built-in ice box and sink. I told him I'd already seen a Westfalia, but he persisted. When I'd asked if it had a heater, he fired it up, and the camper got warm in a hurry. Finally, he suggested we go inside the dealership and talk about it over a hot cup of coffee.

On the way inside, he asked where I worked. I told him the name of the company and he nodded. He carried two cups of "regular" coffee to a table and we sat down. I considered whether I should tell him I drank my coffee black. On a sheet of paper, he began making a list of parts and prices for the camper conversion—pop-up top, jalousie windows, ice box, and more, then summed them, and drew a circle around the total. "That's just the parts. You've still got to add labor." He turned the sheet toward me. "Can I be honest with you, Gizmo?"

"I never assumed you'd be otherwise."

He laughed. "Of course not." He waved his arm vaguely in the direction of the back lot. "The fact is, she's been sitting in my inventory since last fall. And likely no one will shop for a camper before May. Instead of spending all your money on parts, take her off my hands. I'll give you a very good deal, and a fair price for your old bus, too."

I closed my eyes and thought about it. Most of my Christmas bonus was still in the bank. The microbus had done well by me all these years, but that Westfalia would be ideal in Vermont.

"I don't know. I only came into Boston to buy stereo speakers for my 8-Track. Do you know where there's an automotive electronics store nearby?"

"We sell Lear. Take the Westfalia off my hands, and I'll throw in a pair."

Needless to say, I signed the paperwork and returned Monday after work to pick it up. The dealer had even installed the speakers. I only needed to mount my 8-Track and hook up the wires. I did that the following night and thanked my lucky stars I'd bought the new van. The tape deck required a 12-volt system and my old VW only had a 6-volt battery.

Once I had it installed, I needed something to play in it. I drove to K-Mart, which was open until nine, and bought two tapes by the Beatles and two by the Doors. On the way back to my apartment, I cranked the volume up and wailed the words to "Light My Fire."

Except for regular trips to Woody's and my time immersed in orgone, that's about the end of the list of good things that happened in 1968. Now for the bad.

In April, Martin Luther King Jr. was assassinated. The moment I heard the news, I thought, *Shit's gonna hit the fan.* I wasn't wrong.

Civil unrest over segregation and discrimination had been building for years, but Dr. King had kept protesters focused on non-violent resistance—always showing his opposition to be the aggressors. Within a day, riots broke out in a hundred cities. Boston, not so much. The night after King was murdered, soul musician James Brown played a concert in Boston Garden at which he, the mayor, and a city councilor spoke to the crowd about peace and unity. Robert Kennedy, who had joined the presidential race, gave an impromptu speech in Indianapolis on the night of the assassination. The next morning, newspapers credited it with averting riots there. Cities that weren't so fortunate included Detroit, Chicago, Washington, and Baltimore, where some of the worst riots occurred.

Nora, fearful of me living near Boston, asked me to come home for Easter, which was the following weekend. I really wanted to get Woody's take on what was happening, so I assured her I was safe and had other plans, and went to Vermont instead.

Spring was in full force. Nights were still cold, but the days warm. Woody and I sat on his porch.

"What do you think will happen?" I said.

Woody pulled on his face like an ancient prophet. "I think the states will resist implementation of the Civil Rights bill. Many of King's nonviolent followers will become radicalized. George Wallace will use white fear of blacks to split the Democratic Party, giving the Republicans the election this fall."

I hoped not. Robert Kennedy was running, and I anxiously awaited a return to Camelot.

It never came.

Two months later, Sirhan Sirhan shot Robert Kennedy once in the head and twice in the back. I was at work the next morning when a messenger delivering packages told someone in receiving. Word raced through the building. I couldn't believe what was happening to our nation, but my body believed it. I dashed into the men's room and upchucked.

But 1968 wasn't done with us yet. In November, Richard Nixon got elected. Although we had no idea how bad things would eventually get, I started thinking maybe Timothy Leary was right about dropping out.

I called Nora and told her I wouldn't be home for Christmas. I was going to Vermont.

CHAPTER 20

The following July, Dad called me out of the blue. "Hi, son."

"Hi, Dad. Is everything all right?"

"Never better. You didn't come home for Christmas."

"Yeah, I'm sorry, 1968 was a rough year, and I just needed to get away and breathe some clean mountain air."

"Well, your sisters missed you."

"I miss them, too. . . So, your call is a surprise."

"Yeah, we don't talk often enough."

That was probably my fault. True, he never was one for yakking on the telephone, he'd left that up to Mom. But I should have called more often. "Well, Dad, are you keeping busy?"

"Same old, same old. Another day, another dollar." A silence hung on the line for a moment. "So, here's the thing. My vacation is coming up, and this is my first one without your mother. If I stay here, I'd just fix stuff around the house. Then, you know, go back to work at the plant. That wouldn't be much of a vacation."

"No, it doesn't sound like it would."

"So I was thinking . . . I've never seen Massachusetts. Um . . . If I wouldn't get your way, I'd come East to visit my son."

"That'll be great, Dad. I'm sure I can take some time off. I've got a camper now. We'll go camping in Vermont, which is even better. The mountains are beautiful in summer." It was also a chance to show him my new life.

I picked him up at the airport, and we drove straight to the commune. I parked next to Sugar Bear's school bus, raised the roof of my van, and gave Dad a tour of its features.

"I'll say one thing for the Germans," Dad said. "They're damn clever engineers. Amazing how they fit all this inside a VW bus."

I folded down the dinette into a bed for him and set up the overhead bed for myself so we wouldn't have to do it later. Then I took him into the house. The old worn couches and barefoot commune members, which I'd become accustomed to seeing, didn't impress him. Even a houseful of braless women didn't. I'd forgotten how uptight life in the Midwest was.

I had better hopes for Woody. Because he and Dad were almost the same age and had both been through the Great Depression and World War II, I thought they'd click. It turned out to be more like mixing vinegar and baking soda.

Woody, who, from my experience, could talk to anyone about anything, irritated Dad from the moment they met. And Woody, never one to keep silent, kept pushing.

Dad was sour on the whole setup from the beginning, which I might have expected—I had no idea what he'd read and been told about the hippie movement. But somehow he also got it into his head that living in a commune meant you were a communist. On our second night there, after we returned to the camper, he was determined to save me from my folly.

"Gizmo, I'd call this place a brown rice rip-off."

"What do you mean?"

"That long-haired old man gets everyone to chip in money for food, but only ever gives them rice, beans, and seaweed. Seaweed! For God's sake, who eats seaweed? I'll tell you who, the Japs."

"Dad, Woody's doing no such thing. It's not his decision. The whole collective decided to eat vegetarian. And there are lots of vegetables, not just beans. And you've got to admit, it all tastes pretty good."

"Gizmo, collective is just a fancy word for communist. Think about all you've achieved in your life. Consider your security clearance. The government finds out you're spending time with communists, you can kiss that goodbye."

"Dad, we're not communists."

"We? Have they already got you on their hook? Look, son, you don't have to be afraid of these people. Turn them in to the FBI. Your government will protect you."

"Dad! For the last time, they're hippies, not communists." I probably shouldn't have yelled, but the possibility that he might call the FBI on my friends scared me. I took a few deep breaths to cool down and tried to see it from his perspective. What did I know of his loneliness without Mom? "Dad, I'm sorry that you didn't enjoy coming here. It is your vacation, after all. Tomorrow morning, we'll head to Boston." Dad, the conservative patriot, would enjoy Bunker Hill and the U.S.S. Constitution. And baseball. He always listened to games on the radio when I was growing up. "I'll get us tickets to a Sox game."

He smiled. "That sounds good. Besides, they're launching the moon rocket on Wednesday. I don't want to miss that, and these people don't even have television."

Neither did I, but he didn't know that. He hadn't seen my place yet. Truth of the matter, the launch had slipped my mind. But I was proud of our space program, and I wouldn't mind seeing the rocket take off. I had until Wednesday to find somewhere with a TV.

On the way back, we passed the American Legion near my apartment. A sign advertised: "Moon launch pancake breakfast. Watch it here with us!" Problem solved.

My apartment only had one bedroom, so I gave Dad the bed and I slept on the couch. Wednesday morning, we got up early and drove to the American Legion post. I'd never been in one before and didn't know what to expect. A man at the door asked if we were members.

"No," I said.

My dad stepped in. "My son was in the Air Force during the Korean War."

"Korea wasn't a *real* war. Not like ours." He nudged Dad with his elbow. "They only ever called it the Korean *conflict*."

Dad looked like he was going to pop him in the snout. "More Americans died in Korea than in all of World War II."

Neither of us mentioned that Dad had been too old for World War II.

The man shook our hands. "Well, all vets are welcome. I can admit you as guests, but we're only allowed to sell alcohol to members. If you want a drink, hand your money to a member and he'll buy it for you."

God, it wasn't even eight in the morning. Who'd need a drink at this hour?

Apparently, the line of old men standing at the bar with beers in their hands watching the countdown on TV did.

The center of the room had a row of long tables with metal folding chairs. At the head of the room, guys wearing aprons were cooking pancakes on electric griddles and stacking them in a large stainless steel pan. Another manned an electric frying pan full of sausage links. Dad and I picked up our plates from a stack, and the cooks dropped three pancakes and two sausages on each. It reminded me of chow line in the mess hall. At the other end of the table was a crock of butter, jugs of maple syrup, and a tall chrome coffee urn.

We slathered up our pancakes and took seats at one of the long tables. Several color TV sets were situated around the room, all tuned to Walter Cronkite broadcasting from Cape Kennedy. The massive Saturn V rocket sat on the launch pad, veils of thick white vapors pouring down its sides.

The camera panned the full height of the rocket to the top, where three brave astronauts waited to begin mankind's greatest venture.

I thought of President Kennedy, who promised we'd put a man on the moon before the end of the decade. Were he still alive, he'd be so proud.

"Plenty of food left," shouted one of the cooks. "If anyone wants seconds, come on up."

"Dad, you want more?"

"No thanks, son. I'm full. I will have more coffee, though."

We refilled our cups and watched as the countdown proceeded smoothly. I'd call the mood in the room jovial anxiety, if that makes any sense. We were all high on what was about to happen, while crossing our fingers that it wouldn't blow up. Cronkite said, "The Saturn Five is the largest machine ever built. When its five massive engines fire—about thirty minutes from now—they will develop almost eight million pounds of thrust. The first-stage burn will last two minutes and forty-eight seconds, carrying the astronauts at a speed of 5,113 miles per hour."

The camera switched to a close-up view underneath the rocket. Steam-like fumes streamed from the massive rocket cones.

A swell of pride filled the room, as if the men watching had built it themselves. I admit, I had the same feeling. You couldn't help it. We were about to witness the greatest achievement in human history.

When the countdown clock reached one minute, the room fell silent. The bartender came out from behind the bar. Everyone set down their beers and leaned toward the TVs. We held our breath.

The final seconds ticked away. At 9:32, Jack Riley, the voice of Mission Control, announced, "Ignition." Great plumes of orange fire flared beneath the engines, but the behemoth rose only slightly and shuddered. I prayed it wasn't a dud.

Slowly, gravity gave way, and the Saturn V crept past the launch tower. Then suddenly, it was off, racing for the moon. Cameras followed its rise as it pierced a cumulus cloud high above Cape Kennedy and came out the other side.

"Hot Diggity!" someone yelled. It took me a second to realize it was the staid journalist, Walter Cronkite, himself. Those around us let out a sigh of relief and cheers broke out.

Almost in unison, the men in the room decided this called for a celebration and mobbed the bar. The bartender returned to his station and began drawing draft beers as fast as he could.

Dad, too, agreed an event this monumental deserved a celebratory beer, and shoved money into the hand of a man wearing a navy-blue legionnaire cap. "We're guests. Buy us a couple of beers, will you?"

I guess nine-forty wasn't too early to start drinking after all.

While we drank our beers, launch coverage continued. Twelve minutes after entering Earth's orbit, the engines of the final stage fired and pushed the spacecraft onto its trajectory toward the Moon. That merited another round. The crowd grew rowdy and offered frequent toasts to the space program, the brave astronauts. And, of course, Massachusetts' favorite son, President Kennedy.

Dad was on his third beer when he said, "Is there a good barbershop around here?"

"I suppose so. Why? You don't look like you need a haircut."

"No. You do. You look pretty shaggy. Be careful they don't fire you."

I had been letting my hair grow a bit, but truth be told, it wasn't any longer than the Beatles' back in '64 when they first came to the US.

"No, Dad. The company doesn't mind."

By 1969, everyone at my company except the salesmen and top executives had slightly longish hair. It was a sort of badge that distinguished the "creative brains" in engineering from middle-age members of the establishment. And I definitely didn't want the cool hires from MIT to classify me as the latter.

"Well, don't turn into a damn communist hippie."

The American Legion was not a place to discuss this. "You said you'd like to see a ball game. Finish your beer and we'll drive out to Fenway."

On the drive there, I said, "Dad, again, hippies aren't communists."

"That's not what Spiro Agnew says."

Right. If you couldn't trust Nixon's asshole running mate, who could you trust? "I know you mean well, but don't get it into your head to call the FBI on my friends. You won't do my career any favors."

"I won't, but that doesn't mean I approve of them."

I kept silent until we got to the box office. We learned the Red Sox were playing the Yankees in New York that day, but would be hosting the Orioles in a three game home series starting Friday. Dad was flying out on Sunday, so we only bought tickets for the Friday and Saturday games. As I recall, the Sox won both days, and Dad enjoyed himself immensely.

The astronauts landed on the moon Sunday night, and Dad called to say he'd made it home in time to watch it with Mrs. Brockport, a widow who lived on his street. He'd waited until we were almost to the airport before he told me that he'd started dating her.

"I know some people may think it's disrespectful to your mother—that I didn't wait long enough after she died. But I get so lonely living alone, even with all that your sisters do for me."

"I understand." Actually, I preferred bachelor life, but we were of different mind-sets. The least I could do was support his decision. "What do Nora and Sophie say?"

"I haven't told them. You're the first."

"Well, Dad, it's been a year and a half since Mom passed. I think that's plenty long enough. Tell my sisters about Mrs. Brockport. If they object, let me know and I'll talk some sense into them."

CHAPTER 21

A month later, was Woodstock. I wish I could tell you about it, but I never got there. Not for lack of trying. The commune caravanned there, but we only got as far as Gardiner, New York, before we came to a roadblock. I had no idea how much pot Sugar Bear was carrying, but I knew my van was clean, so I cut in front of his school bus, slid open my window and spoke to the policeman manning the barricade.

"Road's closed," he said.

"Is there another road? We're going to the rock festival."

"You and a million other people," the cop said. "Traffic's backed up in every direction. Even the New York State Thruway is closed. You'll have to turn back."

Sparrow frowned. "Can we park somewhere and walk?"

"It's forty-nine miles," the cop said. "Help yourself."

"Sparrow, that's two days on foot. We'll never make it."

He started toward Sugar Bear's school bus. My heart raced. The inside of his bus perpetually reeked of pot. I didn't want the cop to get a whiff. "They're with us, sir, and the bread truck too. If you'll guide us, we'll all three make a U-turn and head back."

He nodded and began directing my turn around with his arms.

"Jump out and ride with Bear," I said. "Tell everyone the situation. I'll come up next weekend."

She ran over and boarded the bus.

A U-turn on a two-lane road was nothing for my VW, but turning the school bus took longer. I waited up the road, watching in my rearview mirror, as Bear swung the bus halfway around, backed up, pulled forward, see-sawing across both lanes, until finally catching up to me. Leaf's bread truck followed. With everyone safely away from the cops, I waved good-bye and turned off on the road to Boston while they continued north to Vermont.

The telephone in my apartment was ringing when I walked in. "Where have you been?" Sophie said. "We've been calling all weekend."

"Woodstock. Is everyone all right?"

"Woodstock? I saw that on the news. The Governor of New York declared it a disaster area. Oh, little brother, what kind of people have you gotten involved with?"

"For crying out loud, Sophie, it's just a music festival. Three days of peace, love, and music. Says so right on the poster."

"When Dad saw the news, he was afraid you were mixed up in that. The people at that place you took him to in Vermont really shook him."

"I thought he got over that before he left. Just a misunderstanding—he confused commune with communist. They're not. They're just peace-loving vegetarians. I hope he doesn't think he'll help me by calling the FBI."

"FBI?"

"Never mind. You said you've been telephoning all weekend. What's wrong?"

"Depends on who you ask. No one's sick, if that's what you mean. Dad is getting married—Louise Brockport—our old neighbor. He wants you to be best man. The wedding is at Christmas. So you tell me, is something wrong or not?"

"I'd say not. Tell him that, of course, I'll be his best man. How are you and Nora taking it?"

Silence.

Finally, Sophie said, "Well, I'm *not* calling her Mom."

"I'm sure she won't expect us to. Just try to be kind to her. She's been a widow a long time and was probably as lonely as Dad's been since Mom passed."

"Gizmo, Nora and I have been helping him. Aren't we enough?"

"He appreciates all that you're doing for him, but it's not the same. You know that, right? Daughter and wife—two different roles."

She sniffed.

"Be happy for him, sis. I'll see you at Christmas. Give the kids a big hug from their Uncle Gizmo."

"Okay. I love you. Bye." She hung up.

CHAPTER 22

By late September, the trees in Vermont were already showing their colors. Saturday morning, Woody and I carried steaming mugs of coffee out to the wood shop where he'd previously told me commune members made furniture to sell for extra income. I'd gotten all their machinery back in working order, but I'd never seen anyone doing any work there. Then again, I only came on weekends.

He set his cup down, opened a drawer in the workbench, and rummaged around in it. Eventually, he pulled out a yellowed sheet of paper containing a hand-drawn sketch and handed it to me. "You think you can build this?"

I had a fairly good idea of what it was, but I asked anyway.

"It's the orgone accumulator we have in the woodshed. There's a woman in Lenox, Massachusetts, who wants one. Now, it's not illegal to own or even to make one, but the FDA can bust you for transporting one across state lines. That's how they got Reich. One of his assistants shipped one out of his lab in Maine while Reich was in Arizona."

I scratched my ear and studied the plan. It was a perspective drawing, with an exploded view showing the sandwiched layers within the walls. The layers were labeled, but the unit measurements were missing.

Woody cleared his throat. "I was thinking you could cut all the pieces here and then assemble them for her there. I understand the law and feel certain the Feds can't make a case over someone carrying pieces of sheet metal and mason board in their van."

"You'll show me how?"

"I didn't make ours. One of Reich's collaborators did. But I understand the principle and we have this drawing. You can figure out almost anything, right? That's why they call you Gizmo."

The idea intrigued me. I'd spent time in Woody's orgone accumulator nearly every weekend I was there, and felt its benefits. It seemed only fitting I should help someone else. "I'll do it."

Woody picked up a carpenter's pencil and began writing a parts list. "Whatever I don't have in our shop, we can pick up this afternoon in Brattleboro."

The plans called for a wood frame of sufficient height, width, and depth to accommodate a person sitting on a bench or chair. I found Woody's tape measure, and we went to the woodshed to measure the interior of his accumulator. From those figures, I could extrapolate the size of the framework and exterior.

We constructed four long rectangular frames using one-by-two pine boards that Woody had on hand. We reinforced the corner joints with metal L braces, and then stood the finished frames upright, forming the four sides. Since I had to travel with it disassembled, we only joined them with duct tape to make sure they fit, and to get measurements for the top and bottom of the accumulator. Once the top and bottom frames were made and tested for fit, we undid the tape and laid all six pieces aside.

Woody had a sheet of half-inch plywood from which I cut a piece for the floor. I spread glue along the bottom frame and nailed the plywood in place.

For the outside of the accumulator, we needed mason board, and for the inside, 27 gauge galvanized sheet metal. Sandwiched in the middle were alternating layers of steel wool and a dialectical material such as fiberglass or sheep's wool. We'd have to drive into Brattleboro for all that.

"The woman we're making this for is a real freak about everything being natural," Woody said. "She won't want fiberglass. I know a store that sells Army-Navy surplus. We should be able to buy 100% wool blankets there. If not, we can try a fabric shop."

We took my van. A contractor's supply sold mason board and the sheet metal. "Do you carry rolls of steel wool that can be cut to size for floor sanders?"

"Sure," the man said. "What grade to you need?"

Woody glanced at the notes he'd copied from the plan. "Very fine, 000 or 0000, if you have it." He also picked up a pair of brass door hinges and a hook and eye.

I opened the camper bed and folded down the dinette, then slid in the four by eight sheets of mason board. The sheet metal was thin and floppy, so we laid it between two of the mason boards, then set the reels of steel wool on top. Last stop was the surplus store where we purchased three white wool blankets that had the word "Navy" imprinted on one end.

It was dusk by the time we got back to the commune. "Let's not do any more until tomorrow," he said.

I backed up to the wood shop. "No, Woody. We've got to unload tonight. My bed is under all this crap."

Two of the women came out to help.

Fine brown fibers from the back side of the mason board had stuck to my bed. Sparrow helped me take the bedding out and shake it off.

In the morning, we cut the mason board to size, then glued and nailed it to five of the frames, all except the bottom piece. Woody tied a blue bandana over his mouth and nose. All he needed was a cowboy hat to look like an old cattle rustler. He handed me a bandana and an old pair of work gloves. "For this next part, you don't want to get any steel wool particles on your skin or breathe them."

I soon saw what he meant as we unrolled the steel wool and cut it to fit the frames. There were fine steel wool particles everywhere. Over the steel wool, we laid a piece of wool cut from a Navy blanket, then another layer of steel wool, and another of the blanket so there were two layers of each. Next, we cut a piece of sheet metal to precisely fit the frame, sandwiching the layers in place within. This wasn't difficult as the metal was so thin we could cut it with tin snips. We nailed it in place with small steel tacks and set it in my camper. One down, five to go.

The last frame held the hinged door. Once it was finished, we removed the pins from the hinges. I'd rehang it after assembling the accumulator in Massachusetts.

It was dark by the time I set the last piece in the camper, and I had to be at work in the morning. So I said goodbye to everyone and started to pull away when Woody stopped me. He handed me the yellowed paper with the accumulator plan. "You might need this. Take care of it. This could be the only set of plans left in existence."

I put it in my box of tapes. I'd store it in back for safekeeping, later. "I won't be here next weekend. I'll be in Lenox."

He nodded. "Right. See you in two weeks."

CHAPTER 23

Lenox was in the Berkshire Mountains, which weren't really very high and reminded me of the mountains outside Paoli, Pennsylvania. Small colonial-style villages dotted Western Massachusetts. Many consisted of little more than a church and a post office. I passed through Stockbridge, which Arlo Guthrie had sung about in "Alice's Restaurant." Not seeing any restaurant, I kept driving.

A sign for Tanglewood announced it was the summer home of the Boston Symphony Orchestra. And I guess that meant something. Growing up in the Midwest and going to college in Texas, I didn't know much about classical music.

In Lenox, I wound my way through a neighborhood of two-story clapboard houses looking for the address Woody had given me. He'd told me the woman ran a yoga center, but the street I was on was residential and there were no business signs. I finally passed a house with a large Om sign painted next to the door. That had to be the place. I backed up and parked in the driveway.

Five painted wooden steps led up to a wide front porch. I looked for a house number, didn't see one, but a black mailbox on the wall read: "Woodbridge." Ah, must be some relation of Woody's. A neatly lettered card taped inside the glass storm door said, "Please leave shoes in the foyer upon entering. Namaste."

No doubt I'd found the right house.

I didn't see a doorbell, so I rapped on the glass. A woman wearing loose, drawstring cotton pants and a white leotard opened the inner door and looked at me. "Yes?"

The leotard was translucent, and her full breasts pretty much filled it. Without a bra, her nipples pushed at the thin material, and her dark aureoles hovered around them like two flying saucers. I pulled my eyes up to meet hers and discovered a bright scarlet dot painted on her forehead. My mind drew a blank. Finally, I glanced at the slip of paper in my hand. "Um . . . I'm looking for someone named Mata Shanti."

"That's me."

"I'm Gizmo. I've come to install your orgone accumulator."

She broke into a broad smile and opened the storm door.

I entered and took off my shoes like the sign said. Her living room was completely devoid of furniture and covered in white carpet. Without the glass door between us, I got a closer look at her. She seemed older than Nora—so too old to be Woody's daughter. Maybe a much younger sister or niece. Still, I couldn't have guessed her age if my life depended on it. Her face was free of wrinkles, not even crow's feet around her eyes. The skin on her neck and arms was like a twenty-year-old's.

"You teach meditation?" I said.

"And Hatha Yoga. Do you practice?"

"I meditate."

She looked at her watch. "I teach a Saturday afternoon class at four. You're welcome to sit in."

"Thank you, that'd be interesting. I don't know how long it will take me to put your orgone box together."

"You mean it's unassembled?"

"Had to be. It's as big as a closet. Show me where you want it."

"I hadn't taken into account its size." She rubbed the middle of her chest, making her breasts jiggle. I found her eyes again. Next, she held up her hands, closed her eyes, and turned in a circle like a radar antenna on an airbase. She was facing south when she stopped. "The porch. We'll have to put it on the back porch."

I followed her down a hallway and through the kitchen to a glassed-in porch. An exterior door led to a lawn carpeted with colorful autumn leaves.

I measured the door with my eyes. "This will do nicely. Is it all right if I drive my van on your grass? I have six large pieces to unload."

She considered the question for a moment before nodding. We chose an inside corner, and she helped me clear her patio furniture out of the way. I moved my van around while she swept the area where she wanted it set up.

I carried in the base and set it far enough from the wall that I could work around all sides. I'd slide the accumulator into place once I had it fully assembled. She helped me carry in the side panels, and I began fastening them together with wood screws. After I set the top on, I realized the assembled accumulator was too tall for me to drive in screws from above.

"Mrs. . . . uh Miss Shanti."

"Just Mata Shanti."

"Okay. Mata Shanti, do you have a step ladder?"

"I don't, but I'm sure my next-door neighbor does."

We walked together to his house, and I carried it back. Her students started arriving, so she left me to finish the work on my own. Once I had a ladder, it didn't take long. Finished, I pushed the accumulator against the corner walls, hung the door, and returned the neighbor's ladder.

I moved my camper off her lawn, went back in the house, and peeked into the living room where two men and four women sat listening. She saw me and motioned for me to enter.

"Sit anywhere. This is Gizmo. He'll be joining us today."

Mata Shanti led a meditation, talking softly all the way through it. Next, she showed us various contortions that she called asanas. After each demonstration, we tried to replicate her example. She'd walk softly among the students, stopping to adjust the position of one person or the other—most frequently me. I'd never seen any of these poses and performed them awkwardly. At the end of the class, the last asana she had us do was lie on our backs, sequentially relax every muscle from toe to head, and then rest. Finally, an asana I excelled at. I fell asleep.

She gently woke me as the others were preparing to leave. Each student held their hands in prayer and said, "Namaste" to her. She replied in kind. When the last student left, I pondered whether I was expected to follow that ritual as well.

She saved me the trouble. "You must be starved. Let me make us something to eat."

I followed her into the kitchen, where she started pulling vegetables from the refrigerator and dropping them into the sink. "Wash those, if you don't mind."

I didn't. At the commune, everyone shared kitchen duties. It made me feel at home.

She set a wok on the stove, turned on the burner, and added oil. As quickly as I washed the vegetables, she chopped them and threw them into the oil to sizzle. She returned to the fridge to get a package of tofu and another of thick udon noodles. These I recognized from Japanese takeout I'd eaten. She dumped them in the wok and poured soy sauce over them as she stirred. "I assume you're vegetarian."

"Not strictly, but I'm used to eating that way at the commune."

"You don't live there?"

"No, I just visit on weekends. I live in Maynard, outside Boston."

She slid dinner onto two plates, and we ate with chop sticks. I didn't have a problem with that. I'd eaten in a lot of Chinese restaurants since moving to the Boston area. Over dinner, she said, "Thank you for building me an orgone accumulator."

"It was Woody, really."

She rolled her eyes. "He's not that handy."

"Why do you say that? He has a whole wood shop."

"Which he gets other people to use."

I had no idea if that was true. I'd only known him a couple of years. But now that I thought about it, I'd never seen anyone use the wood shop before. It just sat there. I also wasn't sure if she and Woody were related and didn't want to put my foot in it if they were.

When we finished eating, I helped wash the dishes. She boiled water and made a pot of herbal tea. "Let's take this out to the porch."

The sun was setting, so she turned on a table lamp and poured a pale yellow liquid into delicate china tea cups decorated with tiny red roses.

I picked up my cup and sniffed. It didn't smell like Chinese restaurant tea or Lipton—which was the sum total of my knowledge of tea.

"Chamomile," she said. "Relaxes you, helps you sleep."

"Mata Shanti. Did you give yourself that name?"

"No. My guru gave it to me. It means Mother of Peace."

"Good name."

"Thank you."

I blew on my tea and tasted it. Not bad. Not tea, but not bad.

"Have you tried it?" She pointed to the accumulator.

"Not that one. In fact, it's my understanding that it takes a while for the orgone energy to accumulate."

"That's right. I meant, have you used an orgone accumulator before?"

"Yes. Woody's."

"I take it you were able to feel something?"

"Oh, yes." I smiled. "What about you?"

"I've known about orgone for . . . many years." She laid her hand on mine. I felt a warm tingling at the tip of my penis. I shifted in my seat and crossed my legs. The sensation stopped.

She nodded toward her new accumulator. "But that box isn't a magic cure-all. Our muscles must be loosened and freed before we experience the true free flow of streaming orgone within us. Since Reich's death, Reichian therapists are rarer than hen's teeth. But regular practice of hatha yoga helps break down the armoring."

"Is that what you teach?"

She smiled demurely. "There are eight branches of yoga. Hatha yoga works on the musculature. Other forms work on the mind, heart, sexuality, or directly with conscious energy. They all require more discipline that the average American has."

"Have you ever tried LSD?"

She pulled her hand away. "Never! My Guru says, 'God is not found with a pill.'"

Not what Timothy Leary preached, but I immediately regretted upsetting her.

She laughed. "Never offer your yoga instructor drugs."

I blushed. "I wasn't offering. I was only inquiring. Truth is, I've only taken it once. But I still remember the experience."

The last of the daylight had surrendered to the night. We sat together in a circle of incandescent light.

She cupped her hand over mine and I grew warm all over.

"There's no reason for you to drive home in the dark."

I was feeling contented and had no urge to get back on the road. "Thank you. Your neighbors won't mind me camping in your driveway?" The area looked pretty high-toned.

"Sleep in the house."

"Really?"

She stood up and carried the tea pot and cups into the kitchen. I followed. She set them in the sink, then turned and embraced me, pressing her lips tenderly against mine. The softest lips ever—like velvet.

Oh.

I recognized the difference between our ages, but I always resented it when younger women rejected me because I was "too old." It'd be hypocritical of me to discriminate against her. So we fell into bed.

And it was bliss. Mata Shanti knew more about making love than any woman I've ever been with.

In the morning, we snuggled, our heads sharing one pillow.

"The name on your mailbox is Woodbridge. How are you related to Woody?" Perhaps I should have asked beforehand, but I hadn't.

"That would be by marriage."

"So he's like your uncle or something?"

"Gizmo, don't be dense. He's my husband."

My God, what would he say when I told him? I'd have to. It wouldn't be fair not to.

She lifted her head and looked into my eyes, as if reading my mind. "Woody and I have an understanding. I don't object to his lovers in Vermont, and he doesn't concern himself about mine. Our relationship is what my friends call an Indian divorce."

"What's that mean?"

"In India, instead of getting divorced, some couples just go live separate lives. Often in separate states or countries."

"But why?" Woody seemed the most liberal of men. I couldn't see him as hard to live with.

"I was of a generation sold on the myth of pleasant suburban domesticity. My women friends acted like doormats and then suffered depression because they felt overlooked."

Like Nora and Sophie?

"Then in 1963, I read *The Feminine Mystique*, and woke up."

"I've heard of it." It was popular among feminists in Cambridge, and I'd seen them carrying copies of it around. "I admit I never read it."

"I'm not surprised. The book was groundbreaking. It examined the many ways in which women in American society were still oppressed."

"But Woody seems so—"

"Larger than life? Exactly. To love in the cosmic realm, souls require equality. If the man makes the woman smaller than himself, his essence will not fit her. If she believes herself larger than him, he cannot fill her."

She rubbed her hand over my heart chakra. "Woody and I gave each other a little room to breathe. I took up Tantric yoga. He took up life in Vermont. So far, it's working for us."

CHAPTER 24

Woody never asked me about my trip to Lenox, and I never told him I'd slept with his spouse or whatever they considered themselves. I wondered that I didn't feel guilty, but I figured they were both adults and obviously made their own decisions about what kind of marital arrangement they had.

Despite our wonderful sex, I didn't keep seeing Mata Shanti. I did take her advice though, and joined a yoga class in Cambridge. Weekend sessions in Woody's orgone box were great, but the yoga exercises really helped free my muscles, which were knotted from spending every day hunched over a drafting table drawing circuit boards. Or could it be from emotions I'd suppressed about Mom's death and Dad's impending remarriage?

Christmas that year nearly got lost in preparations for Dad and Louise's December twenty-sixth wedding day. Nora and Sophie acted bitchy. Should Christmas dinner be at Nora and Tom's, as it had been since Mom's death, or at Louise's, or back at Dad's? Since Louise was selling her home and moving in with Dad, they decided to have Christmas there. Nora wasn't happy, but it was a compromise they all could live with.

The wedding was small, just family and a few close neighbors. Louise had two grown sons, old enough they hadn't been in school with me or my sisters, so it was like meeting strangers even though they'd grown up on our block.

Nora's oldest, Tommy Jr., got a portable tape recorder for Christmas. "He's interested in electronics, just like you were," Nora said.

Tommy recorded the wedding ceremony and played it back for everyone the next day. It sounded pretty decent.

"Let me see that," I said.

He opened the lid and took out a small plastic tape cartridge. "It's called Compact Cassette. This recorder is mono, but you can get stereo decks for your home and car."

I saw the possibilities immediately. I'd been buying albums for my record collection. Then if I liked it, I'd have to buy the same album in 8-Track for my van. If I switched to cassettes, I could just copy an album on tape. Besides, I had a whole stack of beloved 45s that were never going to be released on 8-Track.

Soon as I got back to Massachusetts, I added a tape deck to my home stereo and began transferring my record collection to Compact Cassettes. It was painless. I still frequently had people over to listen to music and could record a cassette at the same time. Everything except my Rock 'n Roll 45s from the fifties—none of my younger friends wanted to hear those. I had to record them when I was alone.

When I had a good number of tapes made, I switched the 8-Track in my van for a cassette player. I put my 8-Track tapes in a box and mailed them to Eddie. Wouldn't he be surprised?

Two weeks later, he called to thank me. "Gizmo, I'm grateful for all the tapes you sent. But, man, you listen to some weird shit."

"Well, just keep the ones you like. I'm sure you can trade the rest at a used record store."

President Johnson may have left office, but his war in Vietnam raged on, and protests against it swelled. In most respects, the new rascal, Nixon, was worse than the one we had before. I didn't listen to the news much, but he supposedly declared Timothy Leary the most dangerous man in America. Quite a statement, considering Leary wasn't ordering the bombing of anybody.

Woody kept the commune decidedly apolitical, neither participating in protests nor opposing them. "I've lived a long while," he said. "For nearly all of it, our country has been in one war after another, and between wars, building weapons for the next."

Yet, I was aware of a change in the wind. Protesters were no longer just against the war. Now they were against the "establishment," the people profiting from war. Then the scope expanded further, until the establishment included those who polluted the environment, advertisers who sold the public useless goods, and landlords ripping off the poor. There were tenant strikes and sit-ins and marches on every campus. College deans were wringing their hands and losing sleep.

Nixon didn't give a shit. He called protesters communist sympathizers. Turning a deaf ear to public outrage, he expanded the Vietnam War into neutral Cambodia. More students protested. In a show of force, the National Guard was deployed across American campuses.

In May, Ohio National Guardsmen at Kent State University fired into a crowd at a student peace rally, killing four. Their deaths triggered massive outrage across the nation. I felt it myself, and was still fuming about it the following weekend when I went to Vermont. All the way up, I thought about how the computers I was designing were being used. Helping corporations exploit consumers. Helping advertising agencies tailor ads more precisely. And I was sure there were some dark sales to the military. No big corporation was going to turn away Pentagon money.

The first thing I said to Sparrow when I got there was, "Jesus Christ, I don't want to be a part of the establishment anymore."

"Then don't," she said. "Drop out. You're halfway there already."

Later that afternoon, I took a long hike into the National Forest. Bell shaped yellow flowers grew wild here, blooming in the warm spring. Boston and big business seemed a million miles away. The commune didn't even own a television. Nixon could be forgotten. By the time I returned from my walk, I'd already quit my job and moved to Vermont, in my mind.

Of course, it took a few weeks to turn that into a reality. I had to give my notice, sell everything that wouldn't fit in the camper, and give Dad Woody's address and phone number in case they needed to reach me.

That call didn't go well.

Nixon had lost favor in Dad's eyes after he called the anti-war protesters "bums" and the father of one of the dead Kent State girls appeared on TV and told the president, "My child was not a bum." But my dad didn't want his son to become a bum, either.

"I won't," I told him. "Really, I've no debt, and plenty of savings." After all, I'd been paid pretty well and lived a frugal lifestyle.

"What will you do when that runs out?"

"I'll . . . I'll . . . make things to sell. You know I've always been handy." Yes! An idea struck me at that minute. I'd build orgone accumulators for people.

"You're an electrical engineer, for Christ's sake. What are you going to make, toasters?"

Well, at least toasters weren't war machines. I didn't say that, of course. But I didn't mention orgone boxes, either.

"I'll be all right, Dad. There's always a need for a guy who fixes things."

"Damn waste of education is all I have to say about it. You ought to have you head examined." And without another word, he hung up. We didn't speak for a long time after that.

I moved to the commune, but Sparrow and I weren't a steady thing. Even though she'd encouraged me to quit my job and live there, she preferred the years when we'd only spent weekends together. Sparrow wanted to vary her men.

Well, what did I expect? Hadn't we always been free?

I spent some hours that Saturday in Woody's orgone box. That night, I unfolded the Westfalia bed, turned out the light, and crawled beneath the covers. Alone. A little later, I heard the door open and shut.

A naked woman with cold feet crawled in next to me. "This is nice."

I knew every curve of Sparrow's body. This wasn't her. "Sunshine?"

She kissed my ear. "Woody said you wouldn't want to sleep alone." She wrapped one leg around me. "Is this all right?"

I think there's only one thing a gentleman can do is that situation. I slid my arm under her and pulled her against me.

*　*　*

If I was going to make a go of orgone accumulators, I needed to learn more about Wilhelm Reich and his work. When I mentioned this to him, Woody lent me several banned books written by Reich. "I know you'll be careful with these," he said. "They are literally irreplaceable."

"What do you mean?"

"In 1956, the US government confiscated every book on orgone Reich ever wrote and incinerated them. Even those in his publisher's warehouse. Same way the Nazis burned Freud's books."

My mouth dropped open. I wasn't enamored of the government anymore, but this? "What about the First Amendment—freedom of the press?"

"I guess they ignored that. Reich appealed it all the way to the Supreme Court, but died before his case could be heard. Besides, his books were already ashes by then."

He tapped the book I was holding. "Except for those copies in private hands."

"I'll treat it like gold."

"Gold is durable. Treat these like orchids—easily damaged and difficult to grow back."

I spent that summer reading Reich's books. My sense of outrage only grew. Just like Ray Bradbury's *Fahrenheit 451*, the government I'd served and defended had actually burned books to prevent information from getting out. Reich's enemies said that he claimed the orgone accumulator could cure neurosis and serious diseases, using fraud as an excuse to ban his ideas. He made no such claim. Only that orgone might help in treatment. He always stressed the need to breakdown suppressed emotional energy armoring our muscles.

Mata Shanti was right. Yoga helped accomplish that.

My van was a little small for yoga, and people were still asleep in the commune living room. So on sunny mornings, I spread a blanket on the grass and practiced outside. Some days, Leaf, Misty, or others would join me. Afterward, little flashes of orgone flitted around the sky—at least to my eyes.

Reich's scientific books were as dense and as difficult as any text I'd ever tackled in college. A more straightforward exposition was his slim volume, *Listen Little Man*. In it, Reich postulated that fascism tries to suppress free love because doing so leads to a population preoccupied with repressed lust, which allows leaders in power to do their misdeeds unnoticed. To me, the inverse proved his point. The current sexual revolution freed young people to pay attention to Nixon's and Agnew's actions.

I felt sorry that Wilhelm Reich had died before the free love movement really started. The least I could do was get off my ass and make a few of his orgone boxes and undo the wrong our government had done him. I returned the books to Woody and drove to Brattleboro to buy raw materials.

CHAPTER 25

That autumn, after the commune's annual Thanksgiving feast, Sugar Bear packed up his bus and headed south for warmer climes. Sparrow went with him. Squirrel had disappeared a month earlier. No one said where.

Dad hadn't spoken to me since I moved into the commune, so I decided not to go there for Christmas. Not that I couldn't afford it—if I drove. Despite having the aerodynamics of a brick, the VW got 32 miles per gallon, and gasoline was 35 cents. So it'd cost slightly over a penny a mile. I was solvent financially. Even though I'd sold only one orgone accumulator, I'd learned that because I spent so little money, I didn't need to make much. I contributed my fair share to the commune and still had savings left.

I exchanged occasional letters with Nora and Sophie. Neither of them got on well with Dad's new wife. Nora missed taking care of Dad, and her depression expanded to fill the time provided. I considered whether I should make an orgone accumulator, take it there, and just shove her in it. A thought I quickly dismissed. I knew from all that I was reading that orgone wouldn't help her until she loosened her armor, and I didn't think her therapist was doing anything more than pushing pills.

One December morning, Misty and I were snuggled in my camper. The heater had the place toasty, when a man threw open the side door, letting in a frigid blast of air. "FBI. Come out of there."

FBI? Had Dad finally called them? I jumped out of bed and stood up, which put my genitals about even with his face. "We're not dressed, sir. As you can see."

He had the grace to blush. "Well, put some pants on and get out here."

I tossed Misty her sweater and jeans, and she dressed under the covers. I pulled on my pants and shirt and stepped outside. I opened a small built-in wardrobe near the camper door and started to reach inside.

"Keep your hands where I can see them."

"I'm just getting my coat, sir. It's freezing." My military days came back to me, and I instinctively knew adding "sir" to everything went a long way.

"I'll get it. You stay out here. Miss, you too. Out now."

Misty zipped her jacket and came to stand beside me. "What's going on?"

"Beats me. Excuse me, sir, what's this about?"

"We have a warrant." He gingerly peeked into my closet, expecting to find—I wasn't sure what—bombs or pot or books or something equally dangerous. He pulled out my winter coat, checked the pockets, and tossed it to me. "Come with me."

Other agents were bringing commune members who also slept in their vehicles. Those who slept in the house were on the porch, shivering beside Woody. They herded us toward black vans blocking the driveway.

While we were being frisked, handcuffed, and loaded into separate vans, teams of agents searched our vehicles and the house. None of them explained anything, but Woody had been served a copy of the search warrant, which he held in his handcuffed hands. Unfortunately, they put us in separate vans, so I couldn't ask him about it.

They drove us to the federal building in Brattleboro, where we were locked in a plain room without even being fingerprinted. The women were put in a separate room. No one questioned us. No one said what the charges were. Woody spoke to one of our keepers and was taken, we knew not where. His parting words were, "Be cool. And don't answer any questions."

At twelve, the door opened, and an officer set a bin of brown paper lunch bags on the floor. Inside each bag was a carton of milk, a cookie, and a plain bologna sandwich on white bread.

Beaner pounded on the door until a man came. He handed him the sandwich. "We're vegetarians, man. Don't feed us this skunk food."

"It's that or peanut butter," the man said.

"Peanut butter," Beaner said.

It took them an hour to bring us more sandwiches. Meanwhile, we drank the milk and ate our cookies. We were a pretty quiet group. Since we didn't know anything, there was nothing to talk about.

About four o'clock, they told us we were free to go. Out in front of the building, the women were waiting for us. Woody hadn't come out yet, and we didn't know if he was the only one they were charging. Everyone talked at once, but no one knew anything.

Woody appeared, looking like a frazzled Einstein. "Don't anybody panic. They're going to bring the vans around and drive us all back home."

"That's the least they should do," Leaf said.

Woody held up his hands. "Just accept the ride and don't say anything in front of the drivers. I'll explain everything tonight at dinner."

When we got home, everyone was starved and set about making dinner, anxious to hear Woody's story. The search had left the place in shambles. Those who weren't cooking started putting things back in order.

I entered Woody's room and asked to use his phone, certain that Dad had turned us into the FBI as a nest of communists.

"Meditate a few minutes first," Woody said. "Events like today bring up a lot of bad energy."

He was right, but meditation wasn't happening for me. I managed a few calming breaths, then dialed. I was cagey about how I approached the subject, not wanting to let on I'd been arrested if he wasn't aware of it. After we talked awhile, I became convinced Dad didn't call anyone. He'd changed sides and now vehemently opposed Nixon, who he kept calling "Tricky Dicky." He asked if I'd be there for Christmas, but I ducked the question, not knowing the repercussions of the raid. We might all be in the clink by then.

Dinner was finally ready. While we ate, Woody explained. It turned out Woody held a law degree but had left practice years ago. Who knew? This information made me wonder how many degrees he had, and if his casual hints about his work in physics and psychiatry had elements of truth as well.

"I phoned a federal judge I knew and was granted an emergency hearing." Woody thumped his chest. "I went through their case like shit through a goose. They had nothing, no probable cause—just the deranged fantasy of an unreliable speed freak. And their questionable search had turned up no evidence."

Good thing Sugar Bear was on the road. They'd have found pot, at least.

"The judge gave the Feds a good scolding and let us go." He added, "I don't think they'll dare bother us again."

"But what was it all about?" Sunshine said. "What were they after?"

"I wasn't going to mention this," Woody said. "Our friend Squirrel became addicted to bennies. I discovered he was dealing them and asked him to leave."

That explained a lot. Squirrel often acted hyper. And had disappeared.

"He got busted by the DEA, and instead of calling me for legal help, he made up a bunch of nonsense about us to get a plea deal."

"Us?"

Woody nodded. "We haven't kept up with the news, but apparently Nixon cannot accept that his constituents will not let him do whatever he wants. Since the shooting at Kent State, it's no longer just students protesting. Mothers and fathers are demonstrating. He's convinced it's a communist conspiracy and has the FBI looking under every rock for hippie agitators. Squirrel told them that's who we were."

"I'll throttle him," Leaf said.

"No," Woody said. "We'll pity him and hope he gets over his addiction."

"Well," Beaner said, "he's not welcome back here."

"Agreed," Woody said.

The conversation continued into the night, including a prolonged discussion about whether we ought to buy a television to stay informed. We voted against it.

When it was time for bed, I found my camper was an unmitigated, discombobulated mess. I didn't have the heart to tackle it, not then. I grabbed a sleeping bag and went into the house. The first time I'd ever shared the living room floor with a dozen people. Apparently, the Feds had left everyone else's vans in a similar state of disarray. We slept like a pile of puppies.

In the morning, I checked the woodshed, afraid they'd axed the orgone accumulator to bits like they had Reich's. It was completely intact, although the door was unlatched and open.

I told Woody.

"They probably didn't understand what they were looking at," he said.

Since everyone's van was topsy-turvy, we decided to help each other out. It took all day. I found the paper with the orgone accumulator plan in a pile of papers on the VW passenger seat. Woody was right. That wasn't what the Feds came for, and they didn't recognize what they'd found.

Beaner and Sunshine put together a veggie stew for supper, and everyone gathered at the table.

Leaf grabbed my bowl before I could fill it and threw my Top Secret ID on the table in front of me. "Looks like we've got a narc among us! Who's Sven?"

"I am . . . but I'm not."

The others leaned in to look at my ID, then scooted away like I had scabies.

Woody stood, walked over, and placed his hands on my shoulders. "Gizmo isn't the narc. I told you, it was Squirrel who brought the heat."

Leaf picked up my ID and waved it in the air. "That doesn't explain this."

"Where did you find that?" Woody said.

"In Gizmo's van, while we were putting things in order."

I snatched it out of Leaf's hand. "This was for access to secure air bases. Most of you are aware that I served in the Air Force. I told you that the first night we met. I've never been a cop, never worked for any type of law enforcement, never intend to." I handed the ID back to Leaf. "Look at the date. That ID has been expired for more than a decade. I can't even remember why I kept it."

Woody patted my shoulder. "He *did* tell us he'd been in service. An old ID tag means nothing. What happened yesterday might make any of us a little paranoid, but that's no reason to turn on each other. Now, everybody show Gizmo we love him."

Leaf mumbled an apology and handed me back my bowl and my ID. Sunshine and Misty hugged me, and Beaner changed the subject. But after that, a sense of distrust always lingered around me. When weekend day trippers came to visit, I'd glimpse whispered conversations that I imagined were about me.

I decided I'd drive home for Christmas after all.

CHAPTER 26

With my hair now grown to shoulder length, I prepared for my family's reaction during my long drive across Interstate 80. Predictably, every adult in my family gave me grief, but my niece and nephews thought it looked cool. And I was good with being the cool uncle.

Dad had settled the issue of where holiday dinners were to be held—his and Louise's house, discussion closed. Her sons came, which made sleeping accommodations tight, so I offered to stay in my van. Nora wouldn't hear of it. She doubled up her two youngest boys and gave me one of their rooms. They didn't mind, happy to get Uncle Gizmo to themselves for a few days.

Nora's psychiatrist was still prescribing "happy pills," and upped the dosage as she'd built up a tolerance by now. Tom had tools in his workshop, but I didn't think building her an orgone accumulator would help. And worse, it would probably freak Tom out, given his objection to meditation. One day, while the kids were gone ice skating, I laid a blanket on her living room floor and taught her yoga postures that I thought would free her armoring. Heading off any possible objection from Tom, instead of calling it yoga, I said they were tension and relaxation exercises that I'd found released anxiety. She was a better student than I was a teacher. Still, I think she learned something.

A few days after Christmas, Louise called me at Nora's. "Some person, I think his name was Bean something, telephoned you. He wants you to call him right away. Sounded important."

"Thanks, I will." I hung up. "Nora, I need to make a long-distance call. I'll pay you."

"Go ahead, but you don't need to pay, little brother."

I phoned Woody to see what the matter was, fearing the worst—Feds hassling us again. It was a hundred times worse than I imagined.

"Woody died," Beaner said.

A vice-grip clamped my heart. "I'm on my way."

It felt like Christmas was cursed. Mom died just after Christmas. Now Woody had done the same. I wasn't sure the others at the commune knew about Woody's wife, so I called information.

"Directory Assistance, what city please?"

"Lenox, Massachusetts."

"I'll connect you, one moment please." Two brief rings. "Lenox, Massachusetts. How may I help you?"

What name would she be listed under? "Uh, do you have a listing for Woodbridge?" I'd seen that name on her mailbox.

"I have an Ida Woodbridge."

Really? Could they have been Ira and Ida? Despite the gravity of the moment, the thought made me laugh. "Any other Woodbridge?"

"No.".

"All right, may I have that number, please?" I scratched it down and disconnected.

"Nora, I've just received some horrible news. I need to put another long-distance charge on your bill."

"I'm sorry to hear that. Do what you have to do. Don't worry about the money."

I dialed the number and let it ring. After seven rings, an exasperated woman answered. "Hello, you'll have to call back. I'm teaching a class."

Okay. I had the right number. "Mata Shanti, wait. Don't hang up."

"Who is this?"

"Gizmo, I built your orgone box."

"Yes, I remember you. Listen, can I call you back after class?"

"You can if you want to talk further, but before you hang up, I need to tell you that Woody has died."

I heard a sob, and then a clunk as her receiver fell.

"Mata Shanti! Can you hear me? Pick up the phone, Mata Shanti."

"Sorry, I dropped it."

"I can understand that. I'm at my sister's, I'll give you her number. Call me within the next hour. I'm leaving for Vermont after that."

In the meantime, I told Nora what had happened and packed the VW, ready to get on the road. Nora made me sandwiches and a fresh pot of coffee to fill my thermos.

Mata Shanti telephoned back and said she'd dismissed her class early. I told her what little I'd been told and suggested she call Woody's number. "Someone there will know more. I'm a thousand miles away, and it's going to take me twenty-four hours to reach there even if I drive straight through."

"Don't do that," Nora said.

I nodded, and told Mata Shanti, "Probably longer. I'll pull into a rest stop and sleep along the way."

Nora nodded approval.

"I'll meet you in Vermont," Mata Shanti said.

After I hung up, I set out, stopping briefly at Sophie's and Dad's to say goodbye. Traffic wasn't bad. They'd cleared the roads of snow, though it still lay in dirty piles along the berm.

Still, it was a long, bleak drive.

* * *

I had been right. No one in the commune was aware that Woody had a wife. At first, they were relieved when she took over the funeral arrangements, because none of them had a clue what to do. Later, they weren't so happy when they realized his estate passed to her and she had no intention of keeping the property.

In subsequent weeks, we discussed offering to buy it from her as a collective. Sunshine thought Sparrow and Sugar Bear would be down with that if they knew. They'd missed Woody's funeral because no one knew how to reach them. Unfortunately, we had no credit and couldn't get a mortgage.

It never would have worked, anyway. Under the terms of his grandfather's lease, the land reverted to the US Forestry Service. Our commune was done for. It was time to go.

For a second, I considered moving back to Massachusetts and asking for my old job back, but I discarded the idea in a heartbeat. I was done working for "the man." Instead, I contacted Mata Shanti and asked if she'd sell me Woody's more portable tools and his books by Reich. I planned to travel and build accumulators along the way.

"Gizmo, just take anything you want. Tell the others they can do the same. He'd want it that way."

I wished I could take Woody's accumulator, but there was no way I'd ever fit it in the camper. Besides, he'd warned me I could be arrested for transporting one across state lines, and I didn't intend to go back in the pokey or stay in Vermont.

A group of the others said they weren't leaving. "We'll squat on this property until someone kicks us off," Leaf said. "I'm betting the Department of Interior has forgotten this old place exists."

I wouldn't have taken that bet. My experiences in Nevada had taught me the government had pencil pushers who kept track of every parcel, even desert wasteland, and Woody's was anything but that. No, eventually they'd find out Woody was dead and merge his property into the National Forest.

With months of Vermont winter still ahead, I decided to follow Sugar Bear's example and make my way to warmer states. I said goodbye to everyone and headed south just as another snowstorm started to move from Canada into New England.

Chapter 27

I left the commune and raced south, trying to keep ahead of the storm. Actually, that's not quite correct. '67 Volkswagens didn't exactly race, they sort of chugged along, sometimes shoved sideways by gusts of wind. I had *Let It Be,* The Beatles' final album, in the cassette deck playing over and over. About six months earlier, it'd been released in conjunction with a movie of the same name, and the announcement that the band was breaking up. Now, with Woody's death, the commune had broken up, too.

When the movie came to Vermont, the whole commune crowded into Sugar Bear's school bus and went to the drive-in theater. On Tuesday nights, they had a special admission price, one dollar for the whole carload. The owner might have balked at admitting a busload of hippies for a buck, but the ticket seller was a sixteen-year-old who didn't care.

"If you want to get high, come find us when you get off," Sugar Bear told her.

I was sure that wasn't wise.

Bear parked, and we spread blankets on the adjacent parking spaces. Drive-ins had speakers on poles between the parking spaces. We cranked the volume up on all those nearest us.

The film was of an impromptu concert on the roof of the Beatles' Abbey Road studios. Some scenes were jubilant, especially when they performed "Get Back." All of a sudden, they were one again, four lads from Liverpool, just having fun making music. But in the back of our minds weighed the knowledge that this was the last time we'd see them together. The movie ended on a pleasant enough note, but on the way home, Misty, then Sunshine, started crying. Even Sparrow turned weepy, and she wasn't that much of a Beatles fan. It felt like the end of an era.

The chorus of the title song filled my camper for the hundredth time, bringing to mind the camera close-up of Paul soulfully singing it. I thought, what choice do we have in this life, but to let things be?

I wasn't sure why all these memories were coming up. The continuously looping *Let It Be* tape? Probably. Or maybe that with Woody gone, I'd never see my brothers and sisters from the commune again.

Wait, that wasn't true. I'd already crossed the Connecticut state line into New York State. In a couple of days, I'd be in Florida and could find Sugar Bear and Sparrow. I wasn't sure where they'd be, but it would definitely be somewhere cool hippies hung out. And they stood out in a crowd.

In the meantime, if I was going to change my head, I needed to change the music. I rummaged through a box of cassettes on the floor next to the driver's seat and pulled out George Harrison's solo album, *All Things Must Pass*. It'd come out just after Thanksgiving, and Sophie had given it to me for Christmas. Because of Woody's funeral and all that followed, I hadn't listened to it that much. Now, the long drive ahead seemed the perfect time. Apparently, all things *did* pass.

I wanted to avoid the snarl of big city traffic I'd encountered when Sparrow and I visited Greenwich Village many years before. If I drove down the western side of New Jersey, I could skip Newark and New York City entirely.

Across the state line, I entered Bergen County, New Jersey, and stopped for gas. While the attendant filled my tank, I studied my road atlas. He tapped on the window and I slid it open, ready to pay him.

"How do you check the oil on this thing?" He looked to be about fourteen.

"I'll show you." I got out. An arctic blast stung my cheeks. I was staying ahead of the storm, but not by much. I opened the engine compartment and pointed. He yanked out the dipstick, wiped it on a blue shop towel, reinserted it, and pulled it back out. "Oil's full," he said. "You want me to check your antifreeze?"

"You'd have a hard time doing that. Doesn't have a radiator."

"What?"

"Haven't you ever seen a Volkswagen?"

"On the street. I've never seen the engine. I just started this job."

I closed the compartment. "How much do I owe you?"

He glanced at the pump. "Three bucks."

I paid him and got back into the van. Snow was blowing, and it was damn cold outside. It wouldn't do to let the VW get too cool. They took forever to heat, and it wasn't safe to run the propane heater while driving. I headed out. At the station entrance, a shivering skinny dude with straw-colored, shoulder-length hair waved his thumb frantically. I stopped and motioned him toward the passenger door. He grabbed an old brown suitcase and a rucksack, tossed them in the back, and climbed in. "Th-thanks," he said, teeth chattering.

I pulled onto the highway. "Where are you headed?"

"G-G-Georgia."

"It's your lucky day. I'm on my way to Florida. What's your name?"

"Sticks."

"I'm Gizmo. You have a driver's license?"

"Of course."

"Can you drive a stick-shift?"

"Absolutely."

"Good. We can take turns. I don't want to stop until we get clear of this snow."

"Fine by me."

It turned out Sticks was a drummer, and pretty good. He retrieved a set of drumsticks from his rucksack and played along with the stereo, using my dashboard like a drum kit. *All Things Must Pass* was a double album that lasted us a good way through New Jersey, but it was a little mellow for Sticks. When it reached the last song and started to repeat, he rummaged in his rucksack and brought out a couple of his own cassettes. "Let's listen to some Allman Brothers."

"Who?"

"Y'ain't heard of the Allman Brothers? Man, they're the real deal."

I hadn't. He had two of their albums, and we listened to them all the way to Pennsylvania. My previous exposure to blues music came from songs English groups like The Animals, The Rolling Stones, and Cream had covered. They were good, but Sticks was right, the Allman Brothers were the real deal. He said they lived in Macon, Georgia, and were the reason he was going there.

We had music in common and talked as we traded off driving. I intended to get as far away from the snow as soon as possible. At our first stop, I folded down the dinette and pulled out the bed so one guy could nap while the other drove.

When we neared Charlotte, North Carolina, Sticks was driving and exited at the sign pointing toward Spartanburg, Greenville, Atlanta. I studied our new route and considered the possibilities. From the map, it looked like Florida was only three or four hours south from Macon.

At the turn-off for Macon, I dropped Sticks off and just kept on trucking.

I crossed the Florida state line and stopped at the Welcome Station, where they served free orange juice. An oversized map of the state hung on one wall. I drank several refills of OJ while I studied it. Suddenly, the words *University of Florida* next to a city a little further on jumped out at me. My experiences in El Paso and Cambridge had taught me that hippies and college towns went together like peanut butter and jelly.

The light was fading by the time I pulled into Gainesville, Florida. January sundown came early. I motored down University Avenue past the campus. At a traffic light, I opened my passenger window and called out to a couple of hip-looking students, "Is there a head shop in this town?"

"For sure, dude. Keep going down University Avenue until you get to Seventh Street, then turn right. You can't miss it."

I parked in front of the Subterranean Circus and went in. The air was heavy with the smell of incense. Psychedelic posters lit with black light adorned the walls. Tables held stacks of dashiki shirts and peasant blouses. A long-haired dude stood next to a display of hookahs. We talked for a minute, and I asked him if Gainesville was a cool place. He assured me it was. I described Sugar Bear and Sparrow and their big converted bus and asked if he'd seen them. He hadn't.

I explained I'd just got off the road and asked if he knew where it'd be cool to park my van for the night. Somewhere the cops wouldn't hassle me.

"Did you pass Mac's Waffle shop on your way here?"

"Maybe. I think so."

"Go back the way you came and turn right on the dirt road next to Mac's. That's the student ghetto. There's a woods across the street from a bunch of shack houses. The people around there are cool. You can park among those trees, and they'll probably let you use their shower."

"Thanks, man. I like this town already."

I followed his directions and parked in this block-long forest. I knocked on the screen door of a house across the street. Somewhere inside, "Brown Sugar" was playing at full volume. A barefoot hippie opened the door with a joint in his hand. I guessed I didn't have to worry about the cops here.

"Hi. I'm Gizmo. That's my VW." I jerked my thumb toward the woods behind me. "I just wanted to make sure it was cool for me to camp here."

He opened the door fully and stepped out of the way. "Come on inside." He shook my hand in some complicated ritual I didn't quite follow, but I faked it. "Frisbee," he said, and passed me the joint. "Cassandra and Rainbow." He pointed to two women on the couch, which was actually a mattress on the floor covered with a paisley Indian bedspread. No doubt purchased from the Subterranean Circus.

I took a toke and handed it back to him. He passed it to Cassandra. Instantly, I felt stoned. "Man, this is some great pot."

Rainbow took the joint from Cassandra and smiled at me. "We call it Gainesville Green—grown right in the area." She patted her hand on the couch. "Take a load off."

We finished the joint and talked. I told them about the commune in Vermont and asked if they knew the whereabouts of Sugar Bear and Sparrow. The girls had never met them, but Frisbee knew a guy named Sugar Bear, though he didn't drive a school bus. Cassandra mellowed and replaced the Rolling Stones with a Moody Blues album. I liked that better.

We listened to one whole side of the album. She got up to turn it over, when I suddenly realized I was very hungry. My last meal was three glasses of OJ at the border. "How's the food at that waffle place?" I said.

Rainbow made a face. "Greasy."

"Oh, it's pretty good when you've got the munchies," Frisbee said.

"Well, I certainly do," I said. "Who wants to eat waffles? I'm buying."

Cassandra jumped up and put her shoes on. I stood and held out my hand to Rainbow. She acted reluctant to go, but once we got there, she ate two.

Mac's was a diner lit with overhead fluorescents. Booths skirted the perimeter of the room. In the center was counter seating with padded round swivel stools like the soda fountain in my hometown when I was a kid. On the business side of the counter were the grill, deep fryer, and waffle irons. Rainbow was right, the place did reek of hot grease. But Frisbee was right, too. The waffles were delicious. He and I ate two apiece.

A stained, ragged copy of that morning's newspaper lay on the seat next to me. I picked it up. An oval logo printed in the upper corner of the front page read: "Gainesville, Florida — We like it here." So far, I did too.

CHAPTER 28

Frisbee and I parted ways with Cassandra and Rainbow outside of Mac's. Both girls had class in the morning. Walking back to his house, I said, "Can I cop a shower at your place?"

"Have at it."

I did. Nothing finer than that warm water spraying on my head after three days on the road. I soaped, scrubbed, and rinsed myself from head to toe. I stepped out and looked for a towel in the cabinet under the sink. There weren't any. I opened the bathroom door a crack and shouted, "Hey, dude, you got any towels?"

"Yeah, it's hanging on the wall by the tub."

It was a pitiful, thread bare specimen imprinted: Property of Holiday Inn. I used it, but told myself that in the future I'd bring a towel from the camper. And maybe leave it behind as a thank you.

Frisbee had another joint going when I came out. He offered me a toke.

"Thanks, but I'm going to crash."

"Cool. See you tomorrow."

The bed in the camper hadn't been put away from the trip, so all I had to do was smooth a few wrinkles out of the sheets and tuck in the blanket. I crawled in and slept hard until midday.

When I woke and stepped outside, the sun was warm. In January. What a wonderful feeling!

I put the bed away, set the dinette table back up, made coffee, and ate the last of the granola. Milk was nearly gone, too. I'd have to shop today. Right after I cleaned the road trip trash out of the camper.

A walk seemed in order. The area sidewalks were full of students, and the coeds were exceedingly lovely. Three-quarters of the year, Boston and Cambridge women favored bulky sweaters, long skirts, and thick stockings. Here, shorts or short skirts were de rigueur—again in January! Tanned, lean legs surrounding me set my heartbeat racing. And everyone I met was friendly.

All around me, I could feel this strange mix of intense resistance to President Nixon and an unrelated optimism about what Yippie leader, Abbie Hoffman, called the "Woodstock Nation." Perhaps it was just because people in their early twenties believed they could do anything, whether or not they knew what they're doing. Certainly, creative spirits were trying everything—everywhere I went among the hippie community, I found bands, theaters, poetry journals, underground newspapers, restaurants, and head shops—all started on very little money, but with loads of enthusiasm, energy, and hard work.

Tucked into little shops near campus, I found sandal makers, record stores, bookshops, a health food restaurant, all owned by hippies. Two places crafted custom-made guitars and string instruments. At each of the various hippie enterprises, I inquired about Sparrow and Sugar Bear. No one knew them. I guess they hadn't discovered Gainesville yet. Their loss.

When I asked about groceries, a student majoring in art history directed me to a health food store that had just opened on Thirteenth Street. The prices weren't cheap, but the people were friendly and the food organic. I bought what I needed and carried the sacks back to my van. I put the groceries away and walked to a 7-Eleven to buy ice for the cooler. While there, I saw a package of index cards on a shelf of school supplies. I bought them.

That afternoon, I sat at the dinette table with the doors of the van open to the Florida sun and wrote out ads for custom-built orgone accumulators. Anyone interested should come to the VW bus parked in the enchanted forest on Ninth Terrace. Most of the hippie establishments I'd visited had community bulletin boards, and I figured the Feds who'd persecuted Reich wouldn't be reading them.

No one came.

The following Tuesday, it rained, and the temperature fell. I had to dig out my parka. "Yeah," Frisbee said when I asked, "January is Gainesville's winter. When they're getting snow up north, we're getting rain here."

Rain and cold continued for days. The propane heater kept the van warm, but miserable weather trapped me in that small space all day. Nightly, Frisbee and I met Cassandra and Rainbow at a nearby bar for "happy hour"—a pitcher of beer for a buck and a half. I made friends with their friends and soon knew a lot of people.

"Is all of Florida like this?" I asked Cassandra.

"No," she said. "I'm from Miami. The temperature there never goes below seventy degrees."

"Ah, that's the Florida I came for."

"Don't freak out," Frisbee said. "These cold spells only happen a couple of times and seldom last more than a week. By February it'll be warm again."

Until Gainesville turned cold, I'd been so enamored with the city that I forgot that I'd come to find Sugar Bear and Sparrow. Cassandra mentioned that there was some sort of hippie folk music and art scene happening in Coconut Grove. Sparrow had long been drawn to folk musicians. That sounded like a place I should check out.

"Where's that?"

"In Miami," she said. "My cousin's bar mitzvah is this weekend. I was going home by Greyhound, but if you drive me instead, I'll show you where The Grove is."

Cold rain continued to strike the tavern window. "Let's do it," I said.

She smiled. "I'm cutting my Friday classes. Pick me up at my dorm, Broward Hall, at eight."

"In the morning? Why so early?"

"Florida's a long state. Miami's a six-hour drive from Gainesville."

"I may not be coming right back to Gainesville."

"That's okay. I can come back on the bus like I planned in the first place."

* * *

Cassandra scored some pot from Frisbee, and we drove most of the way stoned, with her listening to me enthusiastically talk about orgone.

"I like that the name comes from orgasm," she said with a wink. At this point, we hadn't slept together, but I got the feeling that was about to change.

Her parents lived in Kendall, which was southwest of Miami Beach and Coconut Grove. She said she'd take me to the Grove Saturday morning. Friday night, she had to have Shabbat with her parents. Whatever that was.

Kendall was pretty upscale, and I suspected someone would call the cops if I set up my camper there. She took me inside to meet her folks. Mr. and Mrs. Levy were the most liberal parents I'd ever met. They invited me to dinner and told me to put my bag in Cassandra's room.

Shabbat, it turned out, was just Friday night supper fancied up with candles, prayers, and a lot of wine. Good wine. Cassandra had told her mother I was a vegetarian, so at the last minute, Mrs. Levy thoughtfully prepared a vegetable frittata.

Miami *was* warm in the winter, and Cassandra slept in the nude with her widows open. I was sorely tempted, but felt reluctant about having sex in her parents' house. Fortunately, she had no such qualms.

In the morning, I opened my eyes and couldn't believe what I saw. Dozens of parrots, the type northerners keep in birdcages, perched in trees outside my window. Here, wild parrots were as common as robins in the Midwest.

At breakfast, Cassandra's mother asked if I'd slept all right.

"I . . . Er, fine. . ."

"That's nice," she said. "I'm sorry to rush off, but I have to help my sister prepare for the party after my nephew's bar mitzvah. You're welcome to come. The service is at ten."

"Thank you," I said, "but Cassandra and I are going to Coconut Grove to look for my friends."

She turned to her daughter. "No. If you go up there, you won't be back in time to get ready for temple."

"But I promised Gizmo I'd show him the way," Cassandra said.

"It's not that difficult to find. I'll draw him a map." And that's what she did.

With map in hand, I said goodbye to Cassandra and thanked her parents for their hospitality. She walked me out to my van. "I hope you find your friends."

"I hope you enjoy your cousin's party." I kissed her on the lips and left.

Coconut Grove was a mellow place full of cool people. It reminded me a little of Greenwich Village, but with palm trees—just the type of place to find Sparrow. But I didn't. Once again, no one knew the Sugar Bear I was looking for, though apparently there were quite a few hippies with that moniker.

Someone in The Grove told me there was a lot of Jamaican weed being smuggled in through the Everglades. That would certainly be a magnet for Sugar Bear. I checked my road atlas. Florida City, the entrance to Everglades National Park, was only about an hour south.

Florida City wasn't much—a handful of tourist cottage motels, and a road that ran west into the park. I didn't see much point in camping there, so I headed into the park. I drove for a while, seeing no proper campground, so I turned off on a dirt forest service road, parked, and popped up the camper top. The mosquitoes arrived in droves shortly after. The jalousie windows had screens, but the bugs came right through them. I shut all windows, and killed every mosquito I could find.

I didn't get them all. Throughout the night, their high-pitched whine continued to buzz around my head. I got out of bed and rechecked the windows. Everything was closed as tight as it could be. Somehow, they were finding their way through gaps I didn't know existed.

In the morning, I headed back to Florida City, covered with bites that itched like hell. I bought a bottle of calamine lotion and dabbed it everywhere until I looked like I had measles. From a pay phone, I called Cassandra at her parents' house. "I've realized Florida's too damn big to find two hippies in a school bus. They'll have to find me or learn about Woody's death some other way. I'm going back to Gainesville. If you'd like a ride, I can pick you up in about an hour."

"I'll be ready," she said.

She wasn't.

"My daughter is still dressing," Mrs. Levy said. "Come into the dining room and have a bagel."

She smeared a bagel with cream cheese and passed it to me. On the table was a platter of lox, sliced tomato, onion, cucumber, and capers. "Help yourself."

"Thank you. Cream cheese is enough." Either she'd forgotten I was a vegetarian, or thought I was one of those vegetarians who ate fish.

I looked around for something to talk about and spied a hardbound copy of *The Feminine Mystique* in her bookcase. It looked well worn. "I see you've read Betty Friedan."

She glanced toward where I was looking. "Oh, yeah. It was a revelation for women of my day. Your and Cassandra's generation are so much freer, I'm not sure Friedan's observations still apply."

Her assumption that her daughter and I were nearer in age than we were stopped me. I took a bite of bagel to stall. After a minute, I said, "My oldest sister is about your age, but she's the epitome of an unhappy 1950s housewife."

Mrs. Levy retrieved the book from the bookcase. "Then, my boy, you must give her my copy."

"That's very generous of you, but I don't know if she'd read it. She's seeing a therapist and thinks that's the way out."

"Out of patriarchal oppression? Hardly! I'm a mother and a wife, but I that's not all I am."

Cassandra came in and picked up the book. "Trying to turn Gizmo into a feminist, Mom?"

"No. He's already there. It's about his sister."

I thanked Mrs. Levy for the bagel, stood up, and carried Cassandra's bag out to my VW. Meeting the Levys was making me think maybe it wasn't just youthful enthusiasm. Maybe the hippies were changing the world.

CHAPTER 29

Six hours later, I dropped Cassandra off at her dorm and parked in the woods across from Frisbee's where I stayed the rest of that spring. He didn't mind, except one time a cop car rolled slowly down the street, stopped, and backed up.

I had the side of the van open and was sitting outside on a cheap lawn chair I'd bought at Pic & Save for a buck, waiting for happy hour.

The cop in the driver's seat rolled down his window. "Come over here, kid."

I didn't mind him calling me "kid." I was in my thirties, and my friends in their twenties believed the popular adage, "Don't trust anyone over thirty." If people thought I was a kid, it was fine by me. I ambled over.

"You have the owner's permission to camp here?" he said.

"Uh. . . Yeah, my friend lives right there." I pointed toward Frisbee's house. Actually, he was renting. I had no idea who owned the place.

"Let me see some ID."

I handed him my Massachusetts driver's license.

"Snowbird, huh?"

I shrugged. "Do you blame me?"

He noticed my date of birth. "Aren't you a little old to be living in a van?"

"Just visiting. Like you said, a snowbird."

He handed back my license. "Enjoy your stay."

As soon as he drove off, Frisbee came over. "What'd the pigs want?"

I shook my head. "He wasn't a pig. He was much nicer than the cops in Georgia."

"What did he ask you about me?"

"Nothing."

"I saw you pointing."

"Oh, he wanted to know who told me I could park here."

"That was all?"

"Yeah. He told me to enjoy my stay and left. You ready to go to the pub for happy hour?"

Being frugal, I budgeted only seventy-five cents a day for beer. Frisbee and I usually split the cost of the pitcher, and then Cassandra or other friends would buy the next round. A full breakfast at Mac's Waffle shop ran forty-nine cents. Add a dime for a tip. I still had savings and ten bucks that Cassandra's dad had slipped me for gas money—way more than the trip cost me. But I'd yet to sell an orgone accumulator despite having my cards on bulletin boards all over town.

It wasn't just about money. I could fix anything, so, if my bread ran out, I could always pick up some handy work. No, it was more about turning people on to orgone energy, as Woody had done for me. If I couldn't do it here, in hippie heaven, where could I do it?

What happy hours in the pub taught me was that, except for a couple of psychology majors, no one had ever heard of Wilhelm Reich, and even the psych majors had never heard of orgone. The government's book burning had done its job. Maybe it was time for a teach-in. The next day, I put up new cards offering a seminar on orgone energy.

It was a time of burgeoning interest in all things New Age. My van couldn't hold more than a person or two, and I hoped for a bigger audience than that. The University of Florida had a large, grassy, park-like plaza behind the libraries where students congregated. It had benches and would be a perfect place unless it rained. I didn't ask anyone's permission. I just wrote that's where we'd meet.

The first time I spoke, a few passing students stopped to listen. One of them belonged to a student group at a church across from campus. He said the minister was very liberal and let the church fellowship hall be used for everything from coffeehouse hootenannies to protest planning meetings. I met the reverend, who agreed I could use the room on Thursday evenings, except for the week before Easter when the church held a Maundy Thursday supper.

My talks at the church never drew crowds, but people started calling me Orgone Gizmo. I didn't mind. I was flattered. One day, a middle-age man wearing a white shirt and tie came to my van. We talked for a while, after which he handed me a cash down payment for materials.

My first sale.

Frisbee had seen the money change hands and it upset him. He hustled over as soon as the man left. "Who was the honkey?"

"A chiropractor." I was all smiles. "I just made my first sale!"

"If you say so. He looked pretty straight to me."

"No, for real. Look." I showed him the money. "Come on. Let's get a beer to celebrate. I'll buy."

I noticed Frisbee growing increasingly paranoid. A popular nightclub featured topless dancers and "Free Keg Tuesdays." One night a week, the owner would tap a keg and, for a one dollar cover charge, everyone could drink free beer until the keg was empty. The scenery wasn't bad either. But the club had a strict policy of checking everyone's ID at the door, no matter how old they appeared to be.

"You've got to be kidding," I said to the doorman the first time we went.

He wasn't.

The bouncers were huge weight-lifters who didn't take "No" for an answer. I surrendered my license. He checked the date of birth, then wrinkled his forehead as he tackled the difficult mathematical gymnastics of subtracting two integers. Finally, he blurted, "Thirty-six!" and handed back my ID.

Busted! I'd successfully hidden my age until this fool mouthed off. What would this mean for me when word got around? Fortunately, the band was really loud. Maybe the rest of our group hadn't overheard.

Frisbee certainly had, and I don't think he ever completely trusted me after that.

A week later, I was taking a shower at Frisbee's house. When I came out of the bathroom, a law student from UF was there buying pot. Frisbee jerked his head in my direction.

"Do you work for or inform for any branch of law enforcement?" the student said.

My stomach jumped to my mouth. "Me? No. I make orgone accumulators."

"You understand that by denying it, any testimony you might give will be thrown out for entrapment."

"Oh, come on," I said. "Frisbee, just because I'm a couple of years older than you doesn't make me a narc. I thought we were friends."

"Well," Frisbee said, "it pays to be safe. Here, have a joint."

✳ ✳ ✳

Increasingly, all was not peace and love in the hippie movement. A small group of radicals calling themselves the Weathermen began blowing up buildings across the country. They'd started in Ann Arbor, Michigan, then changed their name to the Weather Underground and declared war on the

United States. However, when several members died while constructing a bomb at a house in Greenwich Village, membership dwindled.

Gainesville's laid-back students were late to the party in terms of campus protests that were occurring nationwide. Then, in May 1972, Richard Nixon revealed that we were bombing Cambodia, a country we weren't even at war with, and that he would mine Haiphong Harbor. This sparked protests at hundreds of campuses across America. Coming as it did on the two-year anniversary of Kent State, UF students finally took a stand.

Cassandra and Rainbow came by and told me there was a sit-in at Tigert Hall, the UF administration building. "We're going. Do you want to come?"

It was only six blocks away. I said, "Sure."

By the time we got there, the protesters had spilled out of the building and down the steps. A huge crowd covered the lawn, and part of four-lane Thirteenth Street. Campus police faced off against the protesters. City police and the sheriff's department arrived. Police turned water cannons on the demonstrators. The girls and I were standing beyond their range. Finally, police fired tear gas into the crowd, which scattered the students like wrens. The three of us got caught in a cloud of it and could barely stumble away, coughing, half blind. We made it to their dorm to wash away the effects of the gas.

The long-ago Summer of Love had devolved into violent battles between the government and citizens in the name of peace.

The six o'clock news showed scenes of demonstrator-occupied Thirteenth Street from University Avenue to Tigert Hall, about three blocks. The news anchor reported that eighty state troopers had arrived to support local police, along with a group of volunteers from neighboring Marion County. Oh, great! A redneck invasion. I wasn't sure if I could get across police lines to reach my van on Ninth Terrace.

"You can spend the night in my room," Cassandra said.

"Isn't it against the rules to have men in the women's dorm?"

"The RA on my floor won't care," she said. "She sneaks her boyfriend in all the time."

That night, Cassandra wanted to make love. It may have shown my age, but I felt uncomfortable about doing it while her roommate was in the next bed.

"Don't worry," Cassandra said. "She's asleep."

The siege of Gainesville lasted three days. Coeds returning to the dorm reported scenes of police overreactions reminiscent of Chicago, 1968. I told Cassandra and Rainbow to stay away from the demonstration. I didn't want them hurt. They were cool with that. They said that politics wasn't their scene.

Understand, not everyone in Gainesville was politically apathetic. Fox, a regular at our favorite watering hole, was always up on the latest happenings. One night, about a month after the big demonstration, we were all sharing a pitcher of beer and having our nightly bull session. Fox burst in, all excited. "Did you hear? The cops in Washington caught four men breaking into Democratic National Headquarters. They were hiding microphones to bug the place. Nixon's people claim they know nothing about it, but the Democrats say otherwise."

That reminded me this was an election year—I'd forgotten, which tells you how far out of the loop I was—and I wasn't registered to vote here. First time since I turned twenty-one. But I had no Gainesville address. That'd be a challenge.

Cassandra changed the subject. Final exams were over and she was leaving to backpack around Europe during summer break.

"Alone?" I said.

"Why not?" She stroked the hairs on the back of my forearm. "You could come along."

"I don't have a passport." Or, for that matter, the money—I'd still sold exactly one orgone accumulator.

She shrugged. "Well, I guess I'll see you next semester."

"I've finished the orgone accumulator for that chiropractor. Does anyone want to try it before I deliver it to him?"

"Oh, I do," Cassandra said. "Can it be tomorrow morning? I have an afternoon flight to Paris."

The next morning, I let her sit in the orgone box for a half hour. When she came out, she said, "It's nothing like an orgasm, but I definitely experienced a mild energy." She wrapped her arms around me and kissed me passionately. "I wish we had time to get it on . . . but I'd miss my flight. We can be lovers again in the fall."

CHAPTER 30

I delivered the orgone accumulator to the chiropractor and collected the balance due. But no one rushed to order another. So, I decided to try my luck elsewhere.

The summer of '72, I traveled from place to place, parking my camper outside the houses of friendly hippies or at other communes. Nearly everywhere I stayed, I was older than everyone around me. Occasionally, people noticed it and paranoid accusations that I was a narc would come back up again, so I'd move on.

My transient lifestyle meant my family couldn't reach me. I tried to make up for it by keeping a cigar box full of change in the van and regularly calling home from pay phones. Later that summer, I was at a communal farm outside Ann Arbor, Michigan. It was close to the University of Michigan where, unlike in Florida, people *had* heard of Wilhelm Reich. I sold several accumulators during the time I was there, which would keep me going for a while. By late October, I awoke to fogged windows and frost-covered ground every morning. I was about to head back south when I checked in with Nora and she urged me to drive over there first.

Why not? I hadn't seen them since last Christmas, and Michigan was a hell of a lot closer than Florida. Not to mention, the election was at hand and I really didn't want Nixon to have another term. Years before, I had registered to vote using Dad's address—I probably still was. Besides, his new wife, Louise, worked the polls.

I arrived in time to cast my vote, but Louise insisted I stay in the guest room instead of my camper. "If you're going to use this as your address to vote, you have to live in the house."

"Sure, thanks, Louise."

My vote didn't do any good. Nixon won by a landslide.

"Now that you're here," Louise said, "stay for the holidays. Thanksgiving is right around the corner."

So was winter, but I'd grown up there and knew it wouldn't get really bitter until December or January.

The guest room had been Nora's and Sophie's while we were growing up. My old room was now the sewing room. Louise had redone both rooms in flocked wallpaper, so it really didn't make a difference. It felt good to be out of that cramped van for a few weeks—to be able to get out of bed and step into a hot shower every morning.

Louise's Osterizer blender had broken, and she needed it to make her special cranberry relish. "It just won't be Thanksgiving without it."

"I'm not made of money, Louise," Dad said.

"Let me look at it," I said. "In the Air Force I once made a cocktail blender out of a motor and strips from a tin can."

Louise rolled her eyes and set Dad's breakfast dish in the sink. "You better get going or you'll be late for work." He kissed her goodbye and left.

After I helped her clear the table, I spread yesterday's newspaper over it. I opened the drawer next to the refrigerator where Dad always kept a couple of screwdrivers and a pair of needle-nose pliers. Thankfully, Louise hadn't moved them.

She watched with a mix of fascination and horror as I disassembled the base of her blender and spread the parts over the newspaper. The circuit was simple. Wires were soldered onto the brass terminals of a series of switches and the main hot lead had broken off. I got Dad's soldering gun from the garage, stripped a quarter inch of insulation from the wire, and soldered back it in place. I put the blender back together and tested it. It worked like new. Louise was amazed. She had two grown sons of her own, but I guess they'd never fixed anything for her.

This was clearly Louise's house now, and I didn't want to be underfoot, so I visited my sister, Sophie. Her kids were in school, and she was vacuuming when I arrived. She put the sweeper away and collapsed on the couch. "Gizmo, I'm glad to see you. I've been so bored. Tell me about your adventures."

I skipped mentioning the student riots in Gainesville and talked mostly about the communes I'd stayed at during my summer travels.

"A dozen adults and kids all in one place?" She made a face. "Do the men help, or is all the work left up to the women?"

"Oh, men help with gardening and such, but taking care of the kids is pretty much done by the women."

"Along with the cleaning, cooking, and, I imagine, driving the children to all their after-school activities."

"I wouldn't know," I said. "It was summer. School was out. But at the commune in Vermont, a man did plenty of the cooking."

She stared at the floor, drawing little circles on the carpet with her toe. "It's dull, dull, dull."

"What is?"

"Being a housewife."

I sat back a moment and took an honest look at my sister. Dull was exactly the right word. Sophie had lost the sparkle and sass she'd always had. Like her light was on a dimmer switch. "Have you been sick, Sis?"

"No. Just . . . well, the pills are supposed to help, but frankly, they don't do much."

"Pills?"

She nodded. "I've started seeing Nora's doctor. He gave me the same thing she's taking."

"Is she still on those?" I'd taught Nora yoga to get her off them. Apparently, it hadn't worked. "Downers won't bring you up."

"Downers?"

"Those pills he's giving you and Nora. Some drugs open your mind, and some dull it. Can't you see which these are?"

"They're supposed to be happy pills."

"And are you happy?"

"No, Gizmo, I'm bored out of my mind. When I was in high school, girls were supposed to win the most popular guy, marry him, and have his babies. That was all we'd ever need. But now my kids are in high school. They're seldom home. In a few years, they'll graduate. What then? No more softball. No more PTA."

"Think outside the home. What interests you? What would *you* like to do?"

A tear trickled down one cheek. "I don't know. Something besides this. In my day, girls could be teachers, nurses, or secretaries. I never wanted to be any of those, so I chose Eddie."

"Times have changed. Women are entering all kinds of professions."

"But I don't have any skills."

"I'll bet you have enough to get a job. Remember, Mom sewed Army uniforms during the War."

"No. Eddie wouldn't let me work. He'd be afraid people would think he wasn't man enough to support his family."

"No one would think that."

"He would."

"Well, the town has a new community college. Sign up for a couple of courses. If not to get a job, at least to broaden your knowledge and give you more interesting things to think about."

She shook her head. "I never liked school when I had to go. I don't see having to write term papers again as a step forward."

I'd seldom seen anyone who fought happiness so hard. What else could I do to fix her? I stood up. "Well, if you're bored, let me take you out for a milkshake." Chocolate, the great panacea.

She smoothed her dress and ran her fingers through her hair. "No. My hair's a mess and I'm in this old housedress. It's too much effort to go out."

"For Christ's sake, Sophie, I'm only talking about Al's Diner. They don't require satin and pearls. Besides, you look gorgeous just the way you are."

"No, I don't. Why don't you go visit Nora?"

"Are you trying to get rid of me?"

"You're the one who said you were leaving."

"I was trying to get you out of the house."

Sophie gave me a hug. "Oh, Gizmo, you're sweet, but I need to rest before the kids come home, and then I've got to make Eddie's supper. We'll go for milkshakes another day."

We hugged goodbye, and I drove to Nora's. She was more upbeat. Tommy Jr. was graduating the following spring and had already been accepted at the university. She was poring through the Sears catalog, deciding what he would need for his dorm room.

"Isn't it a little early for that?" I said.

"No. He's starting summer term. I decided his Christmas gifts would be things he can use for school."

"I guess you've forgotten what you taught me about gifts with squeal factor. A seventeen-year-old boy isn't going to be thrilled with a set of sheets."

"No, but he can't sleep on a bare mattress either."

"Well, don't buy him a briefcase. Let me do that."

"Does that mean you'll stay through Christmas?"

I hadn't planned to, but I had nothing else in mind, and Nora quickly talked me into it.

"Only if you'll help me shop for the rest of the family's gifts," I said. Just then, I knew what to give Nora and Sophie.

When I left Nora's I drove into Madison, found a book shop, and bought two copies of *The Feminine Mystique*.

Over the next couple of days, I cleaned my camper, rotated the tires, changed Dad's oil, and filled his radiator with anti-freeze. Anything to keep busy. I offered to put on his snow tires, but he said it was too early in the season.

The day after Thanksgiving, while my sisters and Louise went shopping, Eddie and I played pool at a bar downtown. He was better than me, and if he got to break, he'd clear the table before I got my first shot. I didn't care. I was glad to have a chance to talk to him about my sister's state of mind.

He scratched, and I finally got a turn. I lined up the cue ball and said, "Are you worried about Sophie taking 'happy' pills?"

He shrugged. "I'm not the doctor."

"Neither am I, but they don't seem to be helping. Sophie doesn't look happy."

"She's got nothing to complain about. You want boredom? Try standing at a conveyor line seven hours a day. You going to shoot or talk?"

I hit the eight ball by mistake and it rolled into a corner pocket. "You win. I'd rather talk. Let's get a beer." Eddie never turned down a beer.

"Great! Order us a pitcher while I get a book from the car that I've been dying to show you."

Eddie with a book? Maybe an issue of *Hot Rod* magazine, but not an actual book.

I ordered and chose a booth. A waitress brought our pitcher, filled two glasses, and left. Eddie slid into the booth and handed me a dog-eared paperback. "Gizmo, have you read this?"

I glanced at the garish title in red block typeface, *Chariots of the Gods?* I shook my head.

Eddie's face dropped. "Man, you're into all kinds of far-out shit. I thought sure you'd know all about this."

Beneath the author's name, a list of questions suggested aliens from space had visited the earth in prehistoric times. The typeface looked like it belonged on a poster for a 1950s science fiction movie.

Eddie reached across the table and opened it to a section of photographs of Mayan ruins and Incan gods. "Look at these."

I thumbed through the picture pages.

"I've been waiting to share this with you," Eddie said. "I can't get anyone around here interested. Sophie says you're staying through Christmas. I'll loan it to you. Read it, and then we can have a serious rap before you leave."

Rap? Had hippie slang reached Prairie View? I accepted the book and finished it in a day. Von Däniken's theories were intriguing. So were the pictures. But mostly, I needed something more to keep me busy. I'd vowed years before to limit my visits home to only a few days. I was already at odds with what to do with my time. The rest of the family had their normal routines that didn't include entertaining me.

The local Western Auto hardware store served as the town's substitute department store. In addition to snow shovels and bicycles, they also sold kitchenware, toys, color TVs, and stereos. A few weeks before Christmas, I saw a sign in their window: "Temporary holiday help wanted." Perfect. I'd make a little traveling money and keep out of everyone's hair.

Chapter 31

The previous year, Richard Alpert, Timothy Leary's former colleague in the LSD revolution, returned from India a changed man with a new name—Baba Ram Dass. He'd written a book about his journey toward spiritual enlightenment, *Be Here Now*. Nora gave me a copy of it for Christmas. Needless to say, my sister giving me a book about gurus surprised me even more than Eddie reading any book at all, even a tabloid-level theory about aliens. Change was reaching even the staid Midwest. Both my sisters said thanks for their copies of *The Feminine Mystique*, but I wasn't sure they would read them.

On my drive back to Florida after the holidays, I parked overnight in a lot behind a used bookstore. When it opened in the morning, I went inside to browse. I came across two of Reich's books I hadn't read. The store clerk said no one was interested in them and sold them to me for a dime each. Both books were on the threat of fascism.

In the same bookstore, I saw an ad that a TV special called *In Search of Ancient Astronauts* was going to be broadcast in January. I didn't have a television myself, but Eddie did. I telephoned him with the news. He already knew about it and was anxiously awaiting the day.

By the time I got back to Gainesville, spring semester had already started. On Friday night, I found Rainbow and Frisbee sharing a pitcher at our regular bar.

"Hello, stranger," Rainbow said.

I nodded to Frisbee and slid into the booth next to Rainbow. "Is Cassandra coming later?"

Rainbow made a face. "Europe seduced her, and she's decided to study abroad this semester."

Disappointed, I deflected by showing them one of the books I'd bought for a dime, Reich's *The Mass Psychology of Fascism.* "Have either of you read this?" I'd read it and realized a lot of it still applied—to the Nixon administration.

Frisbee turned it over and scanned the blurb on the back cover. "No, but I bet Fox would dig this."

"I'll loan it to him." I took the book from him and handed it to Rainbow. "Here, read this and compare it to what's going on in Washington."

"I'm not sure when I'll get to it," she said. "I've got a lot of reading this semester. Let Fox have it first."

Throughout 1973, information about the Watergate burglary and the involvement of Nixon's men in covering it up kept appearing in the news. Nixon seemed to be more and more out of control. Adding to the president's troubles, his vice president, Spiro Agnew, was accused of corruption. Agnew took the position that a sitting vice president could not be indicted, but by October, he was forced to resign. The following summer, Nixon also resigned. The Watergate scandal and presidential cover up had finally done him in. I admit I was relieved.

While all that was going on politically, Ram Dass began a series of traveling lectures, transforming youth into spiritual seekers. This lead to an invasion of Indian gurus whose ashrams displaced hippie communes. Although ashrams primarily drew young people, my age was no longer an issue. After all, Ram Dass was four years older than me.

The idea of gurus seemed stranger to average Americans than even the rash of UFO sightings that summer and fall—something I tended to notice in the news thanks to Eddie's interest. From Rochester, New York, to Gulfport, Mississippi, people nationwide were spotting unusual lights and

fast moving objects in the sky. Georgia Governor Jimmy Carter reported one. A man in the Midwest claimed a nighttime UFO "followed me
home."

When I telephoned Sophie, she confirmed Eddie was outside every night,
scanning the skies.

* * *

In 1974, I drove three days out of my way to attend lectures by Ram Dass
at a Tibetan Buddhist institute in Boulder, Colorado. When I returned to
Florida in the fall, I ran into Cassandra. She'd graduated from the university and was now following Swami Muktananda, the latest guru from India
to tour America.

"Muktananda isn't like any of the other gurus teaching meditation,"
she told me. "While others talk about states of higher consciousness,
Muktananda gives you an actual experience of it."

Immediate gratification—always a sure way to win impatient Americans,
I thought.

"He's holding a weekend intensive at a Miami hotel after New Year's," she
said. "You have to come."

"All right, I will." After all, it was the instant experience with LSD that
first sparked my interest in the counterculture.

In January, we met at her parents' house and drove to the hotel together.
The Intensive consisted of morning, afternoon, and evening meditations,
chanting, and talks on Indian scriptures. In the tradition of Indian ashrams, the meditation hall was segregated by gender—women on one side
of the room and men on the other. This meant Cassandra and I couldn't
sit together. Everyone sat on the floor. We were permitted to bring a
small cushion, but seating was tight and we were all rubbing shoulders.
Before programs began, staff would walk through the room, cajoling us
to scrunch together to make space for others.

Muktananda spoke almost no English, so after every few sentences in his native Gujarati, he'd pause while a young Indian woman translated his words for us. His talks were mostly about Shakti, a primordial cosmic energy that makes up and moves through the universe. I thought of Reich's bions.

"Although Shakti is the life force creating and keeping our cells alive," Muktananda said, "there is a dormant accumulation of it sleeping at the base of our spine that, when awakened, rises through the spine to the crown of our head, bringing about enlightenment."

Meditation began with lighting incense, which soon permeated the atmosphere. A long period of chanting eventually quieted to a murmur, and then stopped altogether as the participants entered silent meditation.

The silence didn't hold for long.

I was busy watching my breath, practicing the technique I'd learned years before at the Unitarian Church in Boston, when the room erupted with peals of laughter. In another part of the hall, someone cried, and from elsewhere I heard the hoots of a monkey. My concentration fell apart. I'd meditated in a lot of different places, and absolute silence always ruled. At any moment, I expected the staff to haul the noisemakers outside. No one did.

Who could resist opening their eyes to see the source of the commotion? Not I. In the dimly lit room, Muktananda walked along the rows of meditators, carrying a wand made from a bundle of peacock feathers in one hand. His other hand, he held above the head of each person for a few seconds. Sometimes, he also touched the feather wand to the meditator's shoulder or head.

Okay, maybe the noises were a test of my ability to concentrate. I put my attention back on my breath, determined not to be distracted by chaos. And then . . .

The only way to describe what happened is with an analogy. When I was in college, our electrical science lab had a Tesla coil. This is a high voltage, low amperage transformer circuit whose electrical field can be sensed without touching it.

I was minding my business, concentrating on my breath, when I felt the hair on my arms stand up. Not unlike our college Tesla coil experiments. Muktananda hadn't reached me yet, but he emitted such a strong energy field that I could feel he was close. The next thing I knew, his hand hovered above the crown of my head, and a strong force leaped upward through my spine to reach it. He gave me a gentle whack on the head with his peacock feathers and moved on to the person next to me. But I was no longer there.

In calm stillness, I perceived the universe as an undifferentiated field of energy. Galaxies of stars and grains of sand—all mere energy.

An incalculable time later, a chant of Om started. Others joined in. When the Om faded, the room lights came up slowly. I was blissed out, as my hippie friends said, wishing my sisters could have this experience. But Tom would never let that happen.

Cassandra waited for me at the door. "Wasn't that fantastic?"

I smiled and nodded, but didn't want to chat. "I need to go to my room for a bit. Can we talk later?"

Her face fell. She was anxious to discuss what we'd experienced, but I wanted to give the bliss a chance to sink in.

At lunch, I found Cassandra, and we went through a cafeteria-style line where our plates were filled with traditional Indian foods. It smelled and tasted delicious. We sat at a long table with a half dozen strangers. The room hummed with excitement.

"Shakti is the energy of creation, and she is also consciousness," Muktananda told us through his translator in the evening lecture. "I call her chit-shakti—conscious energy. In other words, the energy making up the universe is one and the same as the conscious-intelligence creating it."

He talked for a half an hour in short bursts, pausing for his translator. After his talk concluded, the group meditated.

During the meditation, instead of properly concentrating on my breath, my mind wandered, pondering whether orgone was the same as chit-shak-ti. Although the effect of the accumulator didn't compare with the jolt I'd felt that morning, both he and Reich described a universal energy. A tap from Muktananda snapped me out of my woolgathering and back to that absolute bliss.

At each subsequent meditation for the rest of the intensive, he walked throughout the room giving us "shaktipat," his name for raising energy through the spine to higher spiritual centers. How quickly we become accustomed to even the extraordinary. I soon found myself anticipating his approach, the upward rush of Shakti, and the resulting experience of light, peace, or bliss.

After the intensive, Cassandra continued to follow Muktananda around the country and tried to persuade me to come with her. But she was prac-ticing celibacy. I was not.

CHAPTER 32

Christmas 1977, I visited my family. My niece and nephews were now grown and either in college or working, but the entire clan had returned home for the holidays. Christmas fell on a Sunday, which meant everyone had Monday off. The last time that happened, Mom died weeks later. Not a happy thought.

The blockbuster film that year, *Close Encounters of the Third Kind*, had opened the previous week. Over Christmas dinner, Tommy Jr. suggested we go as a family to see it the next day. I thought my brother-in-law, Eddie, was about to wet himself with excitement.

Louise, Nora, and Sophie tried to duck out, saying they didn't want to miss the day-after-Christmas sales. Their kids outvoted them, so the next afternoon, we caravanned to the theater, where we discovered a line around the building.

Not to be stymied, Eddie double-parked in front of the ticket window and jumped out of the car. The rest of us idled behind him, holding up traffic. In no time, he was back with a wad of tickets in hand. He ran up to our car and Dad rolled down the window. A blast of cold air rushed in.

"The next two shows were sold out, but I was able to get us tickets for the five-thirty show." He smiled at Louise in the passenger seat. "That means you have all afternoon to check out those sales."

It also meant going to the movie when we'd normally be eating dinner, which I'm sure the women thought strange, but they weren't trying to talk him out of it.

We went back to Dad's house, ate warmed up left-overs. The women went shopping, and the rest of us played cards until Eddie announced it was time to return to the theater. Eddie wanted to get there early to make sure we got good seats. With thirteen of us going, he had a point.

We showed up early, bought buckets of greasy popcorn, and were able to sit together, filling an entire row. The story was about a multi-national group of scientists investigating the sudden appearance of unidentified flying objects in multiple countries. Interwoven through that overarching theme was the tale of Roy, an ordinary lineman for the electric company, played by Richard Dreyfuss. After an alien spacecraft hovers over his truck late one night, Roy grows increasingly obsessed with visions of Devil's Tower in Wyoming. Eventually, he deserts his family and journeys there just in time for the arrival of a large group of scientists and the mother of all UFOs. The ship opens, tiny aliens come out to greet the scientists, and Roy volunteers to go aboard their ship and leave with them.

I was expecting more *Chariot of the Gods* crap about aliens among us, but it was actually a very good film. Despite Roy's abandonment of his family, the ending somehow left us uplifted. Everyone except Sophie.

Eddie dropped us off and drove to the corner store to buy beer. As soon as he was out of the driveway, Sophie said, "Gizmo! How could you?"

"What?"

"That movie you chose!"

"I didn't suggest it, your nephew did. But I thought it was great. Didn't you?"

"No . . . I . . ." Sophie teared up. Apparently not.

I hugged her, gently patting her back. "Aw, Sis, now don't get upset. The point of the movie was that we have nothing to fear from them. Everything will be okay."

She stepped back and wiped her nose with the back of her hand. "If you think that's why I'm upset, you obviously haven't been listening to Eddie these past ten years. He's just about as crazy about UFOs as that guy in the movie, and I'm worried that seeing this will put even more ideas in his head. The next time he hears about a bunch of UFO sightings, he could very well decide to drive across the country and leave me. I don't know what I'd do."

"Well, Sophie . . . your kids are grown, there's just the two of you. You could go with him. Make it a fun road trip."

"I don't have that vagabond blood you do. Besides, if he ever saw a real UFO, he'd do the same thing Roy did—just climb aboard, with no thought of his family. Then where would that leave me? Stuck out in the desert alone, without a husband."

"You talk like you believe UFOs are real."

"Don't you?"

I shrugged. "I don't really care one way or the other. My focus has been on raising my own consciousness. I've never met an alien, nor anyone who has, but I have met a slew of men and women who can move their life force onto higher planes at will."

"Oh, Gizmo, that's crazy talk."

"Says the woman who's worried about her husband leaving on a UFO."

Sophie laughed. "I guess you're right."

I shivered. "Let's go inside."

Just then, Eddie returned, parked, and handed me a case of Schlitz. "Here, Gizmo. I'll get the other one."

"Two cases, Eddie?"

"There's thirteen of us. Do the math."

I guess I wasn't thinking about my niece and nephews drinking, but what college kid doesn't? Besides, the state had lowered the legal age to nineteen.

Sophie walked up onto the porch and held the door open for us.

Inside, Eddie gave everyone a beer and told me to put my case in the refrigerator. I took the bottles out of the cartons and managed to squeeze them between leftovers on every shelf.

Eddie brought me the remainder of his case.

"Refrigerator is full," I said. "We may have to set those out on the porch."

He shook his head. "Too cold out. The beer will freeze."

"At the rate this family drinks, there's little chance of that."

Eddie opened the refrigerator and began moving food around, wedging a bottle here and there. He opened the vegetable drawer at the bottom and laid four bottles over a stalk of celery. "See, plenty of room." With only three bottles left, he closed the door and handed me a beer. "One for you, two for me."

Having just come from the movie, I knew that Eddie would bring up UFOs, and he didn't disappoint. He leaned against the counter and twisted the cap off his bottle. "Tell me, Gizmo, when you were in the Air Force, did you ever work on Project Blue Book?"

I'd heard of Project Blue Book, a program funded by the Air Force to study reports of unidentified flying objects—genuine scientific analysis—and evaluate whether they posed a threat to national security. It was based out of the Wright-Patterson Air Force base near Dayton, Ohio, but I had never been stationed there.

I shook my head. "Sorry, when I was in the service, I never knew it existed."

"But Sophie said you had top secret security clearance."

"I used to, but I only had access to the bases and classified projects I was assigned. The way our government keeps secrets secret is by compartmentalizing. The first I heard of Blue Book was when I was living in Massachusetts. By then it was already shut down."

"I've read the project had over twelve thousand cases of reported sightings," Eddie said. "So why did they shut it down? Or did they? Maybe they moved it somewhere more secure, like Alaska."

"I think it really shutdown, Eddie. They said the majority of cases proved to be natural phenomena like ball lightning or stars, or actual identified, flying objects, like satellites or spy planes."

"But what about the rest?" Eddie finished his first beer and opened his second. "Say that eighty or ninety percent were stars or balloons or airplanes mistaken for UFOs, that still leaves a couple thousand that could be actual UFOs."

Or, sometimes there just wasn't enough evidence one way or another to decide for sure. But it was probably not worth saying that.

My silence didn't slow Eddie down. "There are tons of sightings by commercial and military pilots. These men can recognize a weather balloon. Fighter pilots report chasing craft that can out-fly our fastest jets, make sudden, impossible turns, and just disappear."

"Shouldn't we join the others in the living room?"

"In a minute. Let me ask you one more thing. Why do jets make that sonic boom?"

"Oh, that's easy. When an object moves through the air, it creates pressure waves in front and behind, the way a speeding boat creates a wake in the water. Sound waves travel at 767 miles per hour. When a jet flies faster than that, the waves can't get out of each other's way fast enough, so they compress into a shockwave that we hear as a boom."

"So, anything flying at supersonic speed should make a sonic boom?"

"That's right."

"Reports of UFOs that outran our jets, or were seen from the ground to accelerate to high speed and disappear—none of them ever mentioned a sonic boom. How could that be?"

"I honestly don't know. But, Eddie, remember, I'm an electrical engineer. This is outside my field."

"Yeah, but don't you think that's pretty odd?"

"Maybe the witnesses were in the right place to see something, but in the wrong place to hear anything. The shockwave produced by a supersonic aircraft is conical and continues to trail the plane. So, if you're in the right place, you hear a boom, then someone a mile down the road hears it a fifth of a second later. The cone producing the sound is fairly tight, and a person a mile north of you might not hear it at all because they're beyond the cone's width."

Eddie scratched his head. "But could all twelve thousand sightings be outside the path of the sonic boom? That seems unlikely."

Ninety percent of the twelve thousand were ordinary phenomenon, but again, it didn't seem worth raising the argument.

Sophie saved me when she entered the kitchen. "Hey, you two, are you going to join the rest of us?"

"We are," I said. "Does anyone need another beer?"

* * *

Tuesday, Tommy Jr. came over to Dad's and asked me to go to RadioShack with him.

"You don't have to work today?"

"Nah, I've got the whole week off. At our company, you forfeit any vacation time you haven't used by the end of the year, so I'm using mine now. I'm not due back until January."

Dad was snoring in his recliner. Tommy Jr. gently shook his arm. "Hey, Grandpa, Uncle Gizmo and I are going to RadioShack. Why don't you come with us?"

Dad's eyelids half opened. "What's the temperature outside?"

"Minus six."

"You guys go. I'm warm here."

"It's warm in the car, too," Tommy said. "We're not going by dogsled."

Dad smiled and closed his eyes. "Damn, smartass."

Tommy decided that Madison, having the bigger store, would be our best bet. I still didn't know what we were going there for, but I have always enjoyed browsing electronic gadgets. We parked and walked inside. It was midafternoon and there weren't any customers, just two young clerks playing with a . . . black-and-white TV screen? When we got closer, I saw it had a keyboard.

"I thought since you used to design computers, Uncle Gizmo, you could advise me about this one."

A computer? The ones I worked on in Massachusetts were programmed with a terminal that was its own piece of furniture, using punch cards and paper tape. I picked up a brochure.

The TRS-80 Micro Computer was apparently a new class of computer built around an 8-bit microprocessor, a single chip that replaced a whole circuit board of transistors in the large systems I'd worked on.

"Take it for a spin," Tommy said. "Tell me what you think."

I shrugged. "What are you going to do with it, Tommy?"

"Write programs. It comes with BASIC."

BASIC was a simplified, natural-language programming language that looked a little like English. I glanced through the manual quickly and then sat in front of the keyboard and typed in a few calculation loops to check the TRS-80's speed.

It had a full QWERTY keyboard plus a numeric keypad, but no shift key, so everything you typed was in all caps, just like Teletype terminals I'd used in the Air Force twenty years earlier. I typed RUN, hit the enter key and watched it fill the screen, which only fit sixty-four characters on a line.

I was not impressed. The 8-bit architecture was limited—I'd been working on larger processors since the early sixties. The system used a cassette tape player to load programs and save data—which it probably would have to do a fair amount, since the internal memory was pretty limited. Still, it was not an awful machine, and I could see Tommy had his mind made up, so I asked if I could unscrew the cover and look inside.

The salesclerks wrapped their arms protectively around it. "Certainly not!"

"How much does it cost?" I said.

"Five ninety-nine, plus tax," one of the clerks said.

I gave a low whistle. Granted, that was a hundredth of what a real computer cost, but it was still a lot of bread for an average person to lay out. I pulled Tommy aside. "Can you afford this?"

He bobbed his head like a puppy waiting for a treat. "Uncle Gizmo, this is going to be the next big thing. Stores, restaurants, even tax accountants, haven't been able to afford business computers. They're going to buy these like crazy, and they'll want software to run inventory, payroll, and billing. I'm starting my own company to write programs and sell turnkey systems."

I turned to the clerk. "Does it have floating-point processing capability?" Tommy was going to need that for any accounting programs.

"It sure does," the clerk said.

Tommy looked at me. I shrugged.

"I'll take it," Tommy said.

"Not so fast," I said. "Can we return it?" I still wanted to crack open the case and look at the guts first thing when we got home.

"Of course," the clerk said. "RadioShack has a complete satisfaction policy on everything we sell."

Tommy pulled out his wallet and paid with cash. Kids these days—too much money. I could live in my camper for a year on that six hundred bucks.

CHAPTER 33

Two years later, Dad's driveway was edged with dirty clumps of icy snow we'd shoveled there before his funeral. I set his bowling ball bag next to the pile of stuff we were donating to the Salvation Army.

Louise had gone into a nursing home in March, 1979, and passed away a few months later. When I resumed my travels after her funeral, I made sure Nora always had the telephone number of a friend near wherever I was staying. A wise decision on my part, because after Louise died, Dad only lasted six months.

I looked outside where grass showed through spotty patches of melting snow. "From now on, I'm just going to rip Christmas week right off the calendar."

Sophie's daughter, Patty, stopped wrapping china in tissue paper and looked at me wide-eyed. "Uncle Gizmo! Why would you say such a thing?"

"It's jinxed. Too many people I've loved have died around this time of year. In the future, we ought to just go straight from Thanksgiving to New Year's Day."

"Ma-aa!"

"I'm in the kitchen, helping Nora box up the pantry," Sophie said.

"Please come talk some sense into Uncle Gizmo! He wants to cancel Christmas."

Nora and Sophie appeared in the kitchen doorway.

"I . . . just can't believe Dad's gone," I said, "at Christmas, no less."

Sophie turned back into the kitchen and started sobbing. Nora came over and hugged me. "I know."

"Mom, are you all right?" Patty said.

"I will be," Sophie said, "as soon as I take my pills. Patty, have you seen my purse?"

Nora patted my back. "Listen, I need to go home and start supper. Come over and eat with me and Tom tonight. We can discuss Christmas then."

Sophie entered from the kitchen, pulling on her winter coat. "Sorry, I have to run to the pharmacy. Patty, stay and help Uncle Gizmo. I won't be gone long."

Nora kissed my cheek and both of my sisters left. Patty handed me a tissue-wrapped serving platter, and I packed it in the box of dishes. We worked in silence for a while.

"Uncle Gizmo, you know what your problem is?" Patty was home from college on winter break and imbued with all the wisdom of her Psychology 101 class.

"I'm listening."

"You're Peter Pan."

"Because I'm so youthful?"

"No, because you don't want to grow up."

I stopped packing. "That's harsh."

"But true. You're almost forty and still living like a hippie."

"I am a hippie." Actually, I was over forty, but saw no reason to correct her.

"I feel sorry for you, Uncle Gizmo," she said, sounding earnest beyond her years. "If you don't settle down soon, you may never get a wife."

"Patty, this doesn't sound like you at all. In fact, it sounds like your Aunt Nora."

"Well, my thinking has matured since I started college."

"That's good, but don't be too influenced by what others think. Finish school, and then see what you want to do with your life. There's a lot more out there than you know at this point."

I was right. Patty was echoing Nora who, over dinner that night, floated the idea that I should quit the road and buy Dad's house. Since I'd inherit a one third interest in the property anyway, my sisters would hold notes for their shares, and I'd pay them instead of a bank.

"You'd never qualify for a mortgage," Nora said. "This way you wouldn't have to."

"With your engineering degree, I could get you a pretty good position at the plant," Tom said.

I looked around their dining room and thought about years of stuff Dad and Mom had accumulated that we were just going to give away. Did I want to buy that house and spend years filling it with my own stuff? Or lock myself into a single job—or a wife—for the rest of my life? I shook my head. No thank you to consumerism. No thank you to a wife. I didn't believe in marriage, nor did the women I kept company with.

* * *

The rest of Nora and Sophie's children returned home for the holidays, but the Christmas morning squeals of delight were missing. Gifts were painstakingly unwrapped, and the paper neatly folded, accompanied by a polite "Thank you, just what I needed," or "Oh, this is great."

Dad's memory hung over the whole affair like a dull guillotine.

Staying at Dad's amidst a sea of packing boxes didn't help my melancholy. So when Tommy Jr. showed up and asked if he could crash at his grandpa's, I was glad.

"Is there some reason you're not staying at your mom and dad's?" I said.

"It's too crowded with everyone at home, and I have work to do. I figured I'd get more done here."

"Well, be my guest."

Tommy carried in several large boxes—as if the place didn't already have enough. He dragged the kitchen table nearer to the wall phone and began setting up a new computer. "TRS80 Model II," he said. "It just came out in October."

"Does this mean your software business is going well?" I said.

"Selling like hotcakes, but the Model II has a different system architecture, so I'm having to rewrite all the code." Tommy turned it on and the differences were obvious. First, the screen had better resolution. Whereas the one I'd helped him buy two years before had only sixteen lines of sixty-four character text, this model had twenty-four lines of eighty characters, and both upper and lower case letters. Second, the Model II didn't need a cassette player for programs and data storage. Tommy took a thin, eight-inch rectangular plastic sleeve from a box. It had a large hole in the center, like my old Rock 'n Roll 45s, but unlike a record, it was flexible. Tommy slid it into a vertical slot on the right side of the screen, and a motor whirred.

"Floppy disk," he said. "This baby will hold 256 kilobytes of data."

"Impressive." And I meant it. The memory circuits I'd worked on in Massachusetts only handled four kilobytes at a time.

Next, he plugged in a flat box that had two circular rubber cups on top. "An acoustic coupler modem."

I knew what a modem was from my previous jobs. It enabled computers to send and receive data over regular telephone lines. But I'd never seen one like this. "Can I see it work?"

"Sure." He changed the floppy disk and then dialed a telephone number. "John, I'm all hooked up here. Can you connect the modem on your end?" Tommy fit the handset onto the acoustic coupler and typed a command into his computer. A series of squawks came from the handset, and then characters appeared on his screen, one line at a time.

He nodded toward the screen. "It's not bad, about thirty characters per second if you have a good connection. I have a customer who owns several branch stores and needs daily updates of inventory and sales from each."

"We had a modem where I worked," I said, "but it was wired directly to the phone line."

"This is better for small businesses. You don't need a dedicated telephone line, and you only tie up the phone when you need to. Besides, a salesperson or someone traveling could use any phone, anywhere."

That seemed a little optimistic. I looked at the tangle of cables on the kitchen table and couldn't imagine a traveling salesperson hauling an entire computer set-up into a motel room to submit his nightly sales reports.

When the scrolling display came to an end, Tommy typed, "Save," then removed the handset and hung up the phone. "You should come to work for me, Uncle Gizmo."

"I'm no programmer. My expertise was strictly hardware."

"That's what I need—someone to install the systems in my customers' businesses. I can write the code. There's good money in computers."

It seemed like the whole family was involved in a conspiracy to tie me down.

"Please, Uncle Gizmo, I really need your help. I can't get any programming done because I'm always crawling around under some customer's desk hooking up wires or showing them where the On switch is." He waited a beat. "Besides, you love working with gadgets."

He was right. I loved technology. And I certainly wasn't getting anywhere peddling orgone accumulators. Plus, his company was in Ann Arbor, where I had friends.

"Can we take the cover off?" I said. "I'd love to see inside this thing."

He shut the computer off. "Sure, get a Phillips screwdriver."

* * *

After my sisters and I finished emptying Dad's house and getting it ready to put on the market, I followed Tommy Jr. to Ann Arbor. Once I started working for him, I understood why he'd asked for my help. Small business computer sales were booming. Soon, I not only handled installation but also took on computer repair. I continued to meditate daily, but I no longer had time to make orgone accumulators. Not even one for myself.

My first few months there, the weather was freezing, and I traded my camper for a late-model sedan more suitable to Michigan winters. Even with its defroster on full blast, many mornings I had to scrape ice off the windshield before I could drive anywhere. The worse day was when I had to unfreeze the door lock by heating my car key with Dad's cigarette lighter—I carried it to remind me of him. Once I got the door open, I questioned why I didn't just turn south on I-75 and aim toward Florida like I'd been doing for the last decade. But Tommy was family.

Eventually, spring arrived, lilacs bloomed and faded, then summer came and went. In September, Ram Dass did a benefit at the Michigan Theater to raise money for a medical charity that performed eye surgeries in poor countries. Throughout the seventies, a lot of other gurus had brought their brand of yoga to America, but I hadn't seen Ram Dass in years and decided I'd go. I asked Tommy if he wanted to come along, but he said he had coding to finish.

A crowd of about 850 showed up. Ram Dass looked good. Radiated calmness and had a mischievous twinkle in his eyes. Over the course of two hours, he retold stories of meeting his guru and his own spiritual journey. I'd heard them before. He read passages from seemingly randomly selected authors—Carlos Castaneda, Herman Hesse, Robert Heinlein—and tossed in a few Zen stories that reminded me of Woody. I left the theater, glad I'd come, and happy that Ram Dass was still around doing his thing.

The remainder of 1980 went along fine until December. I remembered telling my niece Patty that we ought to tear the Christmas holidays off the calendar. What happened on the eighth convinced me we ought to skip the entire month and hibernate from Thanksgiving to Groundhog Day. After all, it worked for bears.

I was on my way to install an inventory tracking system for a store on State Street. Morning frost dusted everything. The temperature had almost warmed to above freezing. I turned on the radio to find out if snow was forecast. "Strawberry Fields" was playing. That was a pleasant surprise. I hadn't heard The Beatles on the radio for years. All November, WJLB had been playing Donna Summer and Barbara Streisand. Although pop music had gotten edgier with groups like Queen and Devo, none of the new groups could hold a candle to The Beatles. The disc jockey then segued into John Lennon's latest single, "(Just Like) Starting Over."

The car in front of me was poking along at thirty-five in a forty-five zone. I wasn't rude enough to honk, but I drummed my fingers on the steering wheel. "It's John Lennon music all day," the man on the radio said as he cued up, "Give Peace a Chance." When the last notes faded, the disc jockey announced, "News at the top of the hour." I glanced at the dashboard clock. Was it already nine o'clock? Shit, this slowpoke in front of me had made me late.

"John Lennon is dead," the newsman said. "Shot outside his home in New York City last night at 10:50 p.m."

"No!" I screamed, letting go of the steering wheel and pressing my palms into my eye sockets. The car veered right and rode up onto the curb. I stomped on the brake pedal. It stopped, but stalled the engine.

"Lennon's assailant, one Mark David Chapman, is in police custody. And now, for other news . . ."

I turned the radio off. Another shitty end to a year.

CHAPTER 34

With the success of his computer business, Tommy Jr. regularly attended the largest computer trade show in the world, COMDEX, held annually in Las Vegas every November. In 1981, he brought me along to check out a "Smartmodem" being introduced by some company from Georgia. Instead of having to dial a telephone number, and then put the handset into an acoustic coupler, this modem directly connected the computer to the telephone line. It even allowed the computer to dial the phone number, which would greatly simplify things for our customers.

I hadn't been to Las Vegas since I left the Air Force. The city had certainly changed dramatically since I got my first view of living, moving breasts. Fremont Street, with the Golden Nugget and the Pioneer Club, was a backwater now. Megalithic hotels lined Las Vegas Boulevard for several miles.

We entered the Las Vegas Convention Hall, and I was stunned. COMDEX filled the entire 90,000 square feet of exhibition space with a thousand or more companies pitching computers, accessories, chips, and software. We found the booth for the company that made the Smartmodem. It was everything we hoped for, and installation only required a telephone jack and a serial cable.

We spent the next two days walking aisles of exhibits, dazzled by the innovations, until we felt like our feet would fall off. But the thing everyone was buzzing about was that IBM had just released its first personal computer, and what that would mean for RadioShack, who at that point dominated the personal computer market. Tommy said, "I'm not worried." After three days, we flew back to Detroit with free tote bags full of literature and free pens.

Tommy's computer business had become so successful, his accountant told him for tax purposes he needed to spend a chunk of the company profits before year-end. So he bought himself a big Cadillac with cruise control, gave his employees fat bonuses, and me shares in the company.

That Christmas, he set his new Caddy on cruise, and we drove to Nora's. I'd brought my box of cassettes, and on the way, I commemorated the one-year anniversary of John Lennon's death, by giving Tommy a seven hour musical history of The Beatles. He indulged me.

We listened to everything from "We Can Work It out" to "Let It Be." About halfway home, he turned the volume down and asked me about my years on the road. My nomad life had always held a special fascination for my niece and nephews—I was the cool uncle. Tommy, newly rich, couldn't fathom how I'd gotten by for so many years with no income.

"I think your parents gave you kids the wrong idea about me when you were young. I made money building and selling orgone accumulators."

"Building what now?"

"Orgone accumulators. Orgone was psychiatrist Wilhelm Reich's name for the energy that keeps living things alive. It's the current that causes our diaphragm to move, our lungs to breathe."

"So . . . electrical nerve impulses."

"No. Reich initially thought he'd discovered a special form of electrical energy. But what he was observing had been known to the yogis for millennia as prana or life energy. Most people just don't notice it, the way we don't notice the electricity in our nerves. But with years of meditation using certain yogic techniques, you can increase it to elevate your consciousness."

"Sounds pretty . . . well, sort of out there. Kind of the same territory as Uncle Eddie's UFOs."

"Except that I've actually experienced it. I'm an old hippie and in the course of my travels, I met many yogis who could do some pretty amazing things. And, while Reich wasn't the first to discover prana, what he did discover were devices that could accumulate and then discharge orgone. Unfortunately, his work was destroyed, and he was dead before a new generation became interested."

"So, how did you become interested?"

"I used to live in a commune, and an old man there had one of Reich's orgone accumulators. He let me try it, and I was hooked. He also had a rare mechanical drawing of how to build them. After the commune broke up, I traveled around building accumulators, being one of the few who knew how."

"And you made a living at this?"

"I lived cheap—never needed more than I earned."

"I can't imagine it."

No, cruising the interstate in his brand-new Cadillac, I don't imagine he could.

"Here Comes the Sun" started playing, and I turned the volume up.

By the time we arrived at his mother's, The Beatles had a new fan, even if orgone didn't.

During our Christmas visit, my sisters gave me my share of the proceeds from the sale of Dad's house. When I got back to Ann Arbor, I put the money down on a cute little house near West Park. With a steady job and shares in the company, I easily qualified for a mortgage. Tommy had finally done what Patty could not—made Peter Pan grow up.

* * *

The following June, *E. T. the Extraterrestrial* came out, breaking box office records, and remaining in theaters throughout the summer. I imagined

Eddie going wild over it. Sophie confirmed it during a phone call. "We've seen it so many times, I've lost count. Every time he says, 'Honey, you want to go to the movies this weekend?' I know exactly what we're going to see."

"Well," I said, "at least you're doing something as a couple."

"Yeah. We can recite entire scenes to each other from memory. When are you coming for a visit?"

"Oh, we'll be there for Christmas. Not before. Tommy and I have to go to COMDEX in November."

"Well, I'm sure Eddie will still be talking about *E.T.* six months from now."

I smiled into the telephone. "I'd put money on it."

I'd have won that bet, too. At Christmas, Eddie cornered me for what had become our annual discussion of his latest theories on UFOs. Why he considered me knowledgeable, or even interested, I couldn't fathom—maybe because I was too polite to tell him to change the subject. I was braced for him to gush about the movie, which I had seen by then. Perhaps he'd try to convince me Spielberg wanted to prepare the world to accept that extraterrestrials were living among us. Instead, he took an almost opposite tangent.

"We've known about UFOs since 1947," Eddie said. "That's thirty-five years."

"Has it been that long?"

"At least. Could be even longer. But here's the thing I want to understand. What's their purpose?"

I shook my head.

"They don't take anything. Flying saucers don't shoot down planes or blow up buildings with space-rays like those 1950s movies."

"Not that I ever heard about," I said.

"Moreover, they do not bring help. That little E. T. in the movie didn't talk to the scientists, didn't teach the kids any new science or technology."

Attempting to lighten the mood, I said, "He did build a space transmitter out of a Speak & Spell."

Eddie shrugged it off. "*Chariots of the Gods?* claimed that aliens taught primitive man how to make pyramids. What if they did? How did that help mankind? A bunch of tombs for the very elite?"

"Eddie, are you saying you don't believe in this stuff anymore?"

"No. I still do. There have been too many sightings for too many years. Something from another planet is definitely in our skies; some of them even briefly land. But . . . I guess I'm losing faith in them. If they wanted to help us, we'd be better. If they wanted to harm us, we'd be dead. So what are we, a tourist stop?"

"I . . . don't know. Good questions, though."

"Now, a lot of the UFO groups argue in their newsletters that the technological advances we've made since World War II are based on what we learned from crashed flying saucers. I'm not buying that."

"You're not?" Was my brother-in-law coming to his senses?

"Don't mistake me. There are UFOs. But time and again, the reports say those ships pop in or out of existence, change speed, course, or shape contrary to any known laws of physics. If we had acquired any of that technology, would we have used rocket propulsion to send our astronauts to the moon?"

"I don't have a dog in this hunt either way," I said, "but playing devil's advocate, Eddie, just because mankind learns a scientific principle doesn't mean we can apply it. The ancient Greeks had an early example of steam power, but it took another 1700 years before men began to build railroads and steam ships."

"I get your meaning," Eddie said. "It's like ancient astronauts taught men how to build pyramids, but the Egyptians never figured out pyramid power?"

"No. I'm not saying I believe any of this. But if space aliens exist. . . . I don't know, they might have rules like that old TV show, *Star Trek*, with a prime directive to observe, but not interfere."

"Well, maybe. But fat lot of good that does us."

CHAPTER 35

Tommy and I continued to attend COMDEX in subsequent years, where new products continuously changed the computer industry. Processor speeds doubled every couple of years. In 1983, IBM had released the model XT. It featured an internal five-and-a-half inch hard drive, which held a whopping ten megabytes of data and programs. The following year, the rage at Fall COMDEX was the IBM model AT, yet a growing area of interest was portable computers. The first portables were the size of Nora's sewing machine and weighed at least as much, but given the way chip speeds were improving, I could foresee one the size of a briefcase on the horizon. When we saw the first three-and-a-half inch hard drives, it started me thinking. No matter how small the hard drive, it required a circuit board called a disc controller to communicate with the computer processor. I saw a need.

It had been a dozen years since I'd sat at a drafting table drawing printed circuits. Integrated circuit chips and computer-aided-design software had changed hardware design dramatically. Still, I spent the next year designing a disc controller that fit on a single chip. I was ready to meet with manufacturers in Silicon Valley when Tommy stopped me. "Uncle Gizmo, you can't show this to anybody before you file for a patent."

"Really? Is that necessary?"

He nodded. "Oh, yes."

I guess I was still too much of a flower child to think about people ripping me off. Thank God for my cynical nephew.

"The auto companies patent every minor change they come up with," he said. "Detroit has some of the best patent attorneys in the nation. We'll drive into the city next week and meet with one."

The whole patent application process took another year, and the patent lawyer cost a bundle. But in the end, it was worth it. By 1986, we not only found a company to manufacturer my controller chip, but they would also sell and distribute it under a licensing arrangement. All I had to do was collect the royalties.

Feeling flush, instead of driving home for Christmas, Tommy and I flew. We rented a car at the airport so no one would have to pick us up—Tommy insisted on a Cadillac. When we pulled into his parent's drive, his father met us at the door. "Geeze Tommy, you bought another new Caddy? Your old one was barely broke-in."

Tommy hugged his dad. "Don't worry. It's an airport rental."

I shook Tom's hand. "Merry Christmas."

"Glad you came," Tom said. "But Gizmo, you're his uncle. Don't let him waste money like that. I'd have picked you guys up."

My brother-in-law and his son had two different ideas about money, and I wasn't about to get between them. I just smiled and left to look for my sister.

"Nora," I called, moving into the next room. "We're here."

Patty found me first, wrapping me in a tight hug. When I got a good look at her, she had the post-coital glow of a young girl in heat. "Roger is coming," she said breathlessly.

"Roger?" That might explain the glow.

Nora entered the room. "Patty has a steady boyfriend."

"I've told him all about you," Patty said. "He wants to be an engineer."

My sister rolled her eyes. "A recording engineer."

I kissed Nora's cheek. "Somebody has to make records."

"Hi, Mom." Tommy joined us, sweeping Nora off her feet and twirling her in a circle.

When he let her down, her face was wet with tears. "I'm so happy you're here." She wiped away the tears with her palms. "Patty, please call your mom and tell her everyone is here."

"Not everyone," Patty said.

Nora smiled. "I won't serve dinner before your beau arrives. But do tell your parents that Gizmo and Tommy are here."

The doorbell rang, and Patty dashed out of the room. "I'll get it!"

Nora shook her head. "Love-struck. I'll call Sophie."

Sophie flew into my arms. "Not necessary." Behind her, Eddie, with a twelve-pack of beer under each arm, grinned at me. "Gizmo, how the hell are you doing?"

"Couldn't be better," I said, and I meant it. The family was together, my sisters were happy, and my niece and nephews were growing into respectable human beings. And it looked like no one was going to die this Christmas. Things were good.

I freed one arm from Sophie's clutch and reached out to shake Eddie's hand. Instead, I found myself holding a twelve-pack.

"Take one for yourself and pass them out," he said. "I'll put these in the fridge."

"You want one?" I said to Sophie.

"I'm not supposed to mix alcohol with my medication," she said.

"Neither am I," Nora said, "But I have a glass of wine with dinner. I figure the food absorbs it."

So maybe things weren't as good as they could have been. I looked from one sister to the other. "Are you still on those 'happy pills'?"

"Roger and I will take beers," Patty said from the doorway. Beside her was a tall shank of bone in blue jeans, who didn't look old enough to drink. But what the hell, it was Christmas, and he looked like he needed the calories. I handed them each a bottle.

"Thank you," he said, removing his hand from Patty's ass.

"Roger, this is my Uncle Gizmo."

We shook hands. I gave Patty another beer. "Please, take this to your uncle."

They turned and left as one unit, with his hand again in her back pocket. I looked at Sophie, who was watching them walk away. "I hope she's on the pill."

Sophie exchanged glances with Nora. "Isn't everyone?"

I carried the remaining beers into the kitchen and gave them to Eddie, who was on his knees squeezing them into Nora's refrigerator.

The rest of our holiday went well. I shouldn't have been surprised when, on Christmas day, I opened my gift from Eddie to find that he'd given me a book on UFOs. What surprised me most was that it was *Contact with Space* . . . by Wilhelm Reich. First, I had no idea Eddie knew who Reich was. And second, that any of Reich's books were back in print, let alone a title I'd never heard of.

Family activities, dinners, and celebrations filled the week. It wasn't until the flight home that I had a chance to start reading the book. I opened to the copyright page and found it had been published in 1957 by a tiny press in Maine. Well, that was a year after a federal judge had sanctioned the book burning. So was some brave soul republishing Reich's lost works?

In the book, Reich described his orgone research in Arizona between 1951 and 1956. North America was suffering its second worst drought on record. Among the first to recognize the growing crisis of human-caused climate change, Reich declared it a planetary emergency. With his family and close coworkers, he brought his latest invention to the southwest—an orgone accumulator with an array of projection tubes, which he called a cloudbuster. He'd discovered his device could use orgone to draw atmospheric moisture and direct it to fall as rain. The logical step was to test it where drought was extreme—the area around Tucson.

The period from the mid-1940s all through 1950s was replete with reported UFO sightings, especially in New Mexico, Arizona, and Nevada. Reich's book said that at this point, he'd read only one report on UFOs, and knew virtually nothing about them. His primary purpose in Arizona was to investigate whether projecting orgone into the atmosphere could affect the drought. That is, until one clear night in the desert, when he and his team noticed lights in the star-filled sky. They were neither stars nor planets and did not move like the other celestial bodies. I reminded myself that this was half a decade before the first artificial satellites, so he wasn't seeing Sputnik.

He said the phenomena repeated for weeks, during which he hesitated to turn his cloudbuster upon them. Finally, one night in June, he aimed the draw pipes of his device at the "star" in question and caused it to fade out. There was no mistake about it—three other people had seen it happen. Reich realized these were not stars and began to experiment on the effect his orgone mechanism had on space vehicles, which he called Ea instead of UFO. E for energy, a for alpha or primordial.

I thumbed ahead for a quick peek. The writing was dense with formulas and equations. Had Eddie actually read the book or, after skimming it, decided to give it to me in hopes that I would explain it to him?

The flight attendant announced that we were about to land. I stuck the empty wrapper from my airline peanuts in the book to mark my place. I'd get back into it as soon as I got home.

CHAPTER 36

COMDEX was big from the beginning, but by 1987, it was huge, filling not only the massive Las Vegas Convention Center, but overflowing into hotels that had their own convention spaces, including the Hilton, MGM Grand, and Caesar's Palace. Tommy and I were among the estimated 200,000 attendees. Buses shuttled us between convention locations and hotels. He pursued new hardware and software systems we might sell to our clients back in Michigan. I was supposed to hang around the booth of the company that had licensed my controller chip and answer questions. No one had any, so I mainly drifted around the convention with Tommy, checking in at the booth every so often to see if they needed me.

The computer business had exploded, outperforming bedrock industries like automobiles and steel. Every company at COMDEX had lavish expense accounts. One night, a software vendor who wanted Tommy's business wined and dined us at the fanciest restaurant in Caesar's Palace. The lacquered-hair hostess who seated us had a round face and a rounder bottom, about twenty pounds beyond plump. She seemed vaguely familiar, though I'd never eaten there before. I peeked at her name tag, trying not to give the impression I was leering at her tits. Claudia. No one came to mind.

She handed us menus and left. She was soon forgotten with the arrival of our waitress, a pert young woman dressed in a scanty toga that barely reached the top of her thigh. Her outfit reminded me of Lisa, the beatnik in Greenwich Village who wore only a tee shirt and no panties. Our waitress was, of course, wearing undies, a fact she proved by bending toward each gentleman in our party to take his drink order, and giving the rest of the table a glimpse of her behind as her skirt raised.

Lisa, a name I hadn't thought of in twenty years, loosened a rusty cog in my brain. I excused myself and returned to the hostess station. A lengthy queue of people needing to be seated kept the hostess busy and me waiting. Meanwhile, I studied her, fairly certain, but still with a smidge of doubt. This was in part due to her makeup and hairdo. It crossed my mind that whoever held the Avon and Mary Kay franchises for Las Vegas must be making a fortune. I'd never been any place where women wore so much makeup.

Finally, when all the tables were full and Claudia was merely taking down names, I managed to get in front of her.

"Yes?" she said.

"Hello, Sparrow."

Her eyes widened. "Excuse me?"

"Am I wrong? It's Gizmo."

Her mouth dropped open, then she broke into a broad smile. She stepped from behind her podium and embraced me. "My God, I didn't recognize you. How long has it been?"

I did some quick math. "Seventeen years."

"God, what a memory. How did you remember?"

"How could I forget? You left with Sugar Bear."

Worry lines creased the makeup on her forehead. "You're not still mad about that."

"I wasn't mad about it then. I just remember it because I searched all over Florida for you guys to tell you Woody had died."

"Woody . . . Oh, this is all too much."

A portly man in a three-piece suit nudged me aside. "Excuse me, Miss. We'd like a table."

Claudia/Sparrow smiled at him. "We're full at the moment, but I'll be glad to add you to the list."

"How long is the wait?" he said.

She counted the names ahead of him. "About thirty minutes. If you'd like to wait in the bar, I can send someone when your table is ready."

He nodded and gave her his name and the number of people with him.

She wrote it down and when she finished, she squeezed my hand. "I get off at twelve. I'd love to catch up."

"Me, too. I'll come back then."

I thought midnight would never arrive. After dinner, our party entered the hotel casino to shoot craps and play blackjack. Since I'd lost money here as a serviceman, I'd never been much for gambling. Mostly, I just watched the other guys lose their money. Cocktail waitresses circulated the room keeping the gamblers supplied with drinks, but I didn't want to be bombed when Sparrow got off, so I nursed a Coke. Casinos don't have clocks, and by design, you can't tell if it's day or night outside. I had to keep checking my watch. When both hands met on twelve, I returned to the restaurant.

The place was closed, and Sparrow waited outside. She had retouched her makeup and applied a fresh layer of varnish to her hair. Leaning in, she gave me a brief kiss, sticky with lip gloss, and hooked her elbow through mine.

"Where shall we go?" I said.

"My place. I'd like to change."

She walked me to a parking lot behind Caesar's Palace and stopped beside a ten-year-old red Datsun, made before the company changed their name to Nissan. "You want to drive?"

"I don't know where you live."

She laughed. "Right. Get in."

When we got to her apartment, we didn't immediately fall into each other. Rather, she changed into a velour leisure suit, and we fell into her plush, overstuffed sofa where we talked until dawn. I asked then if I could take a shower. I'd been up for twenty-two hours, but strangely, I wasn't sleepy. In fact, I felt energized. Still, a quick rinse before heading back to my hotel seemed the thing to do.

She handed me a towel and washcloth and told me to make myself at home. While I lathered under a warm spray, I heard water running in the adjacent basin. Pulling the shower curtain aside, I saw her removing her makeup with some thick white goo. She caught me and smiled. Covering her head with a plastic shower cap, she tucked stray curls under the edges, pulled off her top, and unfastened her bra. She slid her trousers and underpants off in one motion and stepped into the shower with me.

Just like old times.

We wasted no time, passionately kissing and touching each other everywhere. She turned off the water and pulled us as one into her bedroom, where she threw back the covers, and we tumbled, dripping wet, into bed.

After vigorous, enthusiastic lovemaking, she rolled off me, swept her hand over the damp sheets, and laughed. "I guess we both get to sleep in the wet spot."

I turned on my side and rested my leg on her thigh. "Who said we're going to sleep?"

Her eyes twinkled, and she kissed me.

I ran my hands over the abundance of her body. No longer the svelte, lithe, barefoot hippie I'd known. Still, within her passion, something well remembered abided. Softly, I caressed her breasts, now twice the size of the years when she never wore a bra. She responded and pulled me onto her, filling my mouth with her tongue. Right. No sleep then.

But this time, after we'd both climaxed, we drifted off into a long winter's nap, not waking until four o'clock in the afternoon.

Sparrow woke me by smothering my face with kisses. "I'm going to work. Sleep as long as you want." She was covered in war paint.

"Call in sick," I said.

"I can't do that at the last minute. Say you'll be here when I get home."

"I need to go to the hotel for clean clothes and to tell my nephew why I disappeared. But yes, I want to see you again tonight. How about if I meet you at Caesar's when you get off?"

"That would make me very happy."

"One more thing," I said. "Tell them you need tomorrow off."

She bit her lip and hesitated.

"I'm only here a few more days. We've got a lot of catching up to do."

"What about your convention?"

"Screw the convention. What are the odds of us running into each other this way? You've got to respect that."

She waggled her fingers in a cute farewell and left.

After I heard the latch of the apartment door click, I lay for a time studying the swirls of plaster on her bedroom ceiling, looking for shapes like one finds in clouds. Feelings long dormant for a girl long forgotten churned my heart, and my mind basked in the serendipity of it all. Sparrow, sweet Sparrow.

Finally, I pried myself loose, smoothed the sheets, and made the bed. I took a quick shower, dressed in yesterday's clothes, and meditated.

I perused the Yellow Pages for the phone number of a cab company when it dawned on me that I didn't know where I was. I rummaged through a haphazard stack of papers on her kitchen counter until I found a Vanity Fair with her address on the label.

By the time the taxi dropped me off at our hotel, Tommy was already back from his day at the convention. "There you are. I was wondering if we should send out a search party."

"It's all good," I said, grinning ear-to-ear.

"You dog. Someone made you very happy."

"You don't know the half of it."

"Tell me about it over dinner," he said. "I'm starved."

I wasn't that hungry, but I realized I hadn't eaten since last night. Living on love, I guess. "Okay, but not with a bunch of vendors, just you and me."

That suited Tommy, who said he'd spent all day talking business and had had his fill. After I changed, we dined at the hotel's "All you can eat for $2" buffet, where I tipped the hostess more than the cost of our meal to seat us at a quiet booth in the back. The seats were upholstered in red Naugahyde and the table was set for four. She took up the extra place settings and told us to help ourselves to the buffet.

Over a leisurely dinner, I tried to explain the wonder of meeting Sparrow here—the last place on earth I would have ever expected her to wind up. That led to trying to describe who she had been to me. Which led to filling him in on parts of my life I'd never explained to a family member before.

Tommy had been quite young when I lived at Woody's and wandered the country in my VW bus. Perhaps he'd overheard his parents or my parents carp about my lifestyle. If he did, it didn't matter. I was just fun Uncle Gizmo, who wore long hair and showed up at Christmas with gifts that brought squeals of delight.

Although we were peers now, the difference in our ages became apparent to me as I struggled to paint a picture of the heady days of the late sixties and early seventies. For Tommy, casual hookups were the norm of his youth, and pot had been decriminalized in Ann Arbor long before he moved there—decades ahead of the rest of the nation. So how could he understand the freshness, the explosion of a freedom previously unimaginable, of the sexual revolution? He nodded and smiled, but I still don't think he fully understood.

Eventually, our conversation returned to the present. Starry-eyed, I told him how we'd talked until dawn and slept the day away.

"Frankly, Uncle Gizmo, it sounds like love at first sight."

"Well, first sight happened twenty years ago, so it's been slow to develop."

"I stand by the love part. I've known you all my life and never seen you so luminescent."

I dismissed the notion and tried to change the topic, but the only thing I wanted to talk about was *her*. So maybe he was right.

After we had hogged the table for hours, the hostess appeared and said she needed it for other customers. Another bribe probably would have let us stay longer, but we simply said, "Thank you," and left.

In the elevator, I considered bringing Tommy along when I went to pick her up. I really wanted him to meet her. But a selfish part of me wanted to see her alone. When we reached our room, Tommy turned on the TV, found a football game, and told me to have a nice night and not stay out too late.

CHAPTER 37

Impatient, I arrived early, and hung out in the restaurant lobby, exchanging smoldering glances with Sparrow. Near closing time, her main duty was to turn away late arrivals. Afterwards, I was prepared to take her to a show or club or something—I wasn't sure what people who lived in Vegas year-round thought was fun. The city was really built for tourists.

Sparrow showed me what she thought was fun when she drove me straight home and dragged me into her bed, picking up where we'd left off that afternoon. Fine by me.

We were like newlyweds on their honeymoon, barely able to keep our hands off each other. However, this time, we did sleep.

We woke late in the morning—apparently normal for those in Las Vegas who work until the wee hours. Sparrow was in no hurry. She had indeed taken the day off. We drank coffee, and she made scrambled tofu.

"Still a vegetarian?" I said.

She nodded. "You?"

"It's gotten easier," I said. "Even restaurants like yours offer a couple of vegetarian entrées, or at least pasta."

She patted her wide butt. "I know. But they're mostly carbs."

I grabbed her hips with both hands, pulled her to me, and buried my face in her bosom. "I don't mind." It was the first time I'd mentioned her Rubenesque figure. And truthfully, though I remembered her being younger and slimmer, I found her fuller shape, no less erotic.

She tilted my head away from her tits and looked into my face. "You don't?"

I sighed. "Must I prove it again?" I lifted her off her feet, sat her on the kitchen counter, pulled open her robe, and commenced kissing her everywhere.

She pushed me away and jumped down. "You see people do that in the movies, but you know, it's not all that comfortable. Let's go to the bedroom."

Afterwards, we spooned, talking our way through our missing years. Like me, her parents had passed away. In her case, her dad died first, then more recently, her mom. They hadn't been close—her parents had been more judgmental of her hippie lifestyle than mine were. But she felt bad about the years of discord.

"It's different for girls," she said. "Parents expect weddings and grandkids, and if you tell them you don't want that, they won't make it easy on you. At least mine never did, right to the end. Even after I was too old to have babies."

Oh. I hadn't thought about that. I was fifty-two. Sparrow must be in her mid to late forties, either in or already through menopause. She'd implied she never had children, but I hadn't asked. Did she want to know my situation?

"Me neither," I said. "No kids. Never married."

She turned over to face me and looked at me without speaking. I couldn't read her feelings or tell what she wanted me to say next. I pulled her closer and said into her ear, "Another thing we have in common, we're both orphans now."

Well, that was the wrong thing to say. She began to sob quietly.

"I'm sorry. I didn't mean it to be hurtful. I was trying to lighten the mood." I pressed my hand on her back and moved it in small circles. "So sorry."

Her sobs changed into soft laughter. "No. That's right, isn't it? If both parents are dead, you *are* technically an orphan." She wiped her tears on my shoulder and pulled us into a tight hug. "We're just two orphans holding each in bed."

After a time, we got up and showered—together. We dressed and took a walk. Las Vegas was warmer than Ann Arbor, of course, but the November wind was actually chilly. We cut our walk short and returned to the apartment to laze away the rest of the afternoon. Our politics and spiritual beliefs still aligned. We liked the same music, books, and heroes. And our memories of the events of the times we'd lived through were like being immersed together in a warm, scented bath. It was as though we'd been together forever.

It didn't take much convincing for Sparrow to call work and ask for a second day off. Her refrigerator contents were sparse, so I asked if we should go grocery shopping and make dinner at the apartment, or go out to a restaurant.

"Restaurant, definitely," she said. "I know a cute little Thai place. It's in a strip mall, but the food is fabulous."

The time had come for Tommy and Sparrow to meet. "I work with my nephew. He's with me at the convention. Do you mind if I invite him along?"

"Of course not."

I called the hotel, told the operator our room number, and Tommy answered on the first ring. I explained what we were doing and handed the phone to Sparrow for her to give him the address.

I butted in while she was still on the phone. "Tell him the dress code."

"Dress comfortable," she told him. "It's in a strip mall. Anything will do. We'll meet you there at seven."

I motioned for her to hand me back the phone.

"Hold on, Gizmo wants to say something . . . I look forward to meeting you, too. Here's your uncle."

"Tommy? Throw my clothes in a suitcase and bring it with you. I'm going to stay here another day."

Sparrow left to get ready. Since I only had the clothes I'd worn here, there wasn't much for me to do. I made the bed and meditated on the living room couch while she "put on her face," as she called it. A half-hour later, she came out of the bedroom wearing a smart black sheath dress with a V-neckline and a string of white pearls.

"Someone's mother raised him right," she said.

"Huh?"

"You made the bed. I noticed it yesterday, too."

I laughed. "Thank the US Air Force for that. An airman with an unmade bunk had to do pushups."

She made a slow turn. "What do you think?"

"Gorgeous. But I thought you said the restaurant was casual."

"It is, but I want to make a good impression on your nephew."

To say Tommy was impressed would be an understatement. He was charmed by her and fascinated to meet someone who had shared his uncle's past life.

She and I had arrived ahead of him, and Sparrow held our table while I waited out front. When his taxi came, I put my suitcase in her car and took him inside to make introductions. From there on, the two of them carried the ball and I just sat back and watched. The food was delicious, and by the time the meal was finished, the two of them had formed a deep connection. When he wanted to call a cab, she wouldn't hear of it and insisted we drive him to the hotel.

It was late when we got back to her apartment. I carried my suitcase in from the car and set it in the bedroom against the wall. Sparrow came in and looked at it as she unzipped her dress.

"I didn't know where you wanted me to put it," I said.

"It's fine there." The dress dropped to her feet, and she stepped out of it. She peeled off a girdle that had her flesh squeezed like packaged cookie dough and fell onto the bed with a sigh.

I kicked off my shoes and lay down beside her.

She propped herself up on one elbow, glancing at my suitcase as if it were an alien artifact. Maybe bringing it wasn't such a good idea after all.

"I'm going to take off my makeup." Giving me a quick kiss, she rolled off the bed and went into the bathroom.

I undressed, pulled back the covers, and got into bed. I heard the shower run.

When she returned, she switched off the light and slid into bed next to me. She smelled like fresh rain. We made love, and afterward she lay with her head on my shoulder and her hair splayed across my chest.

Then an earth-shaking shudder vibrated the entire apartment building. I flipped over and hurled my body protectively on top of her. "Earthquake!"

She laughed, rolled me off, and kissed the top of my head. "Don't worry. It's only a shockwave from an underground nuclear blast. They test H-bombs in the desert north of here."

I pressed her hands against my chest. "Feel my heart racing?"

"It wasn't me doing that?"

After my heart slowed, we eventually settled into a state of deep tranquility. I can't say how long we lay like that—neither of us sleeping, but neither of us speaking, either.

Unbidden, a long-ago conversation with my niece about never having a wife began to swirl in the ether. I shooed it away, but it came back. Something I had read in a New Age book about being open to serendipity. Then, there arose that old saw about never looking a gift horse in the mouth.

Sparrow seemed to sense my thoughts and lifted her head. "Gizmo?"

I turned on my side to face her, but that wouldn't do. I got up on my knees. She rose up to meet me as equals. I took a deep breath and swallowed. When I spoke, my voice was hoarse. "We have been given a gift. A precious gift."

Even in the darkened room, I could see her eyes widen.

"Something neither of us sought has come to us after decades of avoiding it. A new life. A different life."

"What are you saying?"

"That I love you."

"I love you, too," she whispered.

"Let's marry."

"No, you can't be serious." Her voice back at normal volume.

"No? You won't marry me?"

"No, I mean . . . isn't this too sudden?"

"I don't believe it is. Our reunion isn't accidental. What does your intuition tell you?"

She rested on her heels in pensive silence.

"I don't want to go back to Ann Arbor without you," I said.

"And I don't want you to, but that doesn't require a piece of paper."

"I agree. But while it goes against the way we've always lived, something tells me we should get one—and I don't mean our deceased parents' morals or society at large. Something compels me to ask, will you marry me?"

I held my breath and waited. My palms started to sweat. This was worse than a nervous school boy asking a girl to prom. This was the shape of my future. Then she embraced me and whispered, "Yes," into my ear.

We must have kissed a thousand times. Finally, I got up and turned on the light.

"What are you doing?" she said.

"Telephoning Tommy. I need a best man." I tossed the phone book on the bed. "Choose one of those Las Vegas wedding chapels. We'll buy rings tomorrow morning and marry in the afternoon."

"What's the rush?"

"I don't know. But the time is now."

"Are you worried I'll change my mind?"

"No. Are you?"

"Never."

"Good. Is there a girlfriend or someone from work you want to invite?"

"Yes, but I'm not going to wake them at this hour."

"Well, I have to tell Tommy now because he's flying home tomorrow night."

CHAPTER 38

Our wedding was a Las Vegas cliché. We were married in a tiny white chapel—and yes, by an Elvis impersonator who began the service by singing "Can't Help Falling in Love" and ended it with "Love Me Tender." Pure schmaltz. But it was kind of nice.

Tommy was a good sport about giving me time off and flew back without me after the ceremony. Sparrow and I delayed our honeymoon while we arranged for a moving van and packed her things.

"You're going to love Ann Arbor," I promised her. "It's far more educated and liberal than Vegas, and the city council are mostly old hippies."

I had her car checked and the oil changed, then we left when the movers did. We decided to honeymoon along the way. We drove her aging Datsun north through Utah to Salt Lake City, picked up I-80 and followed that through Wyoming, Nebraska, and Iowa. Blustery winter threatened along our route, but we never encountered snow.

On the way, I realized that I now had a wife, a good, steady job, and a home. We wouldn't have children— my sisters had done enough to propagate the species—but other than that, it was exactly the suburban lifestyle that my parents wanted for me right out of the Air Force, give or take children. But . . . this was different. Both Sparrow and I had lived freer lives, choosing our own paths, growing in our own ways. We were richer for it. And now we were choosing this path, not falling into it like my sisters had done. It made all the difference.

At Davenport we detoured north, and I took her to meet my sisters.

Nora and Sophie were pleasant to Sparrow, but I could see that her heavy makeup made them worry what kind of woman I'd married. Women in Prairie View, Iowa, confined themselves to lipstick, and on the rare occasion a smidge of rouge. They were too polite to say anything untoward, but they didn't hesitate to let me know they were upset about our having a wedding without them. They tried their best to get us to repeat the ceremony, in a church, with my niece and nephews in attendance. Neither Sparrow nor I wanted all that hoopla. Besides, where would they find an officiant who sang like Elvis?

My brothers-in-law were nice to her, although Eddie gave me grief about the car. "A Datsun, Gizmo? Sell that heap and buy American."

"I like my little red car," Sparrow said.

Eddie just shook his head. "Ford. Now, that's a real car."

Thanksgiving was around the corner, and everyone tried to persuade us to stay. I begged off, telling them that we had to meet the moving van in Ann Arbor, but promised we'd return with Tommy at Christmas.

Sparrow found my Ann Arbor house charming and said she could see us taking lovely strolls around West Park come springtime. I told her I'd paid off the mortgage with my patent royalties, so if anything ever happened to me, she could live there without worrying.

She kissed me. "Nothing's going to happen to either of us."

"Ever?"

"Ever."

The movers unloaded Sparrow's stuff, and we spent the rest of November maneuvering around stacks of boxes while she unpacked and arranged the house to her liking. We were happy. But after a lifetime of each of us being responsible only for ourselves, marriage took some adjustment.

Ann Arbor had long been a center of feminism, and Sparrow fit right in. By the time we flew to my sister's for Christmas, she hardly ever wore makeup. After we returned from the holiday, Sparrow felt at loose ends. Tommy's business was mushrooming, and I worked long hours. I suggested she explore the many yoga classes and meditation groups in the area. She did. She also found a job as a hostess at a vegetarian restaurant situated in an old house on Church Street. We didn't need the money, but she didn't want to sit at home like a housewife—maybe she'd be a good influence on my sisters. Soon, she knew more about the Ann Arbor scene than I did, taking me to hear local bands, poetry readings, or a visiting swami. In that respect, it was much like when we first met.

Originally from Philadelphia, she was no stranger to winter. When she grew up, the air quality in "filthy Philly" was said to be the equivalent of smoking a pack and a half of cigarettes a day. Still, Michigan's freezing weather didn't agree with her, neither did its dampness. Some days she had difficulty breathing and said one of the reasons she'd ended up in Las Vegas was for the dry desert air.

Over the next six years, she caught frequent colds—summer colds, winter colds—the season didn't seem to matter. One evening, when she was coughing her brains out, she confessed that her father died of lung cancer, and that worried her.

It worried me, too, now. The University of Michigan had the best medical school in the state. I urged her to see a doctor.

"No," she said, "I'll just take NyQuil and stay in bed."

That was when orgone came back into our lives.

It had been decades since I'd built orgone accumulators for a living, but I thought it might help her. Sparrow had introduced me to orgone via Woody, so she was willing to try it. I spent the weekend going through old folders in the attic, searching for the yellowed plans Woody had given me so many years ago, hoping they weren't lost, certain I would never have thrown them out. They turned up in an old manila envelope with my military ID badge, and the registration for my old VW camper—my past summed up in documents. On Monday, I Xeroxed the plans at work, and put the original in a fireproof box where I kept our marriage license, car title, and deed.

Our house originally had a screened-in back porch, which the previous owners had glassed in. It wasn't heated, but it stayed above freezing all year, and Sparrow kept her hanging plants there during the winter. We decided that was the place for the accumulator, and I built it the following weekend. Both of us used it regularly, taking turns. I could sense an increase in what yogis called prana in me, so I knew it was working. But Sparrow only marginally improved.

By our seventh anniversary, Sparrow had lost weight, back to her twenty-year-old self. And then some. I encouraged her to eat more, but having finally slimmed down, she resisted. She suffered bouts of painful coughing and shortness of breath. At last I got her to go to one of those walk-in clinics people call "doc-in-a-box." The elderly retired physician, who worked part time, diagnosed her problem as seasonal allergies and told her she had a reactive airway. Sparrow asked if a warmer, drier climate would help. The doctor said it might.

I told Tommy I wanted a leave of absence to try wintering in the desert like snowbirds. But not Las Vegas. I didn't think the frenetic vibes there would do her any good. So we chose Tempe, Arizona.

We stayed in Tempe from November through April, but her symptoms only got worse, and she began to experience chest pain more or less constantly. I panicked and took her to a doctor in Arizona who gave her an electrocardiogram and a troponin T blood test to see if she'd had a heart attack. The results were negative. He thought her chest pain was caused by all the coughing and prescribed codeine.

When we returned to Ann Arbor, she was thin as a twig, coughing violently, having serious difficulty breathing, and her chest hurt all the time. I got a pulmonologist at UM to examine her. Considering her father's history, the pulmonologist ordered a chest x-ray and a biopsy to check for lung cancer.

What they found was far worse.

The pulmonologist followed up with a CAT scan and another biopsy and then called us to meet at her office after she received the radiologist's report. Lilac bushes outside her office hung heavy with blooms, spreading their sweet fragrance. "Smell that?" I said, trying to inject some optimism.

Sparrow took a deep breath and then coughed.

A nurse called our name, and instead of taking us to an exam room, led us to the doctor's private office. The doctor shook our hands and invited us to sit in two chairs opposite her desk. She looked at her notes and then at Sparrow. "You grew up in Pennsylvania in the 1950s, is that right?"

Sparrow nodded.

Oh, boy, I thought, filthy Philly air pollution.

"Do you know if the home you lived in had asbestos?"

Sparrow coughed. "I have no idea."

"It likely did. Asbestos was used to insulate heating pipes and in drywall and joint compound up until a few years ago."

I knew our house in Ann Arbor didn't have asbestos drywall, but the outside shingles might be asbestos.

"Asbestos-cement shingles were also popular for roofs and siding, but less likely to present risk to the occupants."

"So, her cough isn't from air pollution?" I said.

The doctor's words were soft, measured, and empathic, yet her face bore a sadness that couldn't be missed. "No. Claudia has a rare form of cancer called mesothelioma. It's most often related to exposure to airborne asbestos fibers and dust." She held up a medical textbook drawing of the chest cavity. "Mesothelioma affects the pleura, the lining surrounding the lungs, or the peritoneum, the lining surrounding the lower digestive tract." She laid aside the illustration and folded her hands. "Unfortunately, because a biopsy is the only way to determine whether a person has mesothelioma, it often goes undetected until it reaches an advanced stage."

I took Sparrow's hand and squeezed it. "What now?"

"As pleural mesothelioma spreads in the chest, it puts pressure on everything else in that area. This can cause the complications Claudia is experiencing. Pleural effusion—the accumulation of fluid in the chest—compresses the lung area, making breathing difficult, and causing chest pain. Pain can also be caused by pressure on the nerves and spinal cord. Are you having difficulty swallowing?"

"No," Sparrow said. "But I haven't had any appetite."

"So, what's the treatment?" I said.

"Unfortunately, there is no cure."

"What!" My voice cracked, and my throat closed up. I didn't realize how much I'd been counting on the miracles of western medicine.

Sparrow looked at me warmly and patted my hand. "That's okay, Gizmo. I think I already knew this."

That only made me feel worse. I should be the one comforting her.

"We can perform procedures that may make you more comfortable," the doctor said. "A surgeon can insert a catheter into your chest to drain the fluid. Then we'll inject medicine into your chest to prevent fluid from returning. Considering the gravity of your current symptoms, I suggest we schedule this as soon as possible. It will make breathing easier."

I found my voice. "That's it?"

"This is difficult, I know. But there's no point in sugarcoating it. Mesothelioma is an aggressive cancer and for most people at Claudia's stage, life expectancy is only four to eighteen months. I can order MRI or PET scans to see if the cancer has spread to your lymph nodes or to other areas of your body. If so, those cancers might be treated with radiation or chemotherapy, but that won't cure the mesothelioma."

I looked at Sparrow with tears streaming down my face.

The doctor handed us a box of tissues. "I'm sorry. This is the worst part of my job."

I blew my nose. "I think we should get a second opinion."

"I think you should, too," the doctor said. "Meanwhile, we should get the fluid drained from your chest as soon as possible."

"Yes, please," Sparrow said.

* * *

After her procedure, another pulmonologist and an oncologist both confirmed the first doctor's diagnosis. Because of the earlier misdiagnoses, I needed to be sure. But the oncologist, mistaking my frustration with western medicine for guilt, told me that even if they had discovered it earlier, there was nothing to be done.

* * *

Sparrow passed away that autumn, just before our anniversary. We were married for almost nine years—most of them happy. It was not all I wanted, but it would have to be enough.

The US held an election that month, and Bill Clinton was reelected.

Nora and Sophie insisted I come there for Christmas.

Chapter 39

Our holiday gathering at Nora's that year had, for me at least, a gaping Sparrow-shaped hole in it. However, a harebrained idea of Tommy Jr. kept us both well distracted.

By the mid-1990s, the internet was catching on, and for the first time, emails exceeded the quantity of letters sent through the post office. America Online offered a dial-up service for home users, and Tommy decided to give each of my sisters a subscription and a PC for Christmas.

"You'll love it," he told them when they opened their gifts. "The whole family can keep in touch, and you won't have any long-distance phone bills."

The problem he failed to recognize was that computers were as foreign to my sisters as a toaster is to a cat. The cat might be intrigued to see toast pop up, but has no idea how to work it.

He and I spent the week between Christmas and New Year tutoring them on how to turn on their PCs, connect to the network, and sign in. Nora's husband had computers at the plant by then, so it wasn't that strange to him, but he also had a secretary who operated his, so he wasn't much help, either.

Things didn't improve after we returned to Ann Arbor. I was frequently on the phone with one sister or the other, trying to walk them through the America Online options. Since the service was dial-up, they couldn't actually do what I was telling them until we hung up. In the end, I don't think it saved them any long distance charges, and they probably would have preferred a toaster.

Eddie, whom I would have predicted to be the least computer-literate member of my family, took right to it. America Online had forums and communities on a variety of topics, including one on UFOs. With it, Eddie and his fellows could share mysterious, grainy, flying saucer photos and wild speculation.

Once the World Wide Web started up, web pages became the thing every company wanted to have. Investment bankers went nuts for it, and any company that claimed to have a software product in development that used the internet received ridiculous amounts of funding. By 1998, these financial witch doctors were buying and merging companies at wildly inflated prices, mostly paid in shares of the acquiring company's stock.

We were not immune. Tommy set up a group of programmers to make websites for our customers, and they came up with site development tools that created a distinctive product. Tommy accepted an offer to merge with a larger company at 17 times our present valuation. "Too good to pass up," he said.

For me, the fly in the cream was that our new parent company claimed my disc controller chip patent and the royalties earned from it were company assets. "Don't feel bad," Tommy said. "Once your stock options in the new company have vested, you'll make millions more from capital gains than you'd ever have received in royalties."

I had less than two years before I could draw Social Security, and being rich had never been my goal, so I didn't argue. Besides, we had a new worry, Y2K, the acronym given to the problem that once the calendar reached 2000, computers couldn't differentiate 1900 from 2000.

Because early computers had tiny amounts of memory, programmers always shortened the year to two digits to save space. But when the year rolled over to "00," all hell would break loose. Any calculation that depended on a given number of days—interest, scheduling, even a person's age—would be wrong. Doomsayers fretted that utility power grids and all manner of services managed by computers would fail on January 1, 2000.

The entire computer industry scrambled. Software programs, hardware BIOS chips, every piece of stored data containing a date had to be converted to four-digit years. Once the corrections were ready, technicians had to update programs and data. Overtime became the norm.

With Herculean effort, it all came together. Tommy and I hadn't gone to Nora's that year in case we'd missed something and our clients needed servicing. No one did. He and I celebrated New Year's Eve at Ann Arbor's fanciest restaurant, making sure we were home by midnight. I woke the following morning and turned on the coffee maker. Good. The utility grid hadn't crashed.

Tommy called. "The phones are working. I checked the answering service and none of our customers have called. Looks like we got it. Why don't you come over for breakfast?"

When I got there, he laid an unwrapped box on the table. "A belated Christmas gift from the company."

The cover of the box read: *Research in Motion BlackBerry* with a picture of a palm-size device with a tiny keyboard and a monochrome LCD screen.

"It combines the functions of a mobile phone, pager, and email system in your hand," Tommy said, pulling his out of his pocket.

The keyboard resembled three rows of Chiclets. "How do you type on this thing?" I said.

"You use your thumbs." He held his in both hands and rapidly tapped out a message. "Open up your box."

I did, and he showed me where to turn it on. A moment later, it buzzed. A note from Tommy appeared on my screen.

He pointed to a wheel on the right side of the device. "The screen only shows eight lines of text, but you can scroll it with this wheel."

I moved the wheel and read the rest of Tommy's message: "BlackBerry is more than a fancy pager. You can make and receive phone calls, too. Let's call Mom."

He showed me how to find the phone icon, and we called Nora. Sophie and Eddie were there for breakfast. We wished everyone a quick happy New Year and then hung up. Mobile phone companies used to charge by the minute.

Later that morning, we turned on Tommy's TV and watched the Rose Bowl parade and then the game. Wisconsin beat Stanford. I'd lived too many places to care, but I knew the win made Tom and Eddie happy. So far, 2000 was off to a good start. Nothing had crashed.

Until March.

It wasn't Y2K. It was the dot-com bubble.

After years of raking in billions in venture capital, a lot of internet companies had burned through the money without ever making a profit. The stock equivalent of a run on the bank was inevitable. The NASDAQ peaked in March, then fell by more than 75 percent over the next few months. The crash wiped out more than $5 trillion in market value. My stock options became worthless. I had considered selling them right after our merger, but my accountant advised me not to, otherwise I'd have to pay too much capital gains tax. Well, I didn't have to worry about capital gains anymore. Not that I cared. I'd never set out in life to be a millionaire, and it didn't matter that I hadn't ended up as one.

Our parent company began shedding employees like a Siberian Husky loses hair, replacing high salary employees with people younger and cheaper. My sixty-fifth birthday was near, so when it came, I graciously accepted their severance package. Tommy was sorry to see me go, but since he'd sold the company, he didn't have much sway.

"But I'm keeping the BlackBerry," I said.

"It's only right," Tommy said. "After all, it was a gift."

From the beginning, we'd always had a pension plan. By law, the new company had to honor that. So they paid it as a lump sum. The company's CFO suggested I put it in Madoff Securities, a private equity fund that was generating unheard of returns. "It automatically reinvests all dividends back into the fund. With compounding, that'll double or triple your money," he said.

Well, he was the company's financial expert, not me. Since I was now eligible for Social Security and could live off that, I followed his advice.

CHAPTER 40

Once again living a life of leisure, I drove toward a small town west of Ann Arbor on a sunny October afternoon in pursuit of an orchard that sold fresh-pressed apple cider. Trees costumed in bright hues of orange, red, and yellow lined the road with their leaves piled in heaps on still-green lawns. Raking leaves had always seemed a pointless task to me, and one I hadn't engaged in since I'd been forced to as a child. As if to prove my point, a gust shook the trees and deposited a fresh layer on the ground.

Ahead, an old Volkswagen bus sat near the road. "For Sale," written in white paint, spanned its windshield. I had a déjà vu of finding my first VW in New Mexico and pulled off on the shoulder. A quick walk around it and a peek underneath told me this wasn't the one. Rust had eaten holes in the rocker panels, fender wells, and floor pan. The culprit was salt. Michigan salted its highways to melt ice throughout winter, which inevitably made cars rust. To find an older vehicle without rust, one needed to look in Southern states that didn't salt roads.

I got back in the car and proceeded to the orchard, where I bought a gallon of cider and a dozen fresh donuts. I asked for a plastic cup and carried my purchase to a picnic table outside. The day was sunny but crisp. I filled my cup and took my first sip. Autumn bliss. I opened the bag of donuts and ate one.

I finished my second cup of cider and a third donut while thinking about the VW bus. That one would be too much work to restore. In Florida, though, I'd seen twenty-year-old vehicles in better condition, and the idea of snowbirding again began to take shape. I'd put up with two decades of icy Michigan winters, but there wasn't a damn reason to do it anymore. Plenty of retirees migrated south in November and didn't return until April or May.

Wait. Retiree? Was that what I was? I guess so. In my mind, I felt 25, but my Medicare card meant I was 65.

But Florida would have to wait. Nora and Tom had been married for fifty years, and she planned a big anniversary party for Thanksgiving weekend when everyone would be home, anyway. It was a grand affair, held at the Moose lodge, with a champagne fountain and a slide show of their kids growing up. Patty's husband acted as DJ and played dance music from the '40s and '50s, though where he found those old songs I couldn't guess.

I sat with Tommy Jr. during dinner and told him my plan to winter in Florida. He agreed to check on my house from time to time.

The morning after the party, Sophie and Patty went shopping, and Tom took his sons to look at bass boats, which he had decided would be his and Nora's fiftieth anniversary present to themselves—well, himself, but Nora didn't seem to mind. He invited me along, but I declined, preferring to have time alone with Nora. She'd quit the "happy pills," shifting her focus to the grandchildren her youngest sons had given her. Tommy Jr. had yet to settle down, and I'm sure she blamed my influence.

I hung my coat on a hook by the door and hugged her. She'd made coffee and served it in the living room. We sat on the sofa so we could set our cups and saucers on the coffee table, but this required us to turn sideways to face each other.

"So, you're taking up fishing?" I said.

Nora rolled her eyes. "Tom is."

"Did you ever read that book by Betty Friedan that I gave you?"

"Sophie and I both did. We talked about it, and the author was definitely describing us, the housewives of the 1950s. But Gizmo, Sophie and I never wanted to rock the boat. You were always the one to leap overboard and swim the other way. That just wasn't either of us."

"No, but your shrink pushing pills had me seriously worried."

"We eventually figured that out." She patted my hand. "I know you tried to help, but our problems were beyond your solutions. Women in my day decided in high school what their life was going to be and then had to live with it. We made our choices before women had choices."

"But this is a new millennium. Women can and do make their own choices."

"Like what? Divorce Tom and live on my own?"

"Of course not. I like Tom. But you could show a little more backbone. You don't have to accept a boat you don't want for your anniversary. You could buy him a fishing pole and he could give you something romantic—a necklace, maybe."

"Oh, Gizmo, I'm sorry Sparrow died so young. If you'd had forty or fifty years together, you'd have seen those aren't the things that matter."

I couldn't argue with that.

"Both Sophie and I eventually learned to accept that the men we'd married are the way they are, and to be contented. We're fine now, don't need the pills any more, and really don't want to change anything."

I shrugged. There was nothing I could say to that. I still had two days left here. I looked around Nora and Tom's, seeing if anything needed fixing, but found nothing.

Nora gathered our cups and saucers. "We can go Christmas shopping. There are big sales this weekend."

Since I planned to be in Florida at Christmas, I said, "Sure."

When the weekend was over, I returned to Ann Arbor and winterized my house, shutting off and draining the water and pouring antifreeze in the traps. Then I headed to Florida the first week of December.

I exited I-75 at Gainesville, planning to visit my old haunts. They were hard to find. Two-lane roads to the nearby towns of Archer and Newberry were now four-lane and lined with apartments and shopping centers. Hippie-owned shops and restaurants were gone. But men sporting gray-haired ponytails could still be found at free Friday night concerts.

People I'd known in the seventies were now in their late fifties or sixties, and the majority had moved elsewhere. But Gainesville was still a friendly town, and I had no problem finding old friends and making new ones. I rented a room from a Hare Krishna couple. It wasn't my thing, but they supported my intention to meditate.

My sisters pressured me to come for Christmas, but I'd just gotten to Florida and begged off. They weren't happy about it. I pointed out that their husbands also had retired and they could spend winters in Florida as easily as me.

Nora sniffed. "You don't have kids. We want to be near ours."

"What are you talking about?" I said. "Tommy Jr. has lived in Ann Arbor for over twenty years. That's over 400 miles from you."

Sophie was on the extension. "Eddie and I don't have the kind of money you do. We can't afford to keep two places."

Somehow, they had the wrong impression of my net worth. When the dot-com bubble burst, it wiped out my stock options. Not that I was poor. I'd invested my pension, but I lived off my monthly Social Security.

"Florida is cheaper," I said. Of course, my sisters weren't about to move in with some Hare Krishnas.

Neither of us persuaded the other. I did call them on Christmas day and talked with everyone in turn. The call lasted for a half hour.

The week after Christmas, I found a thirty-year-old mint-green VW Westfalia for sale in Leesburg—about two hours south of Gainesville. It had no rust, but the engine and interior needed work. I spent the rest of the winter rebuilding it. When I finished, it was good as new.

Easter 2001 fell on April 15, so everyone had an extra day to pay their income tax. Not that it mattered to me. My lump sum payout had withheld the taxes, so I didn't owe the government anything more. My sisters called and said I owed them a visit. With the restoration on my camper complete, she was ready for her maiden voyage.

The north still wasn't warm enough for me yet, but the tulips in bloom were lovely. Eddie hassled me for buying another German VW. "Why not a Winnebago? They're made right here in Iowa."

"I don't need a big RV," I said. "Besides, I can fix a VW engine myself."

My brother-in-law was always a die-hard "buy American," but being mechanically minded himself, he conceded my point. "I can't fault you for that. Nowadays, every car has computer chips and electronic whatnots. I had to pay the Ford garage a hundred bucks to stick a plug into a jack to diagnose my last car."

Memories of my carefree hippie days had brought on a case of wanderlust. I asked Tommy Jr. to keep watch on my house in Ann Arbor a little longer and told the Krishna couple in Florida to rent my room to someone else. On a cold, rainy Tuesday, I kissed my sisters goodbye and set out for warm, sunny California.

CHAPTER 41

My first stop was San Francisco. I'd done my Air Force training across the bay southwest of Oakland, but that was long before San Francisco became a hippie haven. By 2001, Haight and Ashbury were tourist traps, and the Grateful Dead were dead—or at least Jerry Garcia. It wasn't that warm there, either. So I rode a cable car because that's what one does, checked out City Lights Bookstore, and meandered south to Palo Alto and then Santa Cruz.

From there, I drove the Pacific Coast Highway to Big Sur and stopped at the Esalen Institute. Esalen had been a hip place in the sixties, and I remembered Sparrow had mentioned being there. That made me nostalgic. They had a restaurant that had a beautiful view and served delicious vegetarian food.

The rest of the summer, I visited National Parks, and camped in those that had vacancies. I hadn't considered that I'd need a reservation to camp, and they were surprisingly full. I will say that every National Park stunned me with its unique beauty, and I understood immediately why someone had decided a particular area was worthy of becoming a National Park.

How different life was now from my vagabond youth. Instead of pay phones requiring a handful of dimes, email and my BlackBerry kept me in almost constant contact with my family. The internet enabled me to check camping availability ahead once I caught on to the trick. And any parts I needed for my VW were only a FedEx shipping charge away.

The house in Ann Arbor had sat empty for over a year now. I decided to rent it out, but not to undergrads. West Park was a quiet area, and I didn't want complaints from the neighbors. My ideal tenant would be a married graduate student or doctor doing a residency at UM.

I returned to Michigan in August and spent a month converting the stand-alone garage. I insulated the whole building. The upstairs storage loft became a studio apartment. Downstairs, I added a bathroom with a shower and built cupboards to store my books, records, and tools. I put a braided rug over the concrete floor and added a couple of chairs that could easily be taken out if I needed to work on the VW.

The whole project was finished by the end of August. I moved in what I wanted to keep, then held a yard sale and sold the rest. Except for Sparrow's orgone accumulator. I hadn't been able to bring myself to use it after she was gone, but I couldn't let it go. But it was too large to move on my own, so I asked Tommy to help me carry it to the garage.

"It isn't fair to ask you to keep checking my place while I'm gone," I said.

"I don't mind—we're family."

"Well, I know you're busy. I've contracted a property management company to rent the house, exclusive of the garage. They'll collect the rent, deposit it into my account minus their fee, and handle any maintenance."

We tipped the accumulator on its side to finagle it out the door. Then Tommy carried one end and I the other.

"What's this thing do, anyway?" he said.

"Recharges a person's orgone energy."

Tommy rolled his eyes. "You sound like Uncle Eddie."

Ouch. "Once we get it into the garage, you can try it if you like."

"Maybe some other time," he said.

After Tommy left, I decided I'd try it myself for the first time in years. I sat inside for well over a half hour, but didn't experience the streaming

I once had. Maybe I hadn't given it enough time to build up a charge, or maybe I was holding on too tight to memories of having made it for Sparrow.

With my house now in the hands of the management company, I decided to take the long way to Florida. My plan was to enter Canada at Detroit, drive to Niagara Falls, then cross into New York state, camp in the Allegany National Forest, and eventually wind my way through the national forests in Pennsylvania and Virginia. If I timed it right, I should be driving through fall colors most of the way.

Well, the trip started okay. I had a pleasant drive through Ontario, spent the night, and saw Niagara Falls from the Canadian side. Its thunderous roar filled the ear, and the nightly illumination dazzled. Truly a wonder. One could take a boat ride right up to the falls from either side. I planned to wait and take the one that departed from the American side.

In the morning, I decided not to bother cooking. So, I closed up the camper and drove to a restaurant near the border crossing where I ate pancakes with genuine Canadian maple syrup. After a final cup of coffee, I entered a never-moving line of cars that seemed to stretch forever. After fifteen minutes, I turned off the engine to save gas.

My BlackBerry rang. It was Nora. "Gizmo! Are you all right?"

"Other than being backed up in traffic, I'm fine. How are you?"

Nora started to cry, which scared me. "I'm so relieved. Tommy Jr. said you'd gone to New York."

"I'm trying to, if this line ever starts moving."

"Don't!"

"Why not?"

"Airplanes are bombing New York or something. This could be Pearl Harbor all over again."

"Nora, Nora, calm down. What are you talking about?"

"Haven't you been watching the news? It's on all the channels."

"I never watch the news."

"Well, you should. They've taken out two or three skyscrapers in New York City, just like Kamikazes in World War II."

What! "No shit!"

"Stay where you are and don't go there. . . By the way, where are you?"

"Niagara Falls, Canada."

"Canada?"

"Yeah, I'd never seen the falls. It's amazing. You and Tom should drive over and see it."

"We're not going anywhere," Nora said. "Our country might be at war. And you should get back home right away."

Always the big sister, giving orders. Still, this sounded serious.

"It doesn't look like anyone here is going anywhere anytime soon." Just then, I saw two uniformed border patrol officers wearing Smokey the Bear hats walking down the line of cars, speaking to the drivers. Cars started to creep forward. "Oh, Nora, it looks like we're finally moving. I'll phone you after I cross the border. Call Sophie and let her know I'm fine."

When one of the officers reached my van, I rolled down my window. "Border is closed," he said. "Follow the other cars. There's a place ahead where you can turn around."

"Closed for how long?" I said. "What time will you reopen?"

He shook his head. "I don't have that information. All I know is there was a terrorist attack this morning. The President was removed to a secure location, and the Vice-President is in charge. But, to be honest, I don't expect he'll let anyone in the country today. The entire nation is on high alert."

That *really* didn't sound good. I could return to the campground and wait for the situation to get sorted out, or drive back to Windsor, where I'd entered Canada, and try to cross there. It had been straight forward when I came over. The Ambassador Bridge spanned the Detroit River, and the border was just a sign halfway across that said, "Entering Canada," or "Entering United States," depending on which direction you were going.

When I restored the camper, I'd splurged on an audio system that played both cassettes and CDs. It also had an AM/FM radio that I seldom used. I ejected the tape I'd been listening to before Nora's call, and tuned-in a local radio station. I quickly realized they weren't telling me any more than the border patrol had. So I put the tape back in and headed for Windsor.

The trip back took less than four hours, but the Detroit border was closed, too. I guess Cheney had locked down the entire nation.

Instead of camping, I rented a motel room so I could watch television. I telephoned my sisters and Tommy Jr. to let everyone know I was stuck in Canada but okay. At 8:30 that night, President Bush addressed the nation from the oval office. He pretty much recapped what the news had been showing on a continuous loop since I checked in: two jetliners crashing into the World Trade Center towers, causing the buildings to collapse. He said, "America was targeted for attack because we're the brightest beacon for freedom and opportunity in the world." That didn't sound to me like a reason for an attack. But he also said, "The functions of our government continue without interruption. Federal agencies will be open for business tomorrow." I hoped that included the border.

The next morning, I woke up early and checked out, hoping to be first in line at the border. Boy, was I wrong. All lanes were backed up as far as I could see. The good news was they were moving—like turtles, but moving. Fortunately, the camper was stocked for a long trip, so between the stop-and-go intervals, I made and ate a sandwich.

It was past noon before I reached the actual border station. An immigration officer came to my window. "Passport."

"I don't have one, never did." Back then, you didn't need a passport to enter Canada or Mexico, and the only place I'd been outside the US was Korea. The Air Force didn't give out passports. They just flew us in and out through military bases.

"Driver license," he said.

I handed it to him.

He studied it for a moment. "Where were you born?"

"Iowa."

"Pull over there and get out of the vehicle." He pointed to an area of marked parking spaces.

Two customs officers exited a gray building and told me to sit on a bench. For the next thirty minutes, they searched every nook of the camper, even the engine compartment. Which was ridiculous. I was a sixty-six-year-old retiree, not a student smuggling pot. Maybe it was the Peace symbol decal on the front of my microbus.

Finally, one of the men said, "Come with me." He led me inside and put me in a room with a table and two standard government-issue straight-back chairs. "Have a seat."

His partner walked in carrying the lockbox, which held my important papers. I tracked my bank accounts and investments in Quicken, but since I traveled most of the year, I kept paper records like my vehicle title and bank statements with me.

"Open it," the man said.

I fished out my key ring, inserted a small brass key, and turned it. The lid popped open.

He emptied the contents on the table and slid a yellowed drawing toward me—the plans for the orgone accumulator. Jeez, I didn't even know that was in there. Why in the world was I carrying that with me? Then again, it'd been forty-five years since the government had burned Reich's books. They couldn't possibly still care about him, could they?

"What's this for?" the man said.

I realized they didn't know or care about orgone, and trying to explain Reich's theories would just complicate things. "What's it look like?"

His partner smirked. "An outhouse."

I saw that made sense from his perspective. I'd best go along with it. "Sure. Primitive campsites in National Forests don't have bathrooms. A fellow might need to build his own privy."

What other extraneous paperwork was in there? I hadn't looked through it in years. I fished through the papers scattered on the table and found my birth certificate. "Here! Look at this." Beneath that were my Air Force discharge papers and Defense Department security clearance. Cripes, what was I carrying that around for?

I handed him those and started putting everything else back in the box. "You're hassling a Korean War vet with a long-standing high-secrecy clearance. I own a house in Michigan, and I'm going there now." I reached over and took my military papers and birth certificate out of his hand.

He nodded, and they sent me on my way. I felt the gratification Woody must have felt after he freed us from the FBI.

The first thing I did after I got to Ann Arbor was to apply for a passport. The State Department wasn't quick, especially then, and I had to wait until almost Christmas for it to arrive. Good thing I had my little studio loft to stay in. The couple renting my house was friendly, but busy. She was doing her residency in urology at UM, and he was a computer science theorist for an automotive semiconductor company based in Ann Arbor. We didn't see much of each other, but when we did, he and I talked about how different the circuits he developed were from those I'd designed long ago in Massachusetts. When he learned I held the patent on the hard drive controller chip, he was impressed, even though more advanced chip techniques had replaced it. "We studied that design when I was in school," he said.

Way to make a guy feel old.

Since I hadn't left for Florida yet, my sisters insisted I come for Christmas. Tommy Jr. wanted us to fly there, saying he couldn't afford the time off to drive. We'd flown there many previous years, so I agreed. Neither of us were prepared for what that involved. After 9/11, as the September attack was being called, airport security screening had gotten intense. Lines at the Detroit Metro airport wound between cattle gates around and around the airport. I had my shiny new passport, but the recent hires of the newly formed Transportation Security Administration were poorly trained, and confusion ruled. It took Tommy and me four hours to cover about a hundred yards and go up an escalator to get to the security screening. Flights were delayed while every bag was searched. Our plane left without us and we had to be rebooked on a later flight. We grabbed subs at Subway, and Tommy called his folks to let them know we'd be late. We still had to change planes in Chicago, and who knew what that would entail?

"You know, if we'd driven your Caddy," I said, "we'd be in Chicago by now."

"I know," he said. "Remember when air travel used to be fun?"

"And easy," I said.

CHAPTER 42

Winter was full on by the time we returned from my sisters'. I took I-75 straight to Florida, foregoing the eastern National Parks and the Blue Ridge Parkway. I'd save those for warmer weather. But that didn't happen.

President Bush spent the year pushing Congress to pass the Patriot Act and drumming up support to declare war on Iraq. Fortunately, I was too old for the Air Force to recall me, regardless of my security classification. Still, everything felt unsettled, and the edges of my wanderlust were fraying. I stuck to family and familiar haunts.

In June 2004, Airstrikes in Fallujah killed dozens, even though a year earlier, Bush had declared, "Mission accomplished!" I'd had enough of waiting for the war to end and was ready to start traveling again.

I meandered north, taking my time. I skipped New York City, but visited Bethel. A sign said it was the site of Woodstock, and a number of aging or wannabe hippies were selling organic this-and-that in a farmer's market.

Continuing northward, I crossed into Massachusetts and decided to call on Mata Shanti. Her name wasn't on the mailbox, and the Om sign next to the door had been painted over. I figured since I was already parked in the driveway, I may as well knock.

A youngish mother, trailed by two small children, came to the door. Keeping the children behind her, she spoke through the screen door. "Yes?"

I gave her my most benign smile. "I'm looking for Mata Shanti. You might know her as Mrs. Woodbridge. She used to live here."

The woman relaxed and nodded. "We bought the house from her."

From her, not her estate, so she wasn't dead. "Do you know where she moved?"

She smiled. "Kimball Farms—an assisted living facility on Walker Street. That's off of US 7 just past where it merges with US 20."

I thanked her and left.

Finding the place was no problem, but I hadn't expected to find Mata Shanti living in an old folk's home. I never imagined her old. Maybe because I still felt like I was twenty inside.

I signed the guest register at reception. An eager young man pressed an information folder into my hand and offered me a tour in case I wanted to consider living there.

"No thanks," I said. "I'm just visiting someone."

"It's never too early to start planning," he said. "Our independent living apartments are connected to the main building by corridors, so residents never have to go outside during inclement weather."

My God, did I look that old? "Could you just direct me toward Mrs. Woodbridge's apartment?"

He pointed down a corridor. "It's the fourth door down that hall—the one with a Sanskrit symbol on it."

There was a button next to her door. I pressed it and waited. I pressed it again. A woman with short white hair, but the complexion of a thirty-year-old, opened the door. I folded my hands in the traditional Indian greeting. "Namaste, Mata Shanti."

She echoed the gesture. "Namaste." Then she waited.

"It's Gizmo. I built you an orgone accumulator once upon a time. I used to live at Woody's."

She held up her forefinger. "Come in. I have to put in my hearing aids." She turned and went into her bedroom. I entered her apartment and closed the door behind me. It was . . . nice. On my right was a small kitchen, and ahead was a decent size living room with a sliding glass door that led to an outdoor patio.

Mata Shanti reappeared at my elbow. "Now, who did you say you were?"

"Gizmo."

She smiled. "I remember. You came to my yoga studio."

I nodded.

"You spent the night. I seem to remember teaching you some Tantric yoga."

It was my turn to smile. "You did, and I never forgot it."

She patted my arm. "I'll make us tea. Let's sit on the patio."

The small patio only held a tiny table and two chairs. We sat in the warm sun and she served peppermint tea. Steam carried its fragrance into my nose as I lifted my cup to sip. "So, when did you stop teaching yoga?"

"I haven't. I teach a class here twice a week."

"No wonder you look so fit."

"You really meant, when did I give up my studio. Only five years ago. But for ten years prior, I struggled. An Indian yogi bought that old Jesuit monastery outside Lenox and turned it into an ashram and yoga teacher training center. That made it difficult for me to find new students. Also, keeping up the house and yard was getting to be too much—especially in winter when it snowed. So, I sold the place and moved here."

"It's nice," I said. Not that I could ever see myself in such a place.

I told her about my brief, tragic marriage to Sparrow. She seemed genuinely sympathetic. I brought up Woody.

A small smile played about her lips. "He had a mischievous nature. For instance, the moment he perceived someone thinking that he looked like Einstein, he'd casually mention, 'I dabbled in theoretical physics.'"

"Did he really?"

"Yes, but he wasn't Einstein. You know that, right?"

I laughed. "Of course not, if only because Einstein was dead. But Woody could talk about anything—physics, psychiatry, orgone, Zen. . . . He once gave me a Zen koan: 'Without the heavens, there are no stars. Without stars, without sun, without moon, what time is it?'"

Fine lines appeared around her eyes as they crinkled with amusement. "Have you figured it out?"

"The speed of light may be a constant, but time is merely a variable. Which actually *is* Einstein."

Her watch beeped. "Speaking of time, it's dinnertime in the main building. We can bring guests. Would you like to join me?"

"Do they have anything vegetarian?"

"I wouldn't live here if they didn't."

After dinner, I walked her back to her apartment, and she invited me to spend the night. "Is that allowed?" I said.

She pulled my head down and kissed me. "This is independent living."

I hesitated. "Mata Shanti, I haven't been with a woman since my wife died."

"And how long ago was that?"

"Eight years."

"You've grieved long enough. Don't get the idea that people in their seventies can't have fulfilling sex." And then she pulled me into her bedroom, and proved it.

The next morning, we shared a light breakfast. She had a class that morning, so we said our goodbyes and I left. Seeing Mata Shanti made me nostalgic, and I decided to go to Vermont and visit the site of Woody's old commune. I pictured the route clearly in my mind, but despite driving a dozen different National Forest roads, I couldn't find the cabin. I felt certain that I remembered the road, but where Woody's driveway should have been stood a white pine forest.

A forest ranger driving a dark green pickup pulled over next to me. "Lost?"

"I didn't think I was, but maybe I am. There used to be a cabin . . . I could swear the driveway was right here."

"Gone, and good riddance," he said. "Back when the park service first acquired that old place, they tried to use it for a ranger home, but too many hippies kept showing up. So they tore it down and let the forest take back the land."

Gone? The house Woody's grandfather built—leveled. A new generation of conifers towered where Sparrow and Woody, and a whole commune had once thrived.

I sighed.

"If you're looking for a place to camp," the ranger said, "your best bet is Greendale. All its sites are first come, first served, and check-out is two o'clock. So if you don't dawdle, you can probably get there when someone's leaving. Just follow this road to 100, and take that north to Weston."

I took his advice and got a site. After I set up camp, I opened my road atlas and studied New England. Sure, I had GPS, but I liked to spread out a map to see the big picture. Although I'd lived up here long ago, I'd never been to Maine—or seen a moose. I could drive across New Hampshire from Vermont and be in Portland in less than three hours. From there, I could head north until I reached moose country.

On the other hand, I could take my time, visit Concord, and camp in New Hampshire's White Mountain Forest, then cross into Maine. Since I was in no hurry, why not? The moose would still be there.

Then, I remembered Reich had a laboratory in Maine. And that set me wondering, was it still there?

Chapter 43

I turned on my laptop to find out about Reich's lab, but the White Mountain campground had no internet service. I had to drive to a town with a library that had internet-connected computers.

My web search turned up Rangeley, Maine, home to Orgonon, Wilhelm Reich's laboratory, which was now a museum. It was only a couple of hours northeast of the White Mountain Forest. I marked the route on my map with a marker.

The next day, I reached Rangeley late in the afternoon and stopped at a diner for directions to the museum. Driving west from town on Highway 16, I passed a golf course on my left. A little farther on, I saw a body of water, and just beyond it, Dodge Pond Road—Orgonon's address. I made a right turn and in less than a minute, came to a sign: Orgonon Wilhelm Reich Museum. I hardly believed it. Woody would have been amazed. He thought everything of Reich's had been destroyed, and here his work was being deliberately preserved. Of course, maybe that meant the authorities had decided it was harmless.

Given the way orgone had not exactly transformed my life, I wondered if they were right. It did make some difference, I suppose, but it hadn't saved Sparrow, hadn't given me yogic powers, and hadn't made me much of a living. In a way, coming here was like revisiting a fad of my youth.

Ahead was a flat-roofed stone building, unusual in Maine where peaked roofs are necessary to shed the 125 inches of annual snowfall. But according to the museum brochure, the flat roof provided Reich and fellow scientists an unobstructed view of "pulsatory movement of the atmospheric orgone energy." I wondered if the roof was accessible to the public. I'd seen those little pinpoints of orgone dancing in the clear azure sky after my first time in Woody's orgone accumulator.

The two-story building sat on a hill. On the right front side, an outdoor patio was supported by a fieldstone retaining wall about eight feet high. This wall gave the illusion that the building was three stories instead of two. A long stairway extended from ground-level past the patio, to a set of double doors on the building's main floor.

The museum was dark, obviously closed for the night. But I was here, so I might as well walk around the 175-acre grounds. Not far from the main laboratory building—now the museum—I came upon something that resembled an anti-aircraft gun from my time in Korea. An array of ten parallel hollow metal tubes of various lengths from 18 to 25 feet extended from a gun-turret-like, pivoting cast-iron frame, taller than I was. A wheel on one side changed the angle of elevation, allowing the tubes to be aimed at any particular point in the sky. Flexible metal hoses were connected to the rear of the tubes but led nowhere.

A groundkeeper approached. "We're closed. You'll have to come back tomorrow."

I pointed to the device. "Is that Reich's cloudbuster?"

He nodded.

"Does it work?"

"Not anymore. The trustees had me disable it after some college kids were caught horsing around with it. They had no idea what they were doing."

"Did you ever see it in action?"

He shook his head. "My predecessor did, though."

I pointed to my camper. "Would it be all right if I parked here for the night?"

He chewed his lip and looked like he was trying to find a way not to say *No.*

"It's completely self-contained," I said, "and I won't leave any litter, I promise."

"Well . . . camping isn't allowed."

"Aw, come on. Come see it. It's got its own little kitchen. Let me make you a cup of coffee. I'd like to hear about this place from someone who's grown up around it." I stuck out my hand. "Call me Gizmo."

He shook hands. "I'm Ron. What kind of coffee you got?"

"Chock Full 'o Nuts."

"Man, I haven't had that in years."

I raised the camper top and brewed a pot of coffee. Then Ron and I sat across from each other at the camper's little dinette and talked. I told him how I knew about Reich and orgone and how I'd tried selling accumulators in the Seventies.

"I never met Dr. Reich," Ron said. "He died before I was born. But his son Peter came here once or twice. Peter remembered going with Dr. Reich when they took the cloudbuster to Arizona. He was a boy at the time, but he wrote a book about it after he was grown."

"I'd be interested in reading that," I said.

"The museum bookstore might carry it, I don't know." Ron stood and shook my hand. He stooped down and stepped out of the van. "Thank you. I enjoyed the coffee and conversation, but I'm sorry. The trustees really don't want anyone camping here. I think you're harmless, but it could cost me my job."

"If I lower the top, it won't look like I'm camped, just parked here waiting for the museum to open."

"Well . . . if anyone asks, you can't say I told you it was okay."

"You haven't and I won't."

After Ron left, I closed the camper top, put out the lights, and sat on the bed to meditate. When I finished, I put an extra quilt on the bed so I wouldn't give my presence away by running the heater. I tucked myself in and slept for a couple hours until I had to go pee. Since I'd gotten older, my prostate had me waking up in the middle of the night, sometimes twice or more. I pulled on jeans, opened the side door, and looked for a convenient tree.

It was damn cold. Shivering, I stood next to a tall maple trying to finish, when a movement at the corner of the museum caught my eye. I hurriedly zipped my fly, hid behind the tree, and watched.

A short figure—maybe four foot eleven—slunk along the side wall toward the rear of the building. He had a slight build, like a twelve-year-old boy who hadn't gotten his growth spurt yet. Could be the groundskeeper's kid. His oversize red and gray plaid flannel shirt definitely belonged to a large man. The shirttail hung almost to the kid's knees, and the cuffs were rolled up three or four turns to make the sleeves fit. That was all I could see before he ducked around the back corner.

I stepped out of hiding and followed. Unlikely he'd tell anyone I was camping where I wasn't supposed to because he seemed to be up to something himself. By the time I reached the back of the building, he'd disappeared.

Though I was a trespasser myself, I felt an obligation to protect Reich's home from some prepubescent vandal or thief. I walked around the building, checking doors and windows. Everything was buttoned up tight, and there was no sign of the kid. I glanced toward the woods and decided he'd probably been sneaking home from somewhere and just using the grounds as a shortcut. I went back to bed.

Two hours later, my full bladder woke me again. Damn prostate. Or maybe it was the coffee before bed. I found the same maple and was doing my business when I see the kid slinking away from the museum. What had he been doing in there for the last two hours? And how did he get in if everything was locked? I didn't know, but I was going to find out. With a dozen giant strides, I came up behind him, clasped him in a bear hug, and lifted his feet off the ground.

He kicked, squirmed, and fought, but I held on. It wasn't difficult. Beneath that bulky shirt, he couldn't have weighed over seventy-five pounds. Holding him from behind, I saw he was bald, like kids with cancer undergoing chemo. I felt bad for him, then.

"Listen, I'm going to let you down. Don't run away. I'm not going to hurt you. I just want to know what you're doing out here in the middle of the night. You can talk to me."

He stopped wiggling and nodded. I lowered him to where his feet touched the ground and let him loose, but kept a grip on one of his arms. "What's your name?"

He turned around and I could see the gauntness in his face. "Zytt."

God! I remembered how bad it felt being called Sven the hen and worse. "Is zit what the other kids call you?"

"It is my name."

"Your folks must have really hated you."

He hesitated a while, looking me up and down. "Among my kind, it is a very honorable name."

"I don't know where you're from, but in America, a zit is a pimple."

"Zo what you half me do, change my name?"

"If it were mine, I'd do it in a heartbeat. Also, I'd work on that accent. You sound like one of the Katzenjammer Kids."

"Who's zat?"

"A newspaper comic strip when I was growing up. A long time ago. You've probably never seen it. The characters spoke with a German accent. Is that where your folks are from?"

He shook his head.

"Well, work on your English. The way you talk will give kids one more reason to tease you. And ever since 9/11, Americans are pretty paranoid about everyone who sounds foreign. You don't want someone to think you're a terrorist or a spy."

"And I should not zound like an alien?"

"Oh, definitely not an illegal alien."

"And what if I am one?"

It took me a moment to realize he'd spoken with the same flat, Midwestern accent I'd been told I possessed. "Wait! What happened to your accent?"

"You said get rid of it." He shrugged. "So I did."

"Just like that?"

He nodded. "English isn't that difficult. There are just a lot of flavors of it—a ridiculous amount, if you ask me. I've been speaking like recordings I heard of Reich. Now, I gather you want me to sound like you."

"That's . . . pretty amazing. By the way, my name is Gizmo."

"Isn't that a mechanical whatchamacallit? Pardon the technical term."

"It's a nickname. My, you pick up things quickly."

"Thank you. Can you let go of my arm now?"

I did. "Sorry. So, what are you doing out here by yourself?"

"I could ask you the same thing."

"Yeah, but I'm not a kid."

"Neither am I. I'm just shorter than you. Now, tell me how you came to be here tonight. No one is ever here at this hour."

All right, maybe he wasn't as young as he looked. I'd heard chemo could stunt kids' growth. He could be a student with a summer job as a night watchman—though Ron hadn't mentioned there being any guards.

"Truth is, I'm waiting for the museum to open in the morning," I said. "I've always admired Reich, and wanted to see it."

He looked like he was raising his eyebrows, but he didn't have any. The chemo had cost him those, too. "You've studied Reich's work?"

"Some, yes. I've read all of Reich's books I could find. If you work here, then you know about orgone and Reich's orgone accumulator?"

Zytt nodded.

"I used to make accumulators for other people. Now that I'm retired, I thought I'd visit his laboratory to learn more than was in the books. And I'm glad I did. For instance, I'd only read about the cloudbuster until Ron. . ." Oops, I'd let his name slip out. I hoped Zytt didn't catch that. "Too bad it's been disconnected. I'd love to see how it operated."

Zytt sneered. "Way too well. They should have disabled it sooner."

"You don't believe in orgone?" I couldn't imagine anyone working here who didn't.

"Oh, I do. But it's like your Einstein is alleged to have said about the Manhattan Project, 'monkeys striking matches.' Look how that turned out."

I was a little shocked at the hostility. "It's easy for kids nowadays to judge. But I'm old enough to remember the horrors of World War II and the swift end the first atomic bomb brought to it."

Zytt shrugged. "Yeah, second bomb, actually. But that wasn't my point. Humanity finally discovers the connection between energy and matter, and what's the first thing you do with it? Use it to blow things up."

"Kids say that now, but you wouldn't even be here if it wasn't for my parents' generation."

"No. I wouldn't even be here if it wasn't for Reich's cloudbuster."

What the hell did that mean? Was he blaming it for his cancer? "Aren't you cold? I am. Let's talk in my camper."

He hesitated. Probably his folks had warned him not to get in vans with strangers. "Yes. All right."

I opened the passenger door for him. "We'll have to sit up front. The seats in the back are folded down for sleeping."

Even though it was a big step up, he hopped in with the agility of youth. I walked around and got in the driver's side.

"Have you really built orgone accumulators?" he said.

"Well, it's almost a decade since I last made one, but I still have the plans and the know-how."

"Could you build one for me?"

"Sure. I guess."

"Great. Then I wouldn't have to come here anymore."

"Wait, that's why you're sneaking into the museum? To sit in the orgone accumulator? I didn't know they still had one. Woody told me the Feds chopped them up with axes."

"I wasn't around then," Zytt said. "But there's one on display, and my nightly sessions in it are what's keeping me alive."

I'd read that one of the FDA's big beefs with Reich was that they thought he was selling accumulators for cancer treatment. I'm sure he wasn't, and I knew from Sparrow's experience it failed as a miracle cure. But obviously, this poor kid thought it was helping him. If it was, I didn't see how I could refuse. "All right. I'll buy the materials and make you one before I leave Maine. Tell me where you live."

He opened the door and pointed to the starry sky.

I laughed. "Bullshit."

"You don't believe me?"

This bald-headed joker might have cancer, but he wasn't above having a laugh at an old man's expense. Probably the only fun he had in the children's cancer hospital. "Close the door. You're letting the cold in."

He shook his head. "Gotta go now. I'll tell you more tomorrow night."

"I don't think the museum will let me stay here twice. It was a bit of a trick this time."

"Meet me at the property entrance tomorrow at closing. I really need you to build me an orgone accumulator." With that, Zytt jumped to the ground and vanished into the night. I shut the passenger door and returned to bed, feeling sorry for the poor kid. If he believed orgone helped his cancer, I'd make him an accumulator. But I wanted his parents' okay first. And why meet at night? The only explanation I could think of was that he must undergo chemo treatments during the day.

CHAPTER 44

Long before the museum opened, I was up, dressed, and ready, leaving no sign that I'd spent the night. I'd had coffee and a quick bowl of granola for breakfast, then drove out to the road and back so there would be fresh tire tracks in the dew-covered road. Ron had done me a favor by letting me stay, and I didn't want to get him in trouble. A long set of steps led up to a pair of wooden doors.

A sign said the museum opened at 1:00 p.m. Ron could have told me that. I could've slept in.

I drove back out and found the Oquossoc campground halfway between Rangeley Lake and Mooselookmeguntic Lake, whose name sounded like a promising place to see a moose. The camp offered large wooded camp-sites, electrical hookups, and public bathrooms with hot showers. I regis-tered for one night.

Oquossoc was a small village within greater Rangeley, but it had its own post office and a grocery store. I stopped there and restocked my larder.

I took my time getting back to Orgonon, yet I was still early. I'd been wait-ing half an hour when a lady arrived and unlocked the doors.

"It's not quite opening time yet," she said, "but come in anyway."

Through the doors, I entered a long hallway. "This building is the Orgone Energy Observatory, where Dr. Reich did his research and had his office and library. On your right is his laboratory. Let me turn on the lights."

The walls were knotty pine, and the ceilings were plywood. Not a style you see much anymore, but popular in the North during the 1940s. I'd seen it in older cabins and motels in Upper Michigan and Canada. Evidently, it was also common in Maine. Large windows gave me a view of a good portion of Orgonon's campus. There was a pond at the far end.

The woman's voice jarred me out of my reverie. "Stairs at the end of the hall lead to the upper level, where Dr. Reich's study, library, and laboratory instruments are preserved as they were in his time. On the top of the building, there is an observation deck with views in all directions and a room Dr. Reich used as an art studio."

"I knew he explored multiple science disciplines, but I didn't know he dabbled in art," I said.

"Oh, yes. He was a man of varied interests. We have some of his paintings and one of his sculptures on display here in the museum. I have to make some calls, but feel free to look around."

I wandered upstairs and into his study, with his lab instruments. I recognized the orgone accumulator right away and compared its construction to my own efforts. Satisfied that I'd done a decent job replicating the master's plans, I was tempted to sit inside, but a velvet rope blocked its door, so I moved on. Several oscilloscopes and other electrical instruments preserved from his time were definitely relics of an earlier period and would have made good props for a 1950s movie. With his genius, I had to wonder what he might have accomplished with twenty-first-century technology.

Display boards held photos and explanations of his many discoveries and experiments. An extensive library covered one wall. On his desk was an autographed photo of Sigmund Freud with a personal message to Reich.

I climbed out on the roof and gazed at the sky, hoping perhaps to see little orgone particles dancing in the sky above Orgonon. Nothing, not even here.

The woman in charge stuck her head up. "Please come back inside. There's no railing, and the museum could be liable if you fall."

"Of course." I followed her back downstairs to the first floor.

Across the hall from the laboratory was a kitchen, bathrooms, and another room.

"That's where Reich's son played while his dad worked," she said. "The property has one cabin, which was used by the immediate Reich Family as a residence. The doctor stipulated in his will that it should be made available to needy children. The trust managing the property donates use of this cabin for four weeks every summer to needy families."

"The caretaker said you have books for sale."

"Yes, our bookstore has reprints of most of his works. While he was imprisoned, nearly six tons of his books and notebooks were ordered banned and burned. Whether they believed his theories or not, they shouldn't have burned the books. That's just un-American."

I couldn't disagree. "Well, I'm glad you're able to print them again. Is it all right if I look through what you have?"

"Oh, please do."

I spent the rest of the afternoon browsing through his books. I'd inherited original editions of some from Woody. Several were still in my camper library. "I don't see *Contact with Space*," I said. That seemed odd because it was specifically about the cloudbuster sitting outside the museum.

"No, that's one of the burned books we never reprinted."

Eddie had given me a copy eighteen years ago. I couldn't remember if I had it with me, so I went out to check. There it was, tucked in a small compartment between Reich's *The Function of the Orgasm* and Robert Heinlein's *Stranger in a Strange Land*. I brought it back inside and showed her. "Here, you're welcome to copy this one."

She held it gingerly. "Wow! An original CORE Press limited edition—very rare, indeed." She gently leafed through the pages and then handed it back to me. "Thank you for showing me that. I don't need to copy it. The trust has it in the archives at the Center for the History of Medicine Library at

Harvard. I don't know if they plan to reprint it, though, so take good care of yours."

The afternoon had flown by, and it was nearly closing time. I looked through the bookstore offerings. There were so many more than Woody had left me. Now that I knew where to order them, I limited myself to two. *The Bion Experiments—on the Origin of Life* sounded intriguing. For something lighter, I chose an autobiographical account of his friendship with A. S. Neill, a progressive educator whose ideas had been very popular with my hippie friends in the 1970s.

She locked up and asked if I'd been to Reich's tomb. I hadn't.

She pointed at a stone structure down the hill from the museum. "There is a bronze bust of Dr. Reich on top, cast from a clay sculpture Jo Jenks created of him in 1949."

I dropped my purchases in the camper and walked to his tomb. It matched the flagstone of the main building, and from its large slab top, the face of a serious scientist stared down at me.

A chilly breeze blew from the pond. Odd occurrence for mid-July, but maybe not for Maine. I silently thanked his effigy for his work and walked back to my van.

The docent locked up the museum, and waved at me as she drove away. I got back in my VW and followed her out to the sign where I'd promised to meet Zytt. He wasn't there yet, so I picked up what I now knew to be my rare copy of *Contact with Space*. I'd started reading it years before on a flight to Detroit, but never finished it. I knew this because my place was bookmarked with an empty airline peanuts bag.

The book described Reich's scientific expedition to southern Arizona to test the ability of his cloudbuster to turn the desert green using the newest developments of cosmic orgone engineering. In it, he offered a natural scientific explanation of the metabolism of the life energy, the nature of primal vegetation, and the nature of the death of vegetation to cause desertification. He referenced an experiment six years prior, testing the interaction of orgone with radioactivity, which had produced profoundly detrimental consequences he named DOR, for deadly orgone radiation.

In Arizona and New Mexico, he was unpleasantly surprised to spot the effects of DOR on the mountains, rocks, and soil. Driving into the desert valley of Alamogordo, New Mexico, Reich's team encountered a layer of DOR in the atmosphere several hundred feet high. He wondered if nearby White Sands Proving Ground was attracting DOR. The book described the area mountains as looking "eaten up" by DOR, with jagged, barren, deep ravines lacking any vegetation.

I'd become lost in reading when the passenger door opened and Zytt pulled himself up and into the seat. "Can we go someplace and talk?"

"How about your parents' house?"

"If I could do that, I wouldn't need you."

"Look, I'm uncomfortable driving an unaccompanied minor around without his parent's permission."

"First, I'm not a minor. Second, they'd gladly give you permission if they could. Now, if we can go somewhere and talk, all will become clear to you."

I didn't like it one bit, but sitting on the side of the road was just as risky. The problem was two-fold. I wasn't familiar enough with the area to suggest a place, and I had no idea what he was up to. He could be running away—from his parents, his doctors, and all the needles. I couldn't blame him, but that didn't mean I wanted to get caught helping him.

As if he could see my unspoken objections, he said, "There's a boat ramp on Mooselookmeguntic Lake that's closed this time of night, and orgone around that lake is profuse."

He spoke with an authority and insight I hadn't often seen in minors. And I had to give it to him, he was really into orgone. Maybe on the way there, I could trick him into showing me where his family lived.

I started the engine and put it in gear.

CHAPTER 45

I parked in an area next to the boat ramp and turned to Zytt. "Satisfied?"

He threw open his door and jumped to the ground. "Let's go down by the water. Orgone is stronger there."

I glanced around, praying some forest ranger or deputy sheriff wouldn't roll up and arrest me for kidnapping. No one did, and Zytt was already standing at the water's edge.

When I joined him, he said, "Okay, listen, I've a good intuition, and though I have no logical reason to back it up, I think you can be trusted with what I am about to tell you."

"I'm sure you can."

"What Reich called orgone has been known by many names. The Chinese call it chi, in India they call it prana or Shakti—"

"I know," I said. "I practice pranayama meditation, and I've met gurus who could channel it."

Zytt nodded. "Good, okay, good, you're confirming my intuition. Then are you also aware that this life energy is consciousness?"

"Yes. Swami Muktananda called it chit-shakti—Conscious-energy." Again, this conversation was well beyond the level of a twelve-year-old. I began to see that I'd fixated on the idea of a kid on chemo and blinded myself to the hints he'd been dropping.

Zytt did an excited little jig. "Good! Good. Then have you experienced it keeping you alive? That may make it easier for you to accept that I neither eat food nor sleep but live by this energy alone."

My mouth dropped open. Okay, he'd just shifted back from reasonable adult to delusional pre-teen.

He grabbed my arm. "Listen, I became stranded without access to my normal resources, which is why I had to use Reich's accumulator every night, primitive though it is." His bony little fingers dug deeper. "You said you can build orgone accumulators."

I pried his grip from my arm. "I haven't made one since my wife died, but yes, over the last thirty years I've made many, and had no complaints."

Zytt inhaled and exhaled several deep breaths.

I waited.

"I have far to travel, and I can't do so without a portable orgone accumulator we can carry with us."

"By 'we,' you mean your family?"

"No, I mean you and me."

There it was. He planned to run away. "Oh, hell no!"

"But Gizmo, you've got to. I have no other transportation, and I'm running out of time."

"Look, you have my sympathy. My wife died from a rare form of cancer. And if I am your only means of reaching some distant hospital, I'll drive you. But not unless one of your parents goes with us."

He sat on the break wall and patted it for me to sit beside him. "I have to remind myself, it's natural for you to be skeptical. But like I told you before, my parents aren't here."

"Well, who is taking care of you now—an aunt, an uncle, an older sibling?" I squatted down next to him. "I'm willing to make you a pint size accumulator, but some family member needs to accompany you across state lines. It can't be a strange man you met at a museum."

He met my gaze. "Again, good intuition. I trust you more than any other human."

"How can you say that? There are six and a half billion people on this planet."

"Actually, six point seven four eight and counting."

I scratched my head. "Maybe you can take the train." On second thought, that wouldn't work. The metal rail car would interfere with orgone accumulation.

"No. I have to travel incognito. You are my best hope." He took a deep breath and looked at the stars. "You said you accept that life force is conscious-energy?"

I nodded.

"And do you believe me when I tell you that I am living purely by that energy?"

Where was he going with this? "I guess so. I mean, in some sense, we are all alive by the flow of conscious-energy within us. Other than that . . ."

"Okay, I can work with that. Relax and let your mind be open to what I am about to say."

I flashed back to Hodae guiding my LSD trip.

"Not everyone sitting on this wall is from here."

"Well, I know I'm not."

"Neither am I, but even more so. That cloudbuster gadget outside the museum is also a 'Spacegun'—an extension of the cloudbuster. Reich used it in Arizona to disrupt the flight path of extraterrestrial ships. Recently, some idiot playing with the one outside the museum unintentionally disabled my vehicle. I ejected and it self-destructed. I've been hiding out since, hanging on by a whisker, but I can't wait much longer. I have to reach another ship. I've learned where one is, but I need you to get me there."

Now I knew I was tripping. "What did you say?"

"You heard me, Gizmo. I am not from your planet. And you need to make me an orgone box so I can survive the journey to the other ship."

Could I accept that I actually met an alien? No. I laughed. "You're just pranking an old man." But even as I said it, I knew he wasn't.

"I assure you I am not." He pointed up. "You see that faint star to the right of my finger?"

"Yes."

"That's not a star. It's a galaxy and my planet revolves around a sun on its far edge. I am almost two hundred by your years. Old enough not to need my parents' permission."

Oh, if only this would turn out to be a fantasy the kid dreamed up to cope with his chemo.

I made one last stab at denial. "And your planet just happens to speak English?"

"Of course not. I am fitted with a neural language processor. It's necessary for my job."

"I'd be interested in seeing that. Show it to me."

"I can't. It's a nano implant in the posterior superior temporal lobe of my brain."

He certainly knew medical terminology. "You said it was for your job. What's your occupation, and why are you here?"

"My field is xeno-anthropology. I'm a fellow with . . . well, the nearest earthling equivalent would be a university. My purpose is simply to observe. Over the last century, your species started creating dangerous, unnatural chemical combinations that have polluted every life form on your planet. None of that was our affair, but it was interesting to anthropologists such as myself. Was its cause corrupted synapses or just egotism gone awry?"

I shrugged. "What can I say? Greed makes men fools."

"So you're going for egotism. Then, about sixty-five years ago, humans started tinkering with nuclear fission. And what did they do with that knowledge?"

I was strangely embarrassed by my species. "Made bombs."

"Right. And nuclear explosions do more than blow things up. Their resulting radiation corrupts orgone into a noxious state."

I nodded. "Reich called it DOR, deadly orgone radiation."

Zytt frowned. "DOR is not only poisonous to all living forms, but it's also detrimental to what you humans consider inert matter."

"I was just reading about that before you came. Reich thought DOR had eaten away the ravines in New Mexico and Arizona."

"And the atmosphere, too," Zytt said. "Remember, matter equals energy. If you release the energy in uranium's nucleus and cause a chain reaction, you also tamper with the cosmic forces that make up its atoms."

"But Einstein said energy can neither be created nor destroyed."

"And he was right, but either state can be changed into a form with undesirable after effects."

"Such as DOR?"

"Yes. The first bomb test, Trinity, destabilized one of our craft and caused it to crash in New Mexico."

"You mean . . . Oh my God, the stories about the Roswell incident are real?"

"Well, yes, but I'm talking about an earlier crash in 1945. Roswell was the second. In both cases, your military recovered the ships and took them to study. Since then, our vehicles have been programed to eject the occupants and self-destruct on impact. That's why we can't just find mine and repair it."

Suddenly, it hit me. I was talking to a person—creature, whatever—who I apparently accepted came from another planet. It was true, everything that Reich had said. It was all true. Then I realized that a lot of what Eddie believed was true as well. The government really did have an alien spaceship in a warehouse somewhere.

I gripped the concrete break wall to reassure myself I was still in touch with some semblance of reality.

Carl Sagan had said that out of the trillions of galaxies, it was only logical to assume that Earth wasn't the only planet with intelligent life. But this little guy sitting next to me was . . . the most important thing that had happened to humanity. Of course, according to Eddie, it had happened hundreds or thousands of times before. Just not to me. I couldn't help feeling like the first pioneer stepping on a strange shore.

Although he claimed to be more than a hundred years my elder, his diminutive size gave me the urge to protect him like a child. The film *E. T.* came to mind. "Can't you just 'phone home' and have a ship sent to pick you up?"

"Intergalactic communications aren't something you can cobble together with parts from RadioShack," he said. "I understand that your military has a secret base out in the Nevada desert where they've stored the recovered vehicles. My only hope is to get to one of them and use its transmitter. Assuming I can get it working."

While the military had never let me in on its secret purpose, I had a pretty good idea the base he was referring to was the one I'd helped build. But I didn't tell him that. Besides, there was little chance we'd ever be able to talk our way onto it.

He gazed at me. Now that I had "spaceman" on my mind, I couldn't help but think of his eyes as somehow alien. Not that he looked like the bug-eyed grays in Eddie's tabloids. More like the little guys that came out of the ship in *Close Encounters*. His species so closely resembled ours that I'd previously attributed his facial differences to missing eyebrows, which I thought were due to chemotherapy.

"I'm trusting you," Zytt said, "because in my situation, I have to trust somebody."

I sighed. Okay, it was all true. I'd just have to deal with it. "I'll do what I can."

A fat tear leaked out of his left eye.

So aliens can cry. Interesting.

"First thing is for me to work on your orgone accumulator. Correct?" I said.

"Yes. Thank you."

We walked to my camper, where I took his measurements. The interior of an accumulator only needed to be a few inches wider than the person in it.

"This is the craziest thing I've ever done," I said. "But since we're doing it, come with me to the campground. There's no point in us having to rendezvous in the woods tomorrow. . . . Or do you need to recharge at the museum?"

He looked out at the lake wistfully. "I think I'll be all right for tonight."

Chapter 46

In the morning, I meditated and then made breakfast. Zytt wasn't kidding. He really never ate—not for the whole time I knew him. He was living proof that all the years I'd spent promoting orgone had validity. If everyone could live on prana as his species did, it would solve world hunger.

The first problem of the day was that all my tools were back in Ann Arbor. I'd been out of the accumulator building business so long I never traveled with them anymore. Did I know anyone in Maine who might let me use theirs? Maybe Ron.

I closed the camper top, disconnected the power, and told Zytt to stay in the back, out of sight. Not knowing how long this project would take, I stopped at the campground office and paid for an extra night.

We got to the museum before it opened. I'd counted on that. Ron was on a tractor mowing the lawn. I flagged him down and asked if he had a workshop I could use to cut some one-by-twos and mason board.

"I don't," he said. "But there is a cabinetmaker in Oquossoc—that's about four miles west on Route 16. He'll do it for cheap. Ask for Carl. Tell him I sent you." He gave me the address.

Back in the van, I made a cut list of finished lengths calculated to fit Zytt's measurements, then drove toward Oquossoc.

I passed the cabinet maker's place and had to make a U-turn. His shop wasn't on the main street, but in a repurposed carriage house behind his residence. I told Zytt to hide in the back while I talked to him. Other than the eyes he'd probably pass for an adolescent boy, but not if anyone looked closer, like I should have.

"When we're done here, remind me to buy you a pair of sunglasses."

An old man with sawdust on his trousers and a pencil behind his ear came out to see what I wanted. I showed him my list and explained I just wanted the pieces cut to the sizes indicated and asked how much he'd charge. "Ron sent me," I added.

Carl wiped his face with a bandanna. "I can rip some two-by-fours into one-by-twos, but I don't have any mason board."

"If you'll point me to a lumberyard, I'll buy everything and bring it back. I just need you to cut it."

He pulled the pencil from his ear and chewed on the eraser. "That mason board will dull my saw blade."

Well, I thought that was bullshit. I'd cut mason board many times. What was he angling for? "Haven't you got an old blade you can switch out to do the mason board?"

He finally admitted that it wouldn't be a problem, but he had other jobs ahead of mine.

"I really have to have these boards cut today. I'm staying out at the campground, and I need to check out tomorrow. What would it be worth to you to put this at the top of your list?"

"This for your camper?"

In a manner of speaking. But I wasn't going to lie, so I just dodged the question. "Well, I need it before I can leave."

We haggled a bit on the price—turned out that was what he was angling for—then I drove to the lumberyard he suggested and dropped everything back at his shop. While he cut the wood, I found a fabric store that sold wool batting. The steel wool and sheet metal I'd gotten at the lumberyard, but I didn't have my tin snips with me either, so I had to buy a pair.

Back at the campground, I laid everything out on the picnic table and began assembling. A light breeze picked up and made fastening the wool in place a challenge. I needed a third hand. And Zytt was right there, sitting at the dinette, watching me out the open door.

When I bought his sunglasses, I'd also gotten him a burgundy stocking cap to cover his head and ears. Time to try out his disguise. No one else was camped close to me, and I thought there'd be no problem.

"Put on your new hat and glasses and come help me."

His oversized checkered flannel shirt, watch cap, and sunglasses made a ridiculous combination, but definitely not alien.

With Zytt's help, we had the accumulator assembled before dark. I set it on the ground next to the rear wheel, and he got inside and closed the door. I made myself something to eat, took advantage of the campground showers, then read until bedtime. Zytt was still in the accumulator when I went to sleep.

I woke at first light, dreaming about the Roswell crash. I'd spent decades dismissing it as tabloid fodder and even now found it difficult to accept. I'd been stationed only a hundred miles from Roswell, and no one on the base ever spoke of it as being real. Yet, the skinny alien sitting at my dinette table watching me eat my breakfast shattered that myth once and for all.

I washed my cereal bowl and poured the remainder of the coffee pot into a travel mug. The morning was cool and damp. I checked the oil and the air pressure in all four tires. When I strapped the orgone accumulator on the back of the VW, we looked like *The Beverly Hillbillies*. But it would get us there.

Maine is so large that it took us four hours to reach Portsmouth, New Hampshire. In part, because I'd detoured to the L. L. Bean store in Freeport to buy Zytt some clothes that fit him, so he'd look less conspicuous. From Portsmouth, we crossed New Hampshire and Vermont to pick up the New York Thruway outside Albany. From there, I planned to follow I-90 through Pennsylvania, Ohio, Indiana, and Illinois. We could have saved a few miles and a lot of tolls if we'd cut across Canada to Michigan and taken I-94 to Chicago, but smuggling Zytt over the border seemed too risky.

Tired and hungry, I stopped for the night at a rest area on the Thruway that had parking spaces for RVs. I unstrapped Zytt's orgone accumulator and set it on the passenger side of the VW, out of sight from other vehicles. A cursory inspection told me it had fared well.

Too tired to cook anything elaborate, I made scrambled eggs. About an hour later, the side door opened and Zytt came in. I wasn't surprised. The average human stays in an orgone accumulator for only thirty minutes. The night I'd seen him at the Reich museum, Zytt had spent about two hours. Either he had a higher tolerance or needed longer sessions to make up for not eating.

He slid onto the dinette seat opposite me. "That orgone box stinks."

I'd built quite a few in my life and never had an unhappy customer. Of course, none of my customers had actual alien technology to compare it to. I closed the book I was reading. "Sorry. I did the best I could."

"Not your fault. The exhaust from your combustion engine fouled the box."

Oh. "I hadn't considered that. Leave it open a few hours to air out and try it again later. Tomorrow I'll strap it on the roof."

That worked better, and the next night he had no complaints. The downside was I couldn't raise the camper top without taking the accumulator off first. So, when I needed to get inside to make lunch or take a quick break, I had to scrabble around hunched over like a hermit crab.

Over the years, I've taken many long road trips—from the first one to Greenwich Village with Sparrow, to Florida with Sticks, several times to Miami with Cassandra, and a lot of car trips with Tommy. I'd found that conversing all day while the highway rolled under them was a great way for people to really get to know each other. Zytt and I were no exception, though it was entirely one-sided. He had the uncanny ability to keep me talking about myself while he revealed virtually nothing about himself. Did he have a wife or kids? Did everyone on his planet live only on orgone, or was he an exception? I never found out. Nor was he keen to share the technical workings of his species' spacecraft with an earthling—especially an engineer.

I had so many questions about space travel and aliens and well . . . the universe. But every time I pried into his life or planet, he'd skillfully redirect me back to my own story—perhaps due to his anthropological training. So, while we cruised along the interstates, Thruway, and turnpikes, I wound up telling him my life story from the beginning.

By coincidence, I reached the part about quitting the Texas engineering firm and moving to Pennsylvania just as we hit the Pennsylvania Turnpike.

"I suppose you had to get away from the DOR surrounding Alamogordo," Zytt said.

"No. I hadn't heard of orgone or DOR at that point. Our country was engaged in an unpopular war at the time, and I decided not to work for the military establishment anymore."

"That would be Viet Nam?"

I nodded. "It didn't work out the way I planned. I thought I was going to design systems for our space program, but my new employer put me on defense department work." I shrugged. "One good thing, that's when I met the woman who eventually became my wife."

"Oh?" Zytt said. "Tell me about her."

Chapter 47

We made good time on the toll roads. At first, the tollbooths worried me. Every time we stopped to pay a toll, I feared the toll collector would spot something odd about Zytt. But he kept his hat and glasses on, and I soon realized the toll booth workers didn't give a shit about the passengers in the cars.

My original impression of Zytt—that he was a kid on chemo—had fooled me in the dark, but it wouldn't hold up if some nosey sheriff wondered about a sixty-nine-year-old man taking a preadolescent boy across state lines. The safest thing would be to not get stopped.

As if my worries were a self-fulfilling prophecy, I awoke the third morning at a rest stop on the Ohio turnpike with two old busybodies threatening to report me to child services for abuse. "Keeping that boy in a dog kennel! You ought to be locked in one yourself," ranted an elderly woman, waving her cane.

Fortunately, Zytt was already inside the camper. I hurriedly lowered the roof and hefted the orgone box on top. "It's not a doghouse," I said, fastening the straps. "It's the boy's pretend spaceship. Do you have a problem with that?"

Her companion had his nose pressed to the camper's jalousie windows, but the curtains were still closed.

I grabbed his shoulder and turned him toward me. "Don't your grandkids ever play astronaut?"

He glanced toward the roof. "That doesn't even look like a space capsule."

"That's what imagination is for. I played cowboy riding a stick for a horse. Didn't you?"

He nodded and took the woman's arm. "Sorry. There's just so much about child abusers on TV and in the paper these days, it makes a person suspicious about anything out of the ordinary."

I put on a calmer face. "I'm sure you had the best intentions, but next time, please ask before tossing around accusations."

"Again, I apologize," he said. "Have a good trip and drive safe."

"You, too." I jumped in the driver's seat and left them in my rearview mirror.

Needless to say, I didn't want that to happen again. At the Toledo exit, I got off the turnpike and detoured an hour north to my garage apartment in Ann Arbor.

I let Zytt in and said, "This is my home base. I'm going shopping for a better disguise. Don't go outside. One of the tenants who rents my house is a doctor and will no doubt try to take you to the hospital for treatment. There's an orgone accumulator I built for my wife downstairs. You're welcome to use it."

I recalled seeing Tibetan monks who stood barely five feet tall. With the right clothes, Zytt could pass for one of them. My first stop was Jewel Heart, Ann Arbor's Tibetan Learning Center. I tried to buy a monk's robe from their store, but the earnest young clerk looked appalled. Apparently, robes were only for those who took vows. To appease him, I bought mala beads and a small bag embroidered with Tibetan symbols. I picked up a brochure advertising an upcoming lecture which had a photo of their Rinpoche.

"May I look at your phonebook?" I said.

In the Yellow Pages, I found a seamstress on State Street, and drove there.

I showed the Tibetan brochure to the proprietor. "How long would it take you to make a simple orange robe—like the Tibetans and Krishnas wear?"

"I don't know," she said. "Let me Google it." She searched her computer and then laughed. "They're just two long, hemmed cloth sheets with a couple of hooks and loops to keep the lower robe from blowing open. The upper part is really just an extra-long shawl." She walked into the back and returned in a moment. "I don't have any orange fabric in stock but, I have plenty of maize and blue. UM colors, you know."

I looked at the man pictured on the brochure. "Maize will do fine. What time can I have it?"

"Well, I need to finish another customer's job before I do yours. Come back at four-thirty?"

"Perfect."

In the meantime, I drove to my old company. The new management had instituted many changes. The first was a security desk where I had to sign in. Tommy also had a keeper, a stiff-neck secretary, who said, "He's with someone. Whom may I say is here?"

"His uncle."

She called him on the intercom, and seconds later, Tommy's door flew open. "Come in, come in. When did you get back?"

"Just today. Can we talk?"

Tommy turned to a young man seated across from his desk. "Fred, we'll pick this up tomorrow." Fred left and Tommy closed the door. He, too, had apparently changed, wearing a suit and tie every day, instead of just at conventions.

"Uncle Gizmo, I wish you'd let me know you were coming. I have business meetings every night, but let's go out Saturday."

"I need to leave before then, but I'd like you to do me a favor."

"Anything."

I took a sheet of paper from his desk and sketched out a plan. I wanted to install a digital camera and microphone outside my apartment, and connect them to a computer and modem. "I can do it with off-off-the-shelf components, but I need someone to write a piece of software to tie it all together."

"Sure. What's the functionality you're looking for?"

"Someone knocking, ringing the doorbell, or the sound of breaking glass would trigger a message to my BlackBerry. I could then dial in from a remote computer and see the video feed."

Tommy whistled. "This could be a whole new product line."

"Probably. And you're welcome to it. Since I travel so much, it will help me keep an eye on my place from wherever I am. I just need you to write me a few lines of code."

"Be glad to, although I don't think I can get to it myself until the weekend. I could have one of my programmers write the code this afternoon."

I bit my lip. "The fewer people who know how it works, the better."

"I get you," Tommy said. "To protect the patent, I'll make him sign a non-disclosure."

Truthfully, after the company claimed rights to my previous patent, I didn't give a fig about patents. I thanked him and left for the electronics store.

By the time I'd bought the parts, it was four-thirty. I returned to the seamstress and paid for the monk's robe. She showed me how to put it on.

Tommy sent a message to my BlackBerry. *The software is ready.*

I can swing by there before I go home, I responded.

I'll leave a disc for you at the security desk.

After I picked up the disc, I bought a sandwich, potato salad, and slaw from Zingerman's Deli—a place I used to frequent before I married.

At the apartment, Zytt was in the orgone accumulator. I ate first and then set up the cameras and computer. I installed the software and edited my BlackBerry number into the program code. Next, I coupled in a thermal imager for nighttime, and the microphone to sense sounds. Zytt came out and watched as I wired everything.

"What's this?" he said.

"Remote security. If the government comes looking for us, they'll probably start here since this is my address of record."

Before dark, I tested the camera. Zytt watched the computer screen while I went outside and approached the entry door. Once the sun set, I enabled the thermal sensor, which I had aimed at shoulder height so a stray dog or cat wouldn't accidentally trip it.

I walked outside and closed the door behind me. My BlackBerry buzzed. Its screen read, "IR 20:57."

"Open up!" I shouted.

Zytt opened the door.

"No, no, I didn't mean for you to do that."

"Then why did you shout?"

"It was a test." I showed him the BlackBerry screen, which now read, "Mic 20:58."

We walked over to the computer and brought up the video feed. The image wasn't great in the dark, but I hadn't wanted to install lights. Then, I thought, Why not? Many people put motion-sensor lights on their porches or garages. One more thing to do before we left. Fortunately, K-mart stayed open until ten.

When I returned with the light kit, my tenant's car was there. I knocked on their door and told them I was installing a motion sensor light on the garage so they'd know what was happening if it went on. "I travel so much and you both work."

The next morning, I started to explain to Zytt what Tibetan monks were, but it turned out he knew about them. So I showed how to put on his robe. I'd puzzled over what shoes were appropriate, but I'd seen Hare Krishnas wear Nikes, so I figured a Tibetan could, too. With his knit hat pulled low over his ears and big glasses, he looked at least a little Asian monkish.

"If anyone asks, I'm going to say your name is Lopsang Rimpoche. And if they ask you a question, answer them in Tibetan."

"Tibetan?"

"Doesn't your neural translator handle dozens of languages?"

"Nine hundred thousand."

"Surely, Tibetan is one of them."

"Ho yo ho," he said.

"What's that mean?"

"Yes, it is."

"Good. Then, let's hit the road."

Chapter 48

Since I-94 passed right by Ann Arbor, I decided to take it to Indiana instead of returning to the Ohio Turnpike. The busybodies had swallowed my lie, but I couldn't chance running into them. They'd already glimpsed Zytt. It'd be hard to convince them the same kid was now playing dress-up as a monk.

In Indiana, we switched to I-90 and followed that west. Our three-thousand-mile drive from Maine to Nevada took us a week, with nightly stops for me to sleep and Zytt to recharge in the orgone accumulator.

Now that he'd heard my life story and accepted that I wasn't some military-industrial-complex operative looking to exploit alien technology, Zytt became willing to share more. Still no personal details about life on his home planet, but about how some things worked, okay, since he knew that interested me.

"You have to understand my field is xeno-anthropology. So, my understanding of technicalities is vague—equivalent to asking one of your sociology professors how Apollo rockets entered trans-lunar orbit. I can give you a general notion, but you wouldn't hire me as a rocket scientist."

Okay, that was fair enough. There were very few computer users who could diagnose and repair their own computers. "Even so, here is a question I've wondered about for some time. Our jet pilots report witnessing UFOs that rapidly accelerate or make abrupt high-speed turns. How do occupants inside your craft survive the G-forces?"

Zytt was quiet for a long while. Did he not know, or not want to tell me?

"Look," I said, "I'm finished with the military. I'm not going to give them your secrets. We're just having a conversation, and I'm curious."

"All right, in broad terms, it works like this. From the jet pilot's perspective, our vehicle suddenly outdistances him, which he attributes to rapid acceleration. Inside our vessel, we don't feel the effect because what actually happened was our engine bent space, and we traversed from one point to another as simply as if you folded a sheet of paper and stuck a pin through it."

"You're talking about Star Wars' hyperspace jumps, aren't you?"

"That was just a visual effect in a film—and not even a very accurate representation. Our engines use magnetohydrodynamic waves—magnetic fields that induce currents in a moving conductive fluid to polarize the fluid into a torus that confines the plasma and reciprocally shapes space in twelve directions."

Wow. If that was an anthropology professor's explanation, what would the engineer's explanation be like?

"This same technology can render our ship invisible, though it can't do both at the same time."

"Can you explain?"

"Are you familiar with what your astronomers call the cosmological redshift?"

"Sure, I've read about it. As the universe expands, the space between objects stretches and any light traveling through that space also stretches, which lengthens the light's wavelength. Since red light has longer wavelengths, scientists called the stretching a redshift."

"Not bad. Anyway, by manipulating the shape of space around our craft, we can shorten or lengthen light waves to a wavelength beyond the visible spectrum."

"That still leaves a physical object that will show up on radar." Radar was something I actually knew a lot about.

"Not if we don't want it to. You're familiar with radio blackouts caused by extreme electromagnetic waves emitted by your sun's corona? Well, the same technology that changes the wavelength of light can alter any electromagnetic wavelength."

"I get it. If bending space stretches the radio waves, it renders the flying saucer invisible because radar is only looking for a specific type of wave."

"I really dislike that term, flying saucer. How would you feel if people called your microbus a butter dish?"

"Sorry. You said earlier your craft can't accelerate and be invisible at the same time."

"That should be obvious. If the engine is bending the space a certain amount during a jump, it can't be simultaneously stretching it differently to alter electromagnetic light waves."

"Ah, that explains something else. My brother-in-law asked me why your vehicles didn't create sonic booms. I'd told him I thought it was because people on the ground were outside the cone of sound. But now I think it's because by bending space, your vehicle is never pushing a rapidly moving cone of air in front of it."

Zytt leaned his head back against the seat and closed his eyes. A very human gesture. "I forget, I'm talking to an electrical engineer. I shouldn't tell you any of this."

"No. I'm enjoying our conversation. But I've got to stop to pee." Damn prostate.

I pulled off at the next rest area to use the restroom and stretch my legs. When I came out, I saw a man pressing his face against the windows of my camper. I headed toward him at a dead run.

"Can I help you, fella?"

He patted my VW. "I used to own one of these back in '78. Still miss it."

I caught my breath and tried to sound casual. "What do you drive these days?"

"A Mercedes. The wife and I gave up camping. We stay in motels now. She says camping wasn't a vacation for her—she still had to cook and clean while I fished."

Well, he could have pitched in. But it wasn't my place to give him marital advice, and I really wanted to get him away from Zytt. "So, you must like German cars. Show me your Mercedes."

"Aw, it's just a car. Show me your camper."

"Uh . . . if I had more time. I'm afraid I've got to get back on the road."

"It won't take but a minute," he said. "I remember how compact they were."

"Sorry, I can't. I'm driving a Tibetan monk who really values his privacy."

Just then, a woman in a pink sundress, standing next to a blue Mercedes, spotted us and started waving. "Harold! Harold, let's go."

"Better do what she says," I said.

He started away, and then called back over his shoulder, "Maybe next time we're at the same rest area."

I'd make sure that didn't happen. I opened the driver's door, jumped in, and slammed it before anyone could see past me.

Zytt wasn't there. I whirled around to look in the back. "Zytt?"

The seat cushion on one side of the dinette table lifted, and Zytt peeked out. He'd squeezed himself into the storage area beneath the seat.

I smiled at him. "That was quick thinking, but I'd already given him the bluff about you being a monk."

"Good, but I'd rather not test that deception."

I switched to I-80 in Illinois and took that to Salt Lake City. If Mr. Mercedes stayed on I-90, we wouldn't have to deal with him again.

There wasn't much scenery to talk about. Just corn. Miles after mile of corn. I looked out at the passing fields. "What about crop circles?"

"Yeah, some of the original ones were ours, though the copycats showed up eventually," Zytt said. "It's caused when a ship pivots too close to the ground. Our pilots are supposed to make turns over water or at high enough altitudes so that they won't leave a mark."

It reminded me of greasers in my high school who loved to spin donuts on the blacktop with their hot rods. Eddie had probably been one of them. I didn't know that for a fact, though—I'd been in service when he'd started dating my sister. But it seemed like something he would have done.

We stopped at a rest area in Iowa near enough to the highway to Prairie View that it made my heart pang not to see my family, but how would I explain my skinny friend to my sisters, let alone Eddie? Of course, Eddie would just about piss himself to meet Zytt.

"You seem disturbed," Zytt said.

"Sorry. I was thinking about my family. They don't live too far from here."

"Are you worried about them dying?"

"No. Why would you ask that?"

"Many humans dwell on thoughts of death. The story you shared of your life had a recurring theme—the death of those you held dear. As if you marked the intervals of your life by someone dying."

I hadn't realized that until he said it. "It's . . . natural. Doesn't your species experience death?"

"All life forms die. It's a side effect of focusing consciousness in physical matter—entropy and all that. But death is merely consciousness loosening its bond to matter. I think the difference is, we see that it's not something to grieve."

"I'm not still mourning the dead. But we humans have emotions, and grief is one of them."

"My species has emotions as well, but we recognize some emotions are not conducive to long-term happiness. When we talked earlier, you said you believed the entire universe to be conscious-energy."

"Yes."

"So those you loved and now grieve for—whether you admit it or not—are just in a different form. Their energy did not die. It just left the state you can perceive with your senses."

"But that's precisely why humans grieve—because we miss them."

"Gizmo, did you love your mother? Your father? Your wife?"

"Yes, yes, and yes."

"And do you still love them?"

"What a question! Of course!"

"Then that love is an expression of you. Love is not transactional. You can continue to love them without them being here to love you back."

"You should write little inspirational booklets for Hallmark." But Zytt was right. Even we knew that energy can neither be created nor destroyed, and since energy and consciousness are one, every conscious being is immortal. Grief was merely my fear of them not being here to love me anymore.

Shortly after a sign welcomed us to Nebraska, an eye-watering stench filled the van.

"Oo-eee," Zytt said. "What is that dreadful smell?"

"Dead skunk on the side of the road," I said.

Matter might be energy that can never be destroyed, but its transformation sure could leave a powerful stink.

Chapter 49

At Salt Lake City, we picked up I-15 south to St. George, Utah. "Have you ever been to Salt Lake City?" I said.

"No. Why?"

"I wondered what you knew about Mormons."

"Not much. My specialty isn't earthling religions."

"Well, they believe a celestial being had their founder transcribe tablets written in an alien language. UFO theorists outside the Mormon faith think this being was from another planet."

"Maybe. Might have been someone trying to push your species in a better direction. Might have nothing to do with us." Zytt shrugged. "Like I said, that's not my area."

"Does your species have religious beliefs?"

"I've already told you what I hold to be true. I believe one contiguous field of conscious energy extends from the smallest subatomic particle to the highest state of pure consciousness."

So he had.

Traffic on I-15 was light, and it only took us four hours to reach St. George. By then, it was twilight, and I intended to approach our destination in daylight, so we stopped for the night. Zytt stayed in the orgone accumulator for the entire night, much longer than he ever had.

In the morning, he didn't seem well. I feared he'd overdone it. I'd never read that one could overdose on orgone, but there was always a first time for anything.

Once we got on the road, I said, "Are you ill?"

"Faltering might be a better word. There's too much DOR here. Can't you feel it?"

No. But I kept eyeing the desert landscape along our route, looking for changes Reich had described. There wasn't an exit from I-15 to the secret base, Paradise Ranch. We'd have to drive to Indian Springs and work our way back.

This was starting to seem like the worse idea ever. Zytt continued to decline, but remained convinced that the secret base stored captured alien spacecraft. I can testify there weren't any when I was there. Then again, that'd been over forty years ago. We couldn't see the former nuclear test area. It was many miles west of the interstate. But I remember the guys at Paradise Ranch joking about radioactive testicles.

"Do you know where you are?" he said.

"Yes. I sure do." Even though we'd shared many secrets, I wasn't about to break the oath I made many years ago when I received my classified security clearance. So, I didn't tell Zytt exactly what I knew about the base, which wasn't all that much.

"One of the questions baffling xeno-anthropologists," he said, "is why the United States repeatedly bombed itself. The only government that ever dropped nuclear weapons on your country was your own."

I'd never thought of it that way.

"In this area we are driving near, your government has set off 928 nuclear bombs."

"Are you sure about that?" I said.

"Oh, I'm very sure—this is my area of expertise. And that's just Nevada. The number is even higher when you include the first atomic bomb test in New Mexico and the twenty-three bombs they tested on Bikini Atoll. That's insane."

I felt a little defensive. "I'm sure they were just trying to understand this new force."

"Okay, maybe the first or second time, maybe even the tenth. But what did they learn on the nine-hundred-twenty-eighth test that they already hadn't known by the nine-hundred-twenty-seventh? No, this was a clear case of madness. Whether they were power mad or something had genetically corrupted their brains, is the question."

"Actually, neither. We had this thing called the Cold War. We were trying to show the other side we could make bigger bombs than they could without actually bombing them. It was called the nuclear deterrent."

"I'd call it, 'which side is the more foolish?'"

"That's pretty harsh."

"Look out your window. You can see where low-hanging clouds of DOR have left their mark."

"I see that now. But the Cold War lasted forty years."

Two hours later, we reached Indian Springs, and I doubled back on an unmarked dirt road. When the road passed between a pair of large signs warning that this was a restricted military area, I told Zytt to hide in the back.

By my recollection, we were still miles from Groom Lake when my path was blocked by a pair of military vehicles. A young MP came over and told me I had to turn back. I explained that I had classified security clearance and had helped build the base.

He wasn't impressed. "I wasn't even born when this base was built, so I can't verify that."

I looked at the young MP, who was probably twenty-two, and I knew what he said was true. From the lockbox of documents I traveled with, I hauled out my military clearance papers and showed him.

He handed them back. "These are hopelessly out of date, and they don't say nothing about you ever having access here."

I took them back. "Yeah, well. Sorry to bother you."

I made a U-turn and drove back the way I'd come. Zytt was sorely disappointed.

"I don't know what you thought you were going to accomplish if we had managed to get in," I said. "Let's say you're right and a couple of crashed space vehicles are on that base—and I'm not saying they are. I never saw one. You told me yourself you're not an engineer. They'd be over half a century old and once smashed into a planet. What could you do?"

"I just want to access the intergalactic communicator."

"That's assuming it even works," I said. "Our scientists have, by this point, no doubt dismantled every part of the ship."

"Well, I won't know if I don't try."

"I'm sorry, I don't think you can."

"There must be another way in," he said.

"I remember a second road," I said. "But it will be patrolled as well."

"Take me there. I have an idea."

Zytt's idea was crazy. He wanted me to drive in as far as possible on the other road until I saw the MPs coming. Then, I'd slow to a stop, and he'd slip out and hide in the mesquite or sagebrush. When they turned me away, I would drive back to just beyond the warning signs and wait for him. He'd sneak onto the base on foot, contact his planet, and meet me back at the VW afterwards.

"That's not going to work," I said. "This is 2004. That base is going to have electronic motion detectors, radar, and probably guards patrolling with dogs."

"Dogs might be a problem," Zytt said. "But the desert is full of coyotes and small creatures. Their sensors couldn't effectively screen for small creatures low to the ground. They'd get false alarms all the time. I'm little. They might not detect me."

"Don't count on it. I'm guessing they'd keep the alien technology behind some serious locks."

"Well, depending on the locks, I think I could find a way around."

We argued some more, but I couldn't talk him out of it. So I circumvented the base and came in on the alternate road. He changed out of his monk's robe into the clothes I'd bought him at L. L. Bean.

I was pretty far inside the perimeter before I saw the MPs on the horizon. I stopped beside some scrub and Zytt crawled away from the van on his hands and knees. As soon as he was clear, I made a U-turn and got them to chase me all the way to the boundary signs. After they took down my information, scolded me, and left, I took the orgone box off the roof and set up the camper. The "keep-out" sign didn't say I couldn't park next to it.

I didn't expect Zytt to be back anytime soon. With his short legs and the DOR making him weak, walking there and back would probably take him all day and night. But no matter how long I had to wait, I would.

And I did. Around midnight, I saw lights rapidly ascend from the direction of the base until they disappeared into the night sky. My silent cheer for Zytt mingled with a touch of loss. I wondered if he'd ever come back, but truth be told, if I were stranded on an alien planet and finally got a ship home, I wouldn't stop to say goodbye either.

With Zytt now safely away, I decided to head back to visit my sisters in the morning. I finally went to sleep.

In the wee hours, something outside poking around the orgone accumulator woke me. It was most likely a curious coyote—not worth getting out of bed for. I wasn't sure what I was going to do with the box anyhow, now that Zytt was gone. It wasn't large enough for a normal-size adult. I could just leave it in the desert and let the coyotes use it for a den.

I didn't fall back asleep right away, but lay pondering what effect an orgone box would have on animals. For that matter, had the local wildlife suffered the effects of DOR? These and other questions I was ill-equipped to answer kept my mind spinning. Finally, I decided to get up and meditate.

I'd just gotten seated and taken a couple of deep breaths when I heard pawing on the camper door. Sniffing around the orgone box was one thing, but scratching the paint on my VW was another. I threw open the side door and shouted to scare the animal away.

Zytt fell across the threshold—half in, half out.

"Zytt! I thought you'd gone."

"Help me," he said weakly.

I lifted him up and laid him on my bed. "I thought you succeeded. I saw a ship take off."

"That was one of your stealth planes."

Zytt's skin had turned a sickly shade of pale. "You don't look well. Let's get you into your orgone box."

He barely lifted his head. "Won't help. Too much DOR in this area. We need to get beyond the range of radiation fallout."

"I think it's over most of Nevada."

"Exactly."

"What about your people? Were you able to transmit a message?"

He shut his eyes. "No. You were right. I couldn't get inside."

"Don't worry. I'll take care of you."

I covered him with a blanket and began closing up the camper. I debated leaving without the orgone box, but decided he'd need it if he survived until we made it to some other state. Radiation from nuclear bomb tests had occasionally reached St. George, Utah. I remembered Zytt started showing the effects after we passed there, so I didn't want to go that way. Arizona was nearest, so I sped in that direction as fast as the microbus would take me.

We camped at the Grand Canyon, and I put Zytt in the orgone box, hoping we were far enough from the DOR to do him some good. But then I remembered Arizona was where Reich had observed DOR's effects on the desert. Also, Arizona hadn't been good for Sparrow, and in retrospect, I wondered if her condition had been exacerbated by the DOR there.

I got out a road atlas and considered our options. California was a possibility, but I wasn't sure how DOR spread. Crossing the continental divide would put us in safer territory, but we'd have to drive through New Mexico, and I didn't know if there was still DOR there from the work they'd done on the atomic bomb.

There was still plenty of summer left, so north seemed the best direction. However, to by-pass New Mexico, I'd need to skip the interstates and take older US highways until about seventy miles west of Grand Junction, Colorado, where I could pick up I-70 to Denver, and from there I-25 would connect me back to I-80.

Zytt and I were heading home.

CHAPTER 50

By the time we had driven through most of Colorado, I was certain we were well beyond the area of radioactive contamination, but Zytt still hadn't improved. I blamed my rush to put distance between us and Nevada, because constant driving hadn't given him any time in the orgone box.

I stopped for the night, unsure what to do for the little guy. He wouldn't make it to Ann Arbor without a lengthy layover somewhere. Had he been done in by the DOR in Nevada, or had this decline been gradually coming on since the destruction of his ship? Obviously, if he lived purely on orgone, his vessel had something more sophisticated than a mason board box layered with steel wool and sheep's wool.

There was another possibility—lost hope. Zytt said his species experienced emotions. How depressed would I get if I was stranded half-way across the universe and failed my one chance to send a distress message?

Surely after two UFO crashes in New Mexico, plus whatever happened with the EA lights that Reich had knocked out, a species advanced enough for intergalactic travel must have a method in place for a stranded anthropologist to signal passing ships. We needed to drive to a state where UFO sightings were presently being reported.

And my sister was married to the very man who could find out.

The choice seemed highly illogical, but family is family, and if there was anyone that I knew I could depend on, it was the two women who raised me. And they'd let us stay there for as long as it took Zytt to recuperate. Likely no one in Iowa had ever seen a Tibetan Rinpoche, and knowing my long-time interest in yoga and meditation, my sisters would never doubt he was a monk. Hell, he could sit in the orgone accumulator twenty-four hours a day, if need be, and they'd just accept that he was meditating.

Nora's husband, Tom, still thought meditation was unchristian, so staying at Sophie's would cause less controversy. Eddie's scrapbook of aliens could make it hard to fool him. But if Zytt kept to the orgone box most of the time, we might pull it off.

I got out my BlackBerry and called her from Wyoming to say I was traveling with a Tibetan monk and could we stay with her a few days.

"Of course," Sophie said. "Where are you now?"

"Cheyenne. It'll be the day after tomorrow before we get there."

"Good. That'll give me time to restock the pantry. Is he a vegetarian like you?"

"You don't need to buy anything for him. He's . . . fasting."

"Fasting?"

"Yeah. It's a thing monks do."

"Gizmo, I know what fasting means, but he's got to eat sometime."

"You might be surprised." I was trying not to lie to my sister—except for the big lie—that Zytt wasn't a visitor from another planet.

Cheyenne was about fourteen hours from my sister's house, and I was tempted to drive straight through, but Zytt looked like he really needed to stop for the night, so we did. He crawled into the orgone box and stayed there. When he hadn't come out in the morning, I opened the accumulator door, and found him sitting very still. But, thankfully, alive.

"Zytt, I need you to get in the van so I can strap the orgone box to the roof."

"I'm feeling very poorly. Just let me stay in here."

"I understand. But I'm taking you to my sister's. Once we get there, you'll be able to sit in the accumulator night and day for as long as it takes for you to recover." I held out my hand and helped him stand up.

When we were about an hour away, I called Sophie to let her know. By the time I pulled into her driveway, Nora and Tom were also there. Eddie had the barbeque going, and their backyard picnic table was laden with summertime foods—potato salad, baked beans, watermelon, sweet corn, sliced tomatoes, and that Midwest standard, Jell-O salad.

After hugs all around, I moved my VW to where it would be well out of the way, then unstrapped the orgone accumulator and hid it beside the camper, out of sight of passing traffic and nosey neighbors.

"What's that?" Sophie said.

"It's a . . . sacred space where the Rinpoche meditates."

"Looks pretty small," she said.

"So is he." I opened the van door and motioned for Zytt to come out.

Wearing his full disguise—maize robe, sunglasses, and burgundy stocking cap—Zytt stood up and feebly stepped out. Everyone gathered around us and stared. Zytt folded his hands together and humbly bowed to each of them, softly speaking in what I assumed was Tibetan.

"What did he say?" Tom asked.

"I'm not sure," I said. "Probably a blessing. May you be at peace. May your heart remain open. May you awaken to the light of your own true nature. Something along those lines."

"Humph," Tom said. But Sophie and Nora were charmed.

"We've prepared some food," Sophie said. "Will you share a meal with us?"

Zytt shook his head. Bowed to each of them again, and entered his orgone box.

"Don't be offended," I said. "I told you on the phone, he's fasting."

She hooked her arm in mine. "Well, I hope you're not. Let's eat."

The summer breeze kept lifting the corners of the tablecloth and threatening to blow away the paper plates and napkins. I indulged the joy of picnicking with my family and momentarily ceased my worry about the ailing alien in the box.

While we ate, my family peppered me with questions about how I met the monk and why I was driving him. I answered as truthfully as I dared. "We met in Maine. He was a stranger in a strange land, who didn't have a car and needed a ride out west. I wasn't doing anything important with my retirement, so why not take him? Rinpoche is a greatly respected title in Buddhism. I thought I could learn a few things from him during our trip."

"So, are you a Buddhist now?" Tom said with a hint of disdain.

"No, Tom, but I've always been open to learning what other cultures have to teach." I tried to say this with as little judgment as I could manage.

I deflected further questions by changing the topic to Tommy Jr. and filling them in on his recent successes.

That evening, the sky blackened with thunderheads. Distant lightning drew ever closer. Sophie came into the living room in a panic. "Gizmo, have you forgotten what Iowa thunderstorms are like? It's too dangerous to leave your friend outside."

She was right. We hadn't faced bad weather on our journey, and I didn't know how the mason board would fare in a torrential downpour. The sheet metal in the accumulator might even draw lightning.

"He needs his cubicle," I said.

"Well, there's space for it in the utility room. Eddie! Put down your beer and help Gizmo carry the monk's box inside."

I should have carried it myself, dammit. When Eddie and I went to move him, Zytt said, "No, not yet. I need more time."

Eddie might not have the education I did, but he wasn't dumb.

"He speaks English!" Eddie said.

"Yeah. He just doesn't like to. Pick up your end. Let's get this inside before it pours."

Zytt followed us in and climbed back into his box as soon as we set it in the utility room. I turned off the light and closed the door behind me. Eddie was bristling with questions, which I managed to deflect. For the moment.

After a hell of a storm that night, we just left the accumulator in the utility room. August was the season for evening thunderstorms, and there was no point in hauling it in and out. That suited Zytt, who remained in there day and night.

I checked on him periodically to see if he was improving. So did Sophie and Eddie, who would crack open the accumulator door and peek in.

"How does he just sit there?" Eddie said. "Doesn't he ever need to stand up and stretch?"

"Discipline," I said. "He's been doing it all his life."

Days passed, and Eddie's suspicions grew. Again, not stupid. "Why does he wear sunglasses in a dark room?"

His curiosity made me reluctant to broach the subject of where UFOs were currently being spotted. But Eddie's UFO message boards were my best bet of finding that information.

Zytt said he was holding his own and even working on accumulating more energy, but he looked worse every time I saw him.

The rest of that week was mostly family time, with all of us gathering every afternoon and evening. My nieces and nephews all lived far away, so having me home was a treat for my sisters.

One afternoon, I went to Tom and Nora's to help Tom replace a signal booster on their TV antenna. We were both probably too old to be climbing rooftops, and Tom could well afford cable but wouldn't subscribe. "Why pay for free TV?" he would say. "All those extra channels are just junk."

The job wasn't difficult. Tom held the ladder as I climbed up and down. I mounted the new amplifier in a weatherproof container on the antenna pole. When I finished, we checked the signal on all three channels he received. He declared it a success and turned off the TV. "Daytime TV has nothing worth watching," he said. I agreed. We carried the ladder back into his garage and had a beer to celebrate.

When I returned to Sophie's, I checked on Zytt.

Oh, crap.

Eddie was squatting on the utility room floor with the accumulator door open, talking with Zytt, who had his sunglasses in his lap.

"No one on earth understands reality or even what is *not* real," Zytt told Eddie. "Nothing is as you see it, or as you conceive it to be. Everything is made of light—the entire universe is a field of energy waves—conscious-energy waves."

They noticed me standing there and Eddie looked at me with daggers in his eyes. "Gizmo, how could you?"

"Well, I . . . we need help, and you're the best person I could think of."

He rocked back on his heels, stood up, and got in my face. "For years, you let everyone in this family treat me like a fringe fanatic, and all along you knew better?"

"I didn't, Eddie, I swear. He and I only met a few weeks ago, and he's . . . well, it's hard to deny reality when it's right in front of you."

"Then why didn't you tell me the truth? You brought a spaceman into my house and tricked everyone into believing he was Tibetan."

"Because no one can know. Eddie, you can't tell a soul. Rumors spread like wildfire. The government will send people to capture him, study him with x-rays, MRIs, and lab tests. They'll hold him until he dies. Then dissect him and put his organs in jars."

Out of the corner of my eye, I saw Zytt shudder.

Eddie still wasn't buying it. "The greatest proof of extraterrestrial life is in a box next to my washing machine, and you expect me not to tell my wife?"

"What would she do with that information?"

"Finally believe I'm not off my rocker."

"Sure, maybe after she freaked out. And you know she'd have to tell Nora, and probably your kids. Nora would tell Tom and their kids, who'd tell their friends. Pretty soon, the information would be out of control."

Eddie looked unconvinced.

"Please Eddie, I swore to protect Zytt's secret. It's not yours or mine to reveal."

"Zytt?"

"That's his real name. Look, you were right. That has to be vindication enough. I'm trying to help him get back home. I figure if I take him where there have been a lot of recent UFO sightings, there may be a way for him to signal one."

"There's not," Zytt said. "I don't carry any type of device that can do that."

"That seems very short sighted of your people," I said. "Even earthlings carry BlackBerries and cell phones."

"What about crop circles?" Eddie said. "If we made a huge crop circle in a field, wouldn't a UFO check it out? I have pictures of some that look like hieroglyphics. Couldn't they act as a signal?"

It sounded like Eddie had swung to our side. "Zytt?" I said.

"It is possible. As I told you, our pilots aren't allowed to do that anymore."

"Okay, Eddie," I said. "I'll make you a deal. Find out where the UFOs are flying and you can come with us, as long as you promise to never speak a word about Zytt. You'll be able to take all the flying saucer photos you want. That'll be your proof."

Eddie nodded. "Zytt seems like a nice guy. I wouldn't want anyone to cut him open. But I have one condition."

"What's that?"

"I have questions I want to ask him."

"That's up to him," I said.

"It's okay," Zytt said. "One or two more."

I grabbed Eddie's arm. "Keep it brief. He's very frail."

Eddie nodded and squatted down in front of Zytt. "Are you a god?"

"No more than you are." Zytt shook his head, a very human gesture he must have picked up from me. "It's pointless to ask these questions until you understand that reality is an undifferentiated field of conscious energy. Aren't you part of this undifferentiated field?"

Eddie wrinkled his forehead. "I suppose, but—"

"So am I. Whether that makes us gods depends on your definition of gods."

"Well, I was thinking about the stories of ancient aliens being the gods of the Sumerians, Mayans, and Egyptians."

"I don't know," Zytt said. "I'm not that old. Ask a different question."

"Why aren't visitors from space helping us?"

"Helping you to do what? Accelerate your technological self-destruction? Humanity started playing with the energy that powers the stars and now can wipe out its own world. Giving advanced technology to a society that isn't mature enough for it always ends in disaster. Xeno-anthropologists have a rule against that sort of thing."

Eddie turned to me. "Gizmo, you were right. It is like Star Trek's prime directive. But the crew of the Enterprise broke that rule pretty regularly."

"I don't," Zytt said. "I'm tired now." He closed the accumulator door.

CHAPTER 51

Eddie kept his word not to tell my sister or anyone else who Zytt really was. He was even careful to refer to him by my made-up Tibetan name. He also reached out to his contacts on the message boards and UFO websites for a likely state with a lot of activity within driving distance. He hadn't told Sophie the purpose of our trip or that he intended to go with us. He even suggested he might get Patty to invite Sophie to visit her grandchildren so we could slip away.

While those plans were underway, I fired up my computer and worked on a collection of documents I'd been building up about orgone devices ever since Woody introduced me to Wilhelm Reich's research. These included plans for the accumulator I'd drawn so others could build them. I'd let the project lapse after Sparrow's death. But conversations with Zytt had broadened my understanding of orgone, and his presence showed how real it was. He also showed me how backward a species we were. Reich's work now seemed more important than ever.

Not knowing what might happen next, I decided it was time to get the information about orgone out before it was lost again. Using the internet and electronic books, I'd distribute knowledge across the World Wide Web so universally that no single government could stamp it out with another book-burning.

Late one night, I was working on my computer, refining various documents to put on the web. Eddie and Sophie were already in bed. Zytt was in the accumulator, where he'd stayed since our arrival.

My BlackBerry buzzed with multiple messages from my jury-rigged home security system. It was fortunate that I was already on the computer because in 2004 the Windows operating system took forever to boot up. Immediately, I established a TCP/IP connection with my home computer. The video feed from Ann Arbor showed men in dark suits outside my door. One of them held up his credentials. "Sven Carson? Federal agents. Open up."

Did he imagine I was in Ann Arbor, looking out my door's peep hole?

"Come on, Gizmo. Don't make us break down your door." He waited a beat, and then stepped aside while burly men in flak gear shattered the door lock.

Okay, it was go time.

I broke the link to Ann Arbor and uploaded documents and ebooks to internet publishing sites as fast as I could. When the upload finished, I disconnected the equipment and fetched Zytt from the utility room. He was still too weak to walk.

"Zytt, we've got to go!" I carried him into the VW, gently laid him on my bed, and covered him with a thin blanket. I dragged the accumulator outside, strapped it to the top of the van, and raced away. Eddie would be pissed I'd left him behind, but this was a whole different mess, and I didn't want him mixed up with the Feds. If the raid turned out to not be about Zytt, I'd keep my word and take Eddie along.

Prairie View wasn't large and soon we were past its modest downtown. Having grown up in the area, I decided to take the back roads I knew so well. I turned onto a small two-lane blacktop that I knew led to dirt roads and small farms.

Boy, was I wrong. Family farms that once ringed the town like a pearl necklace had been bulldozed and reshaped into housing developments, complete with cul-de-sacs and aluminum-sided houses. I realized it'd been fifty-five years since my high school friends and I sped down country roads on hot summer nights.

Eventually, we reached tall corn. Miles of it. Super farms. Another thing that had changed since I left. It was about then that I noticed red and blue lights in my mirror.

"Stop," Zytt said in a weak voice. "Let me off this bus."

"I can't just yet. I'm sorry. I don't know how the cops can be on to us already, but if they are, we need more distance from Eddie and my sister."

The lights still seemed a good way behind us. If I could find a dirt road, we just might lose them. No such luck, but I had noticed gravel-covered culverts in the ditches every mile or so. They weren't roads or even driveways, just places where farm machinery could enter or exit the field.

Good enough for me.

The next one I came to, I shut off my lights and wheeled into the field, knocking corn stalks flat with the front of my bus. I turned parallel to the road and drove a little farther. The corn was fairly tall by that time of summer, and I hoped it might hide the camper from a passing cop car. I rolled down the window and listened. I didn't hear any sirens—helicopters either. Maybe I was paranoid, and they were after someone else.

"I need to get out," Zytt said. "You see the lights?"

"Yes. That's why I drove into the middle of a cornfield."

"Please pick me up and carry me outside. I don't have the strength to walk."

"That seems like the last place I should take you. We need to drive the opposite direction as soon as they pass us."

"Don't argue with me," he said. "I can't be in the camper when they get here."

I got out and opened the side door, but with the accumulator strapped on top, I couldn't raise the roof. I had to stoop down to get inside. I kneeled beside Zytt, tucked the blanket around him, lifted his frail body, and carried him outside.

"Take me away from the camper, into the field amongst the corn."

Okay, I suppose that made some sense. If they spotted the camper hidden in the corn, it'd be empty. Although I wasn't sure how far across the field we'd get with me carrying him.

I glanced toward the road where growing luminosity bespoke the impending approach of the lights. "They're getting closer."

"I know," he said. "I'm bringing them."

Great relief swept over me. "Then it's your people coming to take you?"

"Not in the way you think. I'm leaving my body, and the lights are here to dissolve it."

"You're dying?"

"Pretty soon."

"I thought all those extra hours you've been in the orgone accumulator, you were trying to heal."

"No, Gizmo. I knew I was done in Arizona. My purpose was to accumulate enough energy to manifest the lights that are about to arrive at any moment."

"Well, if you can do that, why can't you undo the DOR?"

"You saw what DOR did to the rocks and soil and mountains in Nevada. You read what Reich observed in Arizona. If DOR can eat a mountain, what chance is there for an alien life form who lives on cosmic energy?"

"Then what's the benefit of these lights?"

"As my consciousness exits my body, the light will convert my remains into infinite particles and waves."

I shook my head, still trying to wrap my mind around his death, let alone pending dissolution. "Why?"

"So you don't have to explain what you're doing with a dead alien. Besides, I don't want a body left behind for your government to dissect and put in jars."

I regretted ever saying that in front of him. "I'd never let that happen. Ever."

"What could you do with my body? If you had it cremated, the crematory people might discover it. If you buried it, someone might find the remains later. No, you've proven a good friend to me, and I'm grateful. I won't leave you with that burden. Trust me. This is for the best. Lay me on the ground now."

And then, Zytt's body fell limp and his life energy left.

"No!"

The lights converged around us, and Zytt's remains dissolved into tiny vesicles of light, which moved in and around each other like a dance. In seconds, the thin blanket that draped over him fell flat. I clutched it with his empty robe to my heart and wept. Beneath where it had lain was nothing but a dusty field. The light gave way to the normal starry night sky, and I sat on the ground in stunned silence for I didn't know how long.

Suddenly, brilliant light flooded the field, blinding me. Had Zytt made some miraculous, _E.T._-like return? I rubbed my eyes, trying to get used to the light.

"What the hell are you doing driving in my field?" an angry voice said. "Are you drunk?"

I stood and turned around. "No."

Spotlights on the roof of a Ford F-350 pickup blinded me. I raised my hand over my eyes to shield them and saw, standing in front of the truck, a large red-faced farmer. "Look at how at many rows of corn you've destroyed. I'm calling the sheriff."

"There's no need for that," I said.

"Well, somebody's got to pay for the damage."

"You're right. I will."

"You will?"

I guess he expected an argument.

"Yes. It'll be worth every penny. I've just witnessed the most amazing phenomenon."

"If you're not drunk, you must be on drugs."

I shook my head and gave him the most outlandish explanation I could think of. The truth. "It was a UFO! Didn't you see it? Lit up your whole field. I'm sorry I messed up your corn, but I just had to pull in for a better look. Damn shame I didn't have a camera."

He kicked a clod of dirt. "Yeah, I saw lights, that's why I came—to find out what you were up to. But for God's sake, don't report this."

"So, you don't want to call the sheriff?"

"No, and don't tell anyone else, either. That'll bring UFO fanatics from all over. Keep your lips sealed, and we'll forget about damages."

I walked over and shook his hand. "I won't say a word. I'm just going to get in my camper and leave."

CHAPTER 52

Still in a state of shock, I drove away from the farmer. In fact, after the arrival of the Feds at my home, the urge to flee rose in my throat like undigested cabbage. I could easily leave Iowa, stay off the grid, and continue my wandering ways. But my better side knew I couldn't. I needed to go back to Sophie and Eddie's to explain my abrupt departure. I was fairly confident the Feds hadn't traced me this far yet. Both my sisters had my BlackBerry number and would have called if anyone had come knocking in the wee hours.

When I arrived, the house was dark. Hopefully, they were still asleep. I put the VW in neutral, cut the engine, and coasted to its previous place. Quietly, I slipped inside and went to bed. But I won't say I slept—much.

I had until morning to figure out what to tell them about Zytt's remarkable disappearing act. Thoughts of what had transpired in the field churned with memories of things Zytt had said about mortality. Meanwhile, I also needed to puzzle out what had brought the Feds to Ann Arbor. It was a bitter pill to swallow, but I had to tell my family about that, too.

Staring at the dark ceiling, my mind readily jumped to other memories. I remembered the year I upset Patty by telling her we ought to rip December off the calendar because we'd lost too many loved ones. But this was August. Did Zytt's passing mean I needed to eliminate that month, too? No. Thanks to his words, I could deal with loss and absence with wisdom instead of grief. The part of Zytt that remained with me would be eternal, so long as I kept it in my heart and mind. The same was true for Sparrow, or Dad, or John Lennon. Energy could neither be created nor destroyed.

For the last hundred years, our species had raced down a technological road, driving on the wrong side of stupid. Humanity needed to make a U-turn, but I wasn't smart enough to see how we'd do it. Maybe Nora and Sophie's grandchildren would be the ones to find a way out.

I'd uploaded everything I'd collected on orgone, including what Zytt taught me about life-giving cosmic energy. Writing it had been tricky because I needed to let the world know we were causing DOR, without killing my credibility by saying that a visitor from space had told me all this.

I eventually drifted off.

The next thing I remember was Eddie standing in my room. "Gizmo, the little guy's not in the utility room, and I see you've put his box on the camper. Is it time to go?"

My head still groggy, I sat up. "What?"

"We aren't ready. The UFO message boards haven't given me a location yet, and I haven't arranged with Patty to have Sophie visit."

"What time is it?"

"Almost nine."

So I'd gotten maybe four hours of sleep. "Is there coffee?"

"You bet, and Sophie is cooking breakfast."

"Ask her to make extra. We need to invite Tom and Nora."

"They get up at the crack of dawn—probably ate already."

"I need to see them before I go, and it'd be best if we all were together."

"So, we are leaving?"

"I'll explain when everyone gets here. Ask Sophie to call Nora. I'll be out as soon as I shower."

Eddie saluted and left.

By the time I showered and dressed, Tom and Nora were sitting in the dining room drinking coffee. Sophie had platters of hot cakes and sausages waiting.

I kissed both my sisters, shook Tom's hand, and took the seat at the head of the table. Eddie began passing the food around.

"Nothing for us," Nora said. "We've just eaten."

Tom put a pancake and two sausage links on his plate. "Well, maybe just a taste."

I didn't think I could eat. I needed to steel myself for what had to be said. I took a sip of coffee and let the caffeine rouse my brain.

"Eddie says you're leaving," Sophie said.

Eddie gave me a worried look.

"Yes. But I wanted to talk to all of you before I left, because I don't know what might be coming my way."

Sophie stopped pouring maple syrup on her pancake and set the bottle down. "Gizmo, you're scaring me."

"I don't mean to. I think it's going to be all right." I took another drink of coffee and tried to think of how to break it to them. Really, there was no other choice than to just come out with it. "I haven't been entirely honest with you, and my deception could affect the whole family. But if you'll bear with me, I'll tell you everything."

That killed everyone's appetite and the sound of forks and knives dropping onto plates filled the space.

I cleared my throat. "What I'm going to share may seem unbelievable, and my approach to it round about, but it's the best way, believe me."

Tom waved his hand. "Okay. You've got our attention. Get on with it."

"All of us are kept alive by a life-energy. The same energy abides in every sentient being."

"Is that from your Tibetan monk?" Tom said.

"No, he comes into the story later. It's from Wilhelm Reich, an Austrian scientist who fled the Nazis and immigrated to America just before World War II. He discovered scientific proof of this energy and invented related technologies to apply it."

Eddie chimed in, "One of his inventions is the cubicle Gizmo's . . . friend . . . meditates in."

"That's right, Eddie. But Reich wasn't the first. Life energy has been known by other names and harnessed by other cultures for thousands, perhaps millions of years."

Tom, a very practical man, raised his eyebrows. "Millions? That's a stretch."

I took a deep breath and looked at Eddie. "For as long as I've known Eddie, I—like the rest of you—called his obsession with travelers from outer space absurd. Eddie, I apologize."

Sophie's jaw dropped. "Gizmo, what are you saying?"

"That he was right, and we didn't believe him."

Eddie smiled like the dog that ate the cat's food.

"Don't get me wrong," I said. "There are a lot of crazies publishing hoaxes—I have no idea why people make up stuff about UFOs when the truth is out there. But beings from another planet have been visiting earth regularly, at least since World War II."

"Long before then," Eddie said.

"Eddie," I said, "he told you he didn't know about that."

"He? Who?" Sophie looked between Eddie and me. "Gizmo, I'm sure Eddie is happy you're on his side, but what changed your mind?"

"Earlier this month, I visited Reich's museum in Maine. While there, I met an extraterrestrial, whom I led you to believe was a Tibetan monk." My words caught in my throat. "I'm deeply sorry I lied. Please forgive me."

"Bullshit!" Tom said. "This fakir is conning you. Bring him in here and let's clear this nonsense up."

"I can't. He's gone."

"Gone?" Eddie said. "Gizmo, you promised to take me with you to see that."

"Eddie, he's not gone in the way you think. He passed away last night. I did my best, but I guess he couldn't survive more than a few weeks without his ship."

Tom leaped to his feet, jiggling the china on the table. "If any of this is true, show us his body."

"I can't. It diffused into particles of light."

"What the hell happened to my logical brother-in-law—the engineer?" Tom said. "This sounds like every other flying saucer story anybody ever told. Conveniently, there's not one shred of proof. Just a cockeyed story."

"There's one big difference, Tom. Hoaxers make up UFO stories to get attention. This case is just the opposite. None of you must ever tell anyone about this."

Tom sat back down in his chair. "Oh, don't you worry about that. I'd be the laughingstock of the senior citizen's center."

"Eddie, that means you too," I said.

Eddie shrugged. "Who would believe me? I haven't even got a photo."

"This brings me to the next part of my story."

"There's more?" Nora said.

"I'm afraid so. Last night, federal agents raided my apartment in Ann Arbor."

Nora and Sophie gasped.

Sophie's voice quivered. "Gizmo, what have you done?"

"I'm not sure. I can only think of three reasons."

"Three!" Nora said.

I nodded. "In 1956, a federal judge ordered that orgone accumulators could not be transported across state lines. One of Reich's assistants disobeyed, and Reich was imprisoned."

"What does that have to do with you?" Nora said.

"That box strapped to the top of my camper is an orgone accumulator, and I've crossed sixteen states, some of them twice. I've also released information on the internet about orgone as well as plans for anyone to build their own accumulator." I stopped and thought for a minute. "But that was after the raid, so that can't have anything to do with it."

"You said three," Nora said. "What else?"

"They might have learned I was harboring an extraterrestrial and came to capture him. But most likely, it was Nevada."

"What happened in Nevada?" Tom said.

"I tried to access a secret military base where Zytt—that's the alien's real name—thought our government might be hiding a crashed UFO."

"That was foolish," Tom said.

"Well, I never actually entered the base. MPs stopped us well before we ever got close. But they wrote down my information."

All this truth telling made my mouth dry. I took a swallow of coffee, but it had grown cold. "Anyway, I couldn't leave without telling you the whole story. It's unlikely the Feds will check here, but in case they do, I needed you to know what it was about."

Nora squeezed my hand. "It'll be okay."

Around the table, everyone fell quiet. Picking at their food and, I guess, trying to reconcile what I'd revealed. Absorbed in thoughts of what might await me in Ann Arbor, I couldn't eat much myself.

A tall grandfather clock stood ticking in the corner of Sophie's dining room. It had been our mother's. I kept glancing at it, growing anxious to leave. Finally, I pushed my chair back and stood up. "Sorry to dash. But if I'm going to make Ann Arbor today, I better go now."

"Gizmo, it's too late to start now," Nora said. "That's a long drive, and you're not as young as you were."

"It's only seven hours. And I've been driving distances like that all my life."

"But you hardly touched your pancakes," Sophie said. "You can't drive all that way on an empty stomach. At least finish your breakfast."

"Sis, I appreciate your cooking, I always have, but I've got to resolve this business with the Feds. I don't want them coming out here bothering all of you. Not on my account."

Nora, like a second mom, patted my cheek. "If you're in trouble, call us. We'll find you a lawyer. Don't try to go it on your own."

"Yes, big sister."

Everyone stood, and they walked me out to my van.

"Hold on a minute," Eddie said. "In the unlikely event this is about that orgone gadget, there's no reason for you to show up in Michigan with it still strapped to your roof."

"Good point." In minutes, we had it off the camper and stowed in his garage.

Sophie's eyes darted between Eddie and me, and her lip began to tremble. "Eddie, what happens if government agents come here and find that?"

"Sis, they're not illegal to own," I said. "But if it makes you feel better, have Eddie take it apart. It's too small for a regular-size person, anyway."

Tom pulled me aside. "What Nora said about the lawyer . . . Don't wait. Hire one before you talk to whatever agency searched your place. And have the lawyer with you when you go to meet with them."

Actually, that was good advice.

But Tom didn't let me go. He hemmed and hawed a bit, then said, "I don't know how you're fixed financially. But lawyers aren't cheap. So if you need money, Nora and I have a good nest egg . . ."

Tom wasn't a hugger, but I gave him one anyhow. "I'm good. I'm touched by your offer. But when I left the company, they paid me a very generous lump sum. I have it invested, and it's grown beyond all expectations."

We walked over to my van. Sophie, who had gone into the house while we were talking, now came running out with a brown paper lunch sack. "I packed you a sandwich, some chips, and an apple for the road. You're going to get hungry later."

I kissed her cheek. "Thanks, sis. Just like you used to make for me to take to school."

Nora joined her and me in a group hug.

I climbed into the driver's seat, closed the door and rolled down the window. I started the engine, stuck my arm out the open window, and waved as I backed out.

"Call us when you get there!" Nora shouted.

"I will."

Feelings of love washed over me as my family stood in the driveway smiling and waving goodbye. Above their heads, little vesicles of orgone lights danced in a clear, azure Iowa sky, the first I'd noticed in many years. Woody would have loved it—probably Reich would have, too.

347

The End

AUTHOR NOTES

Upon reaching the end of Gizmo's story, it might be assumed that I set out to write about an alien. Actually, at the time, a profusion of book banning across our nation brought to mind the case of Wilhelm Reich. The last, and perhaps only, time the US government confiscated and burned a scientific author's books. When I learned of it, my disbelief echoed Gizmo's. *Sure, Hitler burned books, but not my government. We have the Bill of Rights, freedom of the press, don't we?*

Although a work of fiction, this novel contains many factual details. Wilhelm Reich was a colleague of Freud and, in fact, was in charge of Freud's Vienna clinic. The work of Freud, Reich, and Carl Jung form the cornerstone of the field of psychiatry. Their paths eventually diverged. With the rise of Nazism in the 1930s, the Nazis did burn Sigmund Freud's books, but not Reich's. Freud fled to Britain and Reich to Sweden, then Norway, and later to America.

Experiments in Sweden and Norway led Reich to expand Freud's limited notion of libido as a purely sexual drive into a broader concept of life energy present in the whole organism. To distinguish it from libido, he coined the term Orgone. A medical doctor, Reich, had a thorough understanding of biology. During experiments in Norway, he observed under a microscope sterile chemical molecules forming primitive protozoa-like forms that came to life when imbued with orgone.

Nothing suggests that Reich studied or had any exposure to ancient writings of India or China like I have had. It seemed to me that what he named orgone was the same life force energy that oriental texts called prana or chi.

After he came to America, Reich discovered that orgone was not only present in living animals and plants but also in our water and atmosphere. When a period of droughts struck parts of the US, Reich attempted to manipulate weather by means of a device that could direct atmospheric orgone where he wanted it to go. He called it a cloudbuster.

Researching the novel, I came across a report he wrote about phenomena his team witnessed while attempting to end a drought in Arizona. In the 1950s, numerous sightings of unidentified flying objects were recorded. However, Reich stated that he had only read one report, and knew virtually nothing about the phenomena.

Reich and several members of his party noticed several lights in a clear night sky that were not stars or planets and did not move as an airplane would. Curious, he aimed the cloudbuster at one and the light disappeared. The same thing happened when he directed it toward a second light. On other nights, if the unknown phenomena appeared, the cloudbuster also seemed to knock it out. A rigorous scientist, Reich wrote detailed reports and sent them to the Air Force.

That gave me two interesting ideas to work into the book. Orgone or prana is the energy that sustains life, and the cloudbuster apparently affected UFOs. Having just finished the book, you already know where I went with that. A third concept introduced by Zytt, DOR, also came from Reich's research.

Once the atomic age began in earnest, doctors began using radiation to reduce tumors and treat other medical conditions. Reich, always the inquisitive scientist, wondered if orgone therapy and radiation therapy could be combined to combat cancer. So he applied for, and received, a quantity of radioactive material for medical research. The experiment failed. Even a fractional amount of radiation contaminated the orgone negatively and blanketed the lab and surrounding area with a cloud of DOR—deadly orgone radiation. Years later, when conducting his cloudbuster experiments in southwest US, he recognized the DOR effects in areas where nuclear bomb tests had produced radioactive fallout. My descriptions of the land Gizmo and Zytt see while driving through Nevada draw heavily from Reich's written observations of deserts affected by DOR.

Reich was many things, a medical doctor, a founder of psychiatry, a serious scientist, curious and interested in every new direction his experiments suggested. Some disputed his findings, but to this day, none have been disproved. Their alternative was to discredit him. In 1954, the pharmaceutical industry persuaded the FDA to take him to court, claiming he was selling orgone accumulators as a cancer cure. He never said they were. A federal judge issued an order for him to cease and that all copies of his books be confiscated and destroyed. Reich filed an appeal to the Supreme Court but died before his case could be heard. While agents of the government, acting on the initial judge's order, burned his books, the authors of the Bill of Rights must certainly have turned over in their graves. Fortunately, a few copies survived, were eventually reprinted, and are available from the Reich Museum and online booksellers.

Zytt is purely a product of my imagination. I have never met an alien or seen a flying saucer. But I once met Astronaut John Glenn. Does that count? I've also visited the UFO Museum in Roswell, New Mexico.

My research included a series on the Air Force Project Blue Book and a book by J. Alan Hynek, who headed Project Blue Book, and Jaques Vallee, Hynek's counterpart for a similar project in France. Both men are serious, accredited astronomers. I supplemented this with hours of YouTube videos, mostly by people with their own theories. The biggest development after I started the book was the testimony of Navy jet pilots on *Sixty Minutes*, that they have seen and chased Unidentified Anomalous Phenomena—the government's new term to replace UFO. This sparked the release of formerly classified documents of other sightings. Where this leads remains to be seen.

For interested readers, I have provided a bibliography of Reich's books and a few others about orgone and UFOs.

ACKNOWLEDGMENTS

Thank you to fellow members of Writers Alliance of Gainesville who critiqued the book as I was writing it: Ken Campbell, Pat Caren, Penny Church-Pupke, Allison Durham, Skipper Hammond, Bonnie Ogle, and Bob Kamarowski; beta readers, Nancy Dohn and Leo Hines; my editor: Dave King; and proofreader: Pat Caren.

ABOUT THE AUTHOR

Richard Gartee is an award-winning novelist who has authored seven novels, one novella, six collections of poetry, a theatre history, a biography, and seven college textbooks. He has studied eastern philosophy and practiced meditation for over fifty years. A complete list of his available titles, upcoming events, and forthcoming books is available at www.gartee.com.

If you enjoyed this book, please take a moment to leave a short review on Amazon and/or other booksellers' websites. Reviews help to sell books, and sales help an author to keep writing. You can readily find links to other online booksellers' websites by visiting www.lepublications.com and clicking on the Buy Books menu option.

You can sign up to receive updates on new publications by this author at either site or by scanning this QR code:

BIBLIOGRAPHY

Bean, Orson, *Me and the Orgone*, ACO Press, Princeton, NJ, 1971

DeMeo, James, *The Orgone Accumulator Handbook: Wilhelm Reich's Life-Energy Discoveries and Healing Tools for the 21st Century, with Construction Plans*, Natural Energy Works, Ashland, OR, 1989

Friedan, Betty, *The Feminine Mystique*, W. W. Norton & Company, New York, 1963

Hynek, J. Allen, Vallee, Jaques, *The Edge of Reality: Two Scientists Evaluate What We Know of the UFO Phenomenon*, Red Wheel/Weiser, Newburyport, MA, 1975 and 2023

Raknes, Ola, *Wilhelm Reich and Orgonomy*, St. Martins Press, New York, 1970

Reich, Peter, *A Book of Dreams*, John Blake, London, 1973

Reich, Wilhelm, *The Function of the Orgasam*, Farrar, Straus and Giroux, New York, 1961

Reich, Wilhelm, *The Sexual Revolution*, translated by Therese Pol, , Farrar, Straus and Giroux, New York, 1962

Reich, Wilhelm, *The Mass Psychology of Fascism*, Farrar, Straus and Giroux, New York, 1969

Reich, Wilhelm, *Character Analysis*, Farrar, Straus and Giroux, New York, 1963

Reich, Wilhelm, *Selected Writings: an Introduction to Orgonomy*, Farrar, Straus and Giroux, New York, 1960

Reich, Wilhelm, *The Murder of Christ*, Farrar, Straus and Giroux, New York, 1966

Reich, Wilhelm, *Listen, Little Man*, Farrar, Straus and Giroux, New York, 1965

Reich, Wilhelm, *The Bioelectrical Investigation of Sexuality and Anxiety*, Farrar, Straus and Giroux, New York, 1982

Reich, Wilhelm, *The Bion Experiments — on the Origin of Life*, Farrar, Straus and Giroux, New York, 1979

Reich, Wilhelm, *The Cancer Biopathy*, Farrar, Straus and Giroux, New York, 1973

Reich, Wilhelm, *Ether, God and Devil/Cosmic Superimposition*, Farrar, Straus and Giroux, New York, 1973

Reich, Wilhelm, *Children of the Future*, Farrar, Straus and Giroux, New York, 1983

Reich, Wilhelm, *The Invasion of Compulsory Sex-Morality*, Farrar, Straus and Giroux, New York, 1971

Reich, Wilhelm, *Genitality in the Theory and Therapy of Neurosis*, translated by Phillip Schmitz, Farrar, Straus and Giroux, New York, 1980

Reich, Wilhelm, *Early Writings*, translated by Phillip Schmitz, Farrar, Straus and Giroux, New York, 1973

Reich, Wilhelm, *Reich Speaks of Freud*, Farrar, Straus and Giroux, New York, 1967

Reich, Wilhelm, *Record of a Friendship: The conversations of Reich, Wilhelm and A. S. Neill*, Farrar, Straus and Giroux, New York, 1981

Reich, Wilhelm, *Where's the Truth?*, Farrar, Straus and Giroux, New York, 2012

Reich, Wilhelm, *People in Trouble*, Farrar, Straus and Giroux, New York, 1976

Reich, Wilhelm, *Passion of Youth*, Farrar, Straus and Giroux, New York, 1990

Reich, Wilhelm, *American Odyssey*, Farrar, Straus and Giroux, New York, 1999

Reich, Wilhelm, *Beyond Psychology*, Farrar, Straus and Giroux, New York, 1984

Reich, Wilhelm, *Contact with Space*, CORE Pilot Press, 1957. Republished by Haverhill House Publishing, LLC, Haverhill, MA, 2018.

von Däniken, Erich, *Chariots of the Gods?*, Berkley Books, New York, 1968